ECSTASY

Also by Jacquelyn Frank

The Nightwalkers

JACOB
GIDEON
ELIJAH
DAMIEN
NOAH

Published by Kensington Publishing Corp.

ECSTASY

The Shadowdwellers

JACQUELYN FRANK

ZEBRA BOOKS
KENSINGTON PUBLISHING CORP.

ZEBRA BOOKS are published by

Kensington Publishing Corp.
850 Third Avenue
New York, NY 10022

All Kensington titles, imprints, and distributed lines are available at special quantity discounts for bulk purchases for sales promotion, premiums, fund-raising, educational, or institutional use.

Special book excerpts or customized printings can also be created to fit specific needs. For details, write or phone the office of the Kensington Special Sales Manager: Attn. Special Sales Department. Kensington Publishing Corp., 850 Third Avenue, New York, NY 10022. Phone: 1-800-221-2647.

Zebra and the Z logo Reg. U.S. Pat. & TM Off.

ISBN-13: 978-1-60751-585-2

Printed in the United States of America

For my father.

You rescued me when I needed it most,
saved me from the worst of villains,
then demanded I rescue myself when
I spent too much time looking for
someone else to save me.

You're my one true hero.

Vocabulary of Shadese Terms

Please keep in mind no translations are exact. These are meant to guide you to the general implied meaning.

Aiya: Ī-yah: An exclamation of frustration or exasperation (Oh my! Oh yes! Oh no! Oh boy! etc.)

Ajai: Ah-<u>ZH</u>Ī: (The *j* is always pronounced as in *déjà vu*.) My Lord, Sir, Master

Anai: Ah-NĪ: My Lady, Mistress, Madame

Bituth amec: Bi-TOOTH AH-meck: Son of a bitch (or stronger)

Drenna: drehn-NAH: Darkness. The god/goddess of Darkness.

Frousi: Froo-SĒ: A sectioned fruit that grows only in darkness. It carries a great deal of water and plant proteins, making it a good source of energy.

Jei li: <u>ZH</u>Ā-lē: (roughly) A precious one, sweetheart, honey

K'jeet: KĒ-<u>zh</u>ēt: A nightgown, caftan

K'yan: KĒ-yahn: Sister (religious)

K'yatsume: KĒ-at-soo-mā: Your highness (female), My Queen

M'itisume: Mit-Ī-soo-mā: Your highness (male), My King

M'jan: MM-<u>zh</u>an: Brother, Father (religious)

Paj: Pa<u>zh</u>: A pair of light silk or gauze cotton trousers with cuffs tight at the ankles, traditionally worn under any skirt that flows away from the body with movement.

Sua vec'a: Swah VEHK-kah: Stop! Cut it out! Desist!

Names:

Guin: Gwin

Acadian: AH-cā-dē-ann

Rika: RĒ-kah

Killian: Kill-Ē-yan

Xenia: Zuh-NEE-ahh

Malaya: Mah-LĀ-yah

Prologue

Ashla Townsend was afraid to drive on New Year's Eve.

Since this was a well-known fact, she was at a huge loss when she asked herself for the sixtieth time how she had managed to end up being the designated driver for the night. It wasn't that she wanted to be one of the drinking revelers herself, just that she dreaded the idea of being on the roads with the untold numbers of *other* drinking revelers who hadn't taken the time to choose a designated driver.

"Ashla, sweetie, relax," Diana Quaid scolded with knowing sympathy from the passenger seat. She reached to touch soothing fingertips to one of the hands Ashla had clenched around the steering wheel in a legitimate white-knuckle hold.

"I'll relax when we're all at home safe and sound like all those designated driving ads promise us," Ashla qualified with a nervous glance in the SUV's rearview at the four other passengers. They had all finally wound down from the excitement of the party they'd attended, and Cristine, her younger sister, had even fallen asleep against her boyfriend's tuxedoed chest. "We should never have come so far out on New Year's. Or we should have at least gotten a room at the hotel or something."

"Oh, c'mon!" Diana groaned, rolling her eyes. "How could we not go? It was a once-in-a-lifetime chance! To party at the Theodore Hotel with so many rotten rich people? It's one of the hottest parties in the tri-state area. Plus, that guy who gave you the invites is totally into you. He danced with you so many times you're going to have to have a funeral for those shoes."

"Bite your tongue." Ashla couldn't help her grin at that. "These cost three hundred bucks."

"And worth every cent." Diana chuckled. "You looked hot tonight. That man all but grabbed you at midnight to kiss you."

Ashla flushed with the memory, keeping her eyes glued to the road as she recalled the possessive grasp of Samuel Benson's hands on her waist and back as he had pulled her into that kiss. The midnight tradition had allowed him to breach usual dating protocols, and he had taken full advantage of it. Ashla had surprised herself with her willingness to go along with him. Sam's kiss had been one of intensity and impressive skill. Not an entirely unpleasant experience and, now that she thought about it, one she might not be averse to repeating in the future.

"It was just a kiss," she noted aloud with a single-shouldered shrug. "A very nice kiss. It's not as though the Earth moved or heavenly choirs sang."

"God! Ashla, I swear you are so . . . so . . . !"

Diana never finished the expression of her frustration with her tightly wound friend. The oncoming truck that crossed into their lane and hit them head-on at ninety miles per hour killed her instantly.

Chapter 1

Ashla stood shivering in the darkened streets of Times Square.

She was almost used to the total lack of light, and even the eerie absence of sound in a city that ought to have been clamoring with noise, but what she couldn't adjust to was the absolute barrenness of humanity.

How long had she been in this surreal, postapocalyptic version of New York? Had it been a week? Three? She had lost track. One of the most populous cities in America, and she had yet to see a single soul besides herself.

Ashla was a bit hazy on some of the details of when this all had come about, of how and why the world had blossomed into this bizarre, barren landscaping, but she did recall her initial reaction of pure panic. She remembered quite clearly the act of running around to all of the places where coworkers, friends, and even family were supposed to be.

Queens. The Bronx. Eastern Long Island. Eventually here, in Manhattan.

There was no one.

Oh, everything worked all right. Subways. Cars. Machinery. All of it as if the regular occupants of the world would return any moment to pick up and go on just as they always had. Only, there were some strange details missing. There was no television reception or projection. Lightbulbs, neon lights, and anything providing the smallest glimmer of illumination refused to perform their designated functions. That had truly freaked her out in the beginning. The lack of light had made the vast vacant spaces of the city seem somehow claustrophobic and paralyzing. It had gotten better, thank goodness, as her eyes had adapted to the total darkness with a surprising rapidity. She had even grown accustomed to the fact that it always remained nighttime and never turned to day like it should.

Things had definitely improved once she stopped thinking of reasons why there might not be a sun.

Another odd thing was the food. Food was always fresh for the taking, somehow replenishing itself as though invisible workers still carried out their daily duties of stocking and rotating it. She never saw any of it happen, it just did.

In the end, she had realized that the ideal course of action was to not spend too much time thinking about the details. She never got answers when she did, and only managed to scare herself witless in the process. Explanations escaped her for those and many other anomalous details, but she was weary of the constant heart-racing panic that overwhelmed her every time she thought too hard about her shadowed environs. Instead, she learned to enjoy things . . . like foods she'd never tried before, or sneaking into homes in Chinatown just to see how different they were.

There was one light, however. Moonlight. It was the one and only relief to the dark world. The growing cycle of the moon, with its inevitable turn toward fullness, would shed more and more beautifully pale light onto the world around her. Ashla didn't even mind all the spooky shadows it cast in long black and gray streaks. She already knew no one was hiding in them.

In fact, her reality remained completely devoid of humanity, just as it had for the better part of a month now. Two months? More? Even time seemed to have given up on this lifeless wasteland that made no sense to her. She supposed she had given up as well, eventually trudging away from the overwhelming grief over lost loved ones and even abandoning her furious frustration at her suddenly senseless world. Now she simply wandered New York and the rest of the tri-state area trying to amuse herself.

Until then, she had never realized how vital the presence of others could be to a person's sanity.

It had actually been fun for a little while, walking paths and places that were normally so heavily protected by security or warning signs, and examining all the strange inner workings of things she'd never questioned before. At least, it had been fun until she had taken a bad fall in a subway station and it had occurred to her that if she were hurt very badly, there would be no one around to help her; no one to rush her to a hospital for care; no one to care enough to keep her from rotting away from hunger and thirst alone in a dark, tiled tunnel.

She hadn't gone belowground since that particular panic attack. Aboveground might not necessarily be less hazardous, but it was far less enclosing and she took comfort in whatever she could at that point. Ashla's sense of security on the open streets was relative. She was safe from dark, creepy subterranean dangers, perhaps, but she was also left feeling even more alone as towering buildings soared above her, miniaturizing her and making her feel as though she were standing at the bottom of a great abandoned canyon. She had struggled with the ever-increasing fear that someday something might happen and she wouldn't know what to do to help herself.

And then sometimes, some very awful bad times, she couldn't even remember all the names of the people she knew. It was at those times that she truly became frightened. Down deep to the bottom of her soul terrified. Because those were the times when she feared she had simply lost her mind. After all, what other explanation could there be? What could possibly make her forget her beloved sister Cristine? Or even her brothers Malcolm and Joseph? Her parents. It horrified her to think there was anything that could make her forget what it had been like to grow up in her mother's care.

She took comfort that today she remembered it all, and tried not to worry about tomorrow.

Other than all of that . . .

New York City was her playground.

Saks. Barneys. Macy's. Bloomies. Granted, they would have been more fun if there had been some decent light to see by, but she compensated for it by shopping close to windows that filled with moonlight. She walked in whenever she wanted and walked out without needing to pay. Every day she picked a new store to get dressed in. She'd amused herself enough at the department stores, and dazzled herself in the Diamond District, but now she was gravitating back to the retro boutiques she had always loved. She liked the priceless vintage dresses, lace and beads and hand-worked details that were so rare in the modern world. So she made her way to her favorite shop and, before long, was slipping into an ivory gown with a tautly stitched empire waist, à la Jane Austen. It had a silk underlining and hand-crocheted lace over it in a perfect pastel cream. It was unique, delicate and beautiful, the style transporting her back to a time when men fought duels for the honor of a woman.

That was when she heard the first resonant clang of metal on metal.

She was so startled by the sound after so much silence that she threw herself against a wall and hid, her breath panting and her heart pounding for a full minute before working up the courage to sneak to the window.

"Something probably dropped. Toppled over. You're just being a ninny," she lectured herself breathlessly.

It was a plausible idea, right up until the moment she

heard the second crash of metal against metal, the clang reverberating in the dim world and vacant streets. Understanding crystallized when she heard the hard sound of running feet coming toward her, and she strained to somehow hide *and* see what was going on all at the same time.

She glimpsed the dark shape of a man an instant before a second man plowed up into him and they both came flying toward her. Ashla ducked with a scream and barely got her arms up protectively before they barreled through the plate glass window in a shower of shards. Clothing racks and tables disintegrated as they broke the momentum of the two large-bodied fighting men. A sword, of all things, went skidding across the hardwood flooring, bumping to a stop against Ashla's bare toes.

"Oh, yeah, Ash, you are definitely swimming in the deep end now," she muttered to herself as she stared down at the weapon. A sword. Not an Uzi. Not a handgun. A *sword*. Ashla was beginning to realize she had never given her imagination enough credit until she had gone crazy. Now she had to admit that the sword was a neat touch to her little fantasy world. So were the men, for that matter.

She watched with dismay as they grappled with each other on the floor amongst the inventory and glass debris. They were both dark-skinned and had dark coloring. The larger man kept his hair long, whipped back tightly into a plait, the jet color of it gleaming in the weak moonlight filtering into the store. His brawny build filled out his clothing almost to test the integrity of his seams. Denim jeans in black hugged tightly to thickly muscled thighs, biker boots holding his braced feet in place against the floor. His shoulders bulged against the dark gray cotton of his dress shirt, and a necklace of some kind dangled almost tauntingly against the disadvantaged man's cheek below him as they struggled for ownership of the remaining sword.

"Give up!" the brute spat down into the face of his adversary. "You know I will win this!"

"I'd rather kiss the sun," was the gruff, straining reply from the slimmer man. It was true, Ashla observed with concern, that the other man was outweighed and, while of impressive physique himself from what she could tell, he was also outmuscled. This one's hair was close-cropped at the back of his neck and around his ears, but there was a little bit of length to the top as it fell back to reveal a widow's peak. The curve of his hairline made his squared jaw and prominent cheekbones appear deeply exotic. The ebony sheen of his wildly tossed hair set shadows on his already dark eyes, making him appear just a little wicked in his features. The impression deepened as he gave his opponent a slow, amused grin that belied his struggle to keep hold of his weapon. "Give it up, Baylor. You'll not win this. Not today!"

The observation was more like a prediction as a knee levered up between Baylor's braced legs, caught him hard, and sent him flying ass over shoulders above the other man's head. Baylor's back slammed into the floor, forcing a startled cough from him. Free of his opponent, the other man scrambled to his feet but did little more than stagger up against a nearby counter. His sword hung tiredly from one hand, the tip grazing the ground. He raised the back of a broad hand to his nose, which, Ashla realized, was bleeding. For all his determination and bravado, it was clear even to her that he was exhausted and had taken a serious beating. Despite the dusk of his skin tone, she could see the swelling and color of new bruises appearing on his face and battered knuckles.

The one named Baylor was on the floor groaning, trying to recover from a hard shot in the testicles that had to hurt even more than when a woman delivered it. Most men would consider the maneuver fighting dirty, but the weary man had clearly needed every advantage against the behemoth Baylor, and Ashla didn't blame him in the least for resorting to such a brutal tactic.

"You . . . dare . . . to betray . . . our people," the standing man gasped between difficult-to-draw breaths. He was hugging an arm to his side, his ribs obviously hurting him, and Ashla found herself actually worrying that he had broken one or more. She didn't even know him, or what they were fighting about, so why, she wondered, was she starting to show concern for one side over the other?

"There was a time when *you* were considered the traitor, *Ajai* Trace," Baylor growled. "History is written by the one who wins the coup."

Baylor rolled over onto his hands and knees, panting hard and groaning beneath his breath as his movements sent obvious reminders of pain through his reproductive system. He looked up and suddenly Ashla found herself staring into deep eyes of black and menace. But as bad as the scowl initially was, the subsequent grin that showed his teeth was far worse.

"Well, well. What have we here?"

The snide speculation made Ashla cringe, but instincts she didn't understand caused her to lay her shaking fingers to rest against the grip of the sword by her toes. She wasn't going to use it, just . . . she would make sure it stayed out of his easy reach. Her gaze shifted to the other male and she was surprised and unexplainably grateful to see he had straightened and, as though in no pain at all, swiftly grabbed up his own sword and slid sturdily into the space between Baylor and herself.

"Come now, Trace," Baylor drawled slowly as the other man's blade tapped its tip to the jutting point of his chin. The implication was clear. One wrong move and his head would be singing farewell to his neck. "Look at the fear in her eyes. Look at how the Lost one trembles. Don't you get it? It means she can *see* us."

Trace was almost certain it was a trick of some kind. Everyone in their world knew well enough that the Lost *couldn't* see a Shadowdweller. There was one exception, but even that required a ritual, a priest, and a damn good reason to want to make that kind of contact, which on its own was a preposterous likelihood. Still, Trace had glimpsed the cowering Lost girl shortly after they had come in through the window. Her reaction at the time would be understandable. She couldn't see them, but she would certainly see the exploding glass coming toward her.

Trace let his gaze flick to his low right and back again, taking a quick mental picture of the female. It was impossible to miss her, really. She was everything his people weren't. Fair. Blond. Wearing white. Fearful. In fact, he couldn't seem to help himself as he looked back at her once more, getting a better look at just how light and white she seemed. Even her eyes were bright and the fairest shade of blue he'd ever seen.

And they were staring straight at him.

Wide, frightened, but inarguably fixated on *him*.

"Impossible," he muttered aloud.

"Ha! Proof of your idiotic stubbornness," Baylor mocked him.

"You will shut your treacherous mouth, my friend," Trace ground out angrily, using the press of his blade on Baylor's throat to force the other man to sit upright onto his heels. Even despite his quick obedience, the highly honed tip of the blade cut into his skin and started a river of blood flowing down his thick throat. As for Trace, his roaring temper had shifted from betrayed anger to a storm of fury. "Do you think this is how this will end? Do you really think I will merely take you into my custody and march you to your fate at the hands of my regents? After you follow me here to engage my ear in whispered plots and backstabbing sedition meant to pit one regent against the other? A sister against her brother? Oh, no, Baylor," Trace assured in a voice that ground to a low and slow resonance of threat, "I am my Lord Chancellor's vizier, and it is I who advises him, but while I would have you hanged publicly to be made an example of, Tristan would not see you as the threat you truly are.

"His Grace," he continued bitterly, "suffers from the overconfidence of power and strength. A flaw only time will rectify. Also, there is his unshakable foundation of his trust in his sister's loyalty, a factor which makes him laugh off plot-makers like you. It is a mistake many young regents have made. He forgets that voices like yours will always find the ears of the discontented and disloyal whether they succeed at their intended goal or not.

"Their reign is far too youthful to be given such a test, and our efforts at peace with the other Nightwalkers would distract him from realizing that. So no," Trace assured the kneeling man, "this will not end civilly. It will end with my sword severing those seditious vocal cords of yours and keeping you from ever whispering your ill words to a single other 'Dweller."

"It is against the law for one 'Dweller to take the life of another!" Baylor reminded him with a sneer. "A law *you* instigated, if I recall! How steady do you think this political body will ever be when its own lawmakers cannot abide by its own rules?"

"Do not quote my own laws to me, traitor," Trace hissed through clenched teeth, pushing forward on his blade until Baylor squawked in protest. "Or do you forget that an attack on any of the ruling body is considered an act of treason and war? In war, the law is suspended with circumstance and proof of cause." Trace leaned forward to close the distance between their gazes. "Do you forget the dagger you plunged into my back so soon?"

The gasp from the girl on the floor was unmistakable, and Trace cautiously kept pressure on his blade as he glanced toward her again. Sure enough, her eyes were tracking anxiously over the length of his back as if in search of the dagger he had just mentioned.

By the Dark, Baylor was right! The Lost woman could see him! She could hear everything they were saying. It was impossible, his logical mind demanded once again in knee-jerk denial, and yet . . .

Trace looked away. He didn't have time for distractions. He knew Baylor couldn't give a damn about some perceptive Lost. He was just using her to waste time and seek advantage. If Trace waited much longer, he was going to end up giving it to him. He doubled his grip on the hilt of his katana and braced his feet against the steadily increasing weakness of his body. He saw Baylor's entire body tensing exactly like his own was, preparing to act in order to save himself. But Trace knew Baylor was waiting for him to pull back for a swing before moving, and it was a moment of advantage he refused to give, even if it made his task harder and more gruesome in the end.

Trace took a breath, and with a deeply ferocious cry to vent his anger and frustration, he plunged all of his weight forward onto the top six inches of his blade. It was his meticulous maintenance of the thing that did the best part of the work. Before Baylor could so much as flinch in realization, the finely honed blade sawed into flesh and critical arteries. The traitor's gasp of understanding actually bubbled from the cut in his throat, the wet intake of air and blood the only sound in the end. Baylor's hands reached around the blade that was killing him in a last-ditch effort to struggle, but he only succeeded in cutting himself to the bone of his palms.

Trace went to pull his blade free and step back, wanting to let the body fall where it was, as it was, but suddenly his legs turned to rubber and every muscle in his body relinquished the strength he had struggled so hard to maintain. He fell to his knees. Hard. His grip on his sword fumbled and released and a moment later he felt himself tumbling over the hardwood floor.

He knew it was because of the heavy wetness of his own draining blood that this was happening. Frankly, he was surprised he had lasted this long, never mind come out on top of a fight with a brute like Baylor. Trace had to admit it had been utter dread more than anything that had driven him. He had feared that Baylor might succeed in his unlikely plans to drive a wedge between the brother and sister regents. He had feared for the Shadowdweller people as a society if he did.

Then, even as he was aware of the edges of his consciousness fading, Trace felt the shaking touch of warm hands on his shoulders, turning him over gingerly while struggling with his weight. Golden hair, tickling in feathers against her skin, surrounded the woman's head like a nimbus when she leaned over him. The cut was short enough to be a boy's cut, he noted numbly. Why would such a beautiful woman, with hair of such an amazing color, want to cut it all off? He had never understood humans, even when they weren't Lost. Or women, for that matter, of any race. The odds were definitely stacked against him understanding anything about this situation.

"L-let me help you," she stammered, leaning over to cup his face between two soft hands. The skin of her palms brushed beneath his nose briefly, and Trace was caressed by a warm, sweet scent. Like honeysuckle and lilacs. Another anomaly, he noted, because the Lost should have no scent, nor warmth. Those were *living* human traits. The Lost were just lost; souls without the flesh traits of their bodies. But even if he were hallucinating, why would he concoct details like that? Trace didn't think the warm scent of lilacs and humanity was something his own imagination could easily conjure up.

Trace faded after that thought, but found himself jerked back to awareness shortly after when the force of tearing fabric jerked at his body. He lifted his lashes despite their incredible weight and tried to focus on the woman who was struggling at stripping off his shirt.

"Leave me be. I'll be fine," Trace grumbled.

Well, it wasn't entirely true, but it wasn't as if she could do much to help him. He just needed to be left alone for a while. Just long enough so he could catch his breath, regroup, and find the strength to Unfade.

Trace gave no thought to the fact he was completely deluding himself and that he was in very real danger of dying. He also dismissed the knowledge that unconsciousness alone might send him spiraling out of his Fade, and even his pain-numbed senses were warning him that it was still daylight in Realscape. If he lost his grip on the secure darkness of Shadowscape, he would be burned up alive within a matter of moments upon returning.

So much for the idea that his breed was supposed to be immortal. He'd never understood the word "immortal" in that context. Their longevity of youth and the intense hardiness of the species as a whole might make them long-lived and quite difficult to kill, but at the moment he was living proof—or rather dying proof—that mortality was indeed possible. Be it the act of bleeding to death, a beheading, or sprawling into sunlight, his breed was most certainly capable of dying.

Trace knew there wasn't much the Lost one could do for him. He didn't even know why he could feel her in the first place. Also, the little thing was shaking like a leaf with her trepidation. Understandable, granted, considering all she had just seen, but nothing that would inspire him to set his faith in her. Not that he was known for setting his faith in the unpredictability of women lately.

Trace found a pocket of strength within himself, just enough to allow him the advantage of using her existing fear against her. He burst upward beneath her, making her squeal out a scream as he rolled her hard to the floor, following her with the weight of his considerably bigger body pinning her down. Her small hands clutched the front of his shirt, her fists tight against his pectorals, and she instinctively dug her heels against the wooden floor for purchase. This allowed him the unexpected and pleasant comfort of a cradle of soft thighs covered in silk as a resting point for his hips.

He found it strangely provoking, the way she shook so hard and gasped for breath beneath him. The push of the gown she wore accented the extraordinary symmetry of her rising and falling breasts. That scent, that sweet and innocent aroma of tender flowers and springtime warmth arose from her skin to envelop him. To his astonishment, he realized for the first time that this truly *was* a real woman he held trapped beneath him. This was no wraith, no Lost soul only. She felt of soft flesh and heated blood, as alive and vital as he was . . . for the time being. He held her helpless and vulnerable, despite his own weakening stamina, and there was something indelibly primal to that understanding that sent shockwaves of stimulation racing along the surfaces of his flesh.

The thought was actually sexual, Trace realized with a stunned inner laugh at himself. *Of all the times!* Here he was, on the brink of mortality, and all he was thinking of was how delicate and helpless this little blond mouse was . . . and how undeniably provocative she was because of it.

His goal in pinning her to the floor had been to scare her to death so that she would run away screaming and leave him to drop dead in peace. But his desires changed on the fly, and suddenly he was heavily distracted by the bright white and gold of her hair. He reached up for it, fondling one of the silky soft curls between his fingers.

"It never ceases to amaze me how this color seems to glow even in the dark and dim," he murmured, also finding the texture to be supernaturally refined, almost as delicate as cobwebs.

"Please . . . d-don't hurt m-me," she stammered in between chattering of her teeth. "I . . . I can help you!" Her fear was both perplexing and bemusing, but even more so was her offer of help in spite of it. Trace supposed she was bargaining with him, offering him something to make her of value to him so he wouldn't want to do her harm. It was actually quite clever of her.

"What do they call you?" he demanded suddenly, the

hardness of the command in total counterpoint to the fingers still gently stroking her hair.

"Ashla," she said obediently.

Her compliance mystified him. Had she been a Shadow-dweller woman, he'd be nursing a few choice bruises by now, not to mention having his ears rung with tart insults. Trace wasn't used to a woman like this. She seemed fragile enough to break. Small like a child. And yet . . .

"Ashla. You must leave this place. Do you understand? It is not a safe place to be right now." Perhaps for more than one reason, he mused. The possibility that Baylor had arranged to meet companions did exist, and they could turn up at any time, but Ashla's threat might be more immediate than that. Trace pressed a palm to the wooden floor, making to push himself up but succeeding only a little. Still, it was enough to allow him a long appraisal down the length of her curving side.

By the Dark, he groaned inwardly, *I must be losing my mind*. An effect of blood loss. Something. *Anything*. What else could explain this hard surge of predatory need pumping through him? The force of it on his already drained system made him light-headed, and he could feel the room beginning to spin.

"You need to go," he rasped, using one last effort to roll his weight off her. The last thing he wanted was to trap her beneath him as he fell into dead weight and then eventually death. The little Lost rabbit wouldn't be likely to survive such a gruesome and endangering experience.

He sprawled over the floor to her right, closing his eyes when everything around him lurched and spun wickedly. *Damn*, he thought bitterly, *this is an annoying way to die*. Never mind the anticlimactic resolution to his fight with Baylor and the fact that he couldn't warn his regents of bubbling trouble, but to never have a chance to figure out what it was about this woman that so tantalized and intrigued him, that felt like the true tragedy.

*   *   *

Ashla wanted to obey his command to leave with all of her heart. She wanted to run fast and hard until the entire world fell away from her and snapped back into the normal, sane place she was used to and craved so very badly.

But despite all of that, she couldn't find it in herself to leave him like he was. He was obviously injured, and very badly at that. There weren't many things she could count herself any good at, but she had the potential to help him if she had to.

"I'm not going to leave you here without any help," she said with a firm bravado they both knew she didn't feel. She lifted her chin and met his eyes, hoping this would make her determination more convincing.

He chuckled, a dry, breathy sound that went eerily well with the amazingly faceted darkness of his eyes as he looked at her. "There is no help. You'll learn that soon enough," he said.

His defeatist words slid past her barely noticed. She was caught up for a moment in the wondrous way his irises nearly matched the black depths of his pupils, except there was something like starlight in those dark centers, and the black coffee color surrounding them gleamed like painstakingly cut precious stones. She found it impossible to look away until his long, sooty lashes fell over them with his waning con-sciousness.

Ashla shook herself to the ready.

"Who knows, you could be right," she muttered as she leaned over him. "For all I know, that's because you went around chopping all their heads off. And me being the idiot I am, I'm going to try and help you so you can get strong enough to lift your scary sword again and . . . and . . ."

The implication was clear enough. She didn't need to voice what she clearly couldn't. It shouldn't have affected Trace one way or another, what a wraith thought of him, but for some reason the taste her remarks left on his tongue was deeply bitter.

"Look," he growled on labored breaths, indignant emotion fueling him for the moment, "I said I'm not going to hurt you."

"That's what the bad guy tells every stupid woman in all those stupid movies, and she always ends up dead or worse. Which I guess makes me really, *really* stupid." She peeled back the fabric of his torn shirt and turned extraordinarily gray right before his eyes as she took in the scope of the cuts and slices he'd received from both Baylor and the plate glass he'd come through. "Oh, God, I . . ." She gagged low in her throat and reflexively went to cover her mouth, but an inch short of the mark her eyes focused on the blood from his wounds that was soaking her palms and forearms and the movement screeched to a halt. The rusty smell of fresh, abundant blood must have hit her a second after that because she flung herself away from him and vomited violently.

But to Trace's surprise, she turned back to him as soon as she had minimally composed herself. She began grabbing clothing from nearby tables using them to wipe away the blood on his chest. She then applied pressure to the worst of his visible wounds, all the while, continuously weeping huge, silent tears. It was as though the emotional woman and the physical one were acting completely independent of each other's reactions. He was compelled to reach for one of her slim wrists, grasping it and holding it firmly even when she startled hard in his hand. Tears rained off the slopes of her cheeks as her worried eyes flicked up to confront him.

"You do not have to do this. You have every right to be afraid in this strange world you no doubt have little understanding of. And anyway, these wounds are nothing. The mortal blow was in my back, and there is nothing to be done for it. These others are incidental. Listen." Trace squeezed the remarkably small hand he held gently, overcome with the idea that he could shatter her small bones if he pressed too hard. Strange he should think so. The women in his world were strong and powerful, sturdy and bold. He hadn't thought he would even know how to treat a female who might be so delicate, not to mention overly sensitive, as this one surely was. "There's nothing you can do here."

She was already shaking her head in vehement negativity. The defiant stubbornness it signaled simply floored him. What was she thinking? She spoke truth of logic, that from her perspective she had no way of knowing which of the fighting males had been the more just and honorable, that she was likely setting herself up for trouble. She was plainly scared to death to be near him and wanted absolutely nothing to do with his bloody, gored body, and yet she would not take the surcease he offered to her. She wouldn't leave him.

The woman was clearly an idiot.

Chapter 2

Ashla was completely convinced of her own stupidity as she remained firmly by the injured man's side. On the plus side, his kind attempt to release her from obligation had helped her to control her remaining weeping, ratcheting the infernal weakness down to a series of sniffles. As she did so, she began to think more clearly. Ashla slid carefully to Trace's side and bit her lip a moment as she inspected her choices.

"I have to roll you over to see your back. It's going to hurt."

"Yeah. It is. Look, I already told you . . ."

"Well, just humor me! It's not as if you're late for a date or something."

Trace watched her shove at her hair in her pique, her fingers streaking blood through the fair gold strands. He didn't point it out to her, not wishing to potentially bring back her nausea, and simply braced up a knee to help her roll him onto his right side. He didn't need to hear her gasp to confirm what he could already feel. She peeled off the remainder of his shirt to see a river of blood oozing in swift, pulsing rushes down the span of his back. The hole Baylor had left behind was probably an inch or better in width. While the other 'Dweller had been only a fair swordfighter, with his weapon of choice, the dagger, he had always been an absolute killer. The proof being that six inches of steel in Baylor's hand had killed Trace long before Trace had managed to kill Baylor in return.

Ashla bit her lip hard, trying not to react to what she was seeing any more than she already had. The knifing was bad, it was true. It poured out his life in rapid pulses. But just as shocking was the evidence on his back that this had been far from his first such fight or injury. She had uncovered a canvas of scars. Or what should have been scars. They looked strangely smoothed and without texture where they should have been jagged and ridged. They were scars nonetheless, ripped bright pink and pale through the palette of his dark skin, tearing a path up the length of his spine as if some animal had clawed him over and over again. There were other marks as well, a testament to the abuse he had subjected himself to.

But she had to ignore all of that dramatic history and focus completely on the most recent damage. Ashla probed the bloody wound with unsure fingers, gritting her teeth against the feel of the fluid that so quickly became tacky to her touch. She drew a shuddering breath as she realized he was not exaggerating. The wound was horribly mortal. Just the amount of blood he was losing in those few moments told her as much. No medical degree required. She could even feel the warmth of his skin fading beneath her touch as the chill of impending death crept over him.

Something about that struck a fire to a store of anger Ashla hadn't even realized she'd been harboring. Ever since she had awakened to this dark version of the world, she had been unable to escape the feeling of being chilled through. His body warmth was the most comforting sensation she'd experienced in . . . so very long a time. Even in her terror as she had been trapped beneath him for those few minutes, she had wanted to cry with relief just to feel any kind of human contact again. Perhaps it had helped that his had been a powerful and vital contact, a heated energy and dominance that had soaked right through her.

Her instinctive fury was only fueled by the logic of knowing that, just her damn luck, he was going to end up dying on her. She would be left all alone again. Not just lonely as it had often been the case in her lifetime, but well and truly alone. Devastatingly alone.

Ashla had learned to be afraid of a great many things in the world, perhaps even to a degree beyond reason, but the idea of being abandoned in this place again for months or longer . . . the thought of it propelled her beyond a lifetime of cautions and concern like nothing else could possibly have done.

She could help him. She knew she could. Or at least she hoped she could. There were so many factors to consider, not the least of which was that so many things didn't work here as they were supposed to. But how could she not try? How could she allow doubt and questions to stack against the possibility of saving a life?

Ashla spread her palms against the section of his broad back that housed the wound. Her fingers framed the ugly hole, the nails she had painted a ridiculous violet in her previous boredom looking morbid and garish in that moment.

Then she closed her eyes and propelled herself back twenty-two years. She couldn't seem to help herself. It happened every time she did this. She was instantly transported to the very first time she had discovered she could heal with the touch of her hands . . .

. . . and how it had been one of the most horrific experiences of her life, just like every time she had dared to exercise the ability since. The first time, though, that was the one that would never shake free.

She had been only five years old. It was actually one of those cute stories of childhood. Everyone had them, didn't they? A story about a child finding a poor, injured animal and that child's desire to make it better. This in spite of her parents' blunt warnings that the small baby bunny the family dog had dropped triumphantly at her feet would never survive the shock and fear of being mouthed by the retriever. This was to say nothing of the bloody wound in its foot caused by either a canine tooth or the process of the chase. But like any child in that position, she had simply wanted to fix it. She had wanted it with all of her heart. So she had held the rabbit in her hands, against that heart that wanted so badly to help, and felt the small creature go from a distressed ball of limp, shuddering fur to a warm, living animal full of energy and life. It had been an utterly amazing transformation to her.

It was the work of the devil to her family.

Her mother had called her Satan, screamed and wailed as if she was dead, and they had . . .

Ashla closed off the memory, her breath rasping and coming short as if metal was closing around her throat to choke her again. She shut it all away, because if she took the time to think about what this man would do to her when he realized what she could do, she would completely lose her nerve. But her life, her pain, all meant nothing when the only other option was to allow herself to become a murderer by neglect. If she didn't do what she could to save him, she might as well have stuck him with the blade herself.

Trace lay surprisingly quiet. It was surprising to him because he was in a great deal of pain, and while he was known for his patience in most things, agony wasn't one of those things. It was probably his curiosity getting the better of him. He was trying to figure out what she was up to as he listened to her mutter under her breath. To him, it sounded like she kept telling herself to stop thinking.

"Don't think. Don't think. Don't think." A litany. Over and over again. Then, aloud to him, "Listen, this is going to hurt, but you have to trust me, okay?"

Frankly, Trace didn't see a point to any of it, whatever "it" was. However, he couldn't put up much of a protest with his back to her and weakness weighing down his whole body. All he could manage was a listless, unimpressed shrug of his exposed shoulder. What did it matter? Hell, she could strip naked and tap-dance for all the good it was going to do. At least he'd get some entertainment out of it.

Or so he thought until she stabbed her finger deep into the wound Baylor had created. Trace bellowed in agony and tried to haul himself off the floor and out of her sadistic reach, but all of a sudden the little blond mouse who shook at every word he spoke had found the strength of a dozen Demons and kept him forcefully in place as she wriggled her finger down as far as she could into his body.

"By the Dark, are you insane?" he roared, fumbling at his back for her hand. Before he could reach her, however, she yanked it out and shoved him hard onto his back again. He was so heavily occupied with his pained shouts that she climbed up over him without any argument from him that didn't come in the form of curses she probably didn't understand. Not unless she had happened to learn Shadese, the Shadowdwellers' native tongue, in the past five minutes or so.

On a visual-sensory delay of sorts as information filtered through the haze of his hurt, Trace absorbed her actions as she yanked up the long skirt she was wearing, soaking it with bloody handprints while she threw her leg over his hips and settled herself over him as if she were about to ride him into the ground. The fact that he was in too much pain at first to protest, despite the image she made in her strange, pale sort of beauty, only made him angrier.

"Get off!" he gasped at last, reaching for the waif with his jellied arms. He was as weak as a kitten, but he would be damned if he couldn't throw off a sadist bitch no bigger than a ten-year-old.

When she swatted him away as if he were a pesky fly, Trace was ready to explode with frustrated fury.

And then she did the oddest thing, the mere shock of it cutting off his torrential emotions at the knees. The peculiar little blonde ran her splayed hands slowly up his bared belly and chest as she leaned fully forward, just until her eyes were gazing down into his, and her lips were touching his mouth by the space of a hair. Trace caught his breath, holding back his reaction merely by the power of his surprise. He stared up into eyes of blue, so unique to someone like him, and felt her breath and its incongruous warmth as it spilled in rapid rushes over his face. He became aware of her scent again, but this was probably because it was everywhere, warm and weighty and pervasively sweet.

"Trust me," she demanded of him as all of her weight came to lie against him. "This will help."

Trace couldn't even conceive of how to argue with her about that. Old instincts cursed him for ever turning his back on a woman, even if he *was* about to die. But older instincts than that were shifting the focus of his attention, helping to curb the lance of pain constantly running through him. As if he had his father's perceptions and could sense the truth on a higher level, Trace knew that she believed what she was doing could actually help. Ashla was as gentle now as she had been seemingly cruel a moment ago, and the softness of her caressing touch left him off balance and raw with vacillating focuses.

Wraith or not, she had an intriguing little body tucked into that dress, he realized as she slowly began to reach and glide over him; moving like liquid poured over a polished path, she simply flowed. She stroked, she touched. She found every bit of exposed skin she could and painted it with her special brand of delicate attention. All the while she laid herself along his body, warming him in more ways than one.

Trace was left with the inane thought that while he'd never been overly fond of the scent of flowers, he might be persuaded to think otherwise in the future . . . provided he even had a future after this.

The Lost woman continued running her hands all along his bare skin and Trace was struck by how very much it was like a seduction. Her eyes slid closed now and again, her expression one of deep concentration, while at the same time it seemed as though she were experiencing a focused pleasure. It radiated into all her increasingly delicious movements, but it was most reflected in the soft, unthinking sounds she made. She moved in slight rocking motions as she reached to touch his arms, hands, and the tips of his fingers where they lay passively at his sides. Then she reversed her direction, her slightly sticky fingers climbing up Trace's throat and head until they were in his hair. Simultaneously, she sprawled out over him, her full weight, such as it was, resting on him as her legs slid down along the length of his.

"It's all right," she whispered as her lips trailed down his jawline until her cheek was stroking against his.

Trace's confusion and any last remaining instincts to rebel faded. He lifted a hand to the back of her small head, the silky-soft texture of her feathery hair sliding under his fingertips.

"You know," he said hoarsely, "there are easier ways to get a date." But even as he made the facetious remark, Trace felt his entire body shift in sensation. It took him a moment to comprehend that what he was feeling was an actual rush of relief. As the pain bled from him in earnest, he took hold of Ashla by the back of her head and neck and pulled her back until he could see her eyes again. She looked flushed and uncomfortable now, her body stiff all of a sudden as she refused to look directly at him.

"What are you?" he asked on a whisper as he studied her carefully for Nightwalker attributes.

The Nightwalkers were the supernatural races, the night races, those who held the sun in dread and thrived in the darkness and moonlight. His race, the Shadowdwellers, was the epitome of that description. All of the Nightwalker breeds were the caretakers of strange and wondrous powers, rather like the power to heal with a touch.

She was no 'Dweller, of that he was certain. Not with that fair coloring and tiny body structure. She was also far too pale to be a Demon, a race that ran to tan themselves. And Vampires, while pale, were not able to heal anyone but themselves . . . unless a bite was involved. He eliminated Mistrals and Lycanthropes for similar reasons. Besides, only two creatures on Earth that he knew of could enter Shadowscape.

Shadowdwellers and humans.

Specifically, comatose humans.

Shadowscape was a lightless dimension just a step out of phase with Realscape. It was only a step, but it was enough to make the entire 'scape completely absent of the world's population to the perception of anyone there. With concentration, a powerful Shadowdweller like Trace could Fade into the dark of Shadowscape, and Unfade to return to Realscape at will. For 'Dwellers, Shadowscape was the ultimate world away from the painful sear of light that rampantly littered a human-dominated world. The human need for illumination, coupled with the natural course of the sun, had made most of the planet completely unlivable, and often suicidal, for Trace's people. As it was, they spent most of their lives chasing the darkness to places like Alaska and New Zealand, the Arctic and the Antarctic lands where night would fall seasonally without end for months at a time.

Humans were the second occupants of Shadowscape; what Trace's people referred to as the Lost. Trace looked into Ashla's eyes, surprised at the depths of light and emotion within the sky blue pools. Previously, his experiences with the Lost had been chillingly flat. They weren't supposed to be able to see the 'Dwellers—or each other, for that matter—so they never seemed to react to anything around them. To look into their faces was to look into a vacant place, an expression of haunted bewilderment as they tried to solve the puzzle of where they were, how they had gotten there, and how they could possibly get back to the life they had known before. They didn't realize that somewhere in Realscape their bodies had become blanks, empty of soul and consciousness, some illness or trauma having stolen away the tether that tied the Lost part of the person to their now blank body.

The Lost were merely spirits, mental manifestations of the wandering soul. In essence, they were wraiths, images projected by the Lost's own memory of themselves. They had no warmth. No scent. No awareness of the Shadowdwellers and the truths of the dimensional landscape they were now trapped in.

But this one did, he thought as he stared at her.

And this one *healed with her touch.*

Could humans really do such things? Trace's society existed on the same planet as humans, but their interactions were minimal due to the issues of light and its harmful nature. Shadowdwellers, like most Nightwalkers, had no real contact with the dominant species on the planet. They weren't completely ignorant of them, of course. They couldn't afford to be. Humans could be quite deadly as they went about their daily lives, routines, negotiations, bickerings, and wars. Trace was as highly aware of human nature and its capability as anyone because of his position in the Shadowdweller government.

As far as he knew, the ability this woman had just shown was a significant abnormality. Just like everything else about her so far, he realized. Was her unusual talent the explanation to all of the anomalies she represented, all the rules of Shadowscape that she was able to break? Even supposing it was possible for a human woman to heal with her bare hands in the real world, how could that ever be taken across the veil and into Shadowscape, where humans were a manifestation of spirit more than body?

Trace had not meant any insult by his last question to her.

He had genuinely wanted to know what she was—what genus, breed, or species of Nightwalker, to be specific, because to his mind no human could possibly have the power she had wielded.

Just the same, his query visibly took her aback, as if he had landed a smarting slap across her face. There was no mistaking the rush of hurt and horror that flew over her features and now-rigid body. Ashla ripped herself out of Trace's grasp violently, tumbling and stumbling across the floor away from him. Glass crunched and skidded beneath her, making Trace acutely aware of her bare feet, hands, and limbs as she scrambled over the minefield of shards. Trace tried to haul himself up, wanting to stop her, but she was fueled by internal demons he couldn't possibly have understood, and he was still severely weakened by blood loss.

But he was also the man who had defeated an enemy above his own class in weight and strength with a mortal wound in his back all the while they had fought. He wasn't known for accepting weaknesses in himself or others.

In that respect, it baffled him why it was so damn important to him to chase after such a touchy, temperamental creature. But chase her was exactly what he did, after a fashion. It was hardly a chase when it took him so long to get to his feet and then to the door she had bolted through. By the time he managed it, the street was empty in all visible directions, and there wasn't a single hint of sound to help direct him after her.

Trace growled under his breath in annoyance.

It was turning out to be a bitch of a day for him.

What are you?

The phrase rang in her ears with the same knell of a half dozen similar experiences, all with that nasty question ringing through them. It had always been meant to tear away at her, to cut her off at the knees and worse, so it was not possible for Ashla to perceive the possibility that it might be meant some other way.

Satan's daughter.

Witch.

No matter how many times she had sworn her abilities were a gift from God, there was always that nasty voice, usually the voice of her mother, whispering insidious accusations in her ear about how evil she was. Sometimes that whispering mutated into screams, shrill and touched with feverish fanaticism.

She's a witch, cursed by God and mistress to the devil!

All this and more whirled as abusive echoes within her head, propelling her to put as much distance as she could between herself and the man who condemned her. It wasn't until she was beating a hasty retreat down the asphalt that Ashla realized that as lost as she was in this shell so much like her native New York, its lack of people had allowed her, for the first time, to walk around in peace and not feeling like she had a secret she had to hide from everyone. It had been the first time in all of her life where she had not felt like she was lying to everyone around her, hiding her true nature from them out of fear of what they would think or do to her.

All this time she had been griping about being alone, when she had actually been at peace.

Trace was advisor to one of the most powerful and influential people in his world, and he prided himself on his ability to see all angles and sense the thoughts and moods of others. He could anticipate almost any hidden problem that most linear minds could not expect, especially when it was critical that he do so for the good of his entire race. Injured and weak as he was, his perceptions had failed him and he couldn't rectify the mistake quickly enough.

His Good Samaritan was out of his reach in a heartbeat, and now there was nothing he could do to retrieve her or even thank her. He was bewildered as he surveyed the trashed boutique behind him, trying to understand what had happened and, admittedly, taking a few needed minutes to recuperate some strength and balance.

The store he stood by would end up completely destroyed in Realscape as well. There would be some parallel reason for it, either a crime or an accident, something that would create the exact damage and debris, but it would happen.

Usually. On rare occasions there were no apparent reasons for why things moved around or banged and rattled a little. It was the stuff ghost stories were born of, and he supposed that, in truth, it *was* a kind of ghost that caused them. It was either the wraith humans or a Shadowdweller in Fade. It was the law of Shadowscape and other parallel dimensions like it. What happened in one world had to happen in all the others. Anytime objects like buildings shared physical space in dimensions, it was simply the way it had to be. The reasons things happened would change from one realm to another, but the end result would always end up the same. If a tree fell in the woods of Shadowscape, it fell in *every* 'scape.

He looked down at his stained body and torn clothing, one large hand sliding up his chest in a touch inspection of his injuries. He wasn't perfectly healed. Far from it, in truth. But there was no longer any free-flowing blood. He was black and blue all under his skin in large areas, sore as hell, but he was very aware of the change he felt instinctively that told him he was no longer in mortal danger from his injuries. All 'Dwellers, most Nightwalkers for that matter, had the ability to heal rapidly, but he would never have been able to recover so swiftly on his own . . . if at all.

"She saved your life, fool," he acknowledged aloud with bitterness. *How* and even *why* were complete mysteries, but nevertheless . . . it irked him to understand that he had thanked her for it by hurting her somehow.

Trace moved slowly, the deep resonance of his groan joining the other odd echoes that seemed to fill a world of things without the people those things were intended for. He walked out of the debris field and into the empty street. He paused just long enough to search the empty asphalt once more for a glimpse of blond hair, but she was, as expected, long gone.

Trace turned his attention back toward the store and the partially prone body of the regency's enemy. He trekked back to Baylor and reached down to snatch his band of office from around his arm. Trace snapped the bloodied bangle of platinum onto his own biceps, just below the ornate copper one he wore marking him as the royal vizier with its inlay of aquamarine stones. It was tradition to wear the trophy of a defeated enemy beneath the mark of one's office, but in this case it would also serve as a visible warning to others who thought to betray the monarchy.

And by the sound of Baylor's rantings, there were more than a few looking to do just that. Trace needed to get to Xenia and Guin as soon as possible. As the Chancellors' personal bodyguards, they needed to be made aware of the threat nesting so close to the throne. Baylor had been one of the Senate, one of a body of advisors and lawmakers constantly given access to the royals. It would be nothing at all for others like him to surround the monarchy in a single swoop and deal it a blow in the style of Julius Caesar before anyone even realized there was a threat. Even his knowledge of Baylor's treachery was a matter of either pure luck on his part, or pure stupidity on the part of the conspirators.

If they had aspired to include him in their deceitful plots, was it because they had just been critically misinformed, or had they dared and succeeded with others equally high up in trusted ranks? The thought chilled him to his core just as much as it angered him. He gritted his teeth against all pain and weakness and immediately forced himself into lurching progress along the streets of New York.

He didn't go far before heading for the dark tunnels of the subway. Unlike the subways in the "real" New York, there were no yellowed fluorescents and no sparking flickers of electricity from passing trains or friction from brakes on rails. Nowadays, most of these smaller lights went unnoticed in a city, but no light was too small for notice to a Shadowdweller. Only the moon and stars and perhaps the faintest of candle glow was tolerable, but he need not worry about any of it in Shadowscape. In truth, in Realscape, the subways and other tunnel systems like them were a common resource for traveling the human cities that reeked with light—provided one avoided the light-flooded stations and hubs the humans used.

Trace leapt down onto the track, ignoring the speed and efficiency of the trains out of habit. He did very little in Shadowscape that he wouldn't do in Realscape. It wasn't unheard of that something might trigger a spontaneous Unfading. Generally, it happened to youths and weaker 'Dwellers, inexperience and low power resources often denying stability of the Fade state. For Shadowdwellers of Trace's astounding power, however, even severe injury would not jolt them from their Fade. That didn't mean that injury and another added stressor wouldn't, so he took great care as he crossed the length of the city belowground.

Trace paused as a train blew past him on the next track. The vibrations it sent rocketing under his feet were familiar, and, even wounded as he was, he was completely unconcerned about the danger flying by so close to him at such deadly speeds.

He skipped lines some time later, his stride increasing in length and speed as his body continued to heal itself. By the time he exited the Hunt's Point station, he was practically feeling spry.

Now he finally took the opportunity to Unfade.

Because he was so powerful, and because his Fade was so definitive, it took just as much effort to escape the freedoms of Shadowscape as it did to enter them. The key, however, was in sensing light. Or rather shadows. He knew, obviously, to avoid the physical objects that were known for shedding light in Realscape. But it was always important to check for the unexpected. Shadowdwellers had many special senses and abilities, but none was keener than the sense for light and the bodily alarms that went off in anticipation of coming into contact with it. Trace searched himself for these before committing completely to the Unfade. This was what would warn him if he was Unfading into danger.

It was almost always heartbreaking to leave the perfect darkness and liberty of Shadowscape. There was nothing to fear in that world so perfectly made for his kind. At least, not for a while. It was like the twinge of onrushing tears out of the blue, the sensation of releasing his hold on that 'scape. It smarted through his sinuses and behind his eyes, and a weight he didn't feel in Shadowscape insinuated itself back into his chest as he Unfaded into Realscape. His extremities went a little numb, but then sensation rushed back like they were waking from a cramped sleeping position. All of this took place over a span of sixty seconds, and with each ticking moment, sound and the vibration of the real world ebbed into him. Sirens, the rising blare of a passing horn, and even the rousing yapping of provoked dogs—all of it rushed into him, reminding him of how the city could truly be when its population was actually using it.

Then, on the next breath, the transition was over.

But this was all old hat to a man of Trace's longevity. He had learned to Fade and Unfade sometime just before his adolescence, some two hundred-odd years ago. In that time since then, he had skipped dimensions so often and for so many reasons that it was no different to him than using a revolving door to transition from inside a building to outside of one. So as soon as he was back to walking the shadows of the full human city of New York, he continued to his destination.

It only took five minutes for him to find the dingy façade of brick and broken glass he was looking for. To the outside world, it was no different than any of the other abandoned tenements that had become harbors for the homeless and those who were helplessly addicted to crack, crank, or ice. He stepped carefully over the refuse such people left behind them. But in this building, there was an end to the space they could access. After the width of a single room on all sides, outsiders were met with a thick wall of cinderblock and brick. Beyond that, Trace knew, was a second wall just as thick. This was a Shadowdweller safe house. There were only two ways in, and you had to know them to find them. The first was a common way, the entrance he was headed for. The second was an escape, used only in moments of extreme danger or threat of discovery. There were houses like this one all over the world, hidden in plain sight and maintained by caretakers who chose to remain native to the cities in order to provide safe havens for traveling Shadowdwellers who needed to plan their way through them so carefully.

Trace found the entrance after climbing on top of a broken wall. He thrust a hand between etched bricks, the instructions in ancient Shadese, a symbolic language that appeared to be meaningless graffiti to the average outsider, if an average outsider should even dare to enter a neighborhood such as this one. He checked behind himself, all his night-bred senses telling him the nearest human body was rooms away. Reassured, he grabbed the lever behind the brick with his fingertips and with just a squeeze released the latch. The heavy brick wall pivoted away from him on a fulcrum, the weight of it becoming insignificant. It swung only wide enough to let him squeeze into the narrow tunnel between the double walls. He then had to slide sideways several steps before finding the second latch.

As the final doorway swung open, Trace stepped into a completely altered existence. Unlike entering Shadowscape, however, this was more about material improvements. It was like stepping into a sultan's home, lush with riches like velvet and beaten gold for ornamentation. Trace entered the main parlor with a relieved sort of sigh, but kept back from being seen by the general population milling about in conversation.

There was a significant crowd in the room. This was to be expected, since the entire royal household and most of the Senate was migrating north at the present time. Of course, not everyone could be contained in the same safe house, and there would be carefully planned cycles as they all passed through and moved on, but it was posh and prestigious to claim travel with the Chancellors themselves, so it was a much coveted time and place to be. Senators, priests and their handmaidens, and quite a few other upper-class members of their society were blended together. It made the rather large parlor seem much smaller than it was.

It also reminded Trace of just how close-quartered danger could be to the royals at that very moment. The very idea chilled him through as he ran suspect eyes over senators like Garamond and Ethane, who were notorious for siding against the Chancellors whenever they could draw breath. But those were obvious choices and it would be foolish to focus there alone. As it had been during the clan wars, he was going to have to suspect everyone, from Declan the treasurer to Killian the head of security. *Drenna* help them if it was someone like Killian, though. As trusted as he was? As close as he was to the very safety of the twin regents?

Trace caught a familiar pair of eyes across the room. It was easy to spot the house's hostess, really. She was the only one in the room who wasn't dressed in dark blues, browns, or blacks. Instead, she had chosen a brilliant peacock blue satin dress that fell in luscious folds from her slim body. She could afford the luxury of the flashy colors because she rarely traveled outside of her environment of the safe house.

"Valerina," he greeted her as she crossed the room quickly to approach him. Her gray-black eyes roamed his obviously worse for wear body with concern, her brows drawing down expressively.

"My Lord Vizier," she returned, "you are injured. I will fetch you aid."

She raised a hand, ready to snap one of her attendants to attention, but he caught her wrist and eased her arm back down. His dark eyes slid over the others in the room, taking note of who was watching them with interest already.

"That isn't necessary," he assured Valerina. "I'm almost completely healed."

"You will forgive me for saying so, *Ajai*, but that is bull-shit."

Trace couldn't help the half-hitched grin he turned onto her. She lifted a wry brow and gave him a look that reminded him quickly why he liked the sharp-witted woman. She was no-nonsense through and through, and few got away with trying to deceive her. They were good qualities in a woman entrusted to protect untold numbers of 'Dweller lives over the years.

"Be that as it may," he countered, "I have my reasons to use a little discretion."

Discretion and secrecy were other topics she understood well and negotiated with regularity. Her entire life was a well-kept secret from the human world that surrounded her, after all. So, without another word, she turned and led the way to a curtained alcove. She gestured to the door hidden behind the damask fabric.

"Take the hallway to the end, *Ajai* Trace, and use the door on your left. You will find my private bath within. While you make use of it, I will have Raul go to the secured quarters and retrieve some clean clothes from your wardrobe. And before you argue," she continued sharply, holding up a hand to ward him from doing just that, "recall that discretion is your aim. If you enter secure quarters looking like you do and come into the presence of the monarchy thus, you will defeat that purpose."

"But of course," he agreed after a moment, reaching to

take her stubborn hand out of the air and turning it gently up to his lips for a kiss of respect to match his short bow. This brought a smile to sleekly painted lips, the glistening garnet color flattering the clean white of her teeth and the sparkle flashing in her eyes.

"I'll not have you dissatisfied in the slightest while you are in my house, *Ajai*," she said, the statement more like a reprimand that he should even hint otherwise.

"I find the possibility simply preposterous, Valerina. Thank you."

Chapter 3

Why did you leave me?
Why did you shun me?
I never shunned you!
Yes, she said, *you did. You all do. You always do. You are all the same.*
I am many things, my little mouse, but ordinary is not one of them. I am like nothing you know.
Yes, she relented. *You are a man who uses a sword to kill. I have never known anyone like that.*

Trace awoke with a jolt, water raining down on him hot and sharp like a shower of needles. He had fallen asleep on his feet, his exhaustion catching up with him and forcing him into a brief state of dreaming thoughts. Voices dimly whispered in his mind, a barely caught memory of barely realized concepts and visions. His head hurt, ringing with all the effort he had put into the past hours.

And for inexplicable reasons, he couldn't get the image of the young and vulnerable Ashla's final expression of stricken hurt and tragic dismay out of his head.

"Damn," he muttered, reaching to shut off the taps with

hard twists of frustration. Yeah, it had been a hell of a day. And it wasn't over yet. Now he had to find the regents and break the bad news. He was already dreading the conflict. He never knew what Tristan was going to take seriously and what he was going to blow off. It was Malaya he would have to count on, the female Chancellor proving to be the more grounded of the twins. That wasn't to say Tristan hadn't earned his place at the head of the Shadowdweller people, but as Trace had remarked to Baylor, the new monarch suffered from an overabundance of confidence.

Trace walked out of the shower and found the clothing Valerina had promised him resting within immediate reach. He didn't waste any more time than necessary, pulling his clothes on before he was even decently dry. The purpose of the bathing had been to not draw attention and to not alarm anyone by dragging his exhausted carcass into the inner chambers covered in encrusted blood and looking like death warmed over. By the same token, he wasn't out to impress anyone with his grooming.

He quickly exited the bath and found his way down the twisting hallways. In as much as these buildings had once been run-of-the-mill squared-out apartments, it was Shadowdweller style to make a labyrinth of anywhere they lived. The theory was the more corners, the more hidden places they could create, the better to escape light or danger when it came. It had worked too often for them to ever consider changing their ways.

Killian was hanging around the guards who were in charge of keeping everyone out of the royal suites, probably checking up on them to make certain they weren't having any trouble keeping others away. Senators and the like loved to throw their weight around in attempts to get private audiences with the monarchy. However, Killian's men were well trained and quite used to standing up in the face of power threats, the likes of which they could sometimes hand out.

"*Ajai* Trace." Killian greeted him as he approached. He

was smiling, but Trace saw the smile waver and then hold in false position as he got closer to him. Killian had been in and broken up too many brawls in his day not to notice when a man had had a serious shit-kicking handed to him. Despite his healing, Trace knew he was pretty banged up still. But he warned Killian off with a look, and the other guards didn't seem to take notice as he brushed past them.

Killian would have to get caught up later, Trace thought.

He entered the deepest rooms of the craftily constructed safe house, soft and silent in his barefooted steps, partially from habit and partially with automatic respect. He'd begun to hear music and laughter shortly after crossing the barrier that marked the denser line of security in the depths of the house. Now, as he drew closer to the source, both grew in volume and merriment.

When he pushed open the door to the Chancellors' private lounge, he immediately saw the source of this enjoyment. The music was a low throb of steady drumbeats and the overlay of tubular bells, as well as various types of harps and a sitar. Together the overall effect was powerful and playful, a thread of low sensuality marking the beat as it did in most of their music. This was mostly because, next to darkness, the thing they most treasured was the joyous freedom of dance. It had a marked place in their culture, crossing between the genders without prejudice. It had a place in almost every interaction of note, such as special occasions, celebrations, acknowledgments, and flirtations. They used dance to celebrate victory and declare war. They used it to prelude birth and to mourn death. It was even used in some more intricate forms of sex.

As if to demonstrate, a beautiful, lithe dancer swirled across the floor in a billowing frame of dark red skirts heavily embroidered in gold. She was not wearing *paj*, the traditional matching trousers that more conservative 'Dweller females always wore beneath their skirts, so the speed and whip of her dancing became a display of warm, brown skin along long, supple legs. She wore a snug bolero, also in red, with sunflowers of gold embroidered painstakingly on the fabric. Without an under- or over-blouse, the lean muscles of her midriff were on display, as was the lushness of her cleavage. Her flawless skin was gleaming with perspiration from her exertions, the salty dampness wetting the black curling hair along her temples and neck.

Trace glanced to the occupants of the room: the six musicians discreetly separated from the rest of the room by a bamboo and paper partition; the two bodyguards who dogged the steps of the royal twins with every waking moment; and the Chancellors themselves.

Tristan was sprawled back in relaxation amongst an arrangement of pillows on the floor, all of which were made of fine, rich fabrics for his comfort. He was sipping wine from an elegant etched glass with gold inlay and delicately bejeweled with the family crest's four-point stars in precious faceted rubies. Those rubies matched the armband of office around Tristan's significant left biceps, the thick gold cuff making no mistake of the power and prestige of its wearer.

The sister band to match it was gleaming on the arm of the dancer who was gliding and reaching in a breathtaking display of skill and physical endurance by one of the most graceful women Trace had ever known. Trace had no problems with Malaya's enthusiasm for dance, especially when he considered how happy and healthy it kept her, and the pleasure it gave him and others to watch her. However, he thought with a frown, he did take issue with the immodesty of her dress. As a figurehead for her culture, she was expected to uphold a careful balance between the modern world and the traditional one. In this instance, a woman was a thing of exceptional and treasured beauty, but according to tradition she should never allow her dignity to be compromised by being seen in provocative dress in public, thereby opening herself up to criticism and aspersion. The saving grace in this instance was that her audience was limited to himself, her brother, and their bodyguards, who were used to seeing both royals in all manner of dress and undress. Malaya was simply amusing herself and her twin; she wasn't out to rock and shock the rest of their conservative, traditionalist culture.

At least, not at that moment.

Malaya was deeply proud of her heritage and the traditions of their society. She wore full formal dress more often than not, she demanded ritual respect from those around her, and she was devoutly religious. That being said, she had a fierce modern streak running through her that came screaming to the surface every so often. Trace imagined she sated that voracious need for female freedoms by doing things like . . . like dancing in brief, provocative clothing when in relative privacy.

The music stopped and Malaya dropped to the floor in a graceful but heavily panting bow, her folded legs beneath her as her palms and forehead touched the cold marble floor in a gesture of submission and respect aimed at her brother. Again, this was tradition. Had it been Tristan dancing, he would have ended similarly in respect to his sister. Tristan rang the stone of his ruby and platinum ring against the rim of his chalice in salute to his sister.

"Damn me into Light, Laya." He chuckled as he sat up and reached for the pile of rich, silky curls that spilled all around her head on the floor. "You're bound to please your mate beyond speech when he first sees you dance for him. Would that I could find a bride so talented."

Malaya lifted her head, shaking back the heavily curled strands with one of the rich laughs Trace was so accustomed to rolling out of her.

"So you say, my brother," she teased him, "but no woman would have your arrogant ass unless she also had a great talent for patience. She must also like small children in the bodies of full-grown men," she added primly, her folded hands falling into her lap.

"Aye," Tristan agreed with a devilish grin flashing clean and white against his dusky coloring. "Just as you are going to need a man who can tolerate your cheek."

"The only such creature is my twin before me," Malaya declared, stretching forward to briefly give his cheek a warm, nuzzling kiss. Trace recognized it as her apology for publicly teasing him, if you could call the small gathering public. "So I am doomed, as you are, to an eternity of bachelorhood."

"Excellencies," Trace spoke up at last, finally announcing his arrival.

Twin dark heads turned in unison to regard him, and matching smiles appeared. It was uncanny, at times, how much alike they could look and behave, just as it was disturbing how wholly different the twins could be in both thought and action.

"*Ajai* Trace!" Tristan surged up to his feet with ease and speed to greet him with enthusiasm, clasping forearms with him in a firm, gripping familiarity. "Where in Light have you been? One moment you are at my side, the next I can't find you for nearly two days. It's not like you to be unavailable."

Two days.

It was hard to explain how time in differing dimensions worked, and even harder to understand. It wasn't a fixed thing, time. At least, not between Realscape and Shadowscape. Shadowscape time wasn't a fixed factor at all. You never really knew how time was passing in Realscape while you were there, no matter how you tried using technology to track it. What had seemed like no more than a day in Shadowscape to Trace had been two in the realm of the real.

"Forgive me, Tristan, it couldn't be helped." Trace wasted no time in catching the Chancellor's eyes in a steady and serious exchange of intent. "We must talk, *M'itisume*."

Malaya had gained her feet as well and her hands clapped together sharply, the echoing sound full of command as her palm cut downward in obvious dismissal. The musicians scurried discreetly for the nearest exit, while the bodyguards moved closer to their charges.

"Where is Rika?" Trace asked, noting the female vizier's absence for the first time. She was to Malaya what he was to Tristan. There were no absolutes, of course. They often crossed advisory territory. However, for the most part, they each kept their focus on their own Chancellor. The truth of the matter was that their culture was sometimes too divergent when it came to the behaviors of its sexes. Each had critical protocols to adhere to, as well as pitfalls to avoid. Trace and Rika were experts in protocol, social graces and, for want of a better term, spin control. However, they were also trained in the arts of government, diplomacy, and the deadly skills of war. It was no easy position to qualify for, nor was it easy to maintain. But if Trace thought his job was a difficult one, he only need look to his regents to know there was one far more difficult.

Or in this case, two.

Xenia and Guin, understandably, held the next most complicated jobs. The most unusual thing about the bodyguards was the way their respective appointments flouted conventions. That both regents had chosen members of the opposite sex to protect them had stirred up quite a bit of a fuss, and even more snide speculation. It was dying down with time, as most sensationalism did, but it was still a much debated issue when opponents of the Chancellors ran out of things to squawk about.

But regardless of the gossip, no one could deny either warrior as being the best at what they did. Publicly, they were called "bodyguards," but they often did much more than that. Not that placing their lives in the roles as shields to the two hottest political targets in their society wasn't enough, but facts were facts. They were food tasters, inspectors of every detail the regents came into contact with, and always expected to know every detail about anyone who was to be in the royal presence. They were also bosom companions and confidants to their charges, the nature of their jobs making them the most readily available resource to confide in when things came up in the personal life of the Chancellers, who were afforded little privacy and even less trust of those outside the regime. Sometimes the warriors were, at the softest whisper of permission from their masters, private assassins. As the twins grabbed a firmer foothold on their reign, things like that were less necessary, but in the beginning it had been the only way to deal with the most aggressive enemies who had sought their heads.

But the clan wars were over now, for the most part, and for the first time in a great many decades the Shadowdwellers were united beneath a single ruling body. That wasn't to say there wasn't still opposition out there that endangered the stability of the Chancellery, and Trace's encounter with Baylor had more than proven that.

"Rika wasn't feeling well and she retired early," Malaya informed him as she reached for the over-blouse she had shed before she began dancing. She slid on the embroidered charmeuse, pulling it closed around her chest. "What is troubling you, *Ajai*?"

"I have killed Baylor," he confessed softly.

Chapter 4

Trace was wandering the street in the dark, a habit he had when he was trying to think something through. It was like a deadly sort of game, or perhaps the Shadowdweller version of extreme sports. Striding from shadow to shadow, avoiding the rims of light that flooded the city streets. His steps were light and quick, his body movements as fluid as the inky sections of dark that protected him from certain agony—even death if he were exposed long enough or fully enough.

But it wasn't this, nor was it Baylor's treacherous attack on him that nagged at his thoughts and conscience. In truth, he couldn't seem to get the haunting image of the fair and fragile Ashla out of his head. A large part of the issue, he supposed, was his indebtedness to her. The bald fact of the matter was that she had saved his life. And, as Malaya had wisely pointed out a short time ago, she had saved the lives of his regents as well. Had he died in Shadowscape, there would have been no one to warn them of the plot that brewed against them. There was very little information to work from as it was, but very little was far more than none at all.

As a religious woman, Malaya was also fascinated with the Lost woman's ability to see Trace and his enemy, as well as her fascinating corporeal attributes. The Chancellor did not believe in coincidences, but she felt quite strongly about divine providence. To her mind, Darkness had provided the impossible for Trace at just that moment to help him, and it was very hard for him to argue. By the time he had left the royals, Malaya had all but asked him to return to Shadow-scape and try again to seek this woman out, and perhaps some answers as well.

A preposterous idea, of course. The city, and all of Shadow-scape for that matter, was far too enormous to ever hope to run into a single individual again without it being planned . . . never mind the fact that she would probably try to hide from him if she caught the slightest hint that he was looking for her. But if he could thank her for what she had done, maybe then his mind would rest a bit. Maybe then he could focus once again on the more critical issues instead of this grating regret for having upset her.

"Damn," he muttered, running a hand back through his hair.

He stopped where he was, looking around himself and then at the sky. He could sense the coming day, the lightening of the area too miniscule for human perception but an in-grained alarm to all of his Shadowdweller senses. If he crossed into Shadowscape now, he would be trapped within it until the fall of darkness the next night. This, too, he would sense instinctively, which kept him from crossing out into light by accident because his perception of time had otherwise been toyed with by the alternate dimension.

Trace couldn't believe he was actually considering doing this ridiculous thing. But apparently that was why he had returned to the site of his fight with Baylor. He had made up his mind long before he was aware he was even considering the action.

Trace closed his eyes, leaned back deeply into the darkest of shadows, and slowly began to pull that darkness into himself. He could feel the night entering him first, its weakening hold on the world easily felt in the way it vibrated through him like the tantrum of a furious child. Then there was the tart taint of light that trimmed the edges of the shadows, creating them as much as it destroyed them at whim. It cut through his palate like the rusty taste of blood on the tongue, filling him with an overwhelming urge to spit. It passed quickly enough, though, and soon all there was were the wraiths of blackness that tugged and pulled him toward Shadowscape. He held his breath, like a diver swimming through an underwater tunnel that led from one section of a cove to another one that lay hidden beyond it.

He surfaced in Shadowscape with a gasped draw for breath, a reflex when it took a while to cross. The process was drawn out, depending on how dark it really was around the traveler. The lights of the city and the dawn had pushed the limits of what was safe, and it had been much more taxing on his inner energy to leave from such an unsuitable launching point.

But he was safe now, the utter darkness of the 'scape a pure delight. It would rejuvenate him in time, to the point of euphoria. Of course, like anyone else, he would have to leave once he reached that point. There was a reason why 'Dwellers didn't just stay in Shadowscape all of the time, and it fell under the category of too much of a good thing.

Trace looked around himself slowly, orienting his eyesight to the darkness it was intended for. In Realscape, Shadowdwellers were all a little bit "blind." Unless there was perfect darkness as far as their eyes could see, the shedding of light caused an ache and even sometimes a blur in their eyes. They were prone to terrible headaches, quite often full-blown migraines. Still, those were minor weaknesses and were gladly endured for times like these, where perfect darkness spread the world out before them in brilliant, vivid colors and details. He imagined that this was what humans saw in their daylight worlds, only what he could see was probably much better. He had never heard of a human who could easily see for blocks at a time, see in infrared, and even have enough intuitive sight to know what was lying around corners . . . at least for the first couple of feet.

Normally, none of this would have been likely to help him as he looked for a Lost woman in Shadowscape, but *this* woman gave off very real heat and quite vibrant energy.

Still, he was hit with a bolt of surprise when he immediately caught sight of a slight-figured female less than half a block away from where he stood. She had returned to the scene of the fight as well! As delighted by that as he was, Trace couldn't help but wonder why she would do that. Was she looking for him? Or was she merely gawking at the scene of his gruesome act like so many humans always seemed so fascinated with doing?

There was only one way to find out, and because he didn't know for certain how he would be greeted, he approached his target with all the stealth his species was born with.

Ashla walked away from the ruined store at a clipped pace, muttering under her breath at her absolute foolishness. *Of course he wouldn't be there*, she reprimanded herself. No one would stay in such a mess, and surely there were many more places of better comfort to be found in New York City.

The trouble was, she couldn't keep from feeling like she had acted like a total ass. Fear and disorientation had been no excuse. She ought to have kept her cool and shot down his ignorance and prejudice. Why, he had no right whatsoever to look down on her! Especially considering that she had saved his miserable hide! She could have kept her secret and just as well let him drop dead in that store like he'd expected. But no, she had thrown herself open—risked herself, even—and his thanks had been condemnation?

The more she thought about it, the angrier Ashla became. She was frustrated that she had no one to take it out on. She was even more frustrated that she was so desperate for the

company of another human being that she would have probably sacrificed all of her righteous indignation if he would
only promise to keep her company.

It was this thought that made Ashla realize her solitude
was truly getting to her. She would rather keep company
with a man who beheaded people than be alone? Talk about
desperation!

She had been the lonely, isolated sort even when there
had been other people milling all around her, so she knew
the meaning of desperation quite well. When that kind of
solitude became too much to bear, she would cut herself
away from her normal routines and take a wild chance on
something, like going to a New Year's party even if it meant
driving on the most frightening night of the year.

At that subconscious trigger, a wild rush of sudden illness
overran her body. Chills and queasiness overwhelmed her
and she had to stop and brace a hand against the wall for balance as her head spun nauseatingly. Her knees seemed to disappear and in an instant she was sinking toward the ground.

She nearly screamed when strong hands abruptly halted
her collapse, their warm power drawing her back against a
muscular and sturdy body. Even though she was dizzy and
sick, she looked up over her shoulder and into curious dark
eyes. His brow creased with clear concern as he jogged her a
bit more firmly into his hold, a solid arm crossing her ribs to
pin her tightly to his frame.

"I've got you," he assured her in a richly rumbling mur-
mur that seemed to vibrate against her ear and all down her
neck. She couldn't seem to help the little shiver the sensation
provoked, reaching to grasp his forearm instinctively. The
crisp feel of male body hair at his wrist tickled her fingertips, and Ashla was suddenly overwhelmed with a strange
sense of intimacy. Discomforted, she tried to squirm loose
even as she snatched her hands off him and made fists out of
them.

"Be easy!"

It was a command, plain and simple. The sharp jerking of her body in his grasp made that quite clear to her. And that was to say nothing of the dark heaviness of his voice and the way it seemed so obvious that he was used to having his commands obeyed. Considering his talents with a sword, Ashla could see why no one would be compelled to argue with him.

And there it was, beneath the long black coat he wore, the thick buckle of the belt that held its sheath pressing into her backside from where it was slung at a low angle across his hips. This was what made her realize her feet weren't touching the ground. There was no way otherwise, with their disparate heights, that she should find herself within such intimate fitting with him. Ashla's face was washed with an upward wall of heat and embarrassment, her complexion burning as she gasped in a breath.

Coincidentally, as her thoughts were occupied by all of this input that pushed aside her slightest memories of New Year's Eve, her feelings of illness were quickly brought to heel. She took a deep breath, wanting to demand he put her down, to get furious with him, to just explode with all of the stormy emotions she'd been besieged with ever since she had encountered him.

But she didn't do any of it. Ashla simply turned her face away from him, her hard, stressed breathing the only thing being freely expressed as she said softly, "Please, let me go."

"Really?" he asked, his richly resonant voice a prelude to his breath washing warmly over her face. "Because a moment ago I would have sworn you couldn't wait to get your hands on me."

Ashla gasped in a soft breath, trying to twist around in his hold so she could see his face. The way he said that . . . it was almost as if he were suggesting . . .

She squirmed angrily. "Let go!"

"I would," he mused, "if I wasn't worried you'd collapse

to the ground. Also, I think I rather like you this way. It keeps you in one place long enough for me to get some questions answered."

The truth of the matter was that Trace was enjoying the way her temper seemed to swell and grow with every wriggle of her body and every denial he handed her. Not that he was being mean or anything, but it was intriguing to see the streak of fury that ran through his frightened little mouse. It fascinated him that as angry as she clearly was, she refused to unleash herself on him, as he no doubt deserved.

"Please," she begged him, suddenly relaxing into a limp little creature of defeat. "Please don't."

"Don't?" he questioned. "Don't what?" Trace reached up to cup her small chin in his palm, his fingers sinking into the softness of her cheek with such ease that, for a moment, he feared he would bruise her unintentionally. He tilted her chin up, her head falling back against his chest until her pale blue eyes were blinking up at him. The shine in her overbright gaze warned him she was near to tears, so he was infinitely gentle as he looked down on her. "I'll not hurt you, *jei li*," he promised her. "What makes you think I would repay my debt to you in such unfriendly ways?"

Ashla laughed at that, fully aware of the edge of hysteria in the sound just by seeing him frown darkly at it. "Because I saw you use *that* sword to kill someone," she countered with a shudder as her eyes flicked down to the weapon on his hip.

"Is that what worries you, *jei li*? That I am armed?"

Trace reached down immediately for the buckle of his weapons belt. He slid his hand between their pressed bodies, and he found himself by accident gliding his knuckles along the curve of her backside.

She was wearing another dress, but this one was light and thin, some sort of calico or gauze cotton that barely provided a barrier to his touch. The impression was validated when he realized he could feel every stitch of the fabric of her panties. Trace unbuckled his belt and let it, the sheathed katana, and the slightly smaller wakizashi sword fall with a careless clatter to the pavement. Had Magnus seen him treat his weapons in such a disrespectful manner, Trace would have gotten an earful and, potentially, a hard refresher on the subject. The priest had forged the weapons himself, signed his name to them, and honored Trace with the gifts. Magnus very rarely bestowed his masterful weaponry on others. This one had even been specially designed for Trace's unique left-handed style.

But all of that importance faded with surprising speed as the vizier's full attention became quite riveted on the sweet warmth and shape of her provocatively nestled rear. The charge of sexual awareness that crashed through him so suddenly simply took his breath away. He was no stranger to sexual magnetism and all of its energizing benefits, but to find it so unexpectedly in so muted a package completely amazed him.

She was Lost, he tried to remind himself. By all rights, he shouldn't even be able to feel her. Anomalies notwithstanding, she *was* a ghost, merely the apparition of a woman who most likely lay in a human hospital somewhere connected to those brutally cruel machines that kept bodies alive well beyond sense and grace. Far beyond all dignity.

But it was so hard to reconcile all of that with the lushly heated woman he held against himself; the one who squirmed provocatively whether she knew it or not; the one whose scent changed abruptly under the attentiveness of his keen senses, telling him he wasn't the only one affected by all of this.

Drawn in, Trace lowered his nose to her neck, running the tip lightly along the length of it as he drew in a slow, searching breath. "There," he said softly into her fair hair, his gaze fascinated by the gleam of gold and platinum in every flip and wave, "no weapons."

Ashla was quite unsure about that. Her heartbeat raced in

response to the way he held and stroked her. Every touch was both completely innocent and outrageously provocative. Perhaps it was the tone of his deep voice as it caressed her skin, or the way he seemed to breathe deep of her, but Ashla was also quite aware that there was so much more to it than that. She had felt it when she had covered his body in her touch to heal him. She felt it even more now that she was locked against him under his power. Her body instantly responded, a flush of awareness congregating with long-denied hungers inside her. She blushed with dreadful embarrassment when her nipples hardened into prodding points against the arm that still held her close.

"Tell me why you ran away from me before," he suddenly asked, his coaxing query sounding half distracted. Ashla didn't realize that Trace's attention had been snared by the reaction of her body, and that it had made him realize that she wasn't wearing a bra, merely a chemise, the lace of which was quite obvious beneath the scant material of her dress. All it would take was the lifting of his thumb to prepare her for his teasing stroke of touch. Trace was floored by the power of his yearning to do just that. How in all that was Light had this gone from seeking her out to thank her to becoming an exercise in sensual temptation?

More importantly, how was it that he of all people would be feeling this way? For years he had held on to such bitter memories that he could barely stand to touch or be touched by a woman. And now . . .

He shook his head in denial. How could any Shadowdweller even feel in such a way toward a *human*?

Half a human.

If that.

Trace let go of her suddenly, stepping away from her as she stumbled in her sudden, unexpected freedom. Ashla turned around slowly and he could see the shaking of her hands as she ran one through her short, soft hair. She didn't realize that Trace had lost track of his own question as he tried to plow some kind of order to his jumbled thoughts. So she caught him off guard when she answered.

"Because you . . . you shunned me."

Why did you shun me?

I never shunned you!

The haunted whispers of a half-realized memory swirled through Trace's brain, even as he responded with knee-jerk indignation. "I did nothing of the kind!"

"You did! You said 'what are you?' like . . . like I was some sort of . . . of demon!"

"Because I thought you were . . ."

He trailed off before he could tell her he had actually thought that very thing. Not a demon, but a Demon, a Night-walker race of elementals with great powers. But he had certainly never thought of her as the human incarnation of "demon," some twisted beast damned and deceptive. Trace was actually insulted by the idea she would think him capable of such a disparagement, forgetting she had no way of knowing otherwise about him.

"Look," he said irritably, "I have seen things a lot stranger than you, little mouse. Some human girl who can heal may be unique, but certainly not strange enough to make me forget how to treat someone with decency!"

"Then why did you ask it like that? And—" Ashla stopped short, jerking her head and shoulders into a tight sort of attention as her pale, pretty eyes narrowed on him suspiciously. "What do you mean, 'some human girl?' What other kinds of girls are there?"

Oh, Light and damnation, Trace thought with an inner groan at his own massive stupidity. How could he have made such a mistake? Then again, how often did he ever speak with humans in the first place? It wasn't as though he was well practiced in guarding the uses of his language outside of the Shadowdweller society.

"Please," he said, his tone lowering to a coaxing level. "I feel as though we have misunderstood each other from the start, and all I want to do is fix that so I can thank you for what you did."

"You want to thank me?" she asked, her suspicion seeming to deepen. "No questions? No curiosity? You don't find me strange, so it begs the question what have you seen that you do classify as strange."

That was when Trace realized that for all her bundles of fear, little blond Ashla was ounce for ounce as sharp as others might be brave. What she lacked in courage, she clearly made up for in intellect. He had underestimated her in that respect, and now would have to either pull off some dazzling damage control, or . . .

Lie.

Trace was quite good at telling creative truths. He was even better at flat-out lying. He had to be. Not a single ruling body on the planet that he knew of could function on a completely open and fully honest governing style. Secrets were a necessary evil, especially when it protected vital information and key negotiations between touchy cultures; especially when the telling of truths would leave opportunity for enemies to plunge their daggers into the hearts of the monarchy.

Yet now that he was faced with upholding one of the more crucial lies his people perpetuated, the one that secured their anonymity as a race in order to protect them from hers, his tongue seemed to freeze against it. He found himself trapped in a pair of fair blue eyes the likes of which amazed him, the lightness of them completely mesmerizing. What was more, he couldn't escape the feeling that she had had more than her share of liars and betrayers in her life. Trace shook his head, trying to tell himself that he was applying his own impressions onto her without a single shred of proof, but it didn't sway the overwhelming cry of his instincts. How could he force himself to ignore them when he was so used to living by them?

Ashla saw him hesitate, however, and her face wrinkled

with distress and pain. She was so ready to think the worst of him, and probably anyone else as well. It amazed him that so young a woman could be so jaded. He wasn't an expert at judging human age, but he estimated she was not yet out of her third decade. If she'd had the longevity of a Shadowdweller to look forward to, she would have the time to grow out of this bitter stage while still in her youth. She would learn how truly vast life could be, and how insignificant some things became in the face of it.

"Don't bother saying anything if you're going to lie," she said heavily, shaking her head as she turned away from him.

"I'm not going to lie," he said sharply, grabbing her arm and turning her back to him.

"But you thought about it," she accused as she stumbled awkwardly in his hands. She gave a strange little hop before daring him to deny it with the glare of those uncanny eyes.

"Yes. I thought about it," he admitted with a stiff nod. It burned him to confess it to her, and the unfamiliar guilt of it sat very ill on him. He was completely baffled as to why this would be so damn hard for him, but without a solution he had no choice but to be as honest as he could. "Look, there are things I just can't talk about . . ."

"Is one of them the fact that you've talked about thrones and traitors when there are very few monarchies left in this world? Very few of anything, for that matter," she added, gesturing to indicate the dark world around them.

This was when Trace caught the first sight of bright and dark reds streaking her palms. Far too familiar with the look of it, Trace plucked one of her hands out of the air, pulling her forward with a hasty jerking motion that was far rougher than he had intended.

Ashla gasped and squeaked out a startled sound of protest when the dark male so suddenly manhandled her, bringing her with a harsh tug against his chest as he pinned her to him at the back of her waist with one hand and drew her hand to his face with the other. She could swear she almost felt him shuddering with some tightly contained emotion, but his expression was grim and shadowed in the darkness. She felt his heated breath on her palm, the flow of it rushing over the tender cuts and deeper gashes that were there.

His deeply black eyes glittered as they turned to hers, and she got the thorough feeling that he was furious with her for something. She found that rather rich, considering he was the one with a lot of explaining to do after admitting he was more inclined than not to being dishonest with her. But the truth was, Ashla was tired of lies and liars. She was tired of being judged and found wanting. She was mostly tired of feeling like she was the only one in the world who didn't have a clue what was going on. And considering that the world as she knew it consisted of herself and a man who was keeping secrets, she could hardly be wrong.

With a sudden feeling of vertigo, she felt his hand shoving her against her breastbone, pushing her back off balance. She was next aware of the powerful strength of steady male muscles as he simultaneously dipped her and sank to his knee. The way he moved, she realized suddenly, with such ease and vigor, it was as if he had never been injured at all. He couldn't possibly have healed to such a point in the hours that had passed. Even with her healing, there was just no way. She had only taken him so far before she had run from him, and as soon as she was no longer touching him, the effect of her ability would have worn off instantly. As it was, she needed as much skin-to-skin and body-to-body contact as she could manage to pull off a healing of that magnitude.

She clutched his coat at his shoulders as he brought her down to the ground, allowing the cold of the concrete to seep through her skirt against her backside. But the chill was washed away in an instant when she became aware of him catching her dress by its hem and jerking it well above her knees. She yelped a protest, quickly snagging the material and shoving it back down, but all she managed was a hard meeting with his hand as it caught her mid-motion, stopping her in her tracks. More impressive was the softly spoken snarl of displeasure that gave voice to the anger in his eyes. She had never heard a man make such a sound. This time her chills developed larger chills of their own, and she simply froze under the cold of it. Petrified, she started to shake as he pushed her skirt back once more.

She watched with wide eyes as his gaze drifted down over the length of her exposed legs. It was as if the man had more than two hands as he touched her in one jolting shock after another. First on her thigh, then behind her knee as he pried her legs apart, and then her ankle as he raised her shin to his studied inspection. By the time his fingers danced along the sweep of her instep, she could barely catch her breath, and she had to tell herself quite firmly that it was a product of fear as he continued to control and overwhelm her.

Ashla became less convinced of that, however, as he bent over her like a tiger crouching over prey, but only touched her once more, this time with fingers filtering through the hair at her temple. His expression never changed, that black, fearsome glitter still flashing in his eyes, but she no longer felt it in his touch.

"The glass from the shop," he ground out in a guttural voice, the tone reminding her of that primal sound he had made not too long ago. "Your hands, shins, knees, and feet are shredded. Why are you walking around like this? *Drenna*, this must scream with agony, Ashla. Why would you be so foolish . . . ?" He shook his head sharply. "Can you not cure yourself, little healer?"

Ashla didn't know how to respond at first. She had been second-guessing and fearing his every action since the moment she had first laid eyes on him, and nothing about him had prepared her for the potential of his concern. *For her*, no less.

Trace watched her blink dumbly at him from those big blue eyes, the frosted blond of her lashes seemingly dusted in sparkles the way his eyesight interpreted the lightness of them. His tongue was still flooded with the vile taste of his self-disgust as he realized he had been so preoccupied with himself and the damage being done to his own world that he had easily dismissed any potential damage that had been done to her. He had given up the search for her earlier far too quickly and with far too little effort. It had been wrong and thankless, and he despised himself for it the more his gaze tracked over her torn skin.

"I can, but . . . but I . . ."

She hesitated heavily, peeking up at him through the glistening veil of lashes, her shoulder hitched up in a prepared cringe as if she expected the worst of everything from him. And why shouldn't she? What had he shown her of himself, besides thoughtlessness and cruel disregard for anything not important to his own selfish needs?

"Stop," she whispered suddenly, a trembling hand rising to lay gentle fingers over his mouth. "I can't bear it!"

Trace didn't understand what she was talking about, the action, for a moment, as confusing as every other thing about her. Then, all in a rush, he realized that she wanted him to stop berating himself so harshly for his failures. As though she could hear him and it hurt her heart, she was begging him to cease.

"By the blessed Dark, you can read my thoughts!" he whispered fiercely, not even able to conceive of what to feel about that. Trepidation and anxiety were natural, given the vulnerability it left him at, and the people whose deepest secrets he had a hand in protecting, but . . .

"I can*not*! What a ridiculous thing to say!"

"Then explain that remark!"

"Explain yours first!" she spat back, tears burning hot across her eyes and infuriating her even more. "T-the 'human girl' the . . . the 'monarchy' . . . t-the strange . . ." She was making no sense, and they both realized that, but Ashla was too upset to clarify her garble of thoughts.

"Why haven't you healed yourself?" he demanded of her,

the tattered condition of her body winning out over all the issues that pressed down on him.

She covered her mouth and shook her head, as if she needed to physically repress her feelings and to speak would shatter the last shreds of her control. Trace had never before felt so many emotions jumbled all together inside himself. He hardly blamed her for being overwhelmed when he was wishing he himself could give in to the urge to shout that was racing through him again and again. There was something stirring deeply within him, like a part of himself he had never really met before, and the near savagery of the sensation made him want to send it back where it had come from, banishing it to the oblivion of the place where he could continue being unaware of it.

"Dark and Light, this is crazy," he rasped as he ran a hand back through his hair, his other palm curling in reflexive possession around the back of her calf. For a moment he considered he might be feeling the beginnings of Shadowscape euphoria, but quickly dismissed the idea because he knew he had only been there a short time and that effect took at least two days to settle in.

That left only one variable that had changed between this time and all the times before.

Ashla.

"My name is Trace," he said as he moved closer to her, hovering over her half-prone body. She quickly tried to put distance back between them, but the only way to do it was to lie down completely. Ashla's heart thundered beneath her breast as he came so close she could feel his body heat everywhere against her. "I tell you this because I believe I have failed to do so before," he informed her, his words coming as though he were choosing them very carefully. But in spite of his politeness, and contrary to his efforts at a neutral, explanatory tone, Ashla could hear that quality caressing the lower register of his voice that sounded a great deal like the animalistic sound he had made before. "I am a man of importance, intellect, and reason. Do you understand me?"

She nodded quickly, but her gesture only darkened his expression into a storm of annoyance.

"I mean that I am not prone to emotional whims! I don't chase ghosts and engage in fruitless behavior, because I know better! I create my world around me. I shape the progress of my life and the lives of many, many others!"

"Please," she squeaked as he loomed brusque and intense over her. Instinct put her hands to his chest, pushing at him as if her twiggy arms could make any kind of impression on that wall of muscle and masculinity.

"Tell me why you do not heal yourself!"

"Because I can't!" she shouted back at him in response to his demanding growl. "I burned myself out healing you and I won't recover for days! I'm exhausted. Weak. Weaker, I mean. I've always been weak. Always! Too delicate and fragile to give a big jerk like you a decent black eye without breaking my damn wrist! And here! Try this on for size!"

She reached for the buttons lining the front of her dress and, without bothering to free the antique silver shells, she tore it open in two violent jerks that sent silver flying in wild scatters everywhere. This act instantly revealed the chemise she wore beneath, as well as the shimmy of the breasts beneath the silky fabric. She gathered the hem of it and yanked it up, making Trace's entire body stiffen in shock and, undoubtedly, a rapid-fire response of eager anticipation that he had absolutely no hope of controlling, never mind expecting it in the first place. Trace watched as she swept the midnight blue fabric up between her breasts, keeping her modesty somewhat intact even as she bared her entire midriff from the bottom of her sternum to the low line of her panties where they crossed her hips just barely above her pubic bone.

And while that tempting little flash of feminine decadence snared his attention almost instantly, it was quickly disrupted with a scream of subconscious denial in his own brain as information glimpsed from the corner of his dark-sharpened eye roared for notice.

Trace held himself still as a statue as he let his gaze creep up the amazing light and pale plane of her belly, raw emotion roiling to a head the moment he saw the first angry furrow of a wound marring the delicate canvas. Then there was another and another; jagged evil things, fresh and wildly cut as though without rhyme or reason.

And yet . . .

Trace knew the pattern far too well.

He had hold of her in an instant, lurching back onto his knees as he drew her up off the ground. He heard her suck in a single breath and then there was just the fierce grinding of her teeth as she clenched her jaw. She stoically bore him reaching for the back of her dress and stripping it down, her eyes tightly closed and her cheek resting against his biceps where, unknown to her, dual metal bands tried to contain the swell of muscle he was using to support her weight against himself. Ashla let him do these things to her because she knew what he was looking for.

They both knew what he would find.

There, as sure as sunlight, was the exact same dagger wound that had once been in Trace's flesh.

Chapter 5

"*Aiya*." Trace whispered the exclamation in horror and in the hope that his eyes and thoughts were deceiving him. Was this really happening? Was any of this truly existent? His entire psyche's first instinct was to reject every single morsel of information. She wasn't real, therefore the injuries could not be valid, and therefore he should feel no guilt because there was no actual pain inflicted.

The logic should have been a comfort, but it simply was not.

Not while he could feel the smooth, bare warmth of the skin of her back beneath his fingertips and against the whole of his palm. Not while the drip of her tears stained and wet the fabric of his coat. And, he would swear by both the blessed Dark and the burning Light, never could that logic survive when her sweet scent, so laden with the aroma of spring lilacs, drifted up to embed itself into his sensory memory so deeply he knew he would never be able to forget it.

"Why?" he demanded hoarsely. "You had to know this would happen! Why would you do something so stupid? Why would . . ." Trace's voice broke along with the last vestiges of any attempted bravado and composure. He sat down hard on the pavement, his legs sliding beneath her as he drew her up tighter against his chest. He hugged her to himself far too strongly, but he couldn't seem to curb the need or the impulse. His heart was racing until his blood hissed like steam being forced through metal piping. The sound of it all thundered in his ears.

"The wound was mortal. You could have died," he managed at last, his words spurting out between hard, harsh breaths. "And you so small . . . so . . ."

"Weak," she finished for him, the word muffled against his shoulder.

"No! By the life of my liege, *no*! Who that is weak would do such a thing? Who, if they are so weak, would survive the doing? How can that logic stand?" Trace's hand curved up over the back of her head, his fingertips lost amongst roots of gilding and glitter, the possessiveness of the hold wholly intentional this time. "You saved my life, and now I know it was at risk of your own."

Yes. He was sure of it. Even if nothing else was true in this realm for her, the fact that she had intentionally put her life on the line, while believing the whole while that she could die, meant everything. That she had succeeded and survived meant everything *to him*. Now, at last, he understood the wild rip and ebb in the tides of his emotions . . . as well as hers.

In Trace's faith, it was believed that to willingly risk one's life to save another was the ultimate in sacrifice. If, by some chance, they survived the circumstances of the event, the sacrifice and the saved would be forever bonded to one another. Trace had been witness to several 'Dwellers who had formed bonds like this during the clan wars. Like the ethereal force of connected spirits that accompanied twin-born children, the bonded became a rhythm in specific tune with each other. They always became fast friends, no matter if they had been beforehand or not. They always knew when the other was in need.

Magnus and the other priests called them the Sainted.

But all of this applied to the Shadowdwellers only, as far as Trace understood it. What did that make of his undeniable connection to the spirit of a *human* woman? And even if he stretched this explanation to define that much, what explained the wholeness and dimension she presented in Shadowscape when no other human could?

There was also one other thing about the injuries she had sustained Trace needed to consider, but he closed his mind off to it for the moment.

He was afraid of all he didn't know about what it meant to be Sainted. For all he had been raised in Sanctuary with a priest for his foster father, the topic of the Sainted was one of the mysteries of his religion. Magnus would know. As always, his father would have answers where Trace did not. But at the same time, Trace knew what he was feeling, and the surety in his mind that he was on the right track was undeniable.

"I couldn't watch you die," she whispered softly. "I could never be that cold."

She shuddered against him, and he immediately understood that she believed that *he* was that cold. After all, she had watched him murder a man with deliberateness, even while verbally flouting the laws of his own society. It took no imagination for him to understand what she must think of him.

"But even you must have a sense of self-preservation, Ashla," he said quietly. "Where does the risk outweigh the value you place on your own life? If not in the saving of a stranger you consider no better than a common murderer, then where?"

Her reply took time in coming.

"I learned a long time ago not to judge anyone too quickly or too thoroughly, Trace. What I saw as murder, you saw as justifiable homicide . . . at least from what I heard." She lifted her head with a little sniffle and met his gaze, displaying the deep carving of wisdom within her eyes that he had somehow overlooked. "I know nothing about you or the life you come from. I am hardly qualified to pass sentence on you at a whim just because I stumbled into a five-minute cross-section of it. Can't you see how wrong that would be?"

"Yes," he said softly, his hand sliding around the side of her head until he cupped her ear against his palm and stroked his thumb along her distinctive cheekbone. "Especially when your sense of fair play saved my life. Others would not have done what you did. I'm not certain I would have done what you did, and I like to consider myself a man who is well versed in seeing all sides of an issue."

Trace set her back a few inches so he could gently revisit the ugly wounds on her body that matched the ones still healing on his own. He inspected each unsightly place with feather-soft probes of his fingertips. None of them bled, none of them were swollen with infection, but all of them were tender enough to make her flinch in spite of his extraordinary care.

"They are just sore," she explained with a placating touch on his hand. "It's nothing like they felt when you received them."

Now.

The addendum of that single word floated insidiously through his mind, and Trace knew instantly that she was editing the truth to ease his conscience. Trace was fiercely thankful for whatever it was between them that was tattling on her omission. He reached around her slim body to splay his fingers over her entire back, her smallness making him feel as though he were cupping a fragile butterfly in a single hand. He drew her close even as he lowered his lips against her ear.

"But at the moment you take them on, the wounds feel every bit as real as the moment of their inception when you absorb them into your body, don't they?"

Her response was only a short nod, but it was enough. Trace's eyes slid closed as regret trickled through him. He had watched hundreds of lives come and go, hundreds of 'Dwellers willing to accept pain and worse for the sake of their beliefs and their Chancellors, but never had it been like this for him. He knew he should feel gratitude, but it was almost impossible in that moment. Wounds he had barely felt in the heat of the battle, and had paid little mind to since, came back to him with a force and power he could hardly stand. *Now* he remembered every detail of them. *Now* he felt the flaying of flesh under the speed of sharp instruments. *Now* he truly felt a mortal blow to his body.

He at least had had his breed's strength and supernatural power at his beckoning. Ashla had not. She still did not have them.

"Where are you sleeping?" he asked her softly.

Her reaction to the question scraped harshly against him. She suddenly scrabbled with clutches of slim fingers to gather her torn dress back over her body. Trace's hands caught hers with quick gentleness and he drew her back to the warmth and protection of his body.

"It's okay," he tried to reassure her as she refused to look up at him. "In this place, we have only ourselves to count on. No doubt, you have done a fine job for quite some time. But *jei li*, you are injured and in pain, and these wounds could turn wicked before you recuperate enough to heal them on your own. You need help."

"I took ibuprofen," she argued. "I cleaned out all of the glass. I didn't need help."

I didn't need your *help.* The stubborn implication was clear, but Trace wasn't insulted at all. Her pluck came in spurts, and he knew she was afraid of the loneliness echoing in vast quantities all around them, but it was more than fear and bullheadedness that fueled her. He had no idea what she was trying to prove to herself and why, but he wasn't going to let her go off by herself again.

"Look, I have two days before I have to go—"

"Go!" she gasped, her eyes darting up now and widening

with her true feelings at the prospect of being left alone again. "But there is nowhere to go! I've been everywhere, and there's nothing! Except . . . Well, I went to LaGuardia, and . . . it was just . . . all those planes, taking off and landing empty, with no pilots that I could see! I wanted to try it, but it was just too creepy. They were like these great big mechanical ghosts. Everything is like that. Everything works without explanation or even logic. The things I see are impossible. I tried staring at these tomatoes in a bodega, so I could watch what happens to them. I guess I expected them to float away or something crazy like that. I mean, I knew things were being changed constantly. But you have to blink, you know? And when I did, it was suddenly different and I had no better explanation." She stopped suddenly, seemingly realizing that she was rambling in her anxiety. "Where will you go?" she asked at last, her shoulders slumping and her breath decompressing out of her in dejection.

Ah. The million-dollar question. Trace still didn't know how he should answer it. She was under more than enough duress at the moment, and he couldn't see his way clear to telling her that she was no doubt lying just about dead somewhere in the real world. He could also empathize with the way she struggled for understanding and knew he could provide answers that would resolve all of her questions. His urges to be honest with her warred with his fierce new need to protect her.

"I will explain what I can . . . but later. Right now we need to get you into fresh clothing and somewhere comfortable where you can rest. If you won't tell me where you are living, then we will find another place for the time being."

"No, I . . ." She fell quiet for a very long moment, searching herself quite deeply by the look of it. "I suppose it doesn't matter. I'm at the Plaza."

That made him smile at her.

"The Plaza?" he echoed. Then he shrugged with his grin.

"You know what, if it were me, that's probably where I would stay, too."

"They have big windows," she argued a bit petulantly.

"Yeah. Wouldn't want to miss those Manhattan sunrises," he teased her as he gathered her comfortably to himself and rose smoothly to his feet. He hesitated just long enough to glance down at his weapons. He hated to do anything that would disturb her further, but the fact was it wasn't safe for either of them to walk around Shadowscape unarmed. By herself she would be completely dismissed, but because of his presence she would be in danger. Just looking at her proved she could be harmed physically.

Once again Trace quickly forced himself to shut away the insidious whisper within his mind that wanted to contemplate the worst. It wanted to consider his knowledge that what happened in one 'scape, happened in all 'scapes. But . . . for all that he had seen and done in the world, Trace simply couldn't bear the concept of what had to be happening to her defenseless body in Realscape every time she suffered injury in Shadowscape.

He knelt and swept up his swords.

Chapter 6

Magnus strode into Malaya's sitting room without knocking, and the guards posted outside knew better than to gainsay his entrance. The priest was the only other person besides Guin who had unquestioning access to the Chancellor. Even Tristan was not given that freedom of access to his sister. Malaya had the power to bar him from her rooms and presence if she wished it. They had agreed on that when they had agreed to rule as perfect equals. She would not have him bossing her around or forcing conservative edicts on her that would undermine her image in the eyes of others. But they had also agreed that neither of them could bar their bodyguards without the other's approval.

Magnus's access, however, was unique. Tristan was not as deeply religious as his sister was, but he did understand her passion for her faith. He also liked the priest a great deal and respected him as a warrior and a learned man. Because he knew Trace's foster father so well, he had not thought twice about the access Malaya gave him so freely. What was more, he encouraged it. Between her bodyguard and Magnus, she was twice as safe and protected.

Magnus found his student asleep on her chaise, her work stacked neatly on the near table but a pen still clutched in her hand. The priest glanced over at Guin, who sat nearby attentively. It was very likely that all of the papers on the table had still been in her lap when she had drifted off, and that Guin had removed them thoughtfully for his mistress.

"You can never seem to get the pen," Magnus observed.

"Mmm. She grasps the thing like a prized trophy, even in sleep. Wrestling her for it would wake her and defeat the purpose," the gruff guard pointed out.

"Just as well. I wish to speak with you."

Guin raised a black brow and then extended a heavily callused hand to the empty seat across from him. The bodyguard was dressed completely in a dark charcoal gray, a few shades shy of black and proven to be more effective in a wider range of shadows than the more absolute color. Quite often Guin's best talent was in the way he managed to make his six-foot-six frame a part of the background even to other 'Dwellers. He was well known, certainly feared with good reason, and had a reputation for his savage loyalty to his mistress, and yet he could still sit close to Malaya in crowded rooms without attracting too much attention to himself. He was juggling a fistful of dangerous balls between the hand of duty that protected Malaya, and the one that understood she needed as much liberty to move and breathe as he could safely manage.

It was an exhausting concept to Magnus, despite the many things he was used to juggling in delicate balance himself, but at least he was given time to himself and time to sleep in peace. Guin did neither of those things. The guard almost never left her in care of anyone else, and his bed was always at the base of her sealed bedroom door. Had it been his choice, the guard would have probably preferred to be on the opposite side of the door where he could get to her more quickly in an urgent situation, but it was the one issue of protocol that he could not touch. Honor, as well as Malaya's reputation, forbade him from being in her chamber while she slept.

The exception being moments like these where she took her impromptu naps in her sitting room.

"She will take umbrage if we have this conversation without her," Magnus noted.

"Then she will take umbrage," Guin relented with a single-shouldered shrug. "I'll not wake her. She has slept poorly since we left New Zealand, and not at all since Trace came in with Baylor's crest of office 'round his arm."

"That was three nights past." Magnus frowned, that ever-mysterious gleam in his strange gold eyes giving Guin no clue to his thoughts. But luckily for the guard, the priest almost always spoke his mind. "No sign of Trace as yet?"

"None." Guin joined him in his frown. "If he is in 'scape as we suspect, his time must be running low. He will start to succumb to euphoria. If he waits too long, he will lose grasp of how to return to us."

"It is hard to say," Magnus argued. "Time moves so differently there. What is days to us could be a matter of hours to him."

"Yes. And he knows that. He also knows we had plans to move the entourage yesterday."

"Now that is very unlike my son," the priest agreed. "I have faith that wherever he is, for however long he is there, he has the sense to take care of himself. There is time yet before I will become genuinely concerned as far as euphoria matters." Magnus did not point out the obvious, that there were far more treacherous delays than Shadowscape euphoria that might occur. Again, the priest had faith in his son's skills when it came to defending his life. After all, Magnus had taught him everything he knew.

"I do not like disruptions that keep us stagnant," Guin complained. "The longer we remain still, the easier it is for enemies to ferret us out."

"However, if the enemies are like Baylor, if they are members of our own Senate as Trace has reported, then it hardly matters where we go and when. The Chancellors will always end up back in the vipers' nest every time session is held." Magnus finally took a seat, thoughtfully studying the bodyguard for a moment. "Has she given you leave to investigate yet?"

"No," Guin groused, his feelings about it clear in the snap of his voice. "She will not let me leave her. I cannot figure it out. I can't see if she is afraid to be left to the talents of another guard, or if she is in denial about this whole possibility." Guin looked at his charge, his craggy features smoothing with a moment's compassion. "She is devastated by this, you know. She thought we were finally getting past the deceptions and the assassinations. It is so important to her that this monarchy be accepted so it can start to be effective." His dark gaze flicked back to the priest and he shifted almost imperceptibly in his seat, as if with discomfort. "You should have been there, at the Nightwalker conference. She was so delighted, so proud of her part in bringing the Nightwalker breeds closer together. If we begin to squabble internally again, it will ruin the other breeds' trust in us that we can control our people."

"I understand quite well," Magnus said. "She speaks often of the Demons and their King, Noah. She longs for what he has managed to create with his people. The balance, the trust, and the wholesome readiness that tells her he has full confidence that his race supports him. He is a true monarch, respected and revered as such, yet an earthy companion to those he leads. This is what she longs for, for herself and her brother. She doesn't want to hear that it will take a great deal of time and patience to achieve that. I believe she finds it disheartening these days."

"The war was long. Clan against clan, sometimes cousin against cousin." Guin was almost defensive of his mistress.

"It is no easy pill for her to swallow, knowing she was responsible for instigating the largest civil war of our history."

"It was overdue and necessary, as you well know. This race was running wild and stupid. We were little more than mischief-makers and fornicators. We played, we caused trouble, we fucked, and we rolled into our beds thinking we had accomplished something." Magnus sat back with a slowly released breath. "We were rotting away beneath ourselves, the foundations of a once-organized society crumbling down around our idiotic ears. It was time for someone of royal blood to stand up and take responsibility. It was time for us all to grow up and do so. There were hundreds from many powerful clans who agreed with that, and they realized that these twins represented our breed's best and worst tendencies. They represented the best chance of getting as many of our people to identify with them and put faith in them as there had ever been before."

Magnus leaned forward in his seat, resting an elbow on his knee.

"Karri, my handmaiden, once asked me why these dissenters fought so hard against a royal regime and the progress and order a government could bring. Being a woman of faith, she was really asking what they were putting their faith behind."

"And what did you tell her?"

"I said that as far as I knew, they weren't using faith for motivation. That is why we ultimately won, and I believe that with every fiber of my being. Everyone who fought for Malaya and Tristan was investing faith in them. Everyone who fought against them simply wanted things to stay in chaos the way they had been. They were like spoiled children who wanted to stay out and play, refusing to come in when called. The child will bargain and argue and fight to stay out amongst its toys, but after a while even a child realizes that all it is doing is standing outside wasting time and energy arguing rather than playing like it wants to."

Guin chuckled dryly. "So, they can either continue to

fight and never get the time to play . . . or they can step in line and begin to enjoy themselves again, albeit on the parent's terms."

"Something is better than nothing. The opposing lines were bound to crumble when they began to realize they were destroying the very thing they were fighting for."

"I see your point." This time it was Guin that moved forward, his granite-colored eyes a measure in seriousness as they met the priest's directly. "So explain these senators who defy us. These are learned people, logical thinkers who supported us through all of this. Why, suddenly, is there dissention?"

"I was hoping she would release you to find that out, Guin," Magnus said. This time, though, the bodyguard caught the meaning behind the glint flashing over the priest's hard features.

"You suspect something," he confronted him.

"I suspect a great many things," Magnus returned evasively. "But what I sense overall is that this insurrection is very differently motivated then a bunch of whiny children who want to play past dawn because they don't know what's good for them. We have weeded out the pests and brats, so now it's time to face the bullies, I think."

"Bullies . . ." Guin turned his attention to his sleeping charge and Magnus watched the guard's hands curl with repressed fury around the arms of his chair. "You mean, I suppose," he gritted out, "that now that the twins have done all the hard work, some *bituth amec* thinks to coup the throne away from them."

"It's one of the possibilities I have strongly considered," Magnus agreed a bit vaguely. "I've heard things, and I don't like what I hear. However, we'll discover nothing unless your mistress releases you to do what it is you do best. You must find the heart of this insurrection and cut it out."

"I will," Guin promised fiercely. "You must help me convince her."

"I will do my part, but after that it will be entirely up to you. I have another issue pressing me at the moment and it must be handled, so I will have to return later."

"More pressing than the stability of all of our people, Magnus?" Guin was flabbergasted, his astonishment all over his normally staid expression.

"There is a Sinner on the loose in Dreamscape. I believe he upgraded to rapist last night. Until I hunt him down, no one is safe and no one can be protected." Magnus let his eyes drift over Malaya's sleeping posture to make his point. "You can only protect her body in this realm, *Ajai* Guin. The Sinner who illegally steals his way through dreams could seize her, rape her, and kill her before she would even be able to open her eyes. You would not be the wiser, even if you stood watching her for every moment of it."

The heavy wood of Guin's chair creaked in protest as he tried to contain the emotion Magnus's suggestion sent exploding through him. There was loyalty, the priest thought, and then there was Guin. What the bodyguard felt, his passion, belief, and mission in this world, was centered completely on the life and well-being of Chancellor Malaya. Magnus was not privy to all the deepest details, but Malaya had made her impact on Guin a very long time ago in such a way that it was said his entire path of life had changed. There were rumors he had once been a thief, or that he had been a mercenary who had sold his sword to anyone who would pay for it, regardless of reason, as long as the price was right.

How they had met was a mystery even to Malaya's confessor. What had transpired to seal the life-hardened male to the faithful beauty known for her devoutness and optimism for the future of her people was completely unknown to all but the Chancellor and her guard. After nearly five decades had found the duo inseparable and undefeated, despite numerous attempts to take both their lives and their loyalties away from one another, several truths had become quite well known.

No one came near Malaya without crossing by Guin first.

This included her priest and even her very own twin. Any attempt to bypass this arrangement was usually met with steel and death. And Guin's blade, known to be the deadliest in all their society, often made mortal wounds without bothering to ask questions first. The bodyguard's short fuse was legendary, equal only to his astounding keenness to do his mistress's bidding. There were those who called him "The Beast," the implication being that only Malaya's beauty held claim on taming him.

So Guin took any threat to Malaya as a personal affront. When the master swordsman finally flicked his steel-cold stare back to Magnus, he was all but vibrating with the need to kill.

"Rest easy," Magnus reassured him in a low, steady tenor meant to speak to the warrior rather than merely placate him. "This is what I was born to do, and it will be done. Even now my divine senses are coming in tune with any flaws or disruptions he has left behind. Soon, tracking him will be a matter of small effort." Magnus rose to his feet, his hand resting on the hilt of his blade with purpose. "Trust me. Night will not fall again before this Sinner is made to repent."

Guin also gained his feet, but he moved to Malaya's side and lowered into a crouch on powerful legs until he was more level to her. Magnus watched with amazed fascination as the big brute turned kitten gentle just before reaching to brush the thick curls of her hair back from her smooth cheek. The burnished tone of Malaya's skin seemed almost pale in contrast to the dark, scarred hand that stroked against her and caused her to stir at last. For a moment, for just a moment, Magnus thought there was something . . . some quality to the way Guin turned his knuckles against her sleep-softened face that crossed the hard-to-define lines of emotion between devotion and . . . and more. But the priest dismissed the impression as quickly as it came to him.

After all, devotion was pretty much all he had ever been familiar with himself. It would be nearly impossible for the priest to recognize what he had never really known.

Chapter 7

Ashla sat at the window, as if looking out at the darkness beyond, except she had her eyes closed. Her cheek and forehead touched the chilled glass, but she was ignoring the sensory information. In fact, she was turning the burn of cold into the burn of heat in her mind. Closing her eyes tight enough, concentrating hard enough, she could make herself imagine sunlight streaming in on her and the brilliance of the room she knew lay under the cover of shadows behind her. She had adjusted to the darkness enough to see where she was going without breaking limbs or killing herself, and when the moon and stars appeared she could even make out finer details, but she missed colors. Oh, she could figure them all out most of the time, usually with a great deal of focus and debate in her mind, but she missed the brilliance of sunlight on color.

Now, as she concentrated, she could imagine sunlight on red velvet ottomans, or the glint of it on gold gilding. There were azure blues in the bedroom she slept in; teals and sea greens in the huge bath of the Plaza suite.

A distant sound reached her and like the sharp crack of a whip, her thoughts turned to her new and strange companion. *What would Trace look like in sunlight?* she wondered. Would there be flecks of color within his obsidian eyes, that she simply couldn't see in the dark? What of his midnight hair? Would it be that purest jet, still, or would light strike it blue-black? Most of all, she wondered about the color of his skin. Most of the time she was convinced he was of Hindu Indian heritage, but sometimes the smooth duskiness of it seemed tinged with the reddish bronze that distinguished Native Americans. She had fished gently about it, trying to get him to give her small hints or clues by accident, but he was on his guard, apparently, now that he had already made slips of the tongue, and had become the least forthcoming individual she had ever met in her life.

They had spent the better part of two days together in the suite, sharing living space, meals, and even conversation. She had learned nothing and a great deal about him. He spoke at least one other language besides English, but she had no clue what it was. He was embarrassingly well educated. Embarrassing to her, because she had barely made it out of college. Not that she wasn't smart, but she just had never been inclined to book smarts. Trace could quote dozens of famous writers, their works coming to him like old, well-worn monologues. He had clearly spent a lot of time on philosophy and social anthropology because he tended to dissect things in his mind down to their basest elements. But when she asked simple questions like where he had attended school, where he'd grown up, and more, he evaded answering.

He wasn't actually talkative at all, but he had a way of responding to her nervous chatter with single, well-thought sentences that always made her slam on her mental brakes and think. Trace was also a man of great conscience, she came to realize. It mattered a great deal to him that she had suffered because of him. It was clear the idea of it rubbed him raw. He stubbornly refused to listen when she tried to reassure him that she felt fine, and he insisted on taking care of her every need at every moment.

She felt his commitment to repaying what she had done for him in the focused way he performed even the simplest acts. He would serve her a meal, but with a detailed display on her tray of all the best food groups and an emphasis on those foods he swore would help her heal faster. Reading was one of her favorite pastimes, but she couldn't read in the dark. He said his eyes were better than hers and he took all the time she wanted to read to her, unwittingly letting her take far too much selfish pleasure in the sound of his uniquely smooth and deep voice. He was obsessively tidy, she thought, always making sure to put things back where they belonged as quickly as possible.

He could spend hours sitting quietly with his own thoughts.

This was actually one of the creepier things about him. He could sit in the darkness hardly moving, or he would absently toy with his sword and its strangely designed scabbard. Equally eerie was the way he would polish it meticulously. He slept with it within his reach at all times, as if he expected to be attacked at any instant.

Less creepy, but somewhat more chilling, was when he slept.

He had nightmares.

They were awful, violent things. She could tell. She had a front row seat to his nighttime struggles because he insisted on sleeping on the floor of her bedroom so he could be near at all times if she needed him. Only his virulent stubbornness could have won out over her vehement denials and lifelong lessons of mistrust. And because it had, she bore witness each time he fell asleep to the weight of his memories.

Ashla had no doubt that it *was* memories. She was too familiar with the vulnerability that sleep left someone open to, whether they wanted it or not. She had peeped over the edge of her mattress at him, biting her lip in empathetic distress as he had thrashed in place as if tied fast to the floor. He slept without a shirt, so she had seen every single muscle and vein distend beneath his tension-taut skin. His hair would be-come drenched with the sweat that made his skin gleam. He would grind his teeth or grit out low words in that foreign tongue.

Sometimes he would burst out in a horrific shout, a sound like nothing she had heard before. He would inevitably wake himself up with these, and she had to duck quickly back to feign sleep. Then Ashla would listen to Trace as he struggled to calm his breathing, to calm his thoughts. She could feel them racing and churning, wild and painful, like pins and needles on the edges of her skin. At times like those, she felt like an intruder. She felt like she was invading a deeply kept place of privacy that she hadn't earned the right to enter. She thought of her own secret horrors and how she would feel if he were to come upon them uninvited. It was like . . . letting a total stranger watch a pornographic film you had starred in once when you had been young, foolish, and fancied your-self in love with your co-star. It was raw and embarrassing, out of context and poorly representative.

Ashla opened her eyes and looked across the room at the object of her obsession. She found him doing his creepy sit-ting thing, except at the moment he was watching her with very careful attention. The hilt of his sword spun absently between his fingers, the tip of the scabbard nestled in the rug that alleviated all friction as the entire sword flashed and spun with dizzying speed against nimble fingertips. Ashla couldn't help but wonder what he was thinking about.

Trace was toying with a great deal of danger.

On about three different levels.

The first was, of course, the mental gymnastics he had been forced to perform as he had somehow avoided all of his clever charge's probing questions about topics he felt were too sensitive to discuss . . . either for her benefit or for his own.

The second was that he was closing out his second day in Shadowscape. He would be lying to himself if he had claimed not to notice any effects yet.

Which led him to his third point of danger.

He narrowed his eyes on the svelte and fair Ashla as she screwed her eyes shut and thought very hard about . . . whatever she was thinking about. She was always near windows, as if she couldn't bear to be closed within the dimensions of a room. Even a room as enormous as this one was. He imagined that in her other life, she wouldn't live in Manhattan. Not unless she was incredibly rich. Only the well-to-do humans could afford large spaces in the city. He couldn't see her living in anything like the tiny apartments New York offered to everyone else.

But he lived around wealth, so he was able to recognize someone who wasn't used to it. She would discover little details about the suite that amazed or amused her, and the fact that her entertainment was sometimes lost on him told him he was far more used to higher-end amenities than he had realized. It told him that she was not.

But it wasn't these nuances that troubled him just then.

No.

What disturbed him was . . .

Hunger.

His fist clenched closed, suddenly catching his sword mid-turn, the sound penetrating her daydreaming enough to make her twitch just a bit. She wrinkled her small nose, her bottom lip pouting out in an expression of some consternation. Trace watched the moue with a tightly focused stare, noticing every small detail, from the tiny brackets it caused at the edges of her mouth, to the glint of moonlight on the moisture on her full lower lip.

He had never known a frown could be so stirring.

But then again, lately, everything about her seemed to stir him. He was like dust to her wild wind. She toyed with him exhaustively, twisting him one way one moment—like when she thought she was alone and took to dancing around her room to stretch her sore body, unaware that he could see her through the walls in brilliant infrared vision—and another way the next—like when she made him read to her for long periods of time and took so much pleasure in it that her body flushed warm in places that . . .

Trace released his death grip on the katana and began to spin it even faster than before. This time, he didn't even pause to think of how horrified and furious Magnus would be to see him treat it that way. He didn't really care. Instead, all he found himself caring about was something crafted far more beautifully than some piece of steel.

He was convinced that she was made from light itself. It was the only explanation for how toxic her mere presence had become to him. Her scent when she passed by, her heat when she squirmed in response to his voice, the curve of each and every spot on her body that somehow seemed so exquisite; they were all like light poisoning, burning into him fast and deep until he all but shouted with the gorgeous agony of it.

The worst part was that he couldn't blame it all on Shadow-scape euphoria. No. He had tried that. Then he would re-member in quick flashes of heat and memory the way she had felt as she had straddled him in the boutique to heal him, or the feel of her bottom nestling provocatively against him only minutes after last stepping into the 'scape.

Now, however, he knew he was in serious trouble. He knew it by the wild racing of his heart. He knew it by his ever-sharpening senses that fixated on her every detail. And most of all, he knew it by the savage, surging impulses he had to just . . . to just . . .

. . . *plunge* into her.

And then, just because it was the way his luck had been running lately, she had to pick that very moment to turn and look at him. She flashed those hypnotic blue eyes at him, her lips parting a little when she caught him staring at her. Trace's jaw clenched, his entire body tensing against the rushing high that was his desire for her as it pumped through him.

Then he was on his feet, his katana switching hands so he could secure it to his belt on the right side.

"I have to go," he said gruffly, silently cursing himself for the predatory pitch of his tone.

Ashla leapt to her feet, the spry movement telling him how much she had healed in the past two days. She hurried forward, prompting him to throw out a hand of warning to match his barking command.

"*Stop!*"

She came up short, doing as he demanded. Only an idiot would have ignored the warning radiating out of him in huge, overwhelming waves. But she wasn't able to control herself completely.

"Please don't leave!"

She had promised herself for two days that she wouldn't beg him when the time came. Now here she was doing just that without even a semblance of an effort at bravery. Then again, bravery had never been her strong suit. Neither was solitude, despite her inherent mistrust of others.

"I have no choice," he said tightly as he finished securing the sword and looked around himself in a moment of wild confusion. It was actually unnerving to see him this way. He was always so collected, his actions measured and purposeful, always as if they had been thoroughly thought out. That she, a veritable stranger, noticed the difference was terribly disturbing to her, and she knew it would be to him as well.

"Can . . . can you come back?"

Trace looked at her suddenly, the fierceness of his black eyes making Ashla's breath catch in her throat. He could hear the sound of it hitching from where he stood. How was it that he knew just how difficult these questions were for her? There was desperation lacing them, but it was how much she resented her need to ask them that screamed out to him. She was ashamed of herself for her fear of being alone.

Trace had taken two strides toward her before he realized he was moving and drew himself to a halt. He closed his eyes briefly, his hands gripping into tight fists as he struggled for control—and to take in a deeper breath so he could get beyond the lilac scent of her body wash and reach the purity of nature.

"Can you?" she asked more softly this time, taking a step that all but closed the remaining distance between them. After all, he had moved first. He had broken his own barrier.

"I shouldn't," he whispered, probably more to himself than in response to her query. But he was right. He shouldn't. He had repaid her for her help, albeit not nearly enough, and the pressures of his world now took precedence. But those pressures paled in comparison to the intensity of need roiling up from inside him as he finally caught that thread of warm feminine aroma he had been craving.

Trace had flirted with euphoria on more than one occasion, so he was familiar with the effects. The sharpening senses, the shortness of patience, and the urge to give in to impulse were the norm in their abnormality. But he had never felt or heard of anyone else feeling this intensity of primal sexual behavior.

Ashla was taken completely by surprise when a large hand snatched her up by the back of her head and another snaked under her arm to seize the back of her waist. She was swept up against him, lifted to the very tips of her toes to shorten the distance between their heights, and before she could make a single sound, was sealed mouth to mouth with him.

When she gasped in a breath, it was his breath. When she made her sound of protest and surprise, it slid past his parting lips. Ashla reached to anchor herself in any way she immediately could, finding herself latched on to fistfuls of black silk from his shirt.

And after all obligatory reflexes were satisfied, she simply stared up at his eyes as he kissed her.

It was the raw trepidation amidst her soft sky blue gaze that tempered his savagery to passion. What would have brutalized and bruised, gentled just enough to be worthy of a creature so delicate. By forcing him to slow down, by nibbling at what remained of his conscience, impulse mutated into craving. Now the truth of what was between them surfaced, like the explosive puff of flame first put to tinder. Trace's hold on her tightened as his final sense, his sense of taste, was indulged at last. He had obsessed for hours over the question of her flavor, and now he was beginning to know. Just beginning.

He did not actually have the patience for finesse, but skill was automatic as he kissed her immobile lips. He was challenged by her unresponsiveness, an urge as old as time goading him to win her over. Trace did so with the touch of his tongue, the slowest little flicks of sensation that satisfied his need for her essence temporarily while he coaxed her into relaxing for him just a bit. Her stillness and stiffness were proven a lie, however, when she suddenly drew a breath between parting lips, the act full of response and willing surrender despite its simplicity.

Then he was spearing himself deep inside her mouth, filling his dizzy mind with the sweet wetness of her taste and the vibration of the little moan that escaped her. He felt line after line within himself being crossed, then erased; all he had forbidden himself was suddenly fair game as an explosive bolt of light seared him from head to toe, flash-boiling his blood and burning his breath in his lungs until he labored to exchange it with the cooler air of the room.

It was a fruitless effort because it was all sweetly tainted with her scent, each deep draw of oxygen sending him spiraling into an oblivion of action and reaction. He had no sooner begun to explore the fantasy of her mouth than he was turning her away in his hands, spinning her back to his chest so he held her captive against him exactly as he had when he had first held her two days earlier. He ran shaking fingers down the length of her throat, the adrenaline crashing through his body making it impossible for him to hold steady.

Ashla was panting in an effort to catch her breath, but had just as much success as Trace had. She was trapped against him by that steeled arm full of muscle and demand that crossed her ribs tight beneath her breasts. She was still licking the tantalizing taste of him off her lips when she felt his fingertips gliding along the line of her pulse. To further inundate her senses, his hot breaths burned over her ear and neck in wild bursts, and his entire body stood hard as marble against the back of hers.

She tried to tell herself this was all unexpected. She wanted to believe it was completely uninvited. But, neither was true. As if to provide empirical proof of that fact, her breasts were burning with that same wicked sensation from the last time he had held her like this, her nipples puckering into painfully tight points of anticipation as his fingers continued to drift down over her clavicle and then into the V in her blouse that gave him access to her breastbone.

"Are you afraid?" he asked her, his roughened bass writhing through her like an intimate caress.

"I'm a-always afraid," she managed with a hard swallow. "Of everything."

"Fear is healthy, *jei li*. It tells you when you are getting deeper into trouble. It warns you to be careful." She felt his moist lips nuzzle into the side of her neck just beneath the ear he whispered his wisdom into.

"I n-need to be careful n-now?" she stammered, her lips and tongue going suddenly numb and clumsy as he teased her pulse with the sexy slide of his tongue. At the same time, his fingers slipped beneath her blouse and chemise, caressing a flirtatious path over the rise of her breast.

"Oh, yes. Yes, *jei li*, yes."

Trace was left-handed. Had she had time to realize the small detail, she might not have been so taken off guard when, instead of the obvious taunting hand beneath her blouse, the other just beneath her right breast was the one to come cup her fully. His thumb flicked against her nipple, sending a shockingly raw response deep into the center of her already laboring body. Ashla had never felt anything like his electrifying touches in her whole life. Each minute motion as he toyed with her sent jolts of unexpected pleasure pounding into her in rhythm to her heartbeats. Then his opposite hand fulfilled its teasing promise inside her blouse, slipping over her warm skin and finding the bare nerves of her waiting nipple. He stroked over her, shaping and curving his callused fingers around her as he fondled his way to familiarity with her contours and warmth. Every touch was exponential, the arousal he was stirring up climbing to a wild pace inside of her. She couldn't keep quiet or still, her entire body arching into his hands and back against him at the same time. Her hands reached to grasp his forearms and wrists, soon becoming a part of his caresses against her.

Trace was quite through with working in increments. He'd had enough torture, and then again not nearly enough. He was hardly gentle as he slid one hand free of her blouse and suddenly cupped her directly between her legs. He used his bold grasp to draw her back tightly against him, settling the soft, sweet curve of her ass against his raging erection. He unintentionally took hold of her with his teeth when his mouth opened over her neck to release the deep groan of pleasure that rumbled up out of him as he rubbed himself against her. He couldn't hope to count the numerous fantasies he'd had about holding her like this; nor could he have ever expected how far the reality would surpass those mere speculations. If he hadn't been loath to break the erotic contact, it might well have brought him straight to his knees.

"*Aiya*," he hissed against her. "You burn like sunrise."

Ashla gasped as the fingers of the hand cupping her pubic bone burrowed into her a little snugger through the material of her skirt and underpants. He growled low and with unmistakable menace, like a beast guarding his best morsel of food. Or perhaps like one readying to devour that morsel.

"On your knees, *jei li*," he demanded suddenly, no warning or hint of asking for her permission whatsoever.

"*W-what?*"

"Obey me," he said, lowering himself to his knee and forcing her compliance. "Trust me," he coaxed her then, his sensual plucking at her nipple sending her into wild shivers. It was only then that she realized that by forcing her to her knees, Trace had made her brace her legs hard apart. The position opened her up to his exploring touch, a fact he exploited instantly. His fingertips ran the seam he could feel under her skirt, tracing it completely along the inside crease of her thigh. He felt her heart pounding right through her back, felt the way she trembled in response and anticipation.

She was so passive, so pliant; and somehow it felt incredible to feel her succumb to his strength and his aggression, to feel the growing damp heat beneath his fingertips that broadcast her rising arousal.

"Unbutton your blouse, sweetness. I need to see you," he said, his voice as rough as sandpaper. "There you go . . . yes, perfect," he praised her as she raised quivering fingers to do as he bid her. Each encouragement he spoke spurred her from one button to two . . . to three. He didn't stop until she reached the waistband of her skirt. "Good. Very good, *jei li*. Such pretty things you wear, honey, but all I want is to see you without them."

"But the . . ." Ashla turned her face away against his left shoulder, her anxious fingers curling around the metal that embraced his arm beneath the black silk of his shirt. "I'm not healed," she murmured.

"Don't." He followed the barked word with a physical jog of her body. "Do not try to tell me what I will like and dislike about you. These are things a man can discover for himself." He released her sweetly swollen breast at last and began to push aside the fabric of her blouse. He grasped the satiny material of her chemise for a moment of reflected frustration, and the sound he made warned her he was on the verge of literally tearing through the obstacle. She quickly took his hand into both of hers and slid it beneath the bottom hem. This allowed him the temporary pleasure of bare, warm skin while Ashla wriggled to shed everything from the waist up that was in his way.

She had never done anything so bold in all of her life. Oh, she was a bundle of nerves from head to toe, there was no doubting that. Even when she had stripped to show him her wounds, she had not been entertaining a single second of sexual implication or invitation.

Intent made all the difference in the world.

Ashla was riddled with doubt about dozens of points of logic, and each made her question the wisdom in extending even the slightest trust to him. But on the other hand, there was the bald surety she felt from a point of instinct inside of her she had never tapped in all of her life. It was as though she were watching parts of herself being born at last, coming to life in his hands as they shaped her skin and body with a thorough fascination she'd never experienced before. In fact, Trace had shown more power in his desires for her in the past ten minutes than most had shown her even at the point of their climax. It was a potent sort of drug, to be wanted so strongly. So potent that she dreaded doing anything that might disturb the marvelous feeling.

Trace was absently rubbing himself against her, trying to relieve the molten ache kept cruelly confined behind the fly of his jeans. The provocative motion made his thoughts come in sharp bursts of desire. He wanted her hands on him. Her pretty little mouth. He stared down at her pale breasts and their pastel pink nipples and hastily added them to the list. The thought alone made him throb with painful longing.

"I could come just thinking about all the things I want to do to you," he confessed to her hotly against her near ear.

"And when I think of bringing you to orgasm . . ." He shuddered at her back and groaned with his self-created imagery.

But Ashla didn't share his pleasure, and it was harshly obvious in an instant. He could almost feel her skin turning chilled under his touch as she stiffened in his embrace.

"What is it, *jei li*?" he demanded. He snared her chin in his fingers and kept her from shaking her head in negation. He discarded the question, and made it a demand. "Tell me why that scares you so much."

"Because I can't. I can't . . . do that."

"Speak plainly to me, Ashla. Do not be a child about this. Be a woman who demands her lover knows her needs. Speak to me!"

"I can't h-have an orgasm!" She swallowed hard and gasped for breath as color burned bright in her face. "I never could," she finished on a whisper.

Trace couldn't believe what he was hearing. Suddenly, he was disgusted by the selfish ineptitude of human men. No Shadowdweller male would be let loose on the female population without knowing what to do to best please a woman. The same was true for females knowing how best to please a man. Trace had studied sex from inception of his adolescence until his tutors had deemed him ready. At times, they had been some of the hardest learned lessons of his entire education. The methods to teach control alone had bordered on cruelty. But they had been worth every moment of painful denial and every act of discipline he'd borne. He had left each of his women deeply satisfied, always proud of his performance and grateful to his teachers.

A society that would do otherwise was beyond foreign to him—it was barbaric.

And Ashla's feelings of devastating inadequacy were the perfect example of why. That she was near to tears with her embarrassment, not to mention her frustration and disappointment, made him utterly furious. It was enough to severely rattle his own self-righteousness, to force him to realize he had been less than an exemplary lover as he had fallen on her with haste and selfish need. Trace rubbed his face against her hair and breathed deeply for a moment as he gathered control and a few more moments of clear thinking.

I can't do this. Not like this.

He couldn't possibly do justice by her while swept up in the maelstrom of euphoria. Euphoria was all about seeking and gratifying his own pleasure. It was a deep touch of madness that plunged the sufferer into their own world, deeper and deeper until nothing outside of themselves mattered any longer. He was in the earliest stages of this condition and he was already behaving out of character and without honor or consideration. If he stayed long enough to try and make love to Ashla, he would only end up being another disappointment to her . . . and by then he probably wouldn't even care.

Take her anyway, a part of him was already whispering in heated countermand. *Sink into her deep and hard and let yourself explode. The rest will take care of itself!*

Trace groaned at the mere thought of it, and growled in frustration at himself in the same breath. What made it worse was that he was having his damned epiphany right after she had made her horribly painful confession. What was he going to say? *I have to go, but it's okay . . . it's not you, it's me?* He would never make her believe he wasn't leaving her because he thought she was frigid or malfunctioning.

Basically, no matter which way he turned it, he had just royally fucked himself.

Chapter 8

He thought she was a freak.

Yes, of course he did, Ashla thought. He was a beautiful, healthy specimen of manhood, and clearly had the sex drive to match. He had probably never made a misstep in bed in his life, and no doubt had made several dozen beauty queens beg him for return performances.

She had never had sex with the same man twice. Not that she hadn't wanted to, because she had constantly hoped that practice would improve things for her, but what choice had she had when they had smiled at her and told pretty lies to her just before disappearing from her life for good? She had been left with little more than bitterness and the angry feeling that she had somehow been cheated. However, in time, it had become too steady a pattern for her to keep blaming everyone else. She knew that she was the problem.

So she might as well let him know what he was in for from the start.

It was the quietest and stillest he had been all day, and Ashla closed her eyes in an effort to steel herself against whatever was going to come next. It didn't feel very promising when he stood them both up straight and put an inch of distance between them for the first time since this had all started. She swallowed so hard it hurt, and she struggled to blink back the starting burn of tears.

I can hold on until he leaves, she swore to herself. *I can hold on just that long.*

"Ashla, step forward," he said gruffly.

She automatically did as he asked, not realizing that she made him smile because of it. She drew her arms up to cover her breasts, but his hands curling around her biceps prevented her from it.

"I meant several steps, *jei li*," he murmured into her hair.

Nervous and confused, her emotions in a wild uproar, she obeyed once again. Through chattering teeth, she managed to ask the most ridiculous question of all time.

"What does *jei li* mean?"

His hand at her back kept her moving as he countered with, "What does it sound like it means? I don't believe there is an exact translation for it."

"Um, I don't know. Maybe . . . 'sweetheart'?"

"That would be close," he agreed. "However, that term lacks the level of respectful affection that *jei li* requires. In your culture, 'sweetheart' can be used in a derogatory as well as with affection. In mine, *jei li* is reserved for affection only. To use it in an insult would be horribly taboo. It is one of those things that could find you with your tongue cut down the center of its length by morning."

"Oh my God!" she cried, torn between horror and a fascination for a culture that would take the mere usage of a word so seriously. She pressed her hand to the wall for balance and tried to look at him over her shoulder. That was when he placed a hand on her, making her face the wall once more, which actually made her realize for the first time that she was standing in front of a wall to begin with.

Now he fitted himself back against her and slid both of his warm, strong hands down from her shoulders all the way to her wrists and back again.

"Place your palms flat on the wall, *jei li*," he said softly to her.

"On the . . . ?"

"Don't question me," he gently scolded her, a warning rumble of sound vibrating against the side of her neck. "Just do as I ask."

Ashla's heart tripped over its own beat as she raised her trembling hands to obey him. Her palms were damp already as she pressed them to the thick, textured wallpaper before her.

"Higher. Just a little more," he coaxed quietly until her hands were several inches above her shoulder line. Ashla felt strangely exposed by the position, which accounted for the way she jolted under his touch when his hand slid across her bare belly. She felt surrounded by him somehow, certainly under his power, a point proven when he slid his leg between hers from behind her, firmly nudging her feet a distinct distance apart.

Then she felt his fingers slipping around the waistband of her skirt, tracing the line between nudity and clothing very thoughtfully for a moment.

"Every woman," he said in low explanation, "is unique. Each is a complex lock that takes time and knowledge to open. A woman like you, however, is an even deeper puzzle. I would not dare to claim I fully understand you. I couldn't be so arrogant. But I think I have learned just enough to make a start."

"A s-start?"

"A very small start," he agreed.

Trace's fingers slid open the buttons down the back of her skirt one at a time, his touch reaching to stroke the slowly exposed curve of her lower back as he went. Soon the fabric simply slipped away, landing with a flutter around her calves. She tried to lean forward and press her hot face to the wall, but he stayed her with a firm hand, keeping her just as he had arranged her to be.

"Answer a question for me," he said as those leisurely, thorough fingertips of his began to sketch across the top of her panties. "When did you first realize you were inclined toward submission?"

Ashla jolted as if he had given her a good smack on the bottom. She jerked around to face him, but only made it halfway before his masterful hands caught her and sent her shooting back into the stance he had demanded of her. She drew hard for breath, both frustrated and aroused, confused and excited. She didn't know what to feel from one moment to the next! She couldn't even think to formulate the words she knew she should be flinging at him in protest.

"I take it the answer to that would be 'five seconds ago,' " he noted a bit wryly. He sighed, the exhalation skittering down her naked back in a warm wash.

"But I'm not!" she blurted out. "My God, that's the last thing I would ever—!"

He cut her off with a low chuckle, the teasing tips of his fingers sliding into the secret warmth hiding beneath the last small scrap of cotton she wore.

"Really? Are you sure?"

Ashla choked on her response when his smooth caress glided straight through her damp pubic hair and settled in to stroke her in long, wet rubs along the length of her labia.

Trace forced himself to focus on his point, making a mighty effort to control the response of his body and psyche as he felt how slick and hot she was with her unrealized depth of excitement. She was all but naked as she pressed away from the wall and into the length of his rigid body. He had broken such an incredible sweat as he attempted to master himself that his clothing was sticking to his skin almost as thoroughly as she was. He sent his free hand up to seal around her slim throat, tipping her head back so he could see the mind-numbing start to her journey of passion in her eyes.

He was painfully short of time and luck, but he couldn't

ECSTASY: THE SHADOWDWELLERS 99

bring himself to spear her fragile ego with the coldness his departure would cause. His chest hurt with the raging of his breath and blood, but he couldn't stop now.

I have suffered deeper tortures, he thought fiercely to himself, *and survived. I can do this for her. I can be what she needs so desperately.*

He repeated this litany to himself like a desperate sort of mantra. It was about Ashla. It was all about Ashla. He didn't dare take a moment of purposeful pleasure for himself without risking his state of euphoria overtaking him and destroying everything he hoped to achieve.

"Every command I give you, you obey," he said. "What's more, I can feel your skin turn hot as you do. I hear your breath and heart as they race. You tell yourself it is fear that compels you, but I see much more to it than that. I *feel* much more to it than that." He emphasized his point with the seeking swirl of his finger, rimming the entrance to her vagina until she drenched his fingers with a fresh, scorching flood of honey. "You were never frigid," he gasped between his laboring breaths. "No one who responds like this can be labeled so coldly when she is the truth of heat personified."

Trace closed his eyes as her gaze began to cloud with bald response and snowballing surrender. He throbbed with painful need, unable to resist the thrust of his hips against her bottom as he sought for her clit with his thumb and burrowed his first finger inside her. Ashla sucked in a long breath, her tight flesh tensing around the digit that slid deeper and deeper. It took no stretch of his imagination to envision that sensation all around his straining cock.

He cursed in Shadese, a low and dangerous word of warning she didn't comprehend. But even if he had spoken in English, she was far beyond comprehension. Ashla was wriggling in counterpoint to his strokes and circles that tempted her toward a promise of rushing satisfaction. Fear and doubt abruptly hurried through her; it made her awkward and prompted her to struggle out of cadence with what she truly wanted. Unable to predict how much longer he could hold himself in check, Trace was like a force of fury as he kicked his foot against the inside of hers, forcing her legs wider apart even as he ground against her from behind her and within her.

"Don't!" he barked roughly, the command all but a snarl. "Don't doubt. Don't think! Just obey me, *jei li*. Obey my touch. Obey the pleasure I can give you. Accede to your own passions. Searing Light! Blessed Dark! You are so hot it's driving me mad!"

Ashla couldn't grasp the way his thoughts were wildly vacillating. She didn't understand why he didn't stop teasing her and just bury himself in her. It was so obvious by the savage way he burrowed his erection against her that he needed to do just that. She craved what she felt of him, the hardness and the primal urge of thrust that pounded through him. Her nerves were burning at their ends in a blaze of little bonfires, her body weakening and wetting his probing touch until he slid in and out of her with slick successive thrusts of one and then two fingers.

She felt her soul coiling inside her. Her pulse roared as pleasure spilled through her in powerful washing tides. She cried out, fearful and thrilled and swept away in the climbing rush. Her hands shot away from the wall, one grasping his hair at the back of his head, the other seizing his belt near his katana.

"Trace!" she gasped wildly.

"I'm here," he reassured her. "Come, *jei li*. Yes. *Aiya*, that's it. *Please*," he begged hoarsely then.

Ashla felt everything within herself whip inside out in a sudden surge of power and release, forcing a wailing scream from her lips as she seized with overriding pleasure. Her entire brain exploded into short circuits that snapped and crackled through her in violent rushes. Her fists gripped Trace and held him captive against her as her body jerked and went into pleasured spasms.

Trace opened his eyes and watched her flesh and muscle quiver. He stared as the diamond-hard tips of her breasts shimmied with every shudder roiling up through her. Her swollen clitoris pulsed under his thumb and her walls hugged tight around his embedded fingers.

He had never needed to come so badly, not in all of his long life, as he needed it then. As she rode her orgasm to its fullest crest, she writhed like pure sexuality against him. His knees finally buckled and he brought them both down to the floor. Trace groaned in agony as the movement tightened the denim he wore against him. Then, unable to bear it an instant longer, he shoved himself back away from her, away from the lure and the raw temptation of her. He turned his back on the pink flush covering every inch of her sweet skin and the sensual sweat dampening the fair waves of her hair.

But how could he shut her out when he could hear her panting in the wake of pleasure, when he could smell the aroma of her sex . . .

He raised his wet hand up, the smell pervading and delicious as he couldn't resist slowly painting her across his lips. All it took then was the flick of his tongue, and she was inside him. She was inside his memory and senses, inside the insanity of his thoughts and the bright screaming light of craving that seared him with demand.

Ashla was shaking with disbelief and a dozen other causes as she struggled to get her body to work again. Without Trace's supporting muscle, she had become little more than soggy jelly. She was limp, yet vibrating powerfully with aftershocks. She struggled to see where Trace had taken himself to. She didn't need to look far. He was over her again in an instant, pushing her down onto her back in the suite's thick carpeting. He wedged himself between her thighs even as he tore at the front of his jeans. He stripped his belt free and sent the katana flying back into the oblivion behind himself.

"Can't stop," he choked out, his black eyes filled with a

distress she didn't understand. "You are too perfect. So ready. Primed for the pumping."

He came free of his clothing with a primal cry of triumph, his distended phallus falling heavily against her lower belly, the color of it seemingly angry in contrast to her pale skin.

"You don't need finesse any longer, do you?" he wanted to know as he reached between them to snatch off her panties in two quick tugs. "You'll forgive me. You'll forgive me . . ." The last ended on a wild sound of pleasure as he moved them into a position that opened her bared sex into a perfect cradle to catch his cock. Dry, hot, and hard fell into a wet and welcoming flower of flesh. He choked on his own breath as he slid into a beautiful burning bath, drenching himself from root to tip without even thrusting inside her.

But that had to happen. *Now.* That very same instant. He barely even felt her hands clutching at his shoulders. He heard her gasp when he notched the pulsating head of his cock against the opening rim of her sheath. If she thought he would take his time and savor the sensation as she wanted to, she was wrong. He plunged forward deep and hard, forcing a strangled sound to escape her.

Trace shoved into her harder, sinking deeper, suffocating himself tightly inside her. Then it was a matter of wild, off-cadence thrusts that had no rhyme or rhythm to them, except that he was following one craving rush to the next, to the next, to the next. She was so tight that he could barely move, but so wet he couldn't be kept still. He reached up to trap her head between his hands, staring down into her eyes as his impacts shuddered through her harder and harder.

"I need to come inside you!" he gasped stupidly, as if she hadn't already figured out his desperation for what it was. "I need to . . . I need to . . . Ashla!"

I'm sorry! he wanted to scream at her. *I didn't want to be like this! This isn't me! This animal isn't me!*

"Trace."

So soft, so sympathetic to match the comfort in her eyes as she once again lifted fingers to his mouth in an effort to soothe away his self-recriminations and guilt. Her compassion undid him, the last vestiges of civility evaporating as she silently gave him permission to be whatever he needed to be in that moment; man or beast or both.

He crashed forward into her, holding himself deep and deep, feeling her sex twitching around him. He needed to finish this. He needed to be done! The agony of his want was unbearable, spearing right through the heart of his cock and clutching at his tension-hard balls.

"Why can't I . . . ?" he almost sobbed as he resumed his frantic rhythm into her. It made no sense! He had almost climaxed just watching her reach orgasm, but now that he was inside her at last, he felt trapped within himself.

He heard her start to make little mewls of sound, her pleasure slowly resurfacing. Her breasts bounced hard with each impact of their bodies until the taunt of her nipple was too much to ignore. Next thing he had her between his teeth, and then sucked deep into his mouth. She cried out, tensing everywhere around him as her back arched.

It was enough, and he knew it instantly. He knew it by the savageness of the pain that broiled through him and the relief of oncoming release.

"*Aiya!* Oh, baby, yes!" he shouted with exultation just before he burst hard enough to shatter. He continued to bellow triumph in Shadese as he poured himself into her.

By the time his body resigned its efforts, he couldn't even breathe, never mind support his own weight. He collapsed onto her with no regard for her slight frame. In fact, as he swam in the euphoria of his wild orgasm, he took nothing into regard at all.

Chapter 9

"This is ridiculous," Guin snapped sharply as he paced the length and breadth of the room. "It's been five days! You know Trace as well as I do, and he would never keep us waiting if he could help it."

Rika tracked the agitated movements of the bodyguard, keeping note of his location at all times out of sheer habit, but opted to allow Malaya to handle Guin's frustration and fury. It was usually the wisest move, considering that Malaya was the only one who seemed to have impact on Guin when he got in these moods. She liked to call them "caged tiger with a toothache" moods. The imagery was just as suitable now as ever.

The Chancellor glanced up, sighing before turning to tame her tiger.

"What would you have us do, *Ajai*? Trace may not take advantage of it often, but he is a grown male of independence. Yes, it is rude to keep us waiting without word, but he wouldn't be the first to do so."

"It would be the first time for *Trace* to do so," Guin growled impatiently. "Besides, I have another meaning. If he is injured in 'scape, or if he has run afoul of another traitor like Baylor, we owe it to him to discover what has become of him! Five days, *K'yatsume,*" he reminded her with emphasis. "Even at its worst or best discrepancy, if he has been in Shadowscape all of this time he has certainly hit the two-day mark by now."

"And what makes you think he is in 'scape?" she countered. "He could be anywhere on this planet, a victim of a dozen fates as you just pointed out. Why are you obsessing about him being in 'scape?"

"Because I know him! I know how his mind works, and so do both of you!" Guin pointed to the women sharply. "This wraith he discovered will fascinate him. The Lost's unusual properties alone would challenge a mind like his. But add to this that she saved his life and it makes her an irresistible question in need of a reply. Also, *K'yatsume,* you all but demanded he go back and seek her out."

"I did no such thing," Malaya countered almost primly. "I merely suggested it would be a course of wisdom worth pursuing."

"She said, and I quote, 'I am astounded you would let so unique an opportunity pass you by without taking proper advantage of it'!" Guin countered to Rika with a snort. "She baited the poor bastard."

"*Sua vec'a!*" Malaya burst out as she dropped the beading she was working on and got up to cross away from her warden. "You'll not blame me for the actions of a man of free will."

"I'll blame you for being a cunning little manipulator," he shot back at her, striding up on his heels and more than ready for one of the confrontations they seemed to thrive on. Now it was Rika's turn to sigh a little, but it was strictly to herself. If she had prestige for every time they butted heads like this, she'd be royalty herself.

"Of course," Malaya scoffed, "and the fact that a vizier is

a professional manipulator shouldn't have anything to do with his ability to see right through me? I mean no offense, *Anai* Rika," she added quickly to her vizier.

"None taken," the older woman replied.

Rika carefully set aside her own beadwork, placing her supplies in their proper places so they would be easier to retrieve when she continued later on. She and her young mistress often did beading together as a form of relaxation.

This wasn't going to be one of their more successful times.

Rika supposed she should cut into the brewing argument while she still could. Guin and Malaya could nip back and forth at each other for hours, the entire thing simply dissolving into an exercise in wits. Since the female vizier was beginning to find that time was a precious commodity, she intervened with the soft clearing of her throat.

"Trace is in 'scape. Regardless of how he was motivated, we all know him well enough to know that his conscience would not rest well if his encounter with this strange wraith ended as you say it did." Rika turned her face toward where she had last heard their aggressive voices. "Whether he is injured, captive, or any of that, is pure speculation. The only thing I can be certain of is that he is not in Realscape at this moment, nor has he been for several days. You say five, but I am only certain of the past three nights."

"It's been too long," Guin said with low concern, his frown evident in his tone. "He has stayed too long. He must be recovered before his mind is damaged."

"Be easy," Malaya said to him gently, understanding his concern in spite of their bickering. "Trace is strong. He has great power."

"He was injured," Guin reminded her. "Severely so."

"Guin is right. It has been too long," Rika agreed. "We should call for Magnus. He and the other priests can track Trace far easier than we can."

"Rika, would you be able to sense him if you went into Shadowscape?"

"Yes, of course I would. But I'm afraid I cannot help you like that. If he is in euphoria and I touch his mind, I will be intoxicated as well. I am sorry, but that is just the way it works."

Guin made a sound of frustration at that, his hand absently gripping at the pommel of his sword. He knew very little about the type of special abilities certain 'Dwellers like Rika, the regent twins, and the religious sect exhibited, but he had been around the pretty little vizier long enough to know that she would have found a way to help if she could have. Despite her worsening blindness and the increasing frequency of her bouts with illness, she was one of Malaya's most valuable assets and she had been proven unafraid to risk herself when necessary.

"Very well. I will contact Magnus at once."

"I am certain Trace's father is already on the verge of action himself," Rika noted. "Magnus may preach about his son's independence, but there is a tether between them that will never be severed."

"*K'yatsume*, I will send Killian in to be by your side," Guin said to Malaya before giving her a curt bow. The guard then made one of his very rare exits from Malaya's presence, leaving the Chancellor to sit back down near her advisor with a sigh.

"It is interesting to see Guin show so much concern for Trace," Rika remarked. "He is usually quite withdrawn about such things."

Malaya huffed irritably. "He has only noticed Trace's dilemma because he has ulterior motives for wanting him here. Guin wants Tristan's vizier to talk me into assigning him the mission of seeking out Baylor's compatriots. He believes I will listen to Trace or that Trace will make me see the errors of my stubborn ways." Rika waited while her mistress drew out a moment of silence filled with palpable tension and disturbance. "He is angry with me," Malaya said at last.

"Furious, I would say," Rika mostly agreed.

"I don't care," Malaya lied. "If he thinks I am going to let him become a target to a blind and deceptive dagger like Trace did, he is out of his mind. Trace only survived by the grace of Darkness and luck. Let Guin scoff and pout, but I will not release him so he can ferret out a den of deceivers who will all want him dead!" Malaya sat forward in her seat and Rika could hear the agitated jingle of the bangles she wore as she toyed nervously with her own fingers. "If I am a target for an assassination, the worst thing to do would be to cut loose my guard!"

"Killian would replace him. He is trustworthy and quite good," Rika noted. "None could ever match Guin for dedication and undeniable skill, but he would keep you alive well enough."

Malaya gave an unattractive snort. "Why must men insist on such foolhardy escapades? They seem to thrive on sticking their necks out."

"I see. And instigating civil war had no effect on the safety of your neck as you mounted your throne?"

"This is hardly comparable!"

"I think it is perfectly comparable. I also think Guin merely wants to do his job, which is protecting you. I fail to understand why you insist on interfering with the very thing you keep him around for. It also amazes me how you trust this man to protect your life every moment of every day, yet you do not trust him to protect his own."

"Because he doesn't care about his own!" Malaya blurted out. "The man has a death wish!"

"No, he is simply unafraid of death. He welcomes all possibilities, which makes him fearless and all but undefeatable in battle. However, given his position by your side, he does not need to actively seek means of death and danger. They quite readily come to him. This issue of Baylor is a prime example."

"Stop! I am tired of everyone coaxing me to send that man to his death! I'll not talk of this anymore!" The Chancellor's voice was terrible and unmistakable. Rika knew when she had tested her mistress to the limits of her emotional tolerances, so she wisely backed off for the moment. Malaya was very rarely intractable and unreasonable, and the vizier was left to wonder why she was suddenly being so prickly.

A short while later, the doors to the sitting room opened, sending a wash of cool, displaced air against Rika. The scent of incense tumbled in from the corridor, the other parts of the house constantly burning the fragrant powders. Malaya refrained, knowing that Rika depended on her other senses like scent to compensate for her blindness and that the heavy perfumes could have an obscuring effect.

But despite the entrance of sage and sandalwood, Rika still instantly recognized the darkly exotic scent of masculine musk and coriander. There was also the distinctive little chime of metal charms every time Tristan took a step, the sound of the anklet of small gold medallions he wore whenever he was barefoot.

"Sister, we must talk," he announced, the force of his tone telling Rika that his usual playful demeanor had been set hard aside.

"What is it, Tristan?" Malaya was on her feet in an instant, hurrying to meet him in a series of tinkling steps Rika followed all the way across the room with her.

"I am going into Shadowscape with Magnus and the others. Trace is my responsibility and I will not sit by idle while he is missing."

"But . . ." Malaya seemed to check what she was going to say. "Of course," she agreed quietly. "I would do the same if it were Rika missing."

"Fear not. I will have Xenia by my side at all times."

"I feel I should go as well. Guin will want to join you, yet he will not leave my side."

"No, *jei li*, that is not wise. While I have deep respect for your skills as a fighter, I fear this could be a trap baited for one or both of us. After Trace's report about Baylor, I can only assume and anticipate the worst. In this case, it is best we each take separate realms. You remain here with Rika and Guin. If Trace returns, have Rika locate us. I will take Xenia and follow the priests' progress. It should not take long. Magnus and the brothers have tracking in their very souls. They will find him quickly."

"I beg you all to be careful," Malaya said with passion, her jewelry jingling as she wrapped her arms tightly around her brother. "Good luck, my brother. Keep faith. Darkness guide you."

"Darkness protect you, my sister. Stay safe."

Tristan gave his sibling a fleeting kiss before exiting as brusquely as he had entered.

Ashla grunted loudly as she hit the bed, catching air with a hearty bounce. Before she could draw breath, Trace was on her back, his hands sliding over her sweat-slick skin until he held both of her wrists well above her head. She gasped when his teeth suddenly tested her flesh on the back of her shoulder, then the bend of her waist, and then the rise of her buttock. She squirmed as he transferred both wrists to a single powerful hand, leaving the other free to seek her breasts, her belly, and then between her thighs.

He said nothing, only sounds of satisfaction rolling out of him as all her various parts met with his approval. He never stayed anywhere long enough, her head spinning with internal whimpers of disappointment every time he moved quickly on to whatever next struck his fancy. He rolled her over and dove to suck at her breasts, nipping and tugging before squeezing her tight in his hand and rubbing his face all over her, burning her with the shadow of his unshaven face.

"I should . . . yes, I really should . . ." he muttered as he abruptly seized her by her thighs and pushed them wide apart.

"No . . . wait!" she protested.

He ignored her, grabbing the hand she used to stay him and twisting her wrist against the bed.

"Never say no to me," he growled at her, his dark eyes flashing dangerously.

"But I—!"

He cut her off with the wicked darting of his tongue directly at her clitoris, the tenderness she was trying to warn him of making her jolt up against his lips. This only seemed to encourage him as he suckled and nibbled at her until she was screaming with overstimulation. She couldn't help herself as she grabbed at his hair, pushing him back as she tried to wriggle away.

"Hard to get, eh? Want to play, do you?" Ashla was back on her belly with a bounce and he covered her completely, probing at her from behind. "I'm hard, too. See? Feel me?" He pressed into her, thankfully in slower increments than the last time. Or the time before that. In fact, it could technically be considered the gentlest he had been with her since their bout of repetitive couplings had started almost eight hours beforehand. Considering there had been very little in the way of pauses, she was astounded at his stamina. She kept waiting for exhaustion to take hold of him the way it took hold of her, but it never did. He was voracious and inexhaustible. He would ejaculate and then become erect again quickly, or never even lose his erection to begin with.

She had never known anything like it. Ashla had only been used to what Diana liked to call "One-Shot Charlies." They came, they went, end of story.

Not so with Trace. He seemed completely obsessed with having sex with her. He was impossible to deny as he tuned out all her protests of soreness and fatigue. On the one hand, it was irresistible to be wanted so much. To feel him as he grew more and more excited within her, telling her in barely coherent ways how wild she made him. How hot she was. It was amazing and she found it hard to refuse him, even if he wasn't exactly asking.

But there was also the small detail of her failure to achieve another orgasm. There had been that first brilliant explosion of pleasure, unlike anything she'd even dreamed of, but since then even her closest moments had been disrupted for reasons she couldn't fully understand, or because he finished before she could catch up with him. The frustration and disappointment aside, now she couldn't even get close to started because she was so tired and tender.

Yet something inside of her realized he needed her almost with maddening desperation. She somehow knew that to call a definitive stop would be bad for him . . . or for her. Not that she was afraid he would hurt her—not really hurt her—but sometimes she would look into his eyes and, behind the rising wash of ecstasy, he would be struggling with a depth of pain she didn't comprehend. It was as though he didn't want to continue any more than she did, but he simply couldn't make himself stop. Not when it felt so good for him.

She might have envied him his rushes of pleasure if not for that strange valley of angst within him that marred them.

Just the same, she winced when he slowly burrowed into her swollen sheath. But since her face was buried in the bedding, he never saw the expression. Ashla wasn't sure it would even have mattered if he had.

"*Aiya*, you get tighter every time!" he cried out, reaching under her to tilt her pelvis up to receive his downward stroke. She gasped when he hilted well and truly deep inside of her, and then again when he withdrew. Tears smarted in her eyes and she muffled a sob. He felt as swollen as she was, too much to take, but she allowed it just the same.

Maybe he was right. Maybe she was some kind of sexual freak. Why else would anyone quietly bear what he was doing?

By the third stroke there was finally relief. The soreness disappeared, just as it always did, and he began to glide into her with an amazingly swift rhythm. He spoke to her, sometimes in English, sometimes not, sometimes just with noises and rough caresses. It wouldn't take him long, she realized, to reach climax this time. She could tell because of the desperation in his grip, the fierceness growing in his cadence. At least, she prayed that this was the case. Sometimes he would reach his breaking point and nothing would happen. Not immediately, anyway. He would stay trapped in that moment just before release, what looked like torturous pleasure cutting through him like unrelenting knives. It had brought him to tears more than once. It had made him shout like a savage.

He covered her tightly as he moved inside her, his hot, rapid breaths against her neck and ear, rushing through her hair. He was groaning in increasing crests; just listening to him making her body shiver with pleasure she hadn't expected to feel.

"I'm going to come inside you," he promised on a fierce, fast whisper. "I'm going to fill you up, mark you with my scent. Make you . . ." He stopped long enough to roll out a wicked warning growl. "Burn . . . you make me burn!"

Burn was the perfect word for it. For Ashla it was friction and haste that made her burn. For Trace, however, it was his insane demands on a body incapable of keeping up with him . . . and incapable of stopping. His testicles were on fire, his thigh muscles cramped, but there was no denying the glory of heated, wet flesh sucking him with each move he made. Tight. Hot. Wet. Tight. Hot. Wet.

When Ashla moaned, instinctively shifting to get him to hit her where she felt the best pleasure, it unraveled his coherence and coordination. The burn exploded into rushing wildfire, as relentless as he was as he dove into her over and over, with a painfully triumphant cry to mark the harsh spasms of his ejecting seed.

It was an endless minute before he finally rolled away from her, gasping for breath, almost sobbing for it. Ashla couldn't have gotten up if she wanted to, her aching body content to simply lie quiet, but when she shifted position, his hand fell on her hip and he was there, holding her still.

"Don't go anywhere," he rasped.

"I won't," she promised, closing her eyes when his damp hand started to glide up and down the length of her body, as if he took delight in the mere shape of her. She smiled at that, content to feel, for once, that she wasn't too thin, or too hippy, or too delicate. He certainly hadn't been treating her as if she were fragile. It was a dramatic turnaround from the past two days where he had cared for her as if she were made of porcelain. Still, she had been healing, and she might have treated him exactly the same despite his strength and size.

She rolled over and looked at him, her thoughts leading her eyes over all the places he had been injured when they had first met. He healed with astounding speed, because now the wounds were all just new places of salmon scarring streaked over him. Some of the more shallow cuts were even fading entirely.

Beyond that, he was perfect.

She loved the jewelry thing. The dual metal armbands, a strangely knotted and beaded necklace of simple polished copper, and rings on the last two fingers of both hands. The one on the left side might have made her a little nervous, except that it was in the shape of a falcon and looked nothing like any wedding band she had ever seen. Still, would it even matter? What with the way the world was so vacant all of a sudden? He had probably lost everyone just like she had . . . although he had acted as though there was somewhere very important he had to be, and she had gleaned that there were many people there.

Except now he didn't seem to care about leaving. As silent a compliment as that was, it bothered her. The longer he stayed, the stranger he behaved. It was almost as if she were dealing with two different men entirely, the Trace of two days ago versus the Trace of now.

She sighed, shivering a little. She had learned not to bother covering up. He didn't like it. Instead she risked snuggling up to his much warmer body, hoping he wouldn't take it as an enticement.

"*Ajai* Trace."

Ashla screamed, shocked to hear a strange male voice coming from the foot of the bed. Now she scrambled for covers, yanking the comforter askew over her body as she stared wide-eyed at the large male figure standing there with no regard for the intimacy of their situation at all. He was easily taller than Trace, and while just as broad in the shoulders, he was a bit leaner. His long black hair was slicked into a waved tail long enough to curl well below his shoulders. He wore black, but there was an exotic fit and style to his clothing that broadcast possibilities of a Middle Eastern origin. He was quite breathtakingly beautiful for a man, pure eye-candy, as Diana would say. The sensuality of his facial features, from the arrogant tilt of his lips to the dark speculation in his glittering eyes, told her he was a man very used to coming out on top of any situation.

But it was the glint of a metal sword pommel at his waist that made Ashla's heart race. What if this one was like the other one? The one who had nearly killed Trace in that boutique? Trace's weapon was rooms away, back where their sexual marathon had started.

But Trace seemed unconcerned, not even bothering to sit up or display the modesty that she did with an attempt to conceal his nudity. He lazily looked over the intruder.

"*M'itisume*," he greeted the man in return. "Tristan, what brings you to me?"

"You do," the man named Tristan replied as he rounded the foot of the bed a bit. His hand came to rest on his sword, almost as if in challenge. Ashla saw Trace's brow rise.

"That is odd, as I don't recall summoning you, *M'itisume*,"

Trace noted, a certain amount of steel present in his tone. Ashla saw Tristan's step hesitate and his eyes narrow with obvious displeasure at the terminology of Trace's words, but he recovered and moved steadily forward.

"I am here with Magnus."

That made Trace sit up quickly.

"Magnus is here?"

"He is near. We are all here in search of you, my friend. You have been away too long."

"All?" he echoed.

"The priests. Others." Tristan's eyes flicked back to Ashla. Now Trace reacted, banding an arm around her and sealing her to his back behind himself. "It is time to come home, Trace."

"I am going to. I just need a few more hours . . ."

Even Ashla could tell it was a lie. Tristan stepped closer and she squeaked in surprise when Trace jerked forward and gnashed his teeth at the other man, the warning growl that followed giving cause for the armed man to step back again.

"Trace, I have no desire to make a war of this with you, but I am charged to bring you back. Come of your own free will and this can be resolved in peace. Come before you become too ill for us to help you."

"Ill!" Ashla exclaimed in spite of herself. "He's ill?"

"Yes, he is."

"No. I'm not," Trace countered harshly.

"He is ill," Tristan persisted, meeting her eyes. "He just does not realize it. The longer he stays with you, the worse it will become. It puts you both in danger. His mind is in fever, and the worse it gets, the less he will care about accidentally hurting you. Soon, he will be purposely hurting you, though he will not realize it any more than he will care. Trust me when I tell you, the man I know Trace to be would be horrified and devastated to realize he had done you harm."

"The longer he stays with me?" she echoed. "You mean . . . Is this my fault?"

"*Nei, avet* . . . not any more than it is his," Tristan said, the answer evasive and disturbing. "Trace, I implore you to come with me now."

"Trace?"

Trace looked from his adversary of the moment to face his lover. He engulfed the back of her head in his hand and drew her in for a fierce, desperate kiss.

"Don't listen to them. It's all a lie," he said softly. "A trick. To separate us."

"But why would—?"

"*Ajai* Trace!"

Trace jolted at the boom of Magnus's voice but refused to turn and look at him. The intruding men represented a wall of negativity that his mind wouldn't accept. They were an interference to feelings he had fast become addicted to. They wouldn't let him keep her where and how he wanted her. Even now, as he looked at her troubled blue eyes and the brilliant fairness of her hair framing her elegant features, his heart pulsed with renewed desire for her. He caught her wrists and pushed her slight figure down into the bed with a mere shift of his weight.

"All that matters is what I want. I want to stay with you. I want to be with you . . . inside you, where I belong! It's where I belong!" This last was shouted as the two intruding males grabbed Trace by his arms and wrestled to yank him back off Ashla.

Ashla couldn't watch the humiliating and manic picture Trace made as he fought them with all of his strength. She scrambled away the minute she was free and wrapped herself in a sheet, falling to the floor on the opposite side of the bed and hiding her face in the bedding as she burst into terrible tears.

But the instant she heard the crash of breaking furniture she was on her feet and running after the trio as they took their fight into the open areas of the next room. The one whose eyes reminded her of gold, the one called Magnus, had a knee in Trace's back as they forced the struggling man to the rug. The other reached into his boot to flip open a strange-looking pair of handcuffs. It was as if Trace was being arrested, like some kind of criminal.

"But he didn't do anything wrong!" she cried. "You said he was sick!"

"We have no choice," Magnus explained, his voice strained as he used all of his strength to control his captive. "He must be contained or he will hurt himself or someone else. He will never leave willingly, surely you see that."

"I . . . Please, don't! You're hurting him!"

Trace bellowed in fury and pain as his arms were manipulated toward his back. The other male paused in the fight to turn on her with fierce anger.

"If you have a better idea, by all means speak! If not, be quiet and let us handle this!"

Ashla's first reaction was to recoil from that powerful voice and its harsh commands, but even as she cringed, his words rang through her brain.

If you have a better idea . . .

The pile of violent men and their wildly emotional struggles was one of those entities that Ashla had always avoided, wisely knowing when it was best to get out of the way or risk getting injured or worse. But this time she moved forward, her heart pounding as she did so, her spirit aching as if it, too, were in the midst of Trace's struggles. She believed these men. Trace was ill. It explained so much, and yet made no sense at all. But explanations could wait. Right now, they were fighting so hard to contain him, someone was bound to get hurt.

And she did have a better idea.

She reached Magnus first, her hand curving onto his shoulder so gently, so firmly, that he immediately looked up at her. Her gaze was fixed on Trace, so she only felt the way he hesitated and, for just a moment, relaxed. He watched her with intense curiosity as she reached for the bare expanse of

Trace's back. She ran her hand up his scarred spine, and, as if she had injected him with a drug, he went completely still. He was breathing hard, his skin damp from exertion, and he tried to see her by turning.

She touched Tristan on his hand where he held the cuffs, pushing him gently away even as Magnus also backed off. Both men barely understood why they responded to her silent, gentle urgings. Nor did they understand the way she had calmed the madman who had fought them so hard, but now lay docile under her sweeping, pacifying touch.

"Shh," she soothed Trace. "It's okay now."

Ashla laid herself against his back, her cheek touching his over his shoulder as she ran warm hands down both of his arms.

"Don't let them take me from you," he begged her on a roughened choke of words. "They don't understand. We're Sainted. We're . . ."

"Special," she finished for him softly. "I know, Trace. I know. Just promise me one thing, okay?" she asked, her voice trembling a little as he reached to hold her against himself.

"Anything," he swore. "Whatever it takes."

"Promise me . . . that you'll come back to me. Even if it's just once to tell me you're okay. Please . . ."

"But I'm not leaving," he argued.

"Yes, *jei li*, you are."

With only that warning, Ashla closed her eyes and healed him the only way she could think of.

She sent him to sleep.

Magnus watched the small wraith with no little amazement as she petted Trace's hair one last time before moving off his relaxed body. She was perfectly solid, there was no denying it. Magnus had never seen anything like it in Shadowscape before. A human woman. Or rather, a full physical manifestation of a human woman. His eyes traveled over her, his senses opening wide and sinking deep. She felt pain, both physical and mental, in this state, he realized. He could sense the abuse her body had taken at Trace's hands. As she wiped at hot tears quickly, he was amazed to find her holding no resentment toward him for that. The nature of the promise she had wanted to glean from him had told him as much. It was the request of a woman who did not feel the victim— even though she probably should.

Magnus was baffled by Trace's behavior as it was. Euphoria was a very self-contained effect. Rarely did it spill out to affect others in so direct a manner. It was like being catatonically high, a tidal wave of self-created endorphins causing endless pleasure in the brain, even as you just lay there and let it happen. How was it that Trace had managed to transfer all of that into his warped belief that she was the key to his pleasure state? He shouldn't have even been able to coordinate himself enough to impress himself on a woman, never mind doing what he had done to this one.

A human woman.

Well, almost.

Shadowdwellers and humans were not bred to one another. The secrecy of the Shadowdwellers' existence was the first reason for such exclusion. The dangers and difficulties behind controlling a human mate's unthinking use of light were just too risky to be worth it. But most of all, the chance of conception was an unbearable hazard. What would a half-breed baby suffer? Could it bear the light, or would it burn to death in its first cradle as its caretakers unwittingly killed it? No, it was too much of a terrible consequence.

However, he had to admit there wasn't likely to be a danger of pregnancy here. She might seem real in most every way, but the matter that was her body was occupying space elsewhere. The priest had his suspicions that it was her very unique abilities, and the mind that crafted and wielded them, that had allowed her to believe she was a warm, living being in this place, and as a result had projected it to those who really were. But she certainly couldn't get pregnant, regardless of what her mind was capable of creating.

"Tristan, can you clothe him?" Magnus asked quietly, never taking his eyes off the sniffling young woman.

"Yes. Don't be long. I'll need you if he wakes."

"He won't wake up," she injected quietly. "Not for a while. Trace desperately needed sleep. He was exhausted, except . . . except he just wouldn't listen to his own body, so I . . . I made him."

Ashla had intended to do the very same trick half a dozen times over the course of the past hours, but it had seemed so deceptive, so smugly superior, somehow, and undermining. Even now her insides crawled in a cringe for having done it, but she knew in her heart that it was the only way. If she hadn't stepped in, Trace would have been hurt. Badly. She didn't need to know anything about the two men who had come to retrieve him to know that much. She only had to look at the weapons they carried, the artistic intricacy of some and the cold efficiency of others, to know they took the business of fighting quite seriously. Whatever the world had become, wherever they were from, they clearly had learned to walk around always prepared for the worst.

When Magnus approached her, she backed up in fear. There was something deadly and imposing just in his carriage, the hard glint of analytical thinking so obvious in his golden eyes. But the truly frightening thing about him was that she felt a depth to him that others simply did not have. Ashla had been intuiting things about people for as long as she could remember, her inability to control the feelings forcing her to learn how to accept and live with them—unlike her healing ability, which she could choose not to use. However, in all of her life she had never felt anything quite like the chasm of the spirit that she felt from this man. There was no proper way to describe it, but that was the one that came closest.

"What is your full name?" he asked, surprising her with

the simplicity of his query. She had at least expected he would want her to atone or account for what was happening to Trace.

"Ashla Townsend."

"Ashla Townsend," he repeated carefully. "I thank you for your help." He paused just long enough to give her a chill. "You aren't likely to see him again, Miss Townsend. I think I must be fair and warn you of that."

"Why?" The query was heavy with petulance, but she was too shocked and upset by the news to measure her response. "Is he going to die or something?"

"It is possible, but unlikely," he said, instilling no real confidence, and no false hope, either. Ashla appreciated that. It bore a mark of honesty she rarely saw, even if it gave her no comfort.

"But then why can't he come back?" she wanted to know, inescapably realizing there were depths of secrets going on between these three men that they didn't want her to be any part of. Trace hadn't willingly wanted to leave her, no, but neither had he taken the option of bringing her with him.

They didn't want her there, wherever there was.

"It takes time to heal from this, and his mind and body will be too fragile for travels back this way. However . . ."

Whatever he was going to say, he dismissed it after a moment with a shake of his head.

"Hey, look," she sniffed with a shrug of bravado as she turned her head to stare away from him, and, even more pointedly, away from Trace, "I don't expect anything. I just foolishly hope for the impossible. I guess I'm masochistic like that. Excuse me."

Ashla moved away quickly, hurrying to snatch up enough of her clothes to make herself decent before she scurried for the doors. She couldn't stay there and watch them drag Trace away from her, knowing all the while that she had made it possible—even if it was for the best. And she couldn't stay alone in the suite that was redolent with the heady smell of their frantically paced sex. She simply could not bear to find herself once more plunged in solitude, yet with reminders of living with Trace all around her. Even if it had only been two days, they had been the first days in a blend of seemingly endless time that had stood out and claimed themselves wildly different from the others. Everything about them, and the man who had marked them and her as his, had been full of a color and dimension that she had never known before, and that she might not ever know again by the sound of Magnus's warnings.

However, in spite of her preemptive efforts, Ashla would discover the excision taking place was going to be much, much more difficult for her than she had feared.

Chapter 10

It was like a knife that had been plunged through the back of his skull was being slowly pulled free, with jolting jerks every now and again as the tightness of the bone around the blade hindered its removal. He was hot, burning with the purposeful searing of the dual forges on either side of him that first made him sweat and then boiled the sweat so it would burn as it rolled down the length of his skin. It was "black" fire, a fire made of chemically treated wood that burned with dark flames. It had been discovered back in the times before technology, a way of keeping the Shadowdwellers from freezing to death as they were forced to live in places where winter lived the longest, bringing nighttime with it for twenty-four hours a day at times. They could keep warm without poisoning themselves and burning to a crisp just from the ambient light flames gave off.

The fire's true purpose, of course, was to heat the metal chains attached to the manacles that kept him bound to the floor by his wrists, upper arms, thighs, and ankles. He had been forced into a position of subservience, the stone floor digging into his knees and shins until they were raw and numb, but in the grand scheme of things it was the least notable discomfort.

"You are a traitor," that persistent voice whispered from a place close behind him that he could not see. "A fascist who thinks he can twist our people under the dictatorial rule of two pretty little puppets. But they are without you now, faltering and crying out for direction and"—the laugh came with bitter humor—"left only with a half-blind woman to guide them! Poetic, don't you think?"

"Rika has more sight in her smallest finger than an anarchist like you will ever know in all of your days," he ground out in defiant reply, even though it meant speaking with dehydrated and painfully smoke- and heat-seared vocal cords.

"So loyal. Such a good dog." The obligatory hand came out to pat him on the head in two sharp movements that didn't hurt, but hardly qualified as kind or encouraging.

The sound of light fabric sweeping the floor helped him track movement until his captor finally stepped into his visual range, limited by the blinders mask he wore. It was made of leather and rivets, its only purpose to rob him of a key sense, leaving just enough so he could see the tableau of tortures that might befall him where they were set out in an array straight in front of him.

He watched the slide of a slipper and the light flutter of *paj* under her skirt as she came just that far. She never came into full view, never showed her face, and it was an effective frustration. Trace wanted a face to attach his fury to. He had never wanted anything so badly in all of his life.

Except for Ashla. She has skin like a soft dream, so smooth and warm that even the flaws of her healing wounds could go unnoticed. She has a scent I crave, and a taste bordering on the divine. My body aches for her even now, with a more savage heat than either of these forges could rival.

"Perhaps I should reward you for your devotion," she mocked, bending close behind his ear to speak to him in an enticing voice. "What do you suppose you deserve?" Her hand drifted down his neck, forcing him to grit his teeth as his skin crawled in revulsion. He was tied too tightly to successfully shake her off, and he had learned not to waste his energy. In spite of himself, she was training him to act exactly as she wanted him to. The idea of that did far more damage to him than all her devious little tortures did, but he supposed she already knew that. She knew that destroying his mind was the ultimate path to destroying *him*.

"You know," she purred as her teeth bit the rim of his ear, "if you and yours lose the war, it leaves me the option of doing whatever I want to you in the end. Of course, even if it doesn't end, in a year or so you will pass out of usefulness anyway. I mean, by then your information will be obsolete or I will have turned you into my personal pretty little lapdog. I like to say without ego that I have faith in the latter." Trace felt long, elegantly manicured nails running down his spine, the bitch's natural talons on his skin a disgustingly familiar sensation by now. Her touch was meant to be seductive, slow, and searching as it ran back up over his sweat-slick skin.

Seductive is Ashla's touch, the way her hands tremble with her excitement! Ingenuous and shy, her fair features flushing pink with pleasure—that was irresistible seduction! To be tortured with the promise of that for the rest of my days; there would be the power to tame me to a woman's side. And I have barely begun to know her, to feel her. I could barely pause for breath, she so excited me, never mind taking the time to do everything . . .

. . . everything I should have.

"What are you thinking?" his captor asked with genuine and hungry curiosity. "That expression of distress, it was out of place and not of my doing. Tell me, what were you thinking? I speak of war, betrayal, and death, and you don't even flinch. I speak of breaking you and torturing you and a dozen other torments, but you just grit your teeth in preparation. Now, out of nowhere, that painfully poignant expression, eyes downcast, and . . . is it regret clouding those onyx eyes, *Ajai*? Yes, I believe it is. What is it you regret, *Ajai* Trace? Your choices? Your life? That you sacrificed living it for this vain little war of yours? That you may die without spawning a single child to carry on the pride of your family? That you never took a woman to your heart and home?"

Her nails slowly curled under her palm against his spine, and Trace stiffened as the true claws came out. Like a ninja's metal crampons, these strapped around her palm, leaving an exposed set of metal tines that curved up from the back of her hand in four stainless steel blades he knew were sharp enough to cut, but not sharp enough to make the cut painless for even a second. A good blade, a sharp blade, severed nerves so quickly and with such precision that you felt nothing for a decent amount of time. But a slightly duller blade . . .

The tips of the tines nipped into his skin. He couldn't see, but he could feel from experience that she was avoiding the scarring from the last time she had plowed furrows up the length of his back. The scarring dulled the local nerves, and she simply wouldn't have it. She wanted to be sure every nerve was fresh and raw and ready for her. Trace's hands curled into fists as he braced himself against inevitability.

"Tell me to stop, and I will," she whispered softly, her breath cool against his hot skin. "Tell me to stop. No information or begging or anything like that is necessary. Just tell me to stop and I will."

She pushed her fist forward and the blades punctured his skin. The sound of his teeth grinding together joined the hard crack of burning wood and the roar of flames. Now it was no longer sweat, but beads of blood welling from his skin and rolling down his back. He didn't need to see it to know it.

"If you don't, you might start to convince me that you take pleasure in pain of this magnitude. There is no reason not to ask me to stop. You are simply being stubborn or you are truly a masochist. If the latter is the case, then perhaps I should be—"

She abruptly slid her free hand under his arm around his ribs, the crampon on the back of that hand scraping the underside of his arm as she did this, and he felt her kneeling behind him to improve her reach. When her hand rode down the plane of his belly on a direct path, he tensed violently against his bonds. She always kept him nude, so it was easy for her to wrap her fingers around his flaccid sex. The blades on the back of her fist nipped and bit against his thigh, but he doubted it was an oversight on her part. She did nothing without purpose. Nothing without plan. His torturer was quite clever and accomplished and took great joy in her work.

"Hmm," she mused. "Let's see if you really are a masochist."

Blades furrowed slowly into his skin, and she had gone only a couple of centimeters before Trace gave out and let himself roar with pain.

"*Ajai* Trace!"

Trace awoke with a clawing gasp, the violent memory burning him straight through even as he emerged in a completely different reality. He reached out to either side blindly, grabbing for whatever he could, and found himself caught in two sturdy clasps of strong flesh that felt familiar and grounding all at once. By the time he calmed enough to focus, he could see Guin and Magnus leaning over him with dreadful grimness and frank unease in their eyes.

"You're going to be sick," Magnus predicted quietly, already reaching to help him sit up even as Trace felt the sudden onrush of violent nausea wrenching through him like an invading alien force. With his companions supporting him and a handmaiden providing a basin, Trace fulfilled Magnus's prophecy.

Karri, Magnus's handmaiden, quickly left to hand off the basin for another, this one filled with a wash sprinkled with a fresh mixture of herbs and oils in it. She submerged a cloth and then gently bathed his face, neck, and chest. The aroma of the herbs instantly quelled his rebelling belly, and Trace took in his first easy breath in what felt like ages.

A distinctive jarring sensation went through them all, rocking everyone. Trace looked at the narrow room they occupied with widening eyes.

"Are we on the road?" he demanded, his throat scratching harshly against the words.

"For about two nights now," Guin confirmed.

"Two nights?" Trace turned, trying to jerk free of supporting hands even as he kicked for leverage against the mattress of the bed they had him in. "Where are we?" he demanded.

"Canada."

Canada.

North. They were heading north. They had been all along, ever since lighter days had hit New Zealand. The entire royal household was migrating to Alaska via New York after a . . .

"The conference," he said. "What happened?"

"You don't remember it?" Magnus asked.

"I was there?" Trace felt a little ill again as he tried to mine his mind for the missing memory.

"Yes. It was somewhat forgettable. However, do you remember what happened afterward?" Guin asked him. "With Baylor?"

Baylor.

Ajai Trace, word is that the Chancellor's vizier is not content with the immaturity with which his lord is managing the power of the realm . . . that perhaps you wish to see that change so we're not managed forever by a man who is little more than an adolescent at heart . . . or by the hand of a woman.

"Sedition," Trace whispered, just as he had barked it at Baylor right before he had drawn his weapon. He had reacted with emotion, destroying a chance to infiltrate the seditious vein that might be running through the Senate. It had been a foolish and illogical move, but there were times when Trace's mind clicked on reactive cylinders held over from the wars. They were not even a decade out of those conflicts, after all. Almost, but not quite. They had fought amongst one another for centuries, bitching and bickering and scrabbling in territorial wars and such, but the actual blade-to-blade and death-to-death war had lasted twenty years. It was a long time to live at the hub of every plot, every battle, and every defensive strategy. It would be many more years before veterans like him stopped carrying multiple weapons around with them.

His eyes tracked the closest walls near the bed, and sure enough, his katana stood propped in the corner, shining with readiness. To see it was to unlock the memory of the brutal fight with Baylor that had almost cost him his life if not for—

"Ashla! Where is Ashla?"

"Where you left her, my son," Magnus said quietly, "in New York."

Ashla. He had left her behind. The strange little wraith who had healed him in a dire moment, proving herself to be more dimensional than any real human he had ever encountered. She had felt warm to the touch, defying all rules of humans in Shadowscape, and had smelled like . . .

Sex.

Trace felt shock stiffening his body from his feet upward, as if he had stepped barefoot into liquid nitrogen. In a rush of physical sensation and nerve impulses, everything he had felt from the moment he crossed the room to kiss her the first time came crowding over him, making him struggle for breath and composure in front of his colleagues and father.

No! No, you Light-ridden bastard, you did not do this! Tell them to tell you that you didn't do this! You didn't take that fragile and innocent woman to bed knowing it was nothing! That she could have nothing to comfort her, nothing of you to keep beyond those two days because you would never go back! Even if it wasn't actually real, her mind and her heart, wherever they are, believed it was all real. To take her and then abandon her would seem so cold and callous; so insulting. It could play like light cutting into darkness with her frail ego. With the things a mind as powerful as hers is capable of, a resulting depression amidst so much isolation could be enough to . . .

"Kill her," he choked out, starting to struggle in the others' hands. "Let me go!"

They did so almost instantly, and Trace lurched for the nearest route out of bed. He made it only a foot off the mattress before he was yanked back by his wrists. It was only then he realized he was bound in soft restraints at his wrists and ankles.

There was no measure to the black fury the understanding sent pumping through him.

"*You bound me?*" The betrayal, the utter disgust in the phrase slapped hard at both men, and they exchanged troubled looks. "You are damn right to look like the miserable, treacherous bastards you are!" Trace roared at them. "How dare you bind me, after knowing what I went through at that sadistic bitch's hands? How can you stomach yourselves to do such an unholy act? You know! You know I can't bear this!"

But before he could begin ripping at the cursed leather and lambskin bindings in earnest, Magnus stepped up to him and took his shoulder under his hand. He held firm to avoid being shrugged off, and closed his eyes to the outright panic rushing into the eyes of his son.

"You were in Fade for three days, Trace," he said in low, level tones as his special power bled through to Trace, working its magic on him with the quick, ruthless strength the religious man was known for. "Truth is Light," he warned softly, "and it has a vicious burn."

Burn it did, searing through Trace's healing mind, now that it could be reasoned with. Only then did the full scope of his time with Ashla make impact, forcing him to understand that the awful truth of what he had done was far worse than he had originally recalled.

He had become a brigand in the worst sense, stealing what he had wanted, taking everything and selfishly giving nothing. He had been weak, crossed a line he shouldn't have, and then had made it worse and worse with every greedy touch, every inconsiderate invasion into her. *Now* he remembered each wince of pain, each plea to rest, and each and every one of the aborted pleasures he had made her suffer while single-mindedly taking his own.

"No," he ground out in disbelief and tortured guilt, which forced Magnus's power of truth to kick him hard into a rush of confirming memories.

He heard himself begging her with need, felt the glorious redemption he had experienced via his lust every time he had plunged into her. What was perhaps even worse was the understanding that he had promised devotions and unceasing need for her right up to the moment he had forced her to turn against him in order to rescue him. He had been as an animal, intemperate and untamed. He had abandoned skill to biological imperative. He had used and abused a woman who had already been used and abused enough.

Promise me . . .

The phrase whispered through him just as he reached his worst moment of self-loathing.

Promise me . . . that you'll come back to me. Even if it's just once to tell me you're okay. Please . . .

Magnus lowered himself to a single knee beside the bed,

leaning in to speak softly in guidance, as was his calling when it came to the truth. "Truth, like faith, can be a raw thing or it can have a great many layers to it . . . some too subtle or too ethereal for us to grasp on our own. Guilt and loathing of the self is too easy, Trace. For you, at least. Slow yourself. Take a moment." Magnus glanced up to see Guin had long since taken himself to the farthest dark corner in the small room, and Karri was keeping at a discreet distance as well, allowing the priest the privacy needed to do his work with Trace. "You are not a man who easily allows others to see your thoughts or emotions. Not that you are cold or re-pressed, as I sometimes fear Guin is, but that your experi-ences have taught you in hard ways not to give away such an advantage to others.

"When euphoria struck, it struck with a uniqueness to suit the situation you were caught up in. Now, the definition of that in finer details will be up to you to decide, but be very certain you weigh *every* fact and *every* truth. Whenever you ask me, I will help you with this, Trace, but you have never been one who couldn't see everything from all sides."

Trace turned to look into the gold and black eyes settled level to his, aware that he was vibrating in a fine shiver from the wash of physical and emotional feedback he was swim-ming in. He knew that Magnus's power to make others see truth also allowed the priest to see it, to see all of it in all the shameful or exciting details. Magnus was a man designed by Darkness to guide righteous men, and to hunt down and de-stroy those who sinned. That he wasn't passing heavy judg-ment on Trace said a great deal, and it made the vizier listen hard to what he was telling him.

But because Trace was still wildly disoriented and dis-traught, he was grateful when the man he looked to as a fa-ther took the time to slowly clarify his situation.

"Take a moment to consider that you have been in eu-phoric withdrawal for two days before you condemn us for binding you. We would have done otherwise if it was at all possible, but I know you understand it was not. If you had escaped us, raving as you were and as sick as you were physically, you would have been in human hands within hours, if you hadn't damned yourself to burn in Light before that.

"Do not fear so much for Ashla Townsend's state of mind. Yes," he said quickly when Trace's eyes narrowed on him, "she is a brittle creature in some ways, but what I saw was someone who survives great hardships in spite of herself. There is strength in that. There is strength in her. I told her that you would be well, but that it was unlikely she would see you again. I feel that she believed me. She will not suffer from worry over what has become of you, if that is what concerns you."

"What concerns me," Trace informed him as his hands tightened with tension, "is that she and I are . . . I think we are Sainted, *M'jan*. She sacrificed herself for me, and ever since then things have been strange and threaded, as if we've become caught up in a web together. She sees into me!" he told the priest fiercely. "I know it's unfeasible. She is human and . . . and a-a wraith." He swallowed on the word because it didn't suit and felt like a lie. She had felt so real! She *was* real, just not whole. "What happened, with the euphoria focusing so specifically on her, there was a reason for that. A cause. And I think it was the Sainting."

"Even if such an unprecedented Sainting were to take place, Trace, the bond of the Sainted is one of loyalty and connective companionship. Sex and lust are rarely present, although on occasion those who are attracted to each other will mate, but what you suggest is a reach into wild supposition. It is not like you to think without logic."

"It isn't like me to do any of this!" Trace barked back at him. "To stay in 'scape for so long? To take a human woman, or any woman for that matter, as a lover? You can see the truth, Magnus, and now I want you to feel it as well. I have not been able to let a woman touch me since Acadian tortured me. It is a fact, though I have admitted it to no one."

Trace stared hard into the priest's eyes, making certain he knew how serious he was. "That is twelve years, if you wish to count. Nine of peacetime, two after my liberation, and eleven months captive."

"That suggests to me that this euphoric aberration was more about releasing your repressed sexuality," Magnus mused, but it was the thoughtfulness that hovered in his gaze that kept Trace from crying out with frustration. He had to make his foster father understand, at all costs. He would need his help if he was going to get back to 'scape and where he had left Ashla alone within it.

"How can I prove this to you? Can you disprove it to me? I stand ready for either challenge and will be as victorious as I was against Baylor! You believed me about him without proof or witnesses, when you might have thought me just a murderer; why won't you believe me now?"

"Because you are fresh off euphoria, *Ajai*." Guin spoke up from the far end of the room. "Would *you* trust anyone as such? Could you quickly trust the same man who threatened to cut your throat not two days previously?"

Trace's eyes widened at that, his head snapping to check with Magnus for confirmation. The priest's grim nod made his heart sink low into his belly.

"For that offense, I am deeply sorry," he said, his voice tight as the fire of fight drained from his eyes and body. He fell back onto his pillows, his wrists still pulling taut against his bonds.

"Trace, we will untie you once you are lucid twenty-four hours. It is a lifetime for you, I comprehend that, but you see we have no choice and this is the way these things are done. We have learned from the mistakes of the past how best to do this."

"I know," he said quietly, turning to stare at the far wall. "I can bear twenty-four hours, Magnus. I bore eleven months. Another day will not matter."

Magnus couldn't help but be troubled by this deflation of

his son's spirits. He rose to his feet, knowing that it would only add insult to injury to continue to push him. Instead, he gestured to Karri, beckoning the herbalist forward so she could do whatever her skills could provide to ease these next hours for Trace. Karri knew exactly what her priest required of her, their many years of service together making them work in a synchronicity that often led others to believe they were psychically connected. While this happened occasionally between priests and handmaidens, they had not been so blessed. Still, Magnus knew it made no difference to either of them that they had never bonded in such a way.

But Magnus was beginning to understand that perhaps if they had, he might know the seat of Trace's despondency far better. He frowned as he thought that, not for the first time wondering at the wisdom of his order's exclusionary living arrangements. Perhaps if they lived more among the people they ministered to, they could be of even more use than they were. However, there were those in the order that would consider that kind of thinking a show of wavering faith. Magnus was secure in his faith—he had lived nothing else for centuries and had never wanted anything more—but he was always willing to accept that he wasn't the beginning and the end of all knowledge. That would make him a god, and he was a bit more humble than that.

As it stood, there was a great deal about the aberration that was Ashla Townsend to stimulate not only his interest, but his concern. Not just because Trace was being so soundly affected by her existence, but because Shadowscape was. He was a guardian of all 'scapes, save the one he could never survive in, in this mortal form. Lightscape was a Shadow-dweller's hell in any event, the very idea of arriving in such a place the thing of nightmares. Hell had its own guardians as far as Magnus was concerned, and he had no intention of ever knowing them. However, the others he had access to and knowledge of, those were his to protect. The guidance of his people actually took second place to that duty.

What he needed was information. From this he could formulate a workable theory using logic that he and Trace could
both accept and understand. He had no other goal and must
not attach any others to himself. His personal beliefs and
cultural taboos should not play a part in what was true. Also,
his desire to help his fosterling find peace of mind should
not influence him. Magnus kept all of this in mind as he
gained his feet and rounded the bed toward the doorway. He
paused only long enough to trade a strong look with Guin,
who was clearly ready to leave with him.

"Karri, keep him calm, restful, and otherwise cared for."
He wanted to stress to her not to unbind him, but a look
alone took care of that, and he got a sour face from her for
his trouble that said "what am I, stupid?" all over it. Of
course she knew better, Magnus realized, but this was *Ajai*
Trace. His charm and power of diplomacy were legendary.
He knew how to work people's strengths and weaknesses
against them or to his advantage. Karri had been by Magnus's side a long time, had even known Trace since his days
as a young man, and he should trust she knew better, but
there was too much critical need lying in Trace and too much
compassion inside the handmaiden. Together it could make
for unwelcome circumstances. "Just the same," he said aloud,
his tone quite firm with her.

He stepped through the door and left it to Guin to close it
as another solid jolt thudded through the RV. In the next
room was a low circle of two half-moon couches settled low
to the floor. They were separated just enough to allow a path
through the middle between them. The usual exotic fabrics
they favored in their culture hung about or lay draped for
comfort and appeal all around them. This time it was Malaya
who sat sprawled back against piles of pillows, toying with
one of her gold-chained necklaces as she stared vacantly up
at the ceiling. Tristan was on his feet, restlessly pacing the
path between the couches.

"It's enough!" he was saying to his sister, his voice hot

and wired, his hand streaking roughly through his thickly curled hair. "Damn me, Laya, but he has suffered enough for us! Now this nasty business with Baylor . . . leading him back to that Lost and coming to this!" Tristan gestured toward the door the others had exited from, noticing them for the first time and drawing up short. "What has happened?" he demanded, his dark eyes darting from one to the other in an attempt to read their minds from their faces. Since telepathy was not Tristan's special skill, he was only as successful as both neutral faces allowed him to be.

"Lucidity," Magnus offered as if he had expected nothing else. He couldn't have been certain, everyone's tolerance for euphoria differing, but he would have been surprised if a man of Trace's strength and power would have permanently succumbed. He would have been grieved as well. Deeply, deeply grieved. "Karri can take this from here, Tristan. I am needed on a mission elsewhere."

"You're leaving the convoy? In the middle of nowhere?" Malaya spoke up quickly, sitting forward with concern. "But we need you in Elk's Lake! What safeties will you have, going alone and without travel planning? Where are you going?"

"It is best I keep that to myself for the moment." He made the response as if he did this sort of thing all of the time. "Don't worry. I will do most of my traveling in the night and in Shadowscape. After so many migrations, I know the northeast safely well. I will find the houses I need. I only ask you two things. Don't immediately tell Trace I have left. Let him rest and recover some more beforehand. Also, keep him with you here until you reach Elk's Lake, whatever it takes— short of keeping him bound."

"*Drenna!*" Tristan swore darkly. "As if we would!"

"Understand this: if you release him, Trace will flee you," Magnus promised them. "He may be lucid and coming back to himself, but he is a man with an obsession, and this sort of devotion is hard to interfere with. Time should improve matters, as will being back around the usual demands of work and the companionship of old friends. Keep him out of Shadow-scape for at least a week. To return any sooner would risk relapse. He knows this and will expect you to watch him closely, so don't bother being subversive about it."

"The man is anything but an idiot," Guin remarked, "and neither are we. We know what to do."

Chapter 11

Sophia Townsend was a saint.

Or so the nurses at the West End Rehabilitation and Long Term Care Facility thought. She came like clockwork, every Tuesday evening, and never once had she missed one. Not even that time there had been a terrible snowstorm and even the shift nurses had been forced to stay put rather than go home. She had arrived, as always, with coffee in hand and homemade treats for the nurses. In a place like West End, at least on the LTC side of the building, visits from family members were not so regular, if they even happened at all. It usually depended on the length of time involved; the longer the coma or vegetative state, the more time between visits.

Not so with Ashla Townsend's mother. The nurses set their watches by her, making sure her daughter was freshly bathed, dressed, and presented. Sophia arrived punctually at seven, as always, and this Tuesday night was no different. Also as always, she was dressed in perfectly tailored clothing, all freshly pressed and creased where it was required to be, and her hair swept into a smooth, taut chignon. She carried a purse on her arm, always something that coordinated and evoked compliments from other women, and flowers that she would leave in her daughter's room until next week.

"Good evening, Mrs. Townsend," she was greeted, smiles and warmth always awaiting her.

"Good evening, Sandra. Frannie. Jaime. Olivia, how is that baby of yours?"

"Fine. Getting big. Not so much a baby anymore," she said wistfully.

"Oh, they are always our babies, no matter how old they get," Sophia assured her, reaching to pat the head nurse's hand as she slid this week's tray of goodies onto the counter. "Apple strudel this week. I even portioned it with that new sugar substitute, cutting the sugar in it by half. This way you girls can't accuse me of being responsible for your waist-lines!"

"Oh! Mrs. Townsend, you are an angel! And we would never accuse you of anything. Thank you so much."

"You are quite welcome." Sophia's eyes slid to the near hallway, her smile becoming a degree more fixed. "And how is our girl today?"

"Better. Much better. She is healing quite quickly. We still have no idea what caused her to suddenly drop into seizures like that after all this time, but thankfully the tests show nothing is traumatically wrong. I thought for sure she'd have a bleed somewhere, but the neurosurgeon says not."

"Well, I can tell you I feel so guilty, leaving that vase by the bed. The very idea that it was a danger to her all this time . . ."

"Oh, no! Don't feel that way, Mrs. Townsend, please," Olivia begged as she came quickly around the counter to take her under a comforting arm. "There was no way any of us could expect she would knock it onto the floor and then fall out of the bed on the broken glass while seizing. It was just one of those freakish things. Certainly an accident. And anyway, we have a new one in there, except now it's safely on the far dresser. These will look lovely in it." Olivia reached to fondle the petal of one of the lilies. "Her cuts were almost all superficial, and she is healing, as I said. And other than some restlessness and the usual muscle spasms, she hasn't moved a bit. No more seizures."

"I never thought I'd be grateful for my daughter not moving," Sophia remarked wryly. "Well, time marches forward and so must I." She broke free of the other woman, discreetly shrugging and smoothing her suit jacket back into place. "Enjoy your treat, ladies. God bless."

Sophia gave the nurses a little wave as she hurried into the hallway. Her heels snapped an echoing rhythm as she went, marking her steady familiarity with the route.

Her first hesitation came when she realized her daughter's door was closed. For obvious reasons, all the doors on the floor were usually left open. Only need for privacy would alter that. However, Ashla's nurses would have taken care of any issues like that before her arrival. She had made certain they would always know when she was coming so they could make the room bearable before her visit. Sophia despised the smell of human waste, especially the bitter sharpness of urine. She had raised enough righteous fuss in the past with the floor nurses that she no longer needed to worry about encountering such unpleasantries.

So, she was a little hesitant as she touched her hand to the door and pushed it open. The room was pitch black, she noted immediately, the only light coming from the monitor screens. Sophia reached in to fumble for the light switch, but before she could find it, someone from inside the room grabbed her by the wrist and yanked her inside the room. She squealed in natural reaction to her fear, but the sound was lost in the black privacy of the room as the door closed again at the quick urging push of a foot.

She knew she was dealing with a man instantaneously, just by the strength, size, and scent of him. She heard the creak of leather as he moved, and smelled it, too. She was a small woman, it was true, but even so she could tell he was big. Big in height and big across the shoulders as he sealed a gloved hand over her mouth and pushed her back against the closed door.

"Apologies, miss, for the drama, but I need a few questions answered. You will do this for me and I will assure you not to harm you. If you call for help, however, that will change the agreement. Are we clear?"

Sophia stared at his dimly quarter-lit face, the blue from a bedside machine catching him in a muted slash over his left eye and forehead. It was a dark eye, a serious one, and though there was no obvious menace, Sophia had no doubt that the man beyond it was very dangerous—when provoked. She nodded quickly, not at all interested in provoking him.

"Are you a nurse?" he asked as he lifted cautious fingers from her mouth. "Can you tell me about this woman?"

"I am her mother. I know everything about Ashla."

"I doubt that, but I will settle for a few details. What happened to her?"

"A car wreck. Six people in the car, and she was the only one to survive." Sophia glanced toward the bed where her daughter lay peacefully sleeping. She teared up, as she always did, when she thought of the accident. "My Cristine died."

"How long ago was this?" he asked her, not even bothering to offer sympathy for her grief. This made Sophia angry, so there was bite in her reply.

"Two years!"

"And why does she not awaken?"

"I have no idea! She had some kind of brain bleeding thing and didn't wake up from the surgery. She won't die and she won't wake up, so she just lies there. Why do you want to know about some useless vegetable?"

"I don't recall my answering questions as part of this arrangement," he countered. "Tell me about when she was young. Tell me about the healing."

*   *   *

Magnus had the mother securely held against the door, so he felt the rigidity flushing through her. He squeezed her tightly in warning.

"Don't bother to lie or deny. I have seen it with my own eyes."

"Is that it, then? Are you here because I spawned a demon and you think you can somehow gain use of her wicked power? I hope it died along with the rest of her cursed spirit! I hope she is walking in hell for killing my baby! I come here every week and I pray she pays for her sins!"

"Why there, hmm?" Magnus asked with speculation, the low tenor of his voice making the female fury he held trapped look at him wide-eyed. "With your Christian choices of heaven and hell, blessings and curses, good and evil, why do you take this power she has to a place of evil? In your religion, angels heal. God heals. Jesus healed. So why is Ashla not equated with them in your mind? Why do you relegate her to a dark place?"

"Because she is as dark as this room! Black as ink soaked to her soul. She can't help it, I know! She was born a sin! She was born the daughter of the devil." The mother sobbed with a rushing combination of honesty and drama, and Magnus was bemused by her theatrics. He had no doubt she believed every word of her convictions, but there was more to it than that. Luckily, he had the power of truth on his side. She was probably already wondering why she was saying so much to him.

"Born a sin? In my culture, only you can create your own sin. You can't be born with it. But there is always the conception that leaves room for a child to be created in sin. What did you do, Mrs. Townsend? Step out on your husband?"

"Yes," she confessed on a gasp, covering her own mouth with a slap when she heard her own secret slip uncontrollably into the air.

"So you go off for a fuck out of wedlock, and that makes *her* the sin?" he wanted to know, glancing back at the helpless young Ashla.

"Don't you dare use that language with me!" Sophia raged indignantly. "I was a victim! I was . . . I was seduced!" Magnus could tell by how she fought for her words that she was only admitting partial truths. It was useless for her to struggle. He was going to know the truth regardless.

And just like that, it came.

"I was walking home late from work. He was there again . . . always there. In the dark. I could see his eyes and sometimes his build, but he was always watching me. I felt him follow me every night, but he never showed himself. It was a-a flirtation of sorts. I just knew he wasn't going to hurt me. I would find a rose in my path. Or . . . or some other gift. Sweet, romantic things like my husband never gave me. I ignored it all at first, but I was lonely. Neglected. And he was frightening and exciting.

"Then one night he reached for me, drew me into the shadows, told me he couldn't bear not to touch me any longer. And then he did. Right there in the alley. It was so . . ." She swallowed hard. "It was so primal. It would have been like rape if I hadn't been so willing."

"And it was only the beginning," he said for her. "How long?"

"Two months. Every single night for two months. I wanted to stop! M-my husband and children . . . I wanted to stop!"

"And finally you did. But why then? What changed?"

"Something I saw. Felt. A night when he was so hot to have me. Careless, I guess. He didn't hear like he usually did. The car started and suddenly we were caught in headlights. He screamed as if in pain, smoke rising from his burning skin as he ran into the dark. I followed right behind him, yet he disappeared before my eyes into shadows. Then he was at my back, walking out of a space where there had been nothing a moment before. That was when I realized what he was. That was when I knew he was an imp, a demon sent to tempt me into fornication and hell!"

"One who impregnated you with his child," Magnus mused, looking back at the fair-skinned and golden blond Ashla. "So you thought you really had given birth to a devil?"

"Not at first. I hoped it was my husband's baby. She was so fair and loved the light. A good girl. Until that damned rabbit! She took it into her hands and instead of dying as it should have, it leapt out of them fully healed, like magic! I knew then it was demon power that made it happen. I've known ever since. I preached to her, tried to get her to repent against her father's half inside her, but it was no use. She was born with evil in her core, conceived in one of the worst of sins! And now she's murdered my youngest baby and her father as well! He died at Cristine's funeral of a heart attack! Tell me she isn't cursed and I will—"

She broke off from her hysteria of rising words and emotions, the speech justifying her treatment of her daughter freezing in her throat. If Magnus had been another man, he might have relished the realization flooding into her expression. He might have smiled much wider than he did.

"You're like him!" She looked wildly around the dark room. "H-he sent you! You're a-a—"

"You know, we take offense to being called names, just like anyone else," he said on a warning purr next to her ear. It wasn't very forgiving of him to taunt her so, but he couldn't seem to resist.

The question was, was it really a Shadowdweller who had fathered the woman behind him? The dance of light and shadow wasn't only theirs to own. Vampires, and other Nightwalkers, could be just as sensitive under the right circumstances. Vampires could ride shadows quite well. It would account for her pale skin. But in all cases, the ability to bear sunlight was clearly a human genetic quirk she had retained from her wretched mother.

But Magnus was inclined to believe it was a Shadow-dweller. It wasn't unheard of; it was just unwise and difficult to execute such affairs. The woman before him, despite her age, showed the echoes of her youth. She must have been a tempting, beautiful creature then. Especially to one of his kind, with her fairness and blond, blue-eyed features. But whoever Ashla's father was, the act of impregnating a human was unconscionable. The way Nightwalker genetics held so dominantly? As a child she could have died at her first touch of sunlight. The suffering would have been unforgivable. Whoever he was, he had been selfish and irresponsible, and Magnus prayed that this had been a one-time obsession that wasn't ever repeated.

Unfortunately, knowing his race as he did, he was afraid his prayers were useless.

But it did explain a great deal . . . Not the least of which was how Ashla could see them in Shadowscape, and how she could feel so real and fully embodied. It might also explain the very comatose state she was in. It was possible that, without even realizing it, she was actually in Fade.

But for two years?

Two days could drive any of them mad. What had two years done to her? Was she protected by her human half from the euphoric consequences? She hadn't known about Shadowscape or tried to purposely get there, but the trauma of her accident had plunged her into it somehow. Was it possible that his people held the key to helping her find her way out of Fade?

Trace. Trace whom she trusted and who was quite powerfully adept at Fade; he could help her.

"Take her!" the mother whispered fiercely, as if it was a dirty little secret she didn't want her god to hear. "Take her to your hell and free me from this curse! You have my blessings, just take her! Take her back to the devil that spawned her!"

"That, madam," Magnus said icily, "would force me to bring her back to you, and I would never be so cruel to any living being."

With that, Magnus flipped a hand against a nerve cluster behind her ear, forcing her into unconsciousness. She was useless to him now, and annoying besides. She could rant and rave when she woke up, hopefully about devils stealing her daughter so she caused herself a lot of trouble and psychiatric care. At the very least, it would take her the better part of a week to get over the headache he'd just given her. He was going to have to do a bit of penance for that.

Later.

Magnus let the limp woman fall to the floor with a graceless clunking sound as he turned to the bed where Ashla's corporeal self lay. He crossed to her, avoiding the side with the monitors and their stinging light. He slowly examined her, from her lax, drooping toes to her head. She wore some ridiculous pink dress with a matching ribbon tied in her hair. Her hair was much longer in reality, her curls combed flatly into an outward flip at her shoulders that perfected the image of a flawless porcelain doll, or some kind of sleeping princess from a fairy story. Magnus could easily see why the mother had provided such paraphernalia. Her daughter had been imperfect and damaged in her eyes while she had been alive. In this incarnation of near death, she could finally have the angelic daughter she had craved, even while she prayed for her damnation. The priest was sickened by the way Ashla's mother had demented an otherwise beautiful religious structure. He might not share the belief in the Christian god, but he had always appreciated the wisdom and intricate guidance it provided.

He was drawn to the bandages on her small arms, unwrapping one quickly and inspecting the healing wound. Something had injured her recently, but her enhanced constitution should recover quickly. He wondered at her ability to heal outwardly faster than she could heal herself. It wasn't a common trait in Shadowdwellers at all. But she was a hybrid, and that changed everything. Most importantly, it changed her weakness to sunlight. Would she age? Would she be susceptible to the illnesses that haunted their breed, the ones that blinded those like Rika, or worse? What were her senses like? If she was a half-breed, then it was very possible she and Trace *were* Sainted as he had said, though he didn't yet fully understand the nature of how she had risked her life for his son.

Magnus looked to what he did know, and it came down to two very simple facts. The first was that she was in this half-cocked blend of Fade and human coma, but if she was going to have any chance of coming clear of it, it would be with the guidance of Magnus's people. It certainly wasn't going to happen while a poor excuse for a mother sat over her wishing her into hell.

The second fact was that they owed her the other half of her heritage. It was something her reckless father should have ensured, but had not. Whoever he was, he probably didn't care about such trivial details and what they might mean to a young woman who probably felt in her heart that she didn't quite fit in with the world around her, yet never understood why she felt that way. This was a feeling Magnus could truly understand. Those who stood out among others because of their power often endured hard childhoods. It was either an act of cosmic balance designed to temper sensitivities so those of great power would learn what it meant to be bullied by those stronger than themselves, or it was simply a social fact of life and the way jealousy worked within groups of children and adults. Tearing down what you didn't understand was an almost primitive imperative, it seemed. He had lived under that yoke as a child, fighting bullies and spitting adults alike just because he could wield the power of truth. Now, ironically, some of the same people saw him for penances as their priest.

Had Ashla been full-blooded with this healing gift, she would have definitely been claimed as a handmaiden. The

'Dwellers' powers of self-healing were quite remarkable, but she would be far from superfluous. For all their strengths, there were equal weaknesses in the forms of viruses and disease that even their advanced systems could not defeat. If she proved skilled in any healing of those diseases, it would make her as precious as platinum.

His mind was long made up, he knew, but he liked to think on things as he worked out logistics in his head as to how to escape with her. She had no respirator tubes down her throat, just a pressure mask that might gently remind her to breathe. However, a feeding tube existed, along with a half dozen other ready-made access points the humans had used to maintain her vegetating body.

This turned his gut with disgust, but not for the reasons it would Sophia Townsend. Magnus, like Trace, couldn't stomach the idea of being suspended between life and death like this. There was no honor to it, no purpose. For a warrior, it was a dire and dramatic insult. Still, it had kept her alive long enough for one of her people to find her and possibly call her back, the priest admitted. In this case there would be benefit to all of this mechanization of the human body and its functions.

He rapidly disconnected her from the bed and machines, shutting off alarms as quickly as he could when he could find them. He burned his hands in sharp scorches as lights hit them from the machines, but he barely took note. He had the frail body of Ashla Townsend free in minutes, scooping her up from her mattress and heading for the window he had arrived through.

"No small trick, this," he confided to his unconscious companion as he looked down along the nimble route he had taken through the shadows to get there. "But no great challenge, either. Don't be afraid, and rest yourself easy. I will get you down safely. Then, I believe we'll need a Shadow-dweller hospice to tend you a day or two before we make our way to Alaska. The darkness there grows long and beautiful, and Trace will be there waiting for you."

Magnus was undaunted by her silence. Whenever he could, those next few days, he spent time talking to his charge as if she were perfectly part of the conversation.

When Trace was released from the four-point restraints, it was decidedly anticlimactic. He got out of bed and left the room, only to be reminded that they were on the road and confined by speed and motion. Still, it was a thousand times more bearable than that strangling sensation around his wrists and ankles. He had been held by soft lambskin and not burning metal, but it made no difference to the remembered paths in his brain. Bound was bound, whether it was cobwebs or titanium.

He spent his first days of freedom brooding and quiet, letting the landscape of the night go by unnoticed until they came to a stop. The need for fuel compelled them, the only thing exterior of the convoy they stopped for. There was a supply onboard some of the trucks, but that was for later in the trip when gas stations and the like ran scarce, just as people did, which was fine for the Shadowdwellers heading for the colony up at Elk's Lake.

Trace stepped outside, avoiding the station lights, and found relief in a breath of fresh, dark air.

"Trace?"

Trace turned quickly, his hand twitching against his katana even as his brain registered the familiarity of the voice. "*Ajai* Killian. What can I do for you?"

Killian walked up to Trace slowly, very aware of how on edge the vizier must be after all he had been through in the last week. Sometimes, Killian forgot that the swords Trace carried were not just decorative, as some of the more pompous senators and other highborn men liked to play at. Trace had been raised at Magnus's knee, and there was no better warrior alive, nor a better teacher. Baylor must have forgotten this as well, or he might have thought twice about approaching Trace as a target.

It had been a critically bad move.

"It's nothing too vital, actually. The royal convoy is quite secure. My concern is more for the Sanctuary RVs. They are tending to lag behind a bit, slowing us down. I talked to *M'jan* Shiloh about it yesterday, but it doesn't seem to matter much to him. There's been no improvement. When we get separated . . ."

"Things get dangerous. I know," Trace filled in. "Shiloh loves when Magnus isn't around. The power to ignore you probably gives him a hard-on."

"Yeah." Killian chuckled dryly. "He can be a real *bituth amec* when he wants. I just don't see the damn purpose. He will endanger every priest and handmaiden in those vehicles just to . . . what? Show he doesn't have to listen to the second son of a minor clansman?"

"Perhaps. I take it as a reminder that, despite the war resolving, even priests once came from clans and can still hold grudges. But, Killian, I can't do this for you. You have to find a way to snap his ass in line or he'll keep walking all over you."

"How do you propose I do that?" Killian asked with sharp irritability. "Sanctuary runs very segregate from the rest of us. You know that. Even Tristan and Malaya don't have the power to tell them what to do!"

"Government shouldn't rule religion," Trace said automatically. "I appreciate your difficulty. Magnus is, of course, the better leader . . . but he isn't here right now. You can either complain to Magnus once he returns or you can find a way to make your point."

"Complain to Magnus." Killian scowled blackly. "You mean tattle. *Drenna*, this sucks! When I agreed to head security, I didn't realize how much bullshit stupidity it meant dealing with. I thought it meant using my sword and shield to protect the highest echelon of the new realm. Instead, it's dealing with pompous priests and arrogant aristocrats who think they know better than I do because I'm lowborn dirt to them."

"You are a war hero, Kill, and don't you forget that," Trace said sharply. "Don't let them forget that."

"Yeah." Killian smiled slowly and Trace could see a powerfully wicked thought flitting through his charcoal eyes. "How much penance would you figure I'd owe if I pulled my broadsword on the cocky bastard and made him piss himself?"

"That depends on if there was anyone in the room to bear witness at the time," Trace mused with a half grin. "Private humiliation is very different than a public one. But if you do either, you better pray nothing ever happens to Magnus. If Shiloh came into permanent power at Sanctuary, you'd be fucked."

"I think I'd be fucked anyway. Thanks, Trace. If you'll excuse me, I think I'm going to go polish my sword."

Trace chuckled at the implied threat, though with Killian he knew he couldn't be certain if he would or wouldn't assert himself in that way. Killian liked to declass himself when it suited his arguments, but unlike Guin he had been born the second son, or some would say the spare heir, to a clan chieftain. That made him nobility. He could have easily become a senator or a civic leader of choice with an advantage like that. But it was true that when Shiloh was involved, dealing with Sanctuary could get difficult. In the end, Magnus was the final word when it came to it, but whenever he wasn't available, church and state started to butt heads. Trace had tried to warn his father of the obnoxious traits of his subordinate and positional heir, but Magnus had yet to alter anything about the succession. True, it was not his choice alone, but his was the most powerful voice at Sanctuary. However, it was also true that Shiloh had never done anything except be a burr in the royal butt every now and again.

As he had said to Killian, it was a matter of him wanting to flex muscle and feel a little power. But Trace knew what trouble someone who enjoyed those kinds of things could turn out to be one day.

Trace walked back toward the Chancellors' vehicle, his footsteps echoing in the vast dark and cold Canadian night.

Ashla.

Thinking about her was inevitable, and he wasn't opposed to that. He wasn't afraid to face the grievous mistakes he had made with her. But it was hard to reconcile what he had done with what he had felt about physical contact with a woman for twelve years. It had all happened so easily and so quickly. He had crossed the line without hesitation, and it simply baffled him. He wanted to blame it all on the euphoric condition, but he knew he couldn't. He'd been perfectly sane the first time he'd reacted to her touch. She'd caused him terrible pain before healing him, and he remembered the violence it had sent searing in impulses through his mind, but it had skipped past him in a blink when she had begun to touch him.

Perhaps she had begun to heal him far deeper than he had given her credit for.

It was true, he had come a long way since his captivity. He had reconciled a lot, healed a great deal on his own. He trusted women all the time, Rika and Malaya for example, and he enjoyed great affection with his friends as well. He had been physically attracted to others, but . . .

Here the wall was built. Crossing into intimacy with someone was to share vulnerability with them. It meant exposing skin and scars, memories and sensations. It meant overcoming the simplest sensory triggers time and time again, and he simply hadn't been able to do that. It wasn't something he could spring on just anyone. He couldn't subject an unsuspecting woman to the psychosis of his traumatic memories without preparing her very well beforehand, and even then there were no guarantees.

But the euphoria had skipped over it all, like a stone bouncing over calm water. He had dominated Ashla, controlled every
movement she had made, every touch she gave or tried to
give, his psyche's way of managing his issues of vulnerability. His lovemaking had been crude and even perfunctory. He
had taken years worth of satisfaction inside her and given
nothing in return. The idea made him sick to his stomach.

He had known.

Oh, yes, he had known. Sitting in that chair and watching
her, he had known she was just what he needed. She was
something almost impossible to find among women of his
breed. Submissive, easily controlled, too damn sweet and
gentle for words, and all of this in spite of a past he could
smell on her that was as tainted as his own. They had both
survived, risen above what others had tried to do to them, but
they weren't healed yet.

Not yet.

A part of him had known that he would stay. He had
coated it in an internal fight for honor, but she had been too
perfect for a soul crying out for surcease. Succor had awaited
him in a small, delicate little body, and he had known the
woman within would be the perfect balm.

Trace stopped by the RV, leaning back against it as emotion tightened away the space in his lungs, suffocating the
breath from his body. He had walked over the line on purpose. He had wanted to do right by her when he realized how
she had been treated, but by then it was too late already. It
had been too late the moment he had kissed her. At least he had
brought her to her first orgasm before he had completely lost
sense and control. But it was of no comfort as the following
hours replayed in his head. It brought him an overwhelming
mixture of remorse, accountability, and cold understanding,
but it also brought an unexpected rush of adrenaline and
memory-induced excitement. There had been nothing generic
or homogenized about the way it had felt to touch her and
taste her. He could still respond to the memory of her wet

flavor and the feel of her in his hands. His heart raced and he closed his eyes around the recollection of the sensation of sliding into her. He groaned softly at the power of it, knowing it wouldn't have been the same had it been anyone else.

No one would have been so giving. No one would have willingly sacrificed their own pleasure and even their wellbeing physically just to sate the sexual hunger of a madman. But she had somehow known the depth of his need. Beyond the euphoria, beyond the sheer lust, she had known there was a creature as damaged and desperate as she was, crying out for the slightest sign of loyal warmth and intimacy. She had known no one else would do for him, and she had realized only her flawless devotion and unquestioning surrender could have tied them together.

And he had repaid her for it by abandoning her to the dark loneliness she feared and suffered in. He hadn't even left her with the warmth of half-decent sexual satisfaction to carry her through.

"Damn me," he whispered, blinking back hateful emotions as he stared up at the stars. It was one thing to suffer, and it was worse to inflict suffering on another. On an innocent. And she was innocent. Oh, there was bitter knowledge and cold experience within her, but at her very heart she had remained true to innocence. She treated others better than she expected to be treated; she gave what she could and expected nothing in return. All she did was hope. She hoped for respect, or fairness at the very least. She had trusted him with an almost simple naïveté.

"*Ajai* Trace."

Trace turned his gaze to Malaya, giving her a grim sort of smile. "Checking up on me, *K'yatsume*?"

"*Sua vec'a, Ajai.* You are the last being among us who needs regulation, Trace. All I offer is my understanding, as little as it may be to your situation. But here I am just the same. My brother as well, though he will corner you in his own time and way."

"No doubt," Trace agreed. "There are those who think him self-indulgent and cavalier, but you and I know him better. His worst attribute is arrogance, and that will rectify itself in time."

"Quite quickly, I imagine, once the proper woman gets hold of him."

Trace chuckled at that. Malaya was convinced that every problem only needed a good woman to solve it. Especially problems with men at their core. It was eerie how often she could be right about that. Malaya's perspectives and strong feminine politics in the face of their culture's traditionalist values were quite a learning experience. But for centuries the women of his culture had danced in visible submission while ruling their households with iron wills. Malaya was only bringing this fact into a public venue.

"We will reach Fairbanks in the next two or three days. Elk's Lake is only a day farther north. Then we will be home again. I have always loved to chase the dark like this, but I love to be home even more."

"It's the closest we can get to Shadowscape while in Realscape. Hardly perfect, because there is always some bit of light, but far safer than cities and long-burning bright summers in the south," replied Trace.

"And no threat of euphoria, either," she added. She tilted her head, examining his unhappy expression. "Trace, there is nothing for you to be ashamed of. No one could have predicted what would happen to you."

"I had a responsibility to get out, *K'yatsume*. When I stayed I was being selfish and—"

Trace ended with a shake of his head, unable to find words to suit his thoughts and feelings. He had said it all before, to himself and to his regents as they had tried to draw him out of his silence the past few days.

"Well, anyway, I needed to talk to you about something else, *Ajai*," Malaya said quietly.

It was a key phrase and tone that acted like a subliminal

trigger to Trace. He had heard it and others like it so often through the years, and it defined the job that was so important to him. It had the power to shift him out of his self-recriminations almost instantly, guiding his mind and focus onto a completely different track.

"Of course, *K'yatsume*, anything you desire. I will do my best to be of service." Trace gave her a heart-touched bow of respect, even as his eyes darted around to look for Rika. Malaya rarely consulted him without Rika by her side, and even that was a landmark situation. Whatever troubles there were that Malaya and Rika's wits couldn't solve together was either quite complicated or a personal issue one had toward the other.

"Rika and I are a bit at odds about something," she said carefully, rubbing her hands together for warmth as she began to pace a short space in front of him. Malaya rarely showed such agitation in public, and Trace was immediately concerned for the normally composed monarch.

"Define 'a bit,' " he encouraged her.

"An inch less than Guin and I are at odds about it," she said wryly.

"Ah. This is about letting Guin hunt out the other traitors in the Senate."

"Yes. I feel that if you and my brother agree with Rika and Guin, then perhaps the issue is with me."

"Not necessarily in a negative way, *K'yatsume*. You and I have played the part of the tiny, dissenting voice among many before. It can often be the start of a resonating calling, as you have seen for yourself, if your belief in it is strong enough. If you are convinced that you are right, that your reasoning is sound and rational, it shouldn't matter to you what the rest of us think. Of course, you should always be open to arguments. Stubbornness and commitment to conviction are two different things."

"So what *do* you think? What does my brother feel on this? He keeps saying that I must choose what is best to my mind since Guin is my protector, but he says it with such a grim countenance. He is not pleased, though I can't determine what he is most upset about."

"I think that since Guin started campaigning to leave your side, it has forced Tristan to take the matter of this betrayal more seriously. It is often the case with your brother that whatever affects you and your well-being brings out the imperative in an issue for him."

"Yes," she agreed, her lips curling in a sly and contented sort of smile. That was fine as far as Trace was concerned. The twins had cause to be smug in the security of their love for one another. It was a deep blessing all around. Things would have been very different had their relationship gone the way of Cleopatra and her brother Ptolemy. "But you are avoiding giving me the answer I truly want. Please, I beg you not to be as evasive as Tristan is being. If he has asked you to keep countenance, then by all means I won't goad you into breaking faith with him, but if he hasn't, I could surely use some guidance here."

"It is Guin's duty—his calling, he would say—to protect you. There are many ways of doing that. Both by your side and away from it." Trace reached to tag her arm, making her stop her agitated pacing so she would meet his eyes. "If your reluctance to send him away is solely based on your fear for his life, then you are trying to stop a train with a grain of salt. Guin will lose his life one day because he is trying to save yours. It is his destiny and the very definition of everything he stands for. Nothing you do can stop that unless you resign him from his position, and that alone would be enough to cut the life out of him."

"Trace," she whispered in protest, raising a hand to cover her mouth as tears rimmed her eyes. "I can't bear the thought. I . . . I thought it was over. The killing and death. Cousin against cousin. These past years I was growing content that we had all survived. Now I feel like it's unraveling before my eyes.

Baylor is dead, and you nearly lost in the battle. Rika grows weaker and, though she refuses to admit it, I know she is afraid time is growing short for her. Tristan . . ."

Trace's eyes narrowed to hear her speak of death and Tristan in the same phrase. "What of Tristan?" Had he missed something critical during his time of recovery? This was why he hardly ever left the royal household to itself. Things could change on the turn of the wind and everything caught up in a maelstrom.

"You above all others know him just about as well as I do, Trace. This cavalier attitude of his, the amusements, the women, and his laissez-faire approach to his personal life is not right. I trust you to guide him properly, and my faith in you and the man I know my brother to be carries my confidence in him through, but I am concerned. Aren't you?"

"Of course I am. I suppose I'm hoping time will work this out. Sometimes we need to be allowed to make our mistakes and even to act like an ass." Trace smiled when she laughed through her tears, her elegant fingertips sweeping the telltale drops away quickly. "Don't worry. I won't let him embarrass this household, and I won't let him become a danger to himself, this government, or any of its people. Not that I think it would happen anyway. I think . . . I believe he is doing what we are all doing. Now that we have settled into a routine and into security of position, we are left with time to remember the wars and all we saw and did in them. We have time now for grief, for regrets, for answerability to our mistakes. For all of us here, mistakes meant lives lost. It is a burden we all bear differently. This is Tristan's way of coping."

Malaya nodded, probably already having suspected as much. But it was good she had finally voiced her concern to Trace. He had wondered when she would reach her tolerance for the change in her brother. Overall it was such a minor difference, and restricted mostly to his personal life, but he was a public figure now and all behavior became meat for critics to feed on. Tristan had done nothing wrong as yet, but projecting a playboy image wasn't the best thing to do for a young monarch who wished to be taken seriously. Trace would have to focus on this more in the near future.

"And Guin?" he prompted her, bringing them back on point.

"Guin." She said his name softly, almost as if he were a puzzle that baffled her. "I admit I loathe the idea of sending him on a fool's errand that will probably get him killed. However, I understand that someone will have to do this and someone's life may well be lost in the process."

"Are you placing more value on his life than on someone else's?" Trace asked candidly.

"No," she swore. "My heart breaks for every life, whether known personally to me or not. It's just . . . I can't explain it any better than to say I know in my heart that to send Guin into that pit of vipers is to bring death into this house. And I do not necessarily refer to Guin, but I cannot be more specific."

"I see."

Intuition. It was a tricky thing. Especially in Shadowdweller women of significant power. Intuition must always be heeded. Trace believed that. Unfortunately, it had a bad habit of being vague and unspecific. Still, Malaya was being quite specific at the moment, and that raised a serious flag with him. Her majesty's intuition was not like an average woman's. It was far more pinpointed. But if she was being vague, he had to believe she had her reasons. He only wished she would share what those were.

"Then your choice seems sound to me," he told her. "However, it should now be up to you to choose a replacement Guin will trust in his stead, or you will never contain him. He will not disobey you until the very moment he is convinced you will die if he doesn't. Your life is his only loyalty in the end."

"I know. I think I already know who to suggest. Thank

you, *Ajai*. You have calmed my spirit." She gave him a heart-touched bow, a sign of enormous respect. "Let me know if I can ever do the same for you." She straightened and met his eyes as she cocked her head to the side. "And Trace, you might keep in mind that we women are more forgiving than you might expect . . . or deserve. But whatever you think of yourself, you are not meant to be infallible. None of us are. You can strive, and that is good, but you will never succeed, and that is to be expected."

With that, Malaya leaned in to kiss his cheek in warm, brief affection.

As she walked away from him, Trace touched the spot of warmth she had left behind on his face, smiling with be-musement. It never surprised him how wise Malaya was for her age, but it always amazed him how uncanny her timing could be. It wasn't even the advice that marked him most, al-though it played its part. It was . . . it was just the way she had managed to reel him in from his alienated feelings of a self-made pariah. What had happened in Shadowscape did not define all he was as a man. She had reminded him of that just now as she had jolted him back into the importance of his place among them.

And he knew that, as soon as he found the opportunity, he was going to find a way to resolve what he owed to Ashla Townsend.

Chapter 12

Ashla was now quite sure she had gone completely out of her mind.

Maybe it was loneliness driving her over the edge, or perhaps she had just started out nuts from the get-go, but either way she was pretty well convinced she'd lost all of her marbles and they were falling with little plunks through a sewer grate somewhere.

She was in Alaska.

The how and why were once again completely fuzzy, but now, instead of being lost and lonely in the vast emptiness of New York City, she was lost and lonely and freezing her freakin' ass off in the emptiness of Alaska.

Why she would ever do something like this was completely beyond her comprehension. The clothing requirements alone were totally unacceptable to her. She *loved* dresses. However, a dress in an Alaskan winter added up to a hell of an updraft, and she just wasn't that much of a slave to fashion. The clunky boots weighed a ton, the wind blew her around like a dust mote, and she had, like, two percent body fat somewhere on one cheek of her ass. That meant she got really cold really easy even in what others deemed warm weather.

This was ridiculous.

Her insanity was beginning to get on her nerves.

Okay, so maybe there had been a subconscious imperative telling her to just get away from New York for a while, an attempt to rob herself of the temptation to constantly look around for . . . for a man who wasn't going to come back.

They never came back. It was simply a fact of life she should be used to by now. She was a freak, always doing something weird or something wrong, and no doubt by the time he came around from whatever illness it was he had suffered from, he'd be looking back on his time with her like a man with a bad hangover looked at his time spent with some ugly chick at a bar.

It was harsh, but it was for the best that she got it through her head. She had to stop hoping for useless, unachievable nonsense. Especially now, in this unpopulated wasteland of a world that was the dregs of Alaska.

She would have thought maybe her subconscious imperative would have gotten her to West Chester, Ohio, at the farthest. She had gone to a friend's wedding there once and it had been a nice, peaceful little place.

Well, facts were facts and there was little use griping about it. What she needed to do, really *really* fast, was to find an airport and brave one of those creepy planes and get the hell out of the freezer. Luckily, these sorts of things were listed in local phone books. She just had to hope they *had* an airport in Fairbanks, Alaska.

The campground on the outskirts of Fairbanks was closed to the general public, but the Shadowdweller entourage was an exception. The owner never understood why these people always came just as the snow began to fly, but he didn't much care when they were paying him what amounted to a fortune and they didn't even want the electricity turned on.

Trace was busying himself easily. There was always a lot to do with a large company of people who were growing tired of being confined all day and all night, and it made for delicate tempers.

As he helped arrange the camp in a protective circle with Tristan and Malaya at its center, he started to think about the enclave at Elk's Lake that they were heading for. The completely isolated terrain was only reachable with special vehicles made for traveling mountainous snow and ice. When the pipeline had been built in the seventies, it had brought droves of human settlers into areas that had been only for the 'Dwellers' and the human natives' for the longest time. It had forced the Shadowdwellers to move north into terrain that was a bit more inhospitable to the average human. At first it had just been clans forming their little territories on one mountain face or another, but most of that had been destroyed in the wars. Since they had reconstructed into a total colony, they had fortified and condensed their resources and skills into a single entity.

Much of it was constructed belowground, an entire city carved out of the face of the mountain that bore the upper lake called Elk's Lake. It was the type of environment only the hardiest of souls dared to conquer, never mind form complex developments for a migrating society. But it ensured isolation and privacy and no questions asked. To the human who thought to be curious, they were nothing more than a wildlife and geological survey station.

More importantly, it was home to the Senate and was the official political seat of their people. Trace was quite certain that whatever had been brewing over the summer months while session had been exited was bound to rear its head shortly after the royal household arrived. But that was a few days' journey yet. It gave him time to focus on the potential storm and how he would have Tristan ride out his part of it. However, he had a feeling that it was going to dissolve into Guin and Xenia's territory of worry and control in the end. He prayed it wouldn't get quite that close, but after his deadly encounter with Baylor, he wanted to remain prepared for every possibility.

These thoughts were probably why he jolted when a hand fell on his shoulder. Without thinking he grabbed hold of the hand and twisted as he turned around.

"Magnus!" Trace let go instantly, but he could tell the priest wasn't offended or affected by his aggressive movements. "*M'jan,* where have you been?" Trace demanded of him.

"A little side journey," Magnus responded. "And now, it is your turn."

"I don't know what you mean." Trace indicated around the busy campground. "I'm a bit occupied at the moment and I'm hardly able to leave. What journey?"

"I have recovered one of our people from human hands."

Trace felt everything grind to a sudden and quiet halt. Not that any activity around him actually stopped, only he completely quit noticing it as he stared at his father. A Shadowdweller in human hands was a terrible danger to their entire race. It was shocking to Trace that he had heard nothing about it before now, in spite of his illness and relative isolation. Their culture was still clannish, and almost no one would go missing without family or clan noticing and a ripple of alarm radiating through the community.

"What damage has been done?" he demanded.

"The exposure to humans is virtually nonexistent, and you will understand why in a moment, but I am afraid the damage to our kin is extensive." Magnus took Trace's arm and began to lead him toward the rear of the campground. "Now, normally I would never suggest that a 'Dweller coming down fresh off a bad euphoric experience return to Shadowscape so quickly, but this is a unique circumstance and I require your help specifically."

"*My* help?" Trace was incredulous as he was led to the Sanctuary section of the caravan. They passed by Killian, who was standing attentively just outside of one of the larger trucks in the ministers' section of the convoy. Magnus guided Trace forward, and as he stepped inside he immediately felt the sensationalist emotions and interest radiating around the room. *M'jan* Shiloh was there with his handmaiden Nicoya. *M'jan* Daniel, who was another high-level priest, was there as well. *K'yan* Karri and about a half dozen other handmaidens milled about or were settled in soft, supplicating prayer. All were crowded into that single space and just standing there and staring at him intently as he arrived. "I don't understand. With all of the priests and handmaidens here, what could I possibly provide that your experience wouldn't—"

"Now you understand?" Magnus asked softly when all of Trace's logic and reasoning froze in midstream, clogging his every system as he stood and stared at the body laid out carefully on a floor bed before his feet. "There is always an explanation for even the strangest things, Trace," Magnus gently reminded him, "no matter how impossible or improbable it may seem."

"You said . . . kin," Trace choked, forcing the words out of his shock-riddled body.

Different but the same. It was Ashla. *Really* Ashla. Her physical body, lying in a false sleep, her hands folded neatly just below her breasts as if she were ready to be laid to rest, and the softest, slightest rise and fall of her chest. He had an overwhelming urge to laugh fondly at the beautiful blond length of her hair, the curls an unruly tumble and very likely the reason she had preferred to keep it short. Before he could curb the impulse, Trace was on his knees beside her, his fingers stroking through the precious mass of curling silk and light.

"This hair . . . this skin . . ." He slid his fingertips down to trace the pale, gaunt shallow of her cheek. It made him ache to see her so thin. She had been so slender to begin with, but this state had stripped her of every spare store of fat and muscle she'd had. Trace turned eyes that burned with emotion onto the priest. "These are not kin. And one so frail and delicate? When have you known our women to be so?"

"She is kin," Magnus assured him, "but she is half-bred kin. And her frailty is no different than Rika's. Put simply, she is ill. But I think it may even go beyond that, because the woman in Shadowscape was also quite fragile in her projected appearance. Her human half allows her to walk in sunlight, but I believe it weakens her overall strength in the process because she is one of us."

"One of us," Trace echoed in soft disbelief. "But . . . she's been in 'scape for . . ."

"Two years," Magnus provided.

"Great burning Light," Trace rasped out. "Two years?"

"But only her 'Dweller half is there. It is just enough to allow you to feel her and sense her physically, and enough to explain why she could see all of us. She is the first half-breed I have ever seen or heard of who didn't exist solely in supposition and myth, but it is what it is nonetheless." Magnus explained the story Ashla's mother had reported to him, deleting everything after the circumstances of her conception. The woman's contemptible treatment of her daughter was not for him to relay. Not, at least, to anyone other than Ashla, if he even got the opportunity. "It is possible Ashla was thrown into Fade on impact of her accident, a reflex to protect herself, without even realizing what she was doing. Because she is half-human, though, I'm guessing the Unfade is far more difficult than it is for us . . . or it is simply a matter of her not knowing how."

"It could simply be because she doesn't know she can! Magnus, she doesn't even know where she is. She doesn't know any of it!"

"I know. That is one reason why I require your help. I need you to go into Fade and find her. You have a rapport with her; an intimacy that you can utilize to gain her trust and belief. Until she believes all that is true, she cannot navigate her way back to Realscape."

"Magnus, after two years . . ." Trace swallowed noisily and shook his head as he looked at the pale blue veins running in tiny networks along her eyelids. "How do we know she can return at all? How do we know she will be intact when she does? Her mind could shatter from the sudden change." Trace thought of the fear-riddled girl he had first met, and it made his heart race. Was it possible that her easy intimidation was the beginnings of paranoia or some other psychosis she wouldn't be able to shake even in Realscape? Or it could potentially destroy her just to try and force two parts of her together that had been living separately and growing in different directions for so long, like twins separated from a single egg being forced back together after two years outside of the womb.

But even twins grown from separate eggs seemed to remain connected with one another on deep levels that only other twins seemed to fully comprehend. It was also quite clear that Ashla's human half was wasting away without her 'Dweller spirit to supplement it. Whether it happened now or later, she would slip away eventually.

"She has to know the risks; make the choice for herself. I have to tell her . . . everything." He looked up at Magnus. "I mean everything. Light and Dark, the 'scapes, the clan wars, Tristan and Malaya, even the migrations. The diseases. I have to tell her about other Nightwalkers and the dangers we face together."

"Trace," Magnus interrupted him softly, "tell her more than just the ills and monsters in this world. Balance. In everything, balance. Save some of it for afterward. I know it is in your nature to present all sides and to play as fair as you possibly can, but have a care for her fragile state."

"Yes, of course." Trace ran a hand through his hair as he searched the figure lying so still beside him. His mind filled with very different images of her, ones that throbbed with life and movement. The vital pulse of her body and the heat of her rushing breath in his ear; even when she shook with fear and cried her frustrations, she was always every inch alive. Life might frighten her a great deal, yet she plodded forward through it relentlessly and survived, even against obviously tremendous odds. He had only known her after she had become trapped in a world she couldn't comprehend. He could see why anyone would fear something like that. However, not everyone would have been able to just keep going in spite of it all.

Trace stood up quickly, clenching and unclenching his fists for a second, pausing to stretch his neck until it gave a vertebral pop. He closed his eyes, trying to tune out Magnus and all the other priests and handmaidens in the room.

"If I'm not back in twenty-four hours, come after me yourself. Bring Tristan and Guin if you must, but no others," he instructed tightly.

"Fearing the Fade after euphoria is natural, Trace," Magnus murmured. "There is no shame in it."

"It isn't the Fade I fear," Trace corrected him sharply. However, he didn't elaborate as to what it was that clearly had a grip over him.

It didn't matter after a minute, though, because he slowly entered Fade.

Ashla was running down a main street in Fairbanks.

Well, in actuality, she was waddling. She had raided a department store and, about seven layers of clothing later, had achieved perfect warmth. She had sacrificed grace, fashion, and coordination, but damn it, she was *warm*. She had found it all. Sweaters, goggles, parkas, insulated pants, and long johns. She was wrapped in scarves like a Christmas present, her eyes obscured by the mountaineer's sun goggles she wore. In fact, her nose was just about the only thing exposed to the air, and even that was mostly buried under her muffler.

She looked like some kind of bouncing baby girl belonging to the Michelin Man.

"Warm, warm, warm," she cheered to herself as she hurried along the slightly slippery sidewalk. "Think Florida. Aruba. Martinique. I wonder if there is a plane going to Mazatlan. Just as good as New York, only no winter. But then there's that whole nasty water issue. I could try—"

Ashla skidded to a halt when someone suddenly stepped out in front of her. That ever-present urge to scream took over as strong hands curled around her arms. Or tried to. She was rather a pudgy handful at the moment. Recognition didn't set in until she heard a low masculine chuckle rumbling down against her face. It was a bit distorted by her protected ears, but just the same she knew him in a heartbeat.

"Trace!"

She couldn't believe her goggled eyes. There he was, as big as life, exactly as he had been in New York. In fact, he was so exactly the same that she wondered if she was having hallucinations now. The long coat, the samurai sword slung to his belt, his all black clothing and . . .

Everything else.

The shoulders that would have blocked out the sun, had there been sun. The beautiful curve of defined muscle beneath clothing that broadcast how truly breathtakingly fit his chest and belly were. Those amazing, trunk-steady thighs encased in dark fabric that couldn't hide the overwhelming power she knew they were capable of generating.

Inside all of her clothes, Ashla suddenly felt completely naked. She felt his hands running up her arms to her shoulders, the sensation distant and muffled, yet somehow as sharp as ever. She had a total body memory of his touch and of all the endless frustrations it had teased her to. And then she remembered that one moment early on between them where everything had come together perfectly, and her whole body hummed with a quick wash of recall from the orgasm that had blown her completely away.

Suddenly, getting warm was no longer an issue.

"Hello," he greeted her, as if they had planned all along on meeting each other thousands of miles away from where they had last seen each other.

She hit him.

Ashla out-and-out punched him in the arm as hard as she could, even though she knew it was going to hurt her more than it would hurt him. Still, she did it and it felt damn good to do it.

"Ow!" she yelped, shaking out her wrist. "You jerk!"

"Me? I'm not the one who did the hitting!"

"I meant *you big jerk*! As in 'you scared me half to death!' As in 'where the hell have you been?' As in 'I thought you were dead, you big, dumb jerk!'"

"Well, I'm not dead. And I came here as soon as I could. I was ill, *jei li*, and it takes time to recover."

Ashla pouted under her scarf, and Trace felt the effect despite not being able to see it as it radiated from her puffed-up body language.

"I know that," she relented quietly. "I was just . . . scared for you."

"I know you were, and I am so sorry I put you through that. More sorry than you will ever realize." Trace tugged down her layered scarf, simultaneously drawing off her goggles. He breathed a little better the minute he could see her face, the energy vibrating in her eyes a relief to his soul. The half-dead body he had left behind in Realscape had shaken him to his core. He was terrified of the danger of sending her back to it, but he trusted Magnus to know what was best. If the priest said she would die if she didn't come back to Realscape, then Trace believed him. "Are you cold?" he asked with a tease to his tone as he surveyed her getup.

"Not anymore. I don't even know what I'm doing here. This is totally insane. And how on earth did you find me here?" She hesitated as she searched his face and suddenly realized that she was about to learn everything she wanted to know about the world, and that this mysterious man she had taken to her bed knew everything about it. That he'd probably known everything about it all along might have irritated her, except she couldn't recall ever asking him if he could enlighten her.

"Ashla, I want you to come home with me."

He could have knocked her over with a feather. Gaping at him, she released a little giggle. Men simply didn't make requests like that of her. It just didn't happen. But then again, they didn't make love to her like they had crawled through three deserts and she was the proverbial oasis, either.

Trace had.

In fact, as she stared up into his dark eyes, she got the flashing hot feeling that he would do it all over again given half a chance. The thought made her swallow hard, her heart dancing with a quick step. It might have been exhausting and frustrating and downright strange in the end, but it had still been the best sex of her life. And if he had done all of that while he was ill—well, he looked quite healthy now, and it had to make a girl wonder.

There she was, wearing possibly the most ridiculous pile of clothing he had ever seen, and after just five seconds of looking into her eyes, Trace recognized he was pulsing with a euphoria that had nothing to do with Shadowscape, except for the fact that *she* was in it. He had turned his mind away from so much that had happened, deeming it all so unworthy because it had been tainted by his abominable behavior. But he had forgotten about the raw sensual connection they had. Well, not forgotten . . . just pushed it aside. He hadn't done it or her a damn bit of justice. So he didn't understand why she was looking at him like she was. He had, after all, just been the last in a long line of disappointments in her life.

"Before we say or do anything else," he said quickly, "I need to tell you how sorry I am for everything that happened. I . . . I wasn't in my right mind. I know it's a damn poor excuse for how I behaved, but . . . Ashla?"

He stepped forward quickly because she was backing away from him. To his shock, she held up a sharp warding hand, warning him back from her. Her entire expression was cut as though he had just done something unimaginably horrible to her, and he felt his heart race with the closest thing to utter panic that he had ever felt in his life. Not even when Acadian had—

"No, no, *no!*" She spat the denial hard and stomped a booted foot. "I can't hear this. I'm not hearing this!" Ashla turned around and started to waddle off as quickly as she could. She heard him right behind her, completely unhindered by his snug, sexy clothes. They were dark, tailored, and perfect in every way that flattered his gorgeous body, just like everything about him seemed so painfully perfect. He was beautiful to look at, amazing to watch as he moved, both in and out of clothes, and had a deadly sin for a voice. He was smart and assured, his confidence and bravery so obvious and so opposite everything that she was. Because of all of this, she simply couldn't bear listening to him recant every moment he had spent with her. She didn't want to hear his morning-after "it's not you, it's me" speech! So what if he was being considerate enough to bother giving her the damn speech in the first place? So what if that was a step way up for her in male courtesies? She just couldn't bear it.

She made a hard right and hurried up the walkway of the nearest building. She pushed her way into the place and stopped short when she realized she was in a post office, the stark emptiness of the lobby and its walls of post boxes providing her with nowhere to hide and nothing to put between herself and the inevitable. Then she spied the postal service counters. They were pretty high up and she was decidedly out of the high-jump qualifications the way she was dressed, so she should have known better than to go for it.

Panic made people do pretty dumb things sometimes.

Luckily, Trace was much quicker than he looked, which

was saying a lot. He caught her by the arm just as she was about to make a two-inch leap onto a four-foot counter, spinning her around to face him.

"Won't you even allow me to apologize to you? Are you so unforgiving?"

"Oh, my forgiveness has nothing to do with it, and you damn well know it!" she snapped back at him, shoving back her hood and dazzling him with the distraction of her glimmering hair. He still couldn't believe she had even an ounce of Shadowdweller inside of her. "If you want to absolve yourself of everything and make yourself feel better, then fine! Whatever! Thanks. No thanks. Whatever you want. I don't care. Okay? Let's move on, shall we?"

"I'm not absolving myself of anything," he returned with a dark frown. "That's my whole point! I am taking responsibility for the—"

"Great! Wow, you are a stellar example of honorable manhood," she said sarcastically.

"—animalistic and horrendous excuse for lovemaking I subjected you to!" he finished.

"Oh, well, you—" Ashla cut herself off as his words sank in. "W-what?"

"There is no need to mock me," he said stiffly. "I know there was no honor and certainly no respect on my part for what passed between us, Ashla." He reached down and absently gripped the hilt of his sword. "I beg you to understand that I was not myself. Had I been . . ."

"I know," she sighed. "You'd never have done it. Don't you think I know men like you don't pick girls like me? Not for real, anyway."

"*Sutaptu!*" He exploded with the word, a palm shooting out to strike against the counter just beyond her shoulder. "*Deish sata apth atu mename!* Who would dare imply such a thing?" He reached out with his free hand, leather and muscle gripping her hard by the chin and forcing her to look into his furious eyes. "What kind of world did they raise you in, that you would come free of it thinking such bald, black lies? What have I done to make you think me so shallow and—"

His fury seemed to bleed out of him in an instant, his eyes going wide for a moment. She realized then that he was finding, with tormented shame, those faults in his behavior he felt answered his own query. But the truth was, he had treated her like no one else ever had. Since the moment she had set eyes on him, nothing had been usual or normal. And now, when she weeded out her emotions and reconsidered all he had tried to say to her, she realized that he honestly thought himself some kind of villain for his treatment of her in New York. He was expecting her to condemn him! To shun him or whatever it was that women did to men who fell below their standards. She certainly wouldn't know what that was. Below standards, yes; opportunity to tell them so, no.

But regardless, he had hardly been criminally blackhearted.

"You didn't do anything to make me think that," she said gently, a mittened hand reaching to touch him on his chest a little hesitantly. "I just . . . I've learned to expect the worst of everybody and just go from there. I'm sorry, it's wrong for me to do that. You don't deserve to be mistreated for what others have done."

"No," he agreed, "but perhaps I do for what I myself have done." His hand turned and gentled along the side of her face, the leather on his fingers soft and worn from time and familiarity. "You deserved better than what my feverish brain and body gave you, *jei li*." His dark head lowered closer to hers, the longer fall of his hair in front brushing her forehead soft as feathers as his eyes bore deeply into hers. "I want to give you . . ." He stopped, a hard swallow punctuating his change of heart in expressing his thought. But Ashla wanted to beg him to continue it. *What did he want?*

Trace pulled away and looked up at the ceiling, taking a moment to collect himself. She didn't realize the full scope of the internal battle he was waging over her. He had come there with a different purpose, and yet that crucial and critical purpose had dissolved into nothingness as the ghosts of euphoric memory combined with the reality of the chemistry that flared between them in harsh, stunning sparks. But Trace forced himself to keep on task. His time was short. There was no telling how long twenty-four hours in Realscape would translate to where they were, and there was just so much to tell her. It was an amazing burden on his soul to decide where to begin. He had made more than enough mistakes, and any he made now could cost her life.

"Listen," he said instead of untold numbers of other things he felt the urgent need to say, "we haven't much time and there is much to discuss. We should go somewhere more comfortable so we can sit and talk."

"I don't want to go anywhere," she said, the words a bit numb as they came, almost as if someone else were saying them. She tugged off her mittens, throwing them to the ground to emphasize she was staying put. "I want to know what you were going to say just now. Before you stopped and thought about it."

"It's not im—"

"Let me decide what's important," she interjected.

"Immediately imperative, I was going to say. Actually, to me, it is very important. But, *jei li*, what is more important is your life and your safety. I will sacrifice everything, especially my own selfish desires, in order to protect that."

It had to be the most amazing thing anyone had ever said to her. In fact, since she'd never heard anything even remotely like it before, she had no concept of how to react. She realized on some distant level that she should be afraid of his implication that her life was somehow in danger, but all she kept hearing was everything after that part.

Trace's culture was quite formal, for all its seductive ways and freedoms, so he had never actually had a female throw herself impulsively into his arms before. He certainly wasn't expecting it from his little mouse who took orders far better than she expressed ideas of her own, but as her fingers scraped up through the hair at the back of his head and took hold to pull him down to her mouth, he forgot all about that.

He forgot all about everything the moment her lips touched to his. Trace felt her kiss like lightning; from its electric power to its burning bright light, it all scorched a path straight through him. He was inside her mouth before he realized it, and once he did realize it he was absolutely hooked. Had he forgotten the incredible way she tasted? Or had he just been so far gone that first time that he hadn't taken the time to notice the subtle sweetness of her? And damn if she didn't kiss like the flashes of a sudden strobe, sizzling hot pulses that burned beautifully and in Technicolor lights. Her small tongue was gifted and wicked as the shy mouse bowed out of the picture and the woman starved for passion stepped up for notice.

Trace reached up to cup her face in his hands, but he cursed against her lips when his gloves impeded his ability to feel her delicate skin. He kept her mouth, reaching both hands behind her to strip off the offending leather. When he had her back in the cradle of his palms it only fired his desire for more. Only then did he allow himself to realize just how much he had wanted her since the moment he had left her side. Convincing himself that any impulse he'd had for her over the past days had been just dregs of the disease to him, something to be repressed or hidden, he hadn't allowed for the possibility that the power he had felt had been real. So very real. What was more, now that his mind was wholly clear and the euphoria well distant from his actions, all that was left was the vast need between them.

He hadn't thought he could feel anything more powerful than the euphoria-induced obsession for her. Trace was now being taught a sharp lesson in the power of mind and spirit over its own flaws and weaknesses.

"Ashla," he said, meaning something and forgetting what he meant between one kiss and the next, she was that bewitching.

"I don't care," she whispered with half incoherence. "Just don't stop kissing me. Please."

"Ah, *jei li*," he sighed. "How can I say no when you beg so prettily?"

And that was the end of Trace's struggles of conscience. He lost himself in the moment as thoroughly as he could, drinking her into himself however he could, and growling with frustration when her clothing prohibited some of the best ways.

As if she spoke the same guttural language, she began to rip and tug at her garments. Together they shucked off her many ridiculous layers, the sheer number of them allowing the couple to build a wild sort of momentum as they went. He only left her mouth in brief breaks to accommodate the unwinding of her thick muffler. Once it was gone he was sealed back to the divine fire of her kiss.

Ashla had never known kisses could be so stunning. It didn't matter that they had done it before. It was suddenly all new, as if it had been two other strangers who had spent those hours tangled together in the heat of sex. This time, she could feel the exquisite tenderness lacing his obvious hunger. It was all in his hands. Whenever he bared the smallest patch of her skin, he paused to cup and cradle it, to feel every inch and contour he could before reaching feverishly to continue freeing up his access. He clearly didn't realize he had reached her final shirt until he had stripped it off and his hands landed on hot, bare skin.

"Oh, God!" she gasped, the contrast between her overheated skin and his much cooler hands causing the exclamation.

Trace gave no quarter. Now that he had hold of her, he wasn't letting her go until he absolutely had to. Nothing in his lifetime had prepared him for the kind of desire he was feeling. It went so much deeper than flesh, so far beyond the boiling pulse of his blood as it rushed through his starkly livened body. All his dread about how it would be to have a woman touch him, to have *this* woman touch him, once he was in his right mind, simply vanished as her small fingers sneaked over his rib cage and then his back without so much as a flinch echoing into his body movements. He went utterly still, a sensation of total awe and pleasure rushing him as her touch crept up the deeply scarred line of his spine and he not only felt it, but felt it like sweet delight as it radiated to his entire nervous system. He paused to catch his breath against her lips, his throat tightening with overwhelming emotion. He had thought those nerve pathways forever destroyed, tragic casualties of a wicked bitch who would burn in Light for her sins. But try as she had, Acadian had not won. In fact, the smallest wisp of a woman had just defeated months of Acadian's best efforts with a simple touch of her hand.

Trace was so ecstatic about this revelation and the victorious delight that followed that he scooped her up under her arms in both hands and hoisted her with airy ease onto the countertop behind her. This brought her up a good distance in height, relieving the significant difference between them and opening up all new possibilities to his reach and hers. She burrowed her hands into his coat until he took his hands off her long enough to let her push it off his shoulders. The weighty leather plopped heavily onto the floor, but he was already distracted by the feel of her hands at his belt. It was only his weapons belt, but since it buckled directly across the fly of his slacks, he could feel her fingertips stroking against him as she worked the leather free of the clasp.

"*Aiya*," he exclaimed in a heated burst of breath. "How is it that something so simple can bring a man to his knees?"

"But you're not on your knees," she returned, smiling against his lips. She felt the belt come apart in her hands, but she held on to it with her fingers as she laid her palms against him and quite boldly stroked over him through the fabric of his twill slacks. She could feel the ready swelling of his erection clear as day, but she lengthened her search all the same, slowing it down to an infinitesimal caress.

"*Aiya*," he repeated fiercely, "if you keep that up, you'll be on yours," he promised her.

Ashla tsked her tongue at the lewd suggestion, even as he grabbed hold of her hands and made her drop the weapons belt to the floor with a clatter before he pushed it to relative safety behind her back.

"We didn't get a chance to try that," she noted with a provocative feint for his kiss. "Then again, you never ordered me to."

"Oh, I see. And I should have?"

"You're the one who said I was submissive." She gave him a bare-shouldered shrug, drawing his attention to the shell pink bra she wore, which actually looked dark against her moon-white skin.

"I did say that," he agreed, "and you said otherwise, I recall." His fingertips reached to track the path his eyes were taking down over the slope of her breast. One hooked beneath the upper rim of her cup on the left, the low edge of the design bringing him directly across the path of her hidden nipple.

"I-I've had time to think about that," she informed him a bit breathlessly. The change in her voice and in the texture of the nipple he teased made him smile. So did her conversation.

"Oh? Did you come to a conclusion?"

"Yes. I am submissive," she admitted, but then added her caveat, "to you. Only to you." Trace's gaze shot back up to hers in unadulterated surprise, making her grin. "Don't look so surprised. It seems only right since you were the one who figured it out."

"You knew," he said.

"I suspected. Or maybe I considered the possibility. But . . . I never thought . . . it never . . . ." She released a mighty sigh, blowing up the short curls lying against her forehead. "I was never turned on until you started bossing me around. It just came so easily. God, it made me so hot," she whispered as his head bowed to hear her confession. "You don't take orders, whatever it is you do for a living. You give them. I can tell. It comes so naturally to you. But you don't bully. I can tell that, too. I can just sense how you seek to give pleasure with your commands. Well, pleasure for me."

"When I can, yes. But I am not shy about giving the unpleasant commands, either. But that is my work. You, *jei li*, are strictly for pleasure. Everything I do for you, whether you realize it or not at the time, is to bring you pleasure. At least, it is now that I have my head on straight again."

"Yeah, you'll have to tell me about that one day," she said softly as she drew enticing patterns across his shirt with her fingertips.

"I should be telling you about it now. I should be telling you a lot of things."

"It has to wait," she told him, leaning forward to touch soft kisses to the side of his neck. "There's so much I didn't get to do last time."

"Like what?" he asked hoarsely. "No. Don't answer that. If you do, it'll end up being just like last time."

"Hmm. Just like? Hot, sweaty, and awesomely hungry?"

"Primal. Obsessed. Damn me into Light, you are unbelievable. How do you affect me like this?"

"Like this?" she asked, reaching to skip her fingertips down the length of his fly and the turgid flesh beneath. Ashla hardly knew where all this bravado was coming from, but with each daring word he accepted, and even reacted to so strongly, the braver she got. She was almost giddy with it until he suddenly surged up against her and trapped her against the clerk's window.

"So bold all of a sudden," he growled as he caught her mouth with his in long, eating kisses. "Let's see if you're still so sassy when I have my tongue dancing across your clit."

Ashla gasped at the frankly spoken promise, and at the rush of liquid heat it sent oozing out of her body. She suspected that he knew exactly what her reaction had been, and that it was what prompted him to lower his head to her breasts. But instead of the obvious hunt for her most sensitive erogenous areas, Trace touched his tongue to her breastbone, starting in the snug valley between her breasts and then slowly running it upward to her throat. When he reached the little well where the two met, he slowly flicked his tongue around and across it until they were both unmistakably certain of what he was imitating against her. Ashla's imagination went into overdrive as she anticipated what it would be like to have that adept tongue where he had promised her he would take it.

"No one," she breathed in staccato rhythm, "has ever wanted to do that to me."

Ashla regretted the words the moment they left her lips. She could all but hear the squealing sound of hard-applied brakes screaming through the room as his head jerked up. His passion-dark eyes glittered as they went wide in surprise.

"Explain this," he demanded sharply, not realizing how intimidating his royal vizier's tone could be when it appeared in his temper. "You are of an age for sexual maturity. I understand you do not have sexual instruction in your human culture as we do in mine, but you at least have . . . How do you call it? A sexual liberation? A time of experimentation and learning?"

Trace came to realize his mistake exactly five seconds after she did, and only then because he was watching the expressions change across her face in search of the explanation he sought.

"You said it again. You said 'human.' "

Yeah, he sure had.

"Yes," he agreed shortly. "But you said you didn't care and didn't want to talk about it now," he reminded her. "I'm only reminding you of that because I don't want you to think I wasn't planning on being completely honest with you before all of . . . this"—he nodded down to the close situation of their bodies—"took us over."

"Yeah, but I totally didn't get that this whole 'human' differentiation was going to be a part of it!"

Trace took a deep breath and sighed it out. "There's a lot more to it than that. A lot more to this place, and to you as well. I will tell you anything you want to know, whenever you want to know it. Only, if now is when you want the dissertation, I'm going to have to ask you to put a shirt on. You distract me into oblivion like this." He stressed his point by reaching out to shape her breast through her bra, his thumb circling her areola through the fine material a couple of times. When the point of her nipple began to poke out, Trace couldn't seem to resist curling long fingers into the skimpy undergarment until he was lifting her breast up to his lips. He brushed her with breath first, then nuzzled dry lips against her until she made a sound of complaint. "Shall I keep on point?" he asked softly, the double meaning so very bad of him. He was all but throwing away another perfect opportunity to clear this up with her. *Why is this so hard?* It was almost as if he were afraid of something. The idea grated, but he knew it was too keen not to have basis in reality.

But just then, the newly bold little sex kitten he had discovered put just enough curve in her spine to brush her nipple between his lips. It was all the encouragement he needed, her texture riding against his mouth like that, her scent stirring like fresh spring runs through winter-weary blood. She was between his teeth in the next heartbeat, his tongue guiding the way until he held her gently still for the slow tasting he craved.

There was an exquisiteness to it all that left them both moaning in soft disbelief and pleasure. Her fingertips crackled through the crisp hairs on his neck as she held him lightly to his task. She dropped her head back, closed her eyes, and let the sensations simply ride down her body. It was like extreme skiing, or the way she had always imagined it would feel—just you and a feeling of exhilaration you got to ride any way you wanted, except for the times when it took hold and rode you instead.

Ashla's right knee connected to his outer thigh and rode up to his hip, encouraging him to step in those last inches of intimacy. She still wore her boots, denims, and flannels below her waist, but their closeness had a way of burning right through all of that, even allowing her to feel his body heat warming the already heated skin of her thighs.

Trace was fascinated by how temptingly hard such delicate flesh could become as his tongue swirled around it. He sucked her strongly enough to elicit a throaty cry from her, a sound that went so deeply through him that he had to have it again. His hands were peeling away her bra completely even as he switched to the opposite breast and coaxed her to sing out for him once more. It didn't take much for his senses to start filling with feedback that alerted him to her climbing arousal. The scent of her alone was enough to blind him with the need to have her. Trace drew away from her breasts, looking down at the bright red and pink declarations of his presence left behind on her flesh. He was immediately overwhelmed by the possessive sensation slithering through him, a primal satisfaction triggered by the sight of his well-marked claim on her skin.

He spread his hands up her body, riding the curves of her torso quickly because she was so damn petite and his hands seemingly enormous against her. Yet in spite of her smallness, he recalled the energy with which she had taken everything he had so feverishly given her during his euphoric state. In fact, the memory of it raced through him like molten metal, heating and hardening him all the more. It was gorgeous raw material, he realized, and given the proper time and skill, he could turn them both inside out with it.

But you have no time, a voice whispered through his

mind, *and this is far from a proper venue for pleasing any woman, never mind one who is so complex and so deserving of more.*

He had treated her so callously the first time.

He simply could not do it again.

"*Aiya*," he groaned on a whisper of frustration, "you always make me forget myself. Or remember myself. You remind me I am a man with appetites for more than just duty and protocol. I haven't felt this way for years, so it and you overwhelm me." The truth was, even before Acadian he hadn't experienced anything quite like this. "But you make me forget . . . everything," he breathed a bit incoherently as the sight of her in his hands worked exactly as he was accusing her of.

"I like that," she sighed, her sky blue eyes smoky with unspent passion and need, her lashes half-swept and sultry. "I like the idea of you forgetting yourself because of me. Or remembering. Either way."

Her fingers fell to the front of his shirt, and quite quickly she had undone the row down to his navel. He wore a black undershirt, but it was still much more intimate to them both as she ran her hands inside his shirt and over the ribbed fabric beneath.

"I have things to tell you," he said, his breath and words quick and short against the side of her neck. "This place is not appropriate, and—"

They weren't as alone as she thought they were.

Trace's head snapped up sharply, his passion-muddled senses suddenly searing away all extraneous information as a chill ran like an alarm down his spine. He went for his sword—and met with air, recalling too late that it lay discarded on the floor by his feet. It was instinct alone that made him jerk Ashla off the counter as he hit the floor in search of it. He heard and saw the saw-stars an instant later even as he was still in movement himself, their characteristic whine so like the circular saw they had won their name from. Three bladed missiles shot through the space where he and Ashla had just been, coming in from the right and landing in the far wall on the left with three quick and successive thuds.

"Trace!" Ashla cried out in surprise as her back hit the cold tile floor of the post office lobby. He was crouched over her, her legs still framing him as they had when she had been settled on the counter, her hands clinging to his open shirt. Trace wasn't looking at her, though; his eyes were trained back beyond the teller desk even as he slowly drew his sheathed weapon out of his belt and across her body. Ashla released her grip on him, her hands and arms dropping back onto the floor as she watched him with wide, disbelieving eyes. His hands and the weapon both began to part, with only inches to spare between it and her skin as the brilliant metal blade slowly pulled free of its scabbard. She tried not to breathe so hard, as it brought her breasts dangerously close to the exposed edge of the blade if she did. She watched him slowly place the beautifully inlaid sheath down on the floor without so much as a sound. Then and only then did he finally look down at her.

Trace knew Ashla hadn't seen the saw-stars just by the expression on her face after he had drawn his weapon. He could only imagine what she was thinking after having a man throw her to the ground and laying her under a blade, but his position was defensive and would best stop the next missiles that attacked them. Since he couldn't explain this without giving away their location, he gave her a very serious look as he touched a finger to his lips. If she was half Shadowdweller, he hoped that meant she knew how to be quiet. Certainly their unseen enemy had his skills in stealth down pat. Only years of fighting in a war made up of similar attacks had saved Trace's neck and Ashla's just then. His veteran instincts had been their salvation.

He very gently reached to touch her where her legs were clinging to him in reflex. As much as he loved being there, he couldn't afford the restriction. With a coaxing caress down the inside of her knee and thigh, he urged her legs apart and then, as silent as death, he shifted his stance so she was now between his legs and protected by the crouch of his body. Then he reached noiselessly for one of her discarded shirts, his eyes sharp around the room as he slid the fabric into her hands.

"Wait," he mouthed to her, holding his palm out in a staying motion.

By then Ashla was finally realizing that Trace had sensed some kind of danger, and that he *wasn't* into sex games with sharp objects. Knowing both facts, she didn't think she should waste too much time on relief over the latter. She wanted to rush into the shirt he'd given her, but his warning kept her immobile.

It was absolute stillness then, where Ashla feared the sound of her breathing was way too loud and labored. Then, like the sudden springing of a ground spider out of its hidden hole, Trace leapt into motion, the sharp sound of metal ringing out three times to match his successive and swift movements. If not for the sparks flying off the blade of his swift-moving sword, Ashla wouldn't have realized he was repelling a volley of objects with it. At least, not until a fourth one glanced off the floor near her ear, chipping the maroon tile, which flung into her cheek with a painful sting.

Trace saw it all, the silent wince of pain on her face most of all. That she didn't cry out actually made him proud of her, but she needn't have bothered anymore. It was clear they were in their enemy's sights. So Trace quickly moved to free her from between his feet, urging her up and behind him. He hardly blamed her when she practically glued herself to his back between frantic wriggles to get her shirt on. However, it forced him to compensate for the way her hold was hindering him. Every extra thought was a second wasted before reaction time; Magnus's lessons echoing in his head were warning him of that.

He knew better than to go for the door. As much as it looked the fast escape, without knowing how many opponents he faced, he could assume nothing was safe. Not unless he made it safe. He looked around quickly, cursing when he realized that all other exits must be on the opposite side of the counter . . . which was clearly how the enemy had entered the building.

The vizier wanted to know just who that enemy was, and how they could possibly know he was even in Shadowscape. Again, now was not the time to waste thought on it, but he couldn't shut down the suspicion whispering through the back of his brain. He and Ashla needed to move. Had he been alone, he could have shadow-skipped, the unique power the one thing that had kept him alive through treacherous and deadly circumstances—like escaping the clutches of a sadist and coming back from a fight after being stabbed in the back.

But he wasn't alone. And he knew that if a 'Dweller died in Shadowscape, he was dead in every 'scape. He couldn't risk that it would be any different for Ashla than it was for the rest of them. The idea of leaving her body in Realscape as empty as a locust's husk made his skin crawl with rage. At least he thought it was rage. It was dark and it was powerful, but rage somehow didn't seem to be all-inclusive enough to suit the emotion he was feeling. Emotion, however, was even more of a hindrance than thoughts were when it came to reaction, and he forced it all away as his mentor's voice whispered the advice into his mind as clearly as if he were there himself.

It was thinking of Magnus that actually gave him the idea he needed. Magnus would not leave Ashla's side in Realscape until Trace returned. Not until twenty-four hours had passed. The camp, though, was a good distance from where they were and he would never risk making it there and back to retrieve help. Even shadow-skipping couldn't get him there fast enough, and it would be unconscionable to leave Ashla to the wolves hoping they would leave her be because he was the target they wanted. Anyone who would ambush an enemy so dishonorably was unpredictable. The only thing Trace was sure of was that he could take nothing for granted.

Magnus, however, had once told him that if an enemy erased the honor in battle first, then it obligated you to play by his rules. Trace was more than willing to accommodate the advice, but he had one small problem.

He had explained nothing to Ashla.

Trace stepped back with her, drawing her back as far as he dared without completely cornering them. Then he took a deep breath.

"We have a problem."

"Yeah, I can see that!" she whispered harshly. "Why does everyone want to kill you?"

"Because I am a very important part of the government where I come from," he explained in a quick hush. "If they kill me, it begins to weaken a political structure that cannot afford any weaknesses right now."

"Oh," she said contritely. "That explains a lot."

"Hardly," he sighed. "Listen, *jei li*, I have a lot I need to tell you."

"You said that."

"Yes, but now I don't have time to do it the way I should have." He made certain to meet her eyes and drive his sincerity into her mind and soul with sheer force of will. "Remember, I am going to protect you with my last breath. Don't ever doubt that, okay?"

"Trace, don't say things like that," she scolded fearfully, clutching harder at him.

"I have to say it, because I need to leave you here."

"*What?*"

"Shh," he both soothed and scolded. "Just trust me." He turned on his heel, pushing her back against the near wall. He kept both eyes on the lobby and beyond as he briefly kissed her forehead. Then he pushed back away from her, his chest aching as he watched her panicked breathing increase with his distance and he was forced to pry her hands free of his shirt. He stepped back and she moved as if to lunge forward to him. He stayed her by crossing the flat of his blade between them, his expression a warning, the only exception being the angst written in his dark eyes.

When Ashla realized she was the cause of what she saw in his pained gaze, it had the power to keep her still in place against the wall just as he wanted her to do, in spite of the horrible fear coursing through her veins. She gripped the flat metal faces of mailboxes on either side of her. Trace had placed her against a cinderblock break between one wall of them and another.

She watched him back into the darkest corner of the room, his attention torn between where he knew the threat to be, and her. Slowly, shaking all the while, she sank down low to the floor, watching and waiting to see what he was going to do.

It was because she was staring at him so hard that she saw every moment of the way the darkness seemed to just swallow him up. Then, in a blink of her eyes, there was nothing there but walls. She covered her mouth to keep from gasping aloud, her eyes shot with shock and disbelief. She blinked, telling herself he had to still be there. Where else could he go? After all, people didn't just disappear! If they did, then that meant . . .

She really was crazy!

Chapter 13

Trace had tracked the darkest corners of the room in his mind, those moonlight and starlight had left neglected and virtually black. This was the kind of shadow that was absolutely necessary for him to shadow-skip. Basically, it was like Fade, except instead of switching realms, he switched to a line-of-sight location. It was a silent and swift way of traveling across the room or further. Every 'Dweller could skip close shadows to an extent, as long as they connected at even the smallest point, but no one could match the distance Trace could skip to because all he needed was to *see* the other space of shadow. No connecting shadows necessary. It liberated him to move like no one else could; nor did many expect it because it was not a skill he'd advertised.

In this case, it allowed him to come up behind the enemy that had pinned him down. He materialized in the black, coming free of his skip with perfect silence. He took a moment, sensing more than seeing the stealth-guarded figure before him. He could hear beyond this immediate area of utter silence, to the distant sound of Ashla trying to breathe.

He could also sense a second person close by. The area behind the postal workers' station was full of objects and walls that could conceal, but for the most part it was a single, vastly open space. That meant the moment he moved on one enemy, the other could get a clear shot at him.

But when the flash of silver metal in moonlight winked for the briefest second, Trace knew his target was about to make a mark of Ashla. It was clear he wasn't a professional assassin, however. A Shadowdweller assassin knew better than to use unblackened metal in a stealth fight. Trace himself had only recently stopped carrying a blackened blade, an effort at pulling himself away from a warlike guarding and mentality. It wasn't good for the advisor of a peace-preaching regime to be always suspicious of attack and on his guard. He had sacrificed the mindset for the sake of his rulers and their people.

And he would be damned if some back-stabbing *bituth amec* was going to ruin that for him.

Trace moved like a heartbeat, only not so loudly. He was out of the shadows and on his enemy like a silent breeze, ringing him around the throat with one arm while running through his left kidney with the katana. His right arm choked off his victim's warning cry, and he continued to hold him upright in front of himself while scanning shadows for the other operative.

"Where?" he asked the indistinguishable man he held. In the back of his mind he was already trying to fit the shape and build to someone he knew. There weren't many such slight-figured men among 'Dwellers. "Answer," he hissed soft as a breath, "or I show you how easily this steel cuts upward through a body."

The threat became useless an instant later as the sound of saw-stars whined through the air. They entered the chest of his captive in three solid thunks, even without him having to move to guard. It was clear the ruthless killer in the shadows had murdered his own partner rather than have him taken alive or be given opportunity to reveal his location. These stars, unlike the others, were black as night, however, warning Trace that what he was facing now was something vastly different than a scheming senator. Since trained assassins could learn how to throw stars in a curve, and the whine of the flung missile was designed to echo and throw off its locus, he had no idea where they had come from.

All he knew with certainty was that the assassin was skulking in Ashla's side of the building. He had no doubt that had the hired gun been behind him, he wouldn't have wasted the chance to kill him.

This thought was reaffirmed when the buzzing of blades on air whipped past, one clipping his cheek and another the exposed side of his rib cage on the right. The blade sliced almost painlessly through both his shirts and his flesh before it flew in a true line to hit the drywall several feet behind him. The strike sent fire blossoming over his ribs, but he ignored it as he unburdened himself of the body and dove for the deepest shadows nearby. He skipped locations quickly, altering sides of the room even as he still felt the breeze of a star passing so close he knew it would have hit true under any other circumstances. He measured his breath and waited for the assassin to move again and give himself away. He was thankful for the blood-dulled metal of his blade as he readied it for defense or offense. Whichever came first.

"Trace."

It was the faintest whisper, but his keen hearing picked it up easily. Ashla. She didn't realize she could be easily heard by one of his breed.

Because you never told her about your breed, he thought in fierce regret.

It was for this reason that Magnus had always lectured him about keeping focus in a fight. He became aware of a presence to his left barely in time to avoid another dagger in his back. He would be damned if he knew how he had given himself away, but the cunning assassin had seen him, as still as he was. He sidestepped, lunging down low to the ground and shooting out a leg to catch the enemy at his ankles. The assassin dodged the trip, lightly overstepping Trace's leg and flipping his blackened dagger around to expose the heavy counterbalance in its hilt even as Trace reached for the tanto blade he kept concealed in his boot. The eight-inch Japanese dagger allowed him to fight closer than the katana did, which was fortunate since his attacker clipped Trace hard upside the head with his steel just as he drew the short blade and cut it with a right-handed sweep under his opponent's arm, returning the draw of blood across his ribs with one of his own.

The assassin recoiled with a grunt, stumbling back over Trace's still-outstretched leg. The reaction surprised Trace. The hired gun acted as though he had never taken a wound before, and it was highly unlikely that he had never been injured in training. Just the same, he was in full, fast retreat and in the shadows before Trace could catch him. He knew the instant his reach came up empty that the bastard had Unfaded.

As disappointed as he was at the lost opportunity, he needed to take advantage quickly. He resheathed the tanto quickly and ran for the counter at the front of the room. He cleared it in a single lithe vault, his boots hitting the tile on the other side lightly in spite of his weight and speed. Habit. Unfortunately, it made for a very surprised blonde when he suddenly came around to her. She let out a squeal of alarm until she recognized him. Then she just pressed back hard against the wall and looked at him exactly how he would have expected a human to look at him after seeing him disappear before their eyes.

"I'll explain on the way," he sighed. "Right now, we need to get out of here."

What choice did she have? Ashla took his offered hand and let him boost her over the counter. He followed after grabbing up his belt and her jacket. Then he hurried them out the rear exit. Since his enemies had likely entered this way, if there were further enforcements they would be focused on the front of the building, where the couple would have been forced to run had they tried an escape. Trace's sharp eyes picked up two sets of tracks in the otherwise undisturbed snow. He wasn't in a position to round the front and take on any other possible comers, so he hurried Ashla out into the deeper snow in the lot behind the building.

She ran with him, jerking on her coat quickly, her breath clouding fast on the air. She was afraid to stay behind, and afraid to go with him. She had no idea what was going on and felt like she was in some kind of surreal nightmare. After all, how else could you go from sex to samurai swords in sixty seconds, if not in a weird, disjointed dream? Next she'd be eating peanut butter sandwiches with him on a checked picnic blanket while he played the pan flute.

"Where are you taking me?" she whispered in demand, afraid to raise her voice still.

"Somewhere safer."

"And warmer, I hope," she muttered.

"Ashla, this is serious, okay? If we have to freeze out here in order to stay safe, then that's what we will do!"

"That makes no friggin' sense!" she snapped back at him. "You can't call freezing to death staying safe!"

Trace winced when he realized she had a point. He had spoken to her like a child, and she deserved to get mad at him for expecting her to simply shut up and accept the simplistic demand without question. He wasn't used to seeing so much fear in a person unless it was a child. Not that that was any excuse. He had already acknowledged that Ashla had every right to be frightened and thrown off by the unexplained things happening to her.

The unexplained things he was supposed to explain.

"Okay, here's the condensed version of all this," he said as he hurried her onward, watching frequently over his shoulder. "Human beings aren't the only upright walking species on the planet. There are other races . . . You could call them supernatural races. That's how your culture would see them, anyway. We exist, we have lives, jobs, cultures, and we just happen to have special abilities that most humans don't."

"Like the power to heal?"

Trace drew up short, turning quickly to look at her. She was shivering despite her jacket, huddling in on herself for warmth. He hadn't even grabbed his own coat and could offer her nothing more.

Just the same, her quick retort about how her ability to heal fell under the category of supernatural ability made him realize she had been paying much closer attention than he had been giving her credit for all of this time.

"Sometimes. In our species that's a very, very rare ability. Although that could have something to do with how we heal pretty fast as a race."

"Yeah, I saw that," she said, clearly referring to the speed he had healed at early on in their relationship.

Trace cocked his head curiously and looked at her. "I didn't think you'd be this quick to accept all of this. Honestly, I thought you'd be freaking out by now."

"Are you kidding? After running around in this post-apocalyptic hell for God knows how long? I'm ready to believe any explanation at this point. It sure beats no explanation at all. And I'm not saying I'm not completely freaked out, either, because after watching you disappear like that, I have to say I'm really doubting my sanity, but . . . well, I don't see what choice I have. Besides, being born a freak makes me obligated to be more tolerant of other freaks."

"You aren't a freak, and neither am I. You are a woman who has a side of herself she hasn't learned about yet, that's all. And I am a man who is one of an entire race of people who are just like us."

That seemed to arrest her shivers and her attention as her eyes widened a great deal. "'Us?' And just before, you said 'our.' 'Our species.' Are you saying that I'm from—from people like you? And just what exactly are you?"

Trace sighed. He'd never messed up his language use so

much in his life until he had met this woman. And damn if she didn't catch him every time.

"Shadowdwellers. We're called Shadowdwellers. The name comes from the fact that we can't live in the light."

"Any light?" she gasped.

"Save moonlight," he stipulated. "Weak candle glow is a possibility depending on circumstances, but anything stronger is crippling and disfiguring. On exposure to light, a 'Dweller will die in a matter of minutes."

"Oh my God. You mean you've never been in sunlight?"

He shook his head, trying to understand her shock and disbelief. He saw no special qualities in sunlight to be enjoyed. He didn't see reason for her reaction.

"Well, then, I'm certainly not one of-of you. Anyway, I can't be. I know my parents. Trust me when I say they are as Christian white American *human* as they come. And I run around in sunlight all the time, so that proves that."

"You are a half-breed, Ashla," he countered as gently as he could, taking hold of her arm and bringing her forward through the snow again. "Your mother had an affair with one of us and conceived you as a result. She admitted to it to Magnus. He's one of the ones you met when they came for me."

"My mother had a what? Oh." She burst out laughing. "Please! You clearly don't know my mother. Mom has a cross in one hand and a Bible up her butt. She is religious and devout from tip to toe."

"Perhaps she is now. But she was also once a woman who had a forbidden liaison with a total stranger. In fact, I understand it lasted two months. In alleys. On the street. Cars. Vestibules . . ."

"Stop! Just stop!" Ashla had to cover her ears as she halted once more. "Okay, that's just gross!"

"I don't under—"

"My mother!" She removed a hand from her ear to point a finger in his face. "My mother would never have sex in a vestibule! She's an uptight, rigid, cold-hearted bitch who'd sooner castrate a man mentally and physically than she would climb up on him and fuck him! Don't you tell me about my mother. I know exactly who she is!"

"Clearly you don't, or you would know that you are only half human."

Demon. Devil's child. Spawn of Satan. The names reeled through her mind in her mother's ceaseless voice. Sophia had called her those things so often; every time she'd forced her to her knees to pray for a soul her mother swore was damned no matter what. *A demon put his seed inside me, forcing me to birth an imp into God's world!*

Was it because she had known that her father hadn't fathered her? All of her life, had her mother been blaming her for her own sins?

"And as for sunlight, Magnus believes that your human half allows for that. He also thinks you wouldn't be so thin and pale, nor so weak in bone and muscle mass if you stayed out of the light."

"But I've been out of the light all this time," she said a bit numbly. "I'm no different than I was before."

"That's because we aren't in the real world, Ashla."

Hell of a way to tell her, Trace thought bitterly, once more reaching to hurry her along. He began to explain the concept of 'scapes to her before she could even challenge him on his last remark. He told her everything, even how he and Magnus believed she had gotten thrown into Fade during the accident.

"There are two occupants of Shadowscape," he said. "Us and the Lost. The Lost are humans who are trapped in a coma. Their spirits wander this realm as if they live here, completely unaware of the state they are in. You are in Fade, but you are also Lost, Ashla. In Realscape, your body is lying in a deep coma. It has been for two years."

"Years!" She jerked away from him and laughed on the edge of hysteria. "But it's only been a few weeks. I remember!"

"Do you? Everything? And time doesn't move here like it does in Realscape. Sometimes it's longer, others it comes up shorter. It makes up its own rhyme and reason."

"But that makes no sense," she argued. Trace could hear the rising upset in her voice and saw the swim of tears in her eyes. "What about Cristine? The others? Are they all in comas, too? Why don't I see any of these other Lost?"

"Because Lost can't see each other, or 'Dwellers, for that matter. Not usually. That's why Baylor was so surprised by you."

"You were, too," she said softly.

"Yeah. In a great many ways." He didn't want to, but he had to tell her about Cristine and her friends, so he made it quick and succinct. Like ripping off a Band-Aid. He expected anything, but couldn't prepare himself for the way her legs seemed to just fold beneath her, dropping her numbly to her knees. It was like watching all of her spirit deflate in a single explosive moment. Trace quickly kneeled in front of her, reaching to pull her awkward and wobbly figure into his secure embrace. "*Jei li,*" he said gently against her hair, "we have no time to mourn. Not while there is so much danger. I'm sorry, but you have to get up."

"What does it matter?" she asked him numbly. "I'm as good as dead anyway." She turned to look at him suddenly. "You knew all of this. You know I'm just a ghost. You . . . you . . ."

"No! No, honey, don't even think it!" he said fiercely. "You are no ghost. No wraith. You are as real to me as anything. I never once thought that I could expend myself with you and just walk away without conscience! I would never use anyone in such a way! *Never!* In Shadowscape, Shadowdwellers are as real to one another as we are outside of it."

"But you didn't know I was a Shadowdweller, did you? Not until recently."

"You only have my word for evidence, but bear in mind I came here to bring you back. I came to teach you how to get back to your body, how to Unfade like we do. It's your Shadow half that is trapped here, and your human half left alone in Realscape. But the very fact that you ended up in Alaska with your body says you are still very much connected to it. I will bring you out of this place, *jei li*, and I will face you in the Realscape just as I face you now. I will still want you there just the same as I did in that post office. Nothing has or will change that. Not unless you want it to change. Do you understand me?"

Ashla didn't know what to believe. Her mind was overrun with data. Thoughts both awful and amazing swam through her. But through it all, the one thing that sang out truly to her was the sincerity she felt radiating off him like a nimbus. The sensation that she could see into his very thoughts returned to her as it had several times before. Any ideas she had of him using her and easily discarding her afterward like some kind of blow-up sex toy completely vanished. Even as her experience-scarred psyche tried to lecture her to beware, every deep instinct in her told her that he wasn't capable of anything so dishonorable and low. She actually began to feel bad for thinking it in the first place.

She felt dizzy with information, possibilities, and the ever-present fear that now seemed more justified than ever. She didn't know whether to laugh, cry, or scream. What she ended up doing was simply following his lead as he urged her forward through the cold. She was looking at the ground as they went, so it was only a minute before she realized they were leaving tracks in the snow.

"Can't they follow easily?" she asked dumbly.

"Yes. But not for long."

"I don't—"

"Watch," he said, drawing her up close in the darkness of the tree line. "This takes a lot of focus and energy, *jei li*, so I need you to be very still."

He felt her nod as he wrapped his arms around her, bringing her tightly flush against his body. Just like when she had healed him, Trace needed as much contact with her as possible. It helped that she clung to him tightly in response to his hold. Maybe not for his skip, but it helped him because he felt a rush of immediate relief to feel her willingly touch him. There was an acceptance to it that he needed, for some reason. Then he pushed it all aside and focused on the shadows trail he was going to skip through with her. He would never have tried this with a human being, but she was half Shadow according to Magnus, and that was hopefully going to be enough.

Ashla tried her best not to just stand there and shake like a California fault line, but there was little else for her to do, and she dared any other normal girl on the planet to have her life totally turned upside down and face it with steady hands five seconds later.

Her sister was dead and her mother wasn't. When she had thought the world had been destroyed, she had been devastated by one and wickedly at peace with the other. She had felt bad about that, actually. What kind of person is so detached from the woman that gave birth to them that she means nothing to them in death?

Her brothers and sister had been taught for years to shun Ashla, to treat her like the devil her mother preached that she was, but Cristine had never stepped into line. She had somehow managed to walk the line between avoiding their mother's religious psychosis and keeping a place for her sister in her heart. As for her brothers, her oldest brother had had his own mind by the time their mother's accusations started when Ashla was five. While he had not agreed with Sophia's fanatic beliefs, neither had he ever taken a stand for his sister. He had just sat quietly by as Ashla's life turned into hell on earth. Her other brother, however, was cut right from their mother's ass.

Ashla shuddered and locked the thought away, as well as

the awful memories that came with it. She focused instead on the feel of Trace's cold body near her own. It was only then she realized he must be freezing without a jacket on, and the proof was under her hands. He had never felt so cold to her before.

Just then the strangest sensation rippled through her entire body. It was like a pull from inside at first, but then it flashed like the sharp heat she felt when Trace touched her breasts. She flushed, embarrassed as it made her squirm, and then everything inside her turned light and warm. Trace's cold body seemed to fade away against her, but just as quickly it returned. She opened her eyes and realized the entire landscape had changed. She turned to look, but he tugged her back around just in time for her to see everything haze to gray and then reappear back into the crisp white of snow and the even crisper cold.

Now she could see that they were quite far from their original position. She stared up at Trace, who was breathing hard and covered in a sheen of perspiration in spite of his chill body.

"You can t-teleport?" she asked in amazement.

"It's actually called shadow-skipping, and you can probably do it, too, to an extent. If you couldn't, I wouldn't have succeeded in bringing you with me just now."

She watched him carefully as he spoke. He was breathless even though they were just standing still, and he wasn't standing up entirely straight.

"It weakens you. I make it harder because I'm half human."

"Not too much," he said, pausing to swipe a hand across his forehead. "There are more factors than just that, Ashla. Nothing about anything you are seeing is easy to explain. Remember that, please?"

"Trace, you're ice cold. We need to find some shelter." Ashla bit her lip with worry as she looked around. He had brought them completely outside of the edges of town. There were no buildings in sight and it felt like the temperature was dropping even as they stood there. She kept herself close to him, trying to share what little body heat she could possibly offer.

"There's a campground close by. There should be an encampment of vehicles. It's us. My people. There will be RVs with heat."

"But, Trace, how do you know these killers aren't expecting us to go straight there?"

She was right. Of course she was right. Once any pursuers lost track of their trail, they would head straight for the caravan, hoping to cut them off, provided others weren't already there waiting. Trace shook his head, trying to understand how he could make such a deadly mistake. Just bringing her this close was putting them in danger. He tried to think of what to do next, but he was met with a wall of cold and fog in his mind that seemed to gum up his very thoughts.

And then it knocked his legs out from under him.

Ashla cried out when Trace's weight suddenly fell against her and he dropped heavily to his knees in the snow. She watched his weapon fall as he reached out a hand to brace himself from the ground. She tried to help with all of her strength and weight, propping him up.

"What is it? What's wrong?"

"I don't know," Trace replied numbly, trying to focus on her. "I think I'm . . . injured. But it's not deep."

"Injured?" she said, appalled at the very thought. "How? Where?"

Ashla pulled back to inspect him, noting the cut on his face right off and immediately dismissing it as superficial. Then she caught sight of the tear in his shirt under his right arm. She hadn't noticed it before because the blood soaking the fabric kept it stuck to his body. When she looked down at the sleeve of her jacket, she saw the gray material was stained with red. He had let her squeeze him tightly without so much as a flinch to warn her. Now she balanced propping his weight with an attempt to inspect the wound. It was a juggling act doomed to failure. Trace rolled right off her supporting frame and landed on his back in the snow. She couldn't contain her cry of distress as he groaned softly, shaking his head as if trying to shed the injury with pure strength of will. She quickly knelt beside him, pulling back the torn edges of his shirts.

The cut was pretty ugly, long, bloody, and angry, but it wasn't enough to account for bringing a man like Trace to his knees, and she said as much to him.

"Fuck," he swore baldly. "He dipped his blades. It's poison. The bastard poisoned me."

"Poison! What kind of poison?"

"How the fuck should I know?" Trace snapped at her as he forced himself to sit up. The snow was soaking into his clothes and his skin was freezing. They had to get out of there or they would both be dead by morning.

Ashla took no offense to his tone. She would have been testy too if their positions were reversed, and it had been something of a stupid question.

"Okay, listen," she told him, her teeth chattering as she brushed snow from his back. The snow wasn't deep yet for the season, but it was still wet and cold. Two out of the three was bad enough. "I am going to heal you. Then you can find us shelter."

"No! Are you insane? You showed me what happens to you when you heal; you take the wounds onto yourself. That would mean taking in a poison strong enough to knock me off my feet, and I am a full-blooded Shadowdweller! You can't risk that. I'm amazed you survived what you did last time." Trace's fury drained him and he almost fell back again, except she had quickly moved to kneel behind him and supported him.

"We don't have a choice! I'm not strong enough to carry you, and I can't get help! Even if you did the Fade thing and went back, you can't even get to your feet!"

"Ashla, you can't. I've seen your body. Okay? The real physical you in Realscape. You are thin and frail. Magnus says you're losing your life a little more every day." He reached to grab her by her arm, giving her a shake she barely felt. "When he found your body, it was covered in the cuts and gashes you healed off me. Do you understand what that means? It means that whatever happens to you here, happens to you there!"

Ashla shook her head furiously, tears burning hot in her eyes.

"Stop. Stop making me afraid!"

"You should be afraid! Show some damned sense of self-preservation, for *Drenna*'s sake! You can survive without me. Find shelter. In a day or two, Magnus will come looking for me and he will not stop until he finds you. These people don't want you, Ashla, they want me. If they find me here, they will stop hunting."

"Oh my God! Oh, God, you're insane!" she gasped. "You're telling me that you would walk away and leave me dying out in the cold if this was reversed? That it's okay to be that cold-hearted and . . . and selfish!"

"No, *jei li*. It's about being unselfish," he said, his weight growing against her and his voice softening. "You've been cheated out of half your life. You deserve to find out about it and to live in that world. Trust me, when I tell you how beautiful and extraordinary my culture is. I know you've seen a lot of the dark in it, but there's so much that's good, too. My society—there's so much in it that's worth living for. I would never give it up, except for the best of reasons."

He exhaled, his body crumpling weakly against hers. Ashla cried out in denial, tears flowing down her chapped cheeks and sobs ripping out of her chest as she looked around in vain once more for a sign of life, for someone or something to help. Listening to him tout his people and their way of life, hearing his pride in his voice, it made her want to see all of it. *But not without him.* Not after he had gone through so much with her.

Ashla gently slid away from him, laying him back in the snow as carefully as she could. Then she quickly shed the parka she was wearing, feeling his eyes on her the entire time. She knew just by looking at him that he was too weak to put up the smallest fight, so she rapidly unbuttoned her shirt, exposing her bare skin to the freezing air. Then she did the same for him, pushing up his undershirt so his chest was bared. She threw her leg over him, her knees in the snow by his hips. She leaned forward over him and his hands suddenly shot out to grab her arms, resisting her effort to lie chest to chest with him.

"No," he ground out.

"In two minutes you are going to pass out and I am going to do it anyway," she told him with a firm sort of tenderness. "You can't do anything about this, Trace. Just let go, and this time *you* need to trust *me*, okay?"

The idea of Trace trusting a woman would have been preposterous once upon a time, and despite his level of recovery she was still asking a lot of him. Worse, she was asking too much of herself. But she was right. He wasn't going to stay conscious much longer, and she would be free to do anything she wanted once he was out cold and no longer able to protest.

"Listen," he shot out at her. "The Unfade. Before the poison affects you, you have to try it. The large part is done. You know about the truth now, and are aware you are not in Realscape. The awareness is what you need to guide yourself. Inside yourself now you can find the energy that tethers you to your body. That is the energy that powers the Fading and Unfading. Focus there. Make yourself follow the path out, and use that energy to do it. Ignore everything around you. Think of nothing but the path you need to travel. Return to us there. I'll be waiting for you. Do you hear me? I'll be waiting for you."

She nodded and then took hold of the hand holding her back. "Let go," she whispered softly.

He had no choice. His trembling muscles couldn't sustain the grip anymore. His arms fell away weakly and all he could do was watch with wild breaths as she leaned forward against him.

They were both so cold, and yet as her skin connected to his they both made sounds of relief as what little warmth they each had to share was passed between them. Her hand slid over the wound in his side, and his forearms came weakly around her slender back.

"Don't forget."

"I won't," she promised.

She covered his mouth with hers for her very last point of contact between them, closed her eyes, and slid into the gentle kiss as the healing began.

Trace came to with a stiffly indrawn breath.

He had no idea how long he had been out, but he felt like he was frozen to the ground. Just the same, he sat up sharply and looked around. The first thing he noticed, as always, was lights. All of Fairbanks was lit up for the night in the distance. This immediately told him that he had snapped out of his Fade, most likely when he had lost consciousness. He was in Realscape.

He ran numb fingers across his ribs, feeling the jaggedly healing cut. It was barely closed, but it was closed enough to make him realize Ashla had been successful once again. But at what cost? Had he left her there to die in Shadowscape? He knew he was too weakened to attempt a Fade to check. Had she made it back as well? Even if she had, Magnus would have no reason to expect her to resurrect deeply poisoned and would not be prepared.

He hauled himself over to his hands and knees, raising himself slowly out of the freezing ice around his skin. His breed followed the winters, lived where the snow and darkness lived. They were hearty against the cold. But even his race had their limits. He stood up with a rigid stagger, but instead of steadying himself he let the momentum take him forward. Before he could even get circulation to restore itself, he was running for the encampment.

Within a half mile he was racing for the campground at breakneck speed. His boots churned up snow between long-legged strides, and when he hit the borders of the Shadowdweller's temporary settlement, everyone who was out of doors turned to stare as he bolted past. The Sanctuary vehicles were always at the rear of the camp, just as the royals were always protected at its center. Trace had no concept of the image he made running half naked in the freezing night, obvious blood and wounds easily visible on his body, and for once he didn't care. Protocol, image, and custom meant nothing to him as he tore into the RV Magnus had taken him to earlier.

He was gasping for breath, his body having been wrung through injury, poison, and now panic-driven endurance, but he stumbled forward toward Magnus as the priest was rising from a kneeling position beside the palate where Trace knew Ashla's body lay. When the priest caught his weight and momentum and prevented him from stepping forward, Trace felt a horrible dread sink all throughout his body. He tried to push past Magnus, but the religious warrior was not moving.

"Easy, *Ajai*, easy," he urged. "Tell me what happened."

"Is-is she dead?" Trace demanded, pushing against Magnus with force so he could see Ashla.

"Trace . . ."

"*Is she dead?*"

Trace's roar of outright fear and fury shook the room, sinking every priest and handmaiden there into shocked silence. *No one* raised their voice in Sanctuary. And absolutely no one raised their voice to Magnus. There were even a few soft gasps of horror in the background.

"*Sijii asath aptu mesu ne!*"

Magnus thundered out the Shadese warning, vocally slapping back the man he had raised from boyhood. The tone and the command for Trace to gain control of himself were as ingrained in his memory as his recollections of Acadian were, but these were memories of loving discipline and the training lessons that would save his life time and again over the centuries. Trace instantly snapped out of his near-hysterical panic, his eyes and mind clearing as he stared starkly into his father's golden eyes.

"*M'jan,*" he said, his tone spiraling down into much softer calm and respect. He touched a hand to his heart and fed all the desperate emotion in his soul into his eyes as he bowed slightly to the priest. "I am begging you, *M'jan*. Please, tell me if she survives."

"She lives," Magnus said simply in reply, "but she is deathly ill."

"Is she here? I mean . . . is she out of Fade?"

"I believe that she is. She awoke for just a moment and tried to speak, but of course her body is too unused and deficient for speech at the moment. However, if I had to guess, it was your name she tried to say."

"It was?" he asked a bit numbly. The relief washing through him was so profound that it acted like a ricochet in his body. It was Magnus's sure strength that guided him safely to a seat on the floor when he couldn't seem to stand upright any longer.

"Where is Karri?" Magnus demanded as he watched his foster son collapse in mental and physical exhaustion. "Nicoya, bring tea and *frousi* for the vizier. Daniel, warm clothes and blankets. Bring them from my things. Shiloh, if you would please find Karri and have her bring her herbs and medicines?"

"*M'jan* Magnus." Shiloh spoke up in protest to being ordered about all for the sake of some half-breed creature and the priest's favored son. Of course, he couldn't say as much to Magnus without risking trouble. "There are others who can run such an errand for you. I am better useful tending to those other Shadowdwellers who are in need of a priest while so many of us are absent because we are in here, spending time on this."

Trace looked up at the priest and narrowed evil-tempered eyes on him. Whether Magnus heard the contempt behind the thinly veiled insults or not, Trace heard them quite clearly. He felt Magnus close a strong hand around his arm in warning.

"You are correct, *M'jan* Shiloh," Magnus said easily. "However, why not combine your tasks? On your way to your work, find Karri and send her back to me."

"Of course, Magnus," Shiloh was forced to agree. Still, he was happy to just be getting out of the RV, so it was a good enough compromise.

"Poison," Trace thought to add as the door shut behind the exiting priest. "It's poison that affects Ashla. From an assassin's blade. We were ambushed and I was cut. She healed me."

"Not completely. If she had, she would be dead and you would not be sick as you still are. Come now, Trace, and relax. You have abused yourself enough for two lifetimes these past weeks."

"No. Forgive me, Magnus," he said, reaching to grip his forearm in a plea. "I need to see her first. Please. If our places were reversed, you would feel the same."

Magnus wasn't necessarily sure about that. He wasn't one to react to things with such emotion, since he knew it clouded judgment to do so, but neither was the Trace he was familiar with. Although he had not taken to a life of religion as Magnus had hoped he would, Trace had proven himself a steady and logic-driven man. For him to lose that compass in this way, abandoning it to wildly vacillating emotions and waves of instinct, was significant, though Magnus could hardly appreciate how. However, there was no denying that his former student had formed a quick and deep sort of attachment to the half-breed girl.

In the end, there was more than just protocol and manners between priest and vizier, so it was impossible for Magnus to resist the plea when he knew Trace was the type who rarely begged for anything.

When Magnus stepped aside to show him Ashla, Trace had no idea what he had expected. Maybe he had expected that when her two halves rejoined, there would be more color to her skin or obvious signs of increased life in her body, but she looked exactly as she had before, like a porcelain doll left in a spell of sleep and stillness. The only difference was the labor of her breathing and the dampness of her skin as the poison within coursed through her frail body.

"What made you go after her?" The question took them both by surprise, even though Trace had asked it. He hadn't even realized it was brewing in his thoughts. "You didn't know she was Shadow from the start. Why would you leave the caravan at such a critical time to seek out the body of a wraith?"

Magnus turned and stepped away from Trace, moving back to his patient to briefly kneel and check her vital signs. "I hardly think it is an unreasonable action," he replied almost defensively with a glance up at the other religious members in the room. "Did I not give you tasks to do?" he demanded of them. And although he had only given tasks to two of them, the room cleared out very quickly. When they were alone, he looked back at Trace. "She was an anomaly. Certainly worth investigation."

"Immediate investigation?" Trace pushed, unwittingly irritating his increasingly uncomfortable mentor. "In the middle of migration? You knew she was different. How did you know?"

"Is it urgent you know this now?" Magnus demanded irritably. "I see no relevance in how this will help you both to heal."

"Magnus," Trace said, the soft use of the priest's name his only rebuke and response to that.

Magnus sighed and looked at his foster son.

"The Sainting. You swore you had experienced the Sainting with her. You know it is a connection that fascinates me. Since I have never known you to exaggerate or swear to something that wasn't so, I had to believe you felt *something*. Something powerful. If you were Sainted, then I knew there was a good chance she was not fully human. Or rather, that she was part of us. Also . . ." Magnus hesitated a moment, something he almost never did. "The Sainting makes you vulnerable, Trace. The idea of you being joined that deeply to a being lying on the border of life and death was intolerable. Do you have any idea how often Sainted friends take their own lives when the other dies? I have studied this for decades now. If they survive the original sacrifice together, forming that depth of bonded companionship to its fullest devotion, half of them will chase their companions to the grave when the time comes. Perhaps more than that. I don't have the most accurate of records to go by. People know the stories, but the facts are often lost in poetry and lyric. But the fact remains . . ."

Trace actually smiled at that. "You were worried about me."

"Of course I was!" Magnus said gruffly as he gained his feet and paced for a short turn. "You can grow as independent of me as you like, *Ajai* Trace, but no matter how high in this world you place yourself, you'll not escape your roots with me!"

"I have no desire to do so," Trace assured him.

"Well, then, don't act so surprised. It's insulting. I have my reasons for not exposing my feelings in front of those who work with me, but you and I know the truth of it. At least, I should hope you do." Magnus stilled with a deep sigh, looking steadily at the other man. "You are my son, Trace. Blood or no blood, you are my son. I fathered you for decades where you barely left my sight, and I will father you until you step into your final Darkness."

"I know, *M'jan*," he acknowledged softly, giving his foster father a heart-touched acknowledgment. "Thank you for all you have done for us."

"Thank me when she is well, my son. She has a way to go yet."

Chapter 14

Guin walked through the enclave quickly in search of Trace.

He didn't like to leave Malaya for any reason, especially after the second attack on Trace. The dreadful fact was that the streets of the commune could be littered with conspirators, and any one of those close to the upper government could find themselves unexpectedly dead. Every face he encountered, whether he knew them well or not, was shaded with threat in his mind. Since his mistress had not yet given him leave to investigate deeper, all he could do was remain as vigilant as possible.

Guin took the main thoroughfare into the relay tunnel. An old mining shaft from over a century past, the cave entrance had been transformed into the smooth walls of a tunnel that transitioned the sparse exterior commune to the larger and more intricate interior.

Here mine shafts and tunnels that had been exhausted in the search for precious metals had provided the infrastructure to the underground city the 'Dwellers had built of it. It went into the mountain range for miles, and each man-made passage that had been hacked roughly open had since been transformed by engineers and builders into ash-plastered and boot-blackened curves. They led into the naturally warmer belly of the earth, the one true blackness on the planet and the one place where the threat of light had been totally removed.

As Guin strode through, he was crossing the equivalent of a biodome constructed under rock and stone. It had its own independent water supply from underground rivers and lakes, heated water from hot springs, as well as a supply from the freshwater Elk's Lake that stretched out about a half mile below their elevation. With the exception of lights, every modern convenience that was not light emitting, or alterable into such, could be found. Plumbing. Electricity for heat. Even communications technology. It was not, perhaps, flawlessly provided and perfect in its supply/demand quotient, but it was close enough to keep them safe and comfortable. They had learned how to compensate for the rest with things like black fire or natural resources.

There was only one place in the entire 'Dweller city where light could be found, and that was the hydroponics stations. They were set in the lowest and most distant sections of tunneling, and security limited access to it to both protect the products growing in it and those who might accidentally wander in during a "daylight" event. Timers did what Shadowdweller hands could not, and just to be certain, heavy doors sealed it all away. Tristan likened it to humans toying with nuclear power. It was dangerous and deadly, but efficient and necessary in its way. Despite the migrations, there were those who never moved from the city. Since there were so many to feed, and the ordering of supplies and moving them in were restricted by weather allowances, it made sense to be as independent of the outside world as possible.

Despite what Malaya thought, Guin was not as well known as she assumed. She mistook Trace's more congenial presence for Guin's, when it came to that, at times. No one acknowledged Guin who wasn't a guard, which was very different than all the calling out and waving that went on when he was beside Trace or either of the royals. Even the guard acknowledgment was about knowing who their master was, as opposed to anything of a friendly sort. Not that the bodyguard took any offense.

Guin simply wasn't the friendly sort.

He chose his companions on very rare and careful occasions.

At the moment, it was Trace he sought. The vizier had become increasingly distracted since the recovery of the blond half-breed girl, and now he was becoming increasingly scarce as well. Guin hardly understood the man's behavior. Before Baylor's attack, you could not have found another man more focused and dedicated to his work, except perhaps for the man who had raised Trace. Now, at a time when he was probably most needed, his attention was wavering. Not that he was entirely neglectful or anything. He just wasn't there all the time anymore. Guin didn't like change. Not in schedule, routine, or in people. It disturbed the careful plans and patterns he used to predict safety and the behaviors of others at any given moment.

And why was Trace nowhere to be found today? If Guin had his guess, he'd be exactly where he had been every day this week.

Sure enough, as he entered into Sanctuary, he found Trace in his usual spot, leaning against one of the polished columns edging the rear exit of the temple proper. Guin crossed the vast flooring in a clipped rhythm of steps, his boots as sharp as his patience was short these days. Between Trace, Malaya, and Tristan acting so out of logic and character, not to mention traitors milling about with sedition on their minds, who could blame him for being a bit on edge?

Guin was completely disgusted when Trace either didn't notice his approach or outright ignored it, in spite of the fact that he came up directly behind him. Instead, the vizier continued to keep his full attention on the rear courtyard. As always, the scrawny little half-breed human was engaged in some useless activity or another, and Trace was just standing there watching her. He never approached her. Never even let her know he came there each and every day. He just stood and stared, thinking Light knew what, wasting time and focus best spent elsewhere.

"The next time you let me come up on you like that, I am going to yell at the top of my lungs," Guin threatened testily. "At least then she'll know you're standing here like some moonsick cub."

"Thank you for the warning. The next time you come up on me like this I will have to remember to run a dagger through your throat," Trace responded dryly. Then, to prove his point, he reached down to slowly slide his blade back into the sheath rigged into his boot.

Okay, now *that* impressed Guin. The bodyguard tried to remember seeing the vizier move. He realized that he couldn't recollect any movement at all. That meant either he had been too busy grousing in his own mind, or the vizier had been armed all along. Since Guin hardly thought he could ever be that distracted, he realized the tanto had already been in Trace's hand. That struck him as odd, considering where they were. Also, the vizier had grown up in Sanctuary. Why wouldn't he feel completely safe here surrounded by memories and people from his boyhood?

"Well, at least you aren't as stupid as you are behaving," Guin muttered. "Why don't you go and say something to her? Why do you just stand here every day?"

Trace turned his head very slowly and narrowed his eyes on the bodyguard. "Fine advice, coming from you," he shot back.

Guin felt a sickening rush of chill dread as he met the other man's meaningful eyes. Well, he supposed he should have known better. After all, Trace didn't advise the most powerful people in their world for no reason. It was his un- canny insights that had made him invaluable for years. The worst the war had ever gotten for their side had been when Trace was Acadian's prisoner. They had been crippled those eleven months, like a powerful hunting beast suddenly losing a limb. They would have eventually learned to survive, but it would never be the same and it would have taken much longer than they could spare. Tristan's plan to recover Trace, the moment they had learned he was alive and being held prisoner, had been the most critical act of winning the war, in Guin's opinion. Trace had not recovered fully from his ordeal until the war had officially ended, so it hadn't been so much his contribution as it had been the morale change that had made the difference. But even injured to his soul with the horrors of torture, Trace had still played a critical part in the war's final resolution and Malaya and Tristan's assumption of power.

That had been why Guin had started to call him a friend. That and the fact that despite eleven months at that witch's mercy, Trace had never once given away a single piece of intel that would have endangered Malaya.

That meant more to Guin than all the rest.

"Fine. I'm a pot and you're a kettle," he muttered. "It isn't the same, though. *She* isn't untouchable and out of your league. If anything, you are out of hers. I mean, she's just a half-breed, Trace. She isn't even—"

Yeah. That was stupid, Guin thought quickly as he found himself suddenly being shoved back into the huge antechamber behind them. He regained his balance quickly, though, pausing to rub at his chest where the vizier had struck him quick and hard.

"You watch your tone, *Ajai* Guin," he warned with a snarl and a pointed finger as he closed the distance between them rapidly. "I don't care what they say about the way you fight, I will cut your heart out if I can find it!"

Other than Xenia, Trace was the only one he would ever take a threat like that from remotely seriously. Again, he made Magnus the exception from that; however, the priest would never make a threat of that kind to anyone who wasn't a Sinner. Guin was many things, but he was no Sinner.

"Look, I only meant to stress it's different from my situation, okay?" He backed up, taking a defensive posture, holding out a warning hand while laying another on the hilt of his blade. "Come on, Trace, you don't even have your katana. What are you going to do, spit on me?"

"And disrespect the temple? No. But anywhere else and I would have by now." He moved forward again and Guin was forced to step back or engage him.

"Don't be so damn sensitive!" Guin barked in frustration. "We have better things to do than pick fights with each other!"

Luckily, Trace was a creature of habit and logic. Both of those agreed with Guin's point, and he stood down and folded his arms across his chest, though he still glared at him.

"Why *did* you come down here?" Trace demanded.

"I needed to clear some things up. I haven't gotten to ask you for myself and I don't trust secondhand accounts."

"Clear what up?"

"The assassins at the post office."

"Oh." Trace frowned at the memory and within seconds was turning to look back over his shoulder. Guin looked too, but all he saw was the half-breed girl parked on a lounge with a book in her lap. She was currently reading through her closed eyelids, which Guin considered could be mildly intriguing . . . for about half a second. What was the point in watching the half-breed sleep? "What about them?" Trace asked as he started to walk back toward the column he favored.

"We never found the body of the one you killed. That means they dispose of their own dead so they don't get tracked back. So I was thinking the assassin had to be someone noticeable."

"You think it was another senator."

"Maybe. Or something like that. I've been looking, but

until session starts . . . Have you noticed any conspicuous absences?"

"No. Not yet." Trace finally turned his attention to the conversation and to Guin. "And I injured the other one. I was looking for a while to see if anyone favored their side, but after a couple of days they would have healed."

"If that. The scar will last a while, though. That's good thinking. But here's my thought. How many assassins use dipped blades, do you think?"

"How should I know? You and I don't exactly have Shadow-dweller underworld connections, Guin."

"Well, since the end of the wars and you passing those laws about murder penalties, assassins don't announce their trade anymore. But you have to suppose certain tricks are common with those from certain guilds. In the wars, we always knew the Siyth clan by how bloody they would leave the kill."

"And the Svedde clan always strung theirs up," Trace added thoughtfully. "So how do we find out which assassins' guild uses poisons? As you say, they no longer announce themselves, and they certainly won't announce themselves to us."

"I can find a way around that, I think."

"So that has me asking, once again, why are you here? What do you need me for?"

"I need you to tell me exactly who knew you were going into Shadowscape that day."

Trace frowned as he thought about it, and not for the first time.

"Everyone in the Sanctuary RV. They were the only ones who knew why and when and where. Anyone else who watched Magnus fetch me would have had to make an extremely wild guess, considering I was still fresh off euphoria. But . . ."

"But?"

"But there were only priests and handmaidens there," he

said as he turned back to look at the sleeping blonde once more.

Suddenly, everything clicked in Guin's mind. Trace's long visits down to the temple, his in-hand dagger, all of it. He wasn't just mooning after the girl, he was protecting her. Trace believed someone in Sanctuary was a traitor.

"Who was there? Be specific."

Trace listed everyone quickly, again proving he had thought this over many times already.

"And Magnus, of course."

The look Trace shot him said he had total faith in the loyalties of his mentor. Guin was inclined to agree, but he didn't have the luxury of being certain of anything without proving or disproving it first. It was simply the methodical way to do it, and the only way he could ensure Malaya's absolute safety. Especially when he considered the access the priest had to the Chancellor. No one save himself, Tristan, and Rika had the access Magnus did.

And no one was quite so deadly, either.

The fact of the matter was that the priest was a trained killer, and he had trained others to do the very same thing. The man before Guin was his best example. It was true, there was usually a higher calling for those he trained, and all of Magnus's work was the work of the gods, but it wouldn't be the first time in the long history of their people when a zealot's mind had turned good works into a personal and warped crusade. In all truth, Magnus was the leader of a powerful army of men and women, all with special gifts and all in charge of the education of most of the city's young people.

Darkness and Light spare them if Magnus ever decided to turn on them with that power at his beckoning.

Guin highly doubted anything of the kind, of course. He had spent the past fifty years in close quarters listening to the man's wisdom as he had counseled Malaya through the most difficult times in her life. He couldn't claim a single instance where Magnus had tried to control the mind of his young charge rather than let her control herself. It was one of the things that had come to change Guin over these last decades. He had been a man of very little faith in anything but his sword until Malaya had found him and shown him her world, where so many outstanding people were working together to make a better place for their breed on a planet overrun with humans and light.

Trace was wrong about one thing, though. Guin knew much more about assassins and their workings than he was given credit for. Some things had changed, but others never would. The guilds would probably always exist and they would always kill for a price or their own cause. It was one of the remaining thorns in the new regime's side. Guin had no doubt that if anyone could defeat the ancient brotherhood it would be these people, but it wouldn't change traditions, codes, and people who had been around since time was time.

"If you don't mind, I am going to work my way through that list of names, though I may need your help with it. You know this world far better than I do," he acknowledged, glancing up and around at the temple ceilings and their gleaming tiles.

"I did. Not so much now. Time has gotten away from me, Guin. It's playing nasty tricks, too. When I was raised here, I would have sworn that the touch of corruption could not ever breach these walls. I guess I just assumed that because Magnus was so highly placed both here and in the royal confidence, it was still impossible."

"Magnus's weight of power and responsibility may be the very reason why this has escaped his notice. He spends more time counseling the royals and their entourage since the recovery after the war than he does here. With good cause. It did a lot of damage to morale and spirits, as you are well aware."

Trace ignored the reference. "Even so. Magnus trained most of these people. I know what that is like. I can't imagine ill and wickedness coming out of such devotion and discipline."

"People change. Times change. And every single man and woman in here comes from a clan, Trace. They say you can never shed the grains of your birth, nor your loyalty to your clan."

"Is that what you think?" Trace queried. "That this is a clan-motivated uprising?"

"I told you, I will dismiss only what I can disprove. Until then, everything and everyone is under suspicion to me. Present company excluded."

"Yes, I doubt I'd poison myself," he retorted dryly.

"I've seen everything, so that wasn't what excluded you."

"What does?" came the astounded query.

"Your girlfriend over there," Guin said, surprising him visibly.

"How do you figure?"

"Two reasons. First, you're so distracted by her that you couldn't possibly coordinate an overthrow of the government that you actually helped create."

"And the second?"

"That you wouldn't overthrow the government you helped create. You had your chance to do it the way you wanted and you were very exacting about the horse you backed. If the war didn't change your loyalties," he noted, stressing "war" instead of "Acadian," "then nothing will."

"I don't know about that," he said with a grin. "There's always the love of a good woman to change a man." He gave the guard a sly look.

"Don't be a smart-ass."

Ashla was very much aware of every moment Trace spent watching her. The connection that had formed between them was stronger now than it had been in Shadowscape. Like a homing beacon, it told her when he was coming, when he was getting closer, and especially when he was there. The feeling was like sparkles inside her, the internal equivalent to soda pop bubbles up her nose. She wondered why he didn't feel it, too. If he had, then he wouldn't think she was ignorant of his presence, would he? Or maybe he was gambling that she hadn't figured out what the feeling meant yet.

Either way, he never approached her, never announced himself, and never so much as stepped out of hiding to wave at her. He simply stuck to the darkest corners, spent his time watching over her, and then left.

Ashla had no idea what to make of him.

She played along for two weeks, pretending not to notice a feeling that all but overwhelmed her, and tried not to keep mulling over why he was keeping his distance, because all of the answers she arrived at were so disheartening and disappointing. In the end, they all boiled down to the same thing. He was checking up on her to see she was okay, easing his conscience for the mistakes he had made with her, and pushing her off onto others.

Even after these weeks, she still felt like she was in the wrong body. Hell, the wrong everything. Her hair was longer than she'd kept it since childhood, she was wearing strange clothes that ranged from religious uniforms to what amounted to harem outfits. She felt cold all the time because she was still thin, and in the beginning her atrophied muscles had made movement all but impossible. Her natural healing talent had quickly helped cure almost all of it, except the thinness of her bones and body. Magnus said that was something only time out of sunlight and good foods could cure. And even that was his best guess, she could tell.

No one knew quite what to make of her, either. They tended to whisper a lot around her, or outright speak another language. Ignorance of Shadese was something she was going to have to rectify if she was going to hang around with these people in the future.

She wasn't exactly sure about that part yet, either. Of course, she had no worthy family to return to, and her only friend was dead. Her job and anyone she knew was gone by two years. Magnus had been kind and righteously pissed off as he'd relayed all he had experienced with her mother, but she was used to her mother's zealot opinions about her, so she hadn't reacted much.

Not much.

Sometimes she thought she was in a state of shock still from all of this. Oh, she was very glad that the world wasn't really devastated by some mysterious global phenomenon, but considering how isolated she was feeling again in spite of being surrounded by people taking care of her, she wondered if she was going to feel that way no matter what she did. She was learning about new races—or rather, very old ones. Learning that Demons, Vampires, and Lycanthropes were real unnerved her a bit, but Magnus said they were good guys for the most part, and she was inclined to believe him.

She was figuring out other things, too. The political structure, Trace's importance there, the migrations—she had even realized that she was staying in some kind of a religious house, and the very handsome and kind Magnus was some sort of a priest.

Kind of a waste, if you asked her. The man was beautifully handsome and amazingly magnetic, both attributes probably making him the spiritual leader that he was. He was patient, kind, and incredibly considerate. Intelligent, too. She had actually thought him to be quite the hottie early on, until she had realized he was a religious figure. She had sighed and labeled that under the "All the best ones are gay, married, or . . ." category. To think that he wouldn't pass that on to a child or make someone a fairly lucky girl was just a shame. Then again, maybe their priests *were* allowed to have sex. She wasn't sure. Everyone seemed pretty austere and tightly wound up in tradition and protocol, so she tended to doubt it.

But she had also never seen a priest walk about fully armed before, and she never saw Magnus without his beautiful weaponry. She had recognized the artistic exquisiteness of the scabbards as being very similar to the ones Trace carried. Both men seemed to favor Japanese-style weapons.

The one thing she was certain of since coming back to her "full" existence was that there was a great deal for her to learn and explore now. Knowing that there were whole cultures in the world that had "freaks" just like her in them made her feel a lot less alone than she ever had before. She just wished she didn't look so obviously like an outsider. She always drew attention when she passed by, even though she had not gone outside of the Sanctuary proper yet. All of the attention and furtive whispers felt a little too much like ... like her childhood; like she had felt every day of her adult life as she had concealed parts of herself she had been raised to dread. She didn't like being an anomaly, and here she couldn't hide it like she had been able to among humans.

It made her worry her lip as she thought to Trace again. He had said and done a lot of things in Shadowscape, and she wondered if he was regretting all of that now. If he was such a public figure, maybe it wouldn't be such a great idea to be seen hanging around a half-breed girl like her. Apparently it was an unspoken law that Shadowdwellers and humans were an off-limits combination. She was the product of some kind of felony or something, as if she didn't have enough problems. To top it off, she was pale and blond in a population that was consistently dark-skinned and ebonyhaired. She was a minority of one, and she was deeply out of her element.

Not to mention the women around her were giving her a serious complex. They were incredible. Tall, strong, and curvaceous, they had a dramatic dark beauty that was enhanced by the East Indian way they dressed. Exotic silks in deep colors adorned smooth skin ranging in shade from mocha to burnt sienna. They had amazing complexions, black and russet khols to draw out their sultry eyes, and though they were from a conservative culture, they had powerful wills and decided opinions on what they wanted.

Ashla was none of those things. Not even close. If Trace was used to women like that, what had he ever seen in her?

"Ashla," Karri greeted her warmly as she entered the court-yard from the east. "How are you this evening?"

"Feeling at a bit of a loss," she sighed honestly.

"Really? About what?" The handmaiden quickly sat down beside her, laying a comforting hand on her knee.

"About Trace," she answered baldly, figuring she didn't have anything to lose at that point. Besides, Karri was kind of like a nun, wasn't she? There was probably some confidentiality clause or something.

"Ah. I saw he was here again. He still hasn't approached you?"

"I don't think he wants to," she said with a shrug. "He doesn't strike me as the shy type, so I have to assume he just doesn't want to."

"No, Trace is anything but shy," Karri agreed knowingly. Too knowingly, in fact. Ashla felt a sensation of quick and hot jealousy whip around in her belly as she stared at the clean and simple beauty of Karri. She wore the midnight blue sari of a handmaiden, as she almost always did, with her hair drawn back into a tidy plait. She wore bangles and a col-lared necklace of gold, also as most of the others did, and her nails were painted to match her uniform. She wasn't heavily adorned and wore no make-up, but she was still young and pretty. "He grew up here, you know."

"Here? You mean *here* here? In the temple or whatever you call it?"

"Temple or, most often, Sanctuary. Sanctuary is all inclu-sive, and temple is more directed toward the central build-ing."

"Thanks," Ashla said, feeling as stupid as she did every

time she made one of these faux pas. "So he lived in Sanctu-ary?"

"Yes. He is Magnus's son."

"His son! But . . . isn't he a-a priest? Aren't they sup-posed to be celibate or something?"

"Trace is Magnus's foster son. We rarely make that dis-tinction, though, as it is considered rude. Magnus sees Trace as he would his real blood, and so should we. As for celibacy, Magnus is no more or less restricted from sexual congress as any married man is, barring religious events that require he be. Sex is a very natural instinct and serves great purpose in life. It makes no sense for a religious leader to give guidance about sex, family, and relationships when he has none of his own. Instead of a wife, however, he is given a handmaiden."

"You mean—you have to have sex with him whenever he wants to just because you are assigned to him as his hand-maiden?"

"No! Oh no. Consensual sex is paramount in all relation-ships. I am not obliged to sleep with him any more than he is obliged to sleep with me. It only means that until death dis-solves our religious bond of priest and handmaiden, I am simply his only choice, should he desire to expend sexual energy. He is also my only choice. However, we both reserve the right to decline at all times. It is hard to explain without getting into great religious detail, and you don't look like you have patience for that today."

"Honestly, you're right. I'd rather you tell me what you know about Trace so I can try and figure him out a little. I doubt I will have any success, but . . . I still want to try."

"Well, what would you like to know?" Karri threw a covert look toward the main temple.

Here was the challenge, actually. Ashla didn't want to fish for information from someone else. She wanted to ask *Trace* this stuff, or at least be able to hang out around him long enough to figure some of it out for herself. That would have been nice.

Just the same, she found she couldn't ask any of the personal questions burning in her mind. *What happened to his parents, making him a fosterling? How old was he when this happened? How old is he now?*

"Is he married?" It was such a gauche-sounding and stupid little query that her face burned with embarrassment. "Joined, I mean. You call it 'joined,' right?"

"Yes. Just like your human weddings, joinings are great celebrations, usually involving the whole city. And no, Trace is not joined. He isn't the type."

"The type?" she echoed.

"To settle into a monogamous, familial relationship," the handmaiden explained. "He is too much engaged with his duties and the development of the government. He is career obsessed, I think you call it."

That was easy enough to see, Ashla thought with a sigh. She remembered the fight with Baylor and all he had said so heatedly to the other man. It was clear Trace was devoted to his role and his loyalties to his government.

"Well, does he have children?"

"No. It is considered shameful to bear children without a joining. It must seem old-fashioned, I know, but the shame is attached to the inconsiderate parents who ought to have taken precautions against it. Shadowdwellers enjoy sex freely, Ashla, and we choose our desires openly. There is never any shame in that. However, we also believe a child is best raised within a strong family unit with joined parents to guide it. It is shameful to spread seed or give birth without taking great care in planning the results. Especially when it is so easily preventable in today's society."

"I see." She flushed, thinking of how reckless she had been with Trace before she had realized she hadn't been so reckless after all. Trace, of course, had not been concerned about it. She had been little more than a ghost to him. A wraith couldn't get pregnant, so what was there to worry about? "So . . . sex is neither taboo nor special? I-I mean, you're used to enjoying each other and moving on."

"That is usually the case among single Shadowdwellers, yes. We live much too long to limit ourselves and our experiences. You will see. You will live a long life, too. And there will be many among us who will find you fascinating and exciting."

"You mean a freak," she snapped suddenly, standing up with restless anger as she folded her arms around her clenching stomach. "Like all those stupid erotic stories about making love to an alien. Just because I look and act different, men around here are going to want to nail me, just to say they did it with the half-breed!"

"Well, of course we are all fascinated by you, Ashla. It is hard to resist curiosity over the unique. There is also great honor to be gained if you can claim to have given great pleasure to such an extraordinary being. But—"

"Oh my God! I think I'm going to be sick." She turned away and covered her mouth as tears burned hot in her eyes. Was that what had happened? Did Trace have his bragging rights now? Was he just coming around now to point to his butterfly in a jar and show her as a great conquest?

"I've upset you," Karri said worriedly. "This wasn't my intention. Please, I apologize, *Anai* Ashla. There are many women here who would love to be the center of such attention. They would thrive on having so many lovers to experience." Karri stood up and wrung her hands as she came up behind Ashla. "It is not just you, *Anai*. For instance, a woman who has had Trace for a lover would have incredible prestige in the eyes of other men and women. In our culture, the women would respect her and the men would desire her for themselves. The same would be true for any man who the Chancellor Malaya chose for a lover. For a woman so powerful and highly placed to select him would give him high desirability to others, and the respect of his peers. This is to say nothing of the experience itself. Trace was trained from his youth in the ways of pleasure and gratification. Magnus saw to it he had the very best tutors. We are all trained in the ways of lovemaking when we are young, but such valuable education as Trace or the Chancellors received is only given to an elite class."

Ashla wished the handmaiden would shut up. Karri meant well, but the more she said, the more of a nightmare this was becoming. She didn't want to think about all the lessons and women and prestige Trace had gained or given throughout his already extensive life. What he must have thought of her! With her ridiculous awkward experiences and her admitted failures at achieving orgasm. Ashla couldn't decide what was worse, thinking of his amusement at that, or thinking of how easy it had been for him to use his "lessons" on her to make her perform on command. How smug and blasé he must have been!

"Excuse me, I'm not feeling very well."

Ashla rushed out of the courtyard. She didn't want to burst into blubbering tears in public. She was enough of a sideshow as it was. And she absolutely wasn't going to let Trace watch her—

As though just thinking his name had conjured him, Ashla ran full-force into his body, and his hands and arms immediately closed around her. She squeaked in utter dismay as she became trapped in an instant in the place she least wanted to be.

What was worse was how incredibly good it felt to feel his strength around her again. His hands fitted to her arms and back in smooth sweeps that made her whole body groan with relief. He also smelled even better to her now than he had in Shadowscape. Everything came sharper and deeper, as if her senses had only been half complete and torn apart between the two 'scapes. His warmth, the scent of leather and exotic male musk, and as she looked up, even his eyes seemed a richer, more velvety black.

"*Jei li*," he said softly, his eyes searching her face with such intensity and sincerity that she almost forgot everything she had been feeling an instant ago. But all it took was a single thought, a single understanding that he had been "well educated" in the ways of women, and she shoved away from him with a cry.

"Ashla, what is it?" he demanded, refusing to let her go even as she squirmed so violently she was likely going to injure herself.

"Let me go! Just go away!"

"What did she say? Ashla, tell me what Karri said to upset you!"

"I'm not telling you anything!" she screamed in his face. "Why should I? Why do you care? You haven't even talked to me for over two weeks! You lied to me. You . . . *you used me*! I was so stupid!"

"Enough!"

The furious roar came an instant before Ashla was plucked off the ground and thrown over a leather-clad shoulder. She screeched and kicked, not caring if it sent her crashing on her head. It would probably feel better than she felt right then anyway. She had never been so mad, though God knew she had been hurt that much and more before. Most of all, she was furious with herself for walking right into the lies and the bullshit all over again, proving she would never, ever learn her lesson.

Through the fury of her flying hair, Ashla saw a door slamming closed behind them. Then she felt herself sailing through the air and landing on a soft surface. She scrambled for footing and posture, but she felt him grab her by her chin and face and shove her back down as he pinned her arms behind her back and forced her legs still beneath one of his.

"I said enough!"

"Fuck you!"

"As appealing an idea as that would normally be, I think

not," he retorted dryly. "Now why don't you calm down and tell me what in the searing Light this is all about?"

"It's about you being a total pig! Get off me!"

Ashla had never realized how good it would feel to simply scream at somebody. Just demanding what she wanted instead of tucking tail with a whimper and running away was such a rushing and different experience. Granted, she wasn't getting anywhere, but it still felt better than begging the world's pardon that she was breathing its oxygen.

"Did you just call me a—?"

"Pig! Swine! A filthy, disgusting animal!"

Trace pushed the wild curls of her hair off her face. Her eyes were shut tight, but there was no mistaking the cold fury on that normally meek and docile face. Something about it just made him want to smile, but she would probably pop a stroke if she caught him at it.

"Fine. If we agree on that for the moment, would you care to go into more detail?"

Her eyes flew open and she stared at him incredulously. "Are you *humoring* me? Oh! Get off my legs! I swear I am going to kick your nuts through the roof of your mouth!"

"Given that choice, I think I'll stay right where I am, thanks. And seeing as how I am bigger, heavier, and stronger than you, I'm guessing I can wait out this little snit and stay right here until you answer my questions. What do you think? Wait!" he said when she opened her mouth wide to reply. "I know. I'm a pig. Want to tell me what I did to earn such voluble praise from you?"

"You're a liar! And a-a con artist! Your entire sex sucks! You only think with your dicks and don't give a shit who you hurt in the process!"

"I beg your pardon?" he demanded, the vibration in his voice a warning of his rising temper to those who knew him. "Like women are any better? Deceitful, evil sickness wrapped in pretty packages. Using wiles and sweetness instead of swords to cut us deep. You sidle in close with your painted perfection and practiced tricks, and then stab us in the back once you are sure we are at our most vulnerable!"

"Oh, that's rich, coming from a trained whore!"

"*What did you say?*"

The furious roar rushing against her was like nothing she had ever felt or heard before. She watched with stunned, wide eyes as his eyes shot black lightning through her, his entire powerful body bunching up over her in a threatening cloud of muscle and fury.

She was shocked he didn't hit her, because he certainly looked like he wanted to. Actually, he looked like he wanted to beat the crap out of just anyone. Or everyone. A sensible fear finally spoke up inside her, warning her too late that she had gone too far. Ashla found herself with a finger pointed in her face and a looming maelstrom of masculine outrage right behind it.

"I have borne more nightmare reality than you will ever be able to comprehend *because* I refused to whore, Ashla Townsend, so do not ever speak to me in such a manner ever again! No one would dare accuse me of such a thing, and I realize now I want no part of anyone who does!"

He sprang back from her, almost as sharp as a crack of thunder as the length of his coat snapped with the turn of his body. Ashla sat up, breathing hard as he stormed in long strides toward the door.

"Why did you have sex with me?" she demanded loudly. "Because I was easy and convenient or because you wanted a thrill with a strange, white-skinned blonde?"

Trace stopped short and whirled around on a heel to face her again. If anything, he looked even madder. Ashla bit her tongue and wished she'd just let him walk out. She wasn't good at confronting people. Hell, she *never* confronted people in the first place!

"I cannot believe the things you think of me! What, in all of this time, have I done to make you think these things of me?" he challenged her. "Was it when I nursed you well, or when I saved your ungrateful little backside from oblivion that you became so convinced of my treacherous nature?"

Ashla flinched at that. Especially when he began walking back toward her again.

"Answer me!" he bellowed in a sharp burst of fury.

"She said that it would give you prestige because you slept with me!" she yelled. "That men here would want me because I'm unique and d-different! Everyone stares at me! They whisper and talk in a language I can't understand like I am an exhibit at the zoo! I hate it! I hate all of this! I didn't ask to be different!" She broke in a sob. "I don't want to be different!"

Trace's anger bled away like water whirling in a rush down a drain. "Who told you that? Karri?" he asked, his voice rasping in the wake of their shouting match. "That it would give me prestige to sleep with you?" He stepped closer, his hands clenching into brief fists. "I am the royal vizier, Ashla! I damn well have plenty of prestige on my own! I don't need to fuck around with you to get more! And to be quite frank with you, my performance with you was nothing to be bragged about. I failed you miserably as a lover. Worse than I thought, if this is truly what you think of me. I have one thing," he said, his breathing harsh as he held up a single finger, "one thing that has never been taken away from me, and that thing is my honor. I lost everything. Pride. Well-being. Trust. Sensitivity. All of it, gone. All of it, except for my honor. No one questions my honor. Do you under-stand me? No one!"

"But that's just it. I don't understand! I don't understand any of this world or you!" she cried softly.

"I know you don't, and that's the only reason I am still standing here," he told her, pointing a shaking finger to the floor for emphasis. "The *only* reason."

He turned away, running both hands back through his hair and down his neck. She watched him compose himself a little more before he shrugged out of his coat and threw it onto a divan. For the first time, she noticed she was in a very large room with a bed in its center and a great many chaises and divans scattered all around it. It was really quite beautiful, with all of its splendid silks in unusually brilliant colors. Everyone she had met so far dressed so darkly, even the décor reflecting a life lived in shadow. All of the color was completely dazzling and unexpected.

"Do you know what it means to be tortured?"

Ashla gasped, her attention shooting back to him sharply as her heart raced in mad fear. Her voice locked tightly in her throat and her pulse sprinted out of control.

Trace saw it all. Especially in the way her eyes widened all the way down to the black of her pupils.

"That was supposed to be a rhetorical question," he said softly. He came back to the edge of the bed and reached to gently take her chin in his hand until she was looking up at him, tears dropping down her face with every blink. "But it isn't, is it? You know the answer."

She tried to look away, to shake her head . . . but she couldn't, and it had nothing to do with his hold on her.

"Maybe torture is too strong a word for it," she whispered.

"Maybe. But if it was, it wouldn't have made you react like this. Don't underplay what happened, *jei li*. It makes it harder to recover from when you don't see it as it truly was. When you deny even the smallest aspect of it, it stays inside you and festers."

"H-how do you know that?" she asked, already devastated because she didn't want him to be able to answer that. She didn't want anyone to know what she knew and to feel what she felt, but she especially didn't want *him* to know it.

"Because there was a time when I was a prisoner of war, *jei li*," he said gently, as if it could soften something so harsh. "For eleven months they tried to get information out of me." He briefly closed his eyes and corrected himself. "For *six* months they tried to get information out of me. For the last five, I was just a whole lot of amusement."

"Your nightmares," she whispered. "That's what they are from."

He looked at her with momentary surprise, and then gave her a wry little smile and a nod. "I'm sorry. Did I keep you up?"

Ashla laughed at the absurdity of the question. As if it mattered if she had lost a little sleep when he had clearly suffered so much? She sniffed and grabbed the hand that held her with both of hers, pulling him until he sat beside her.

"No. You didn't." What an idiot she had been, she thought. How could she have thought such awful things of a man who worried about such insignificant details of her comfort? In fact, when she thought back on everything, those hours in bed with him had been the only time he had taken anything for himself. All the rest of the time he had been focused on her and concerned for her well-being.

And even in those selfish moments, he had been sick, she recalled suddenly. If he hadn't been, he had said, he would have done right by her.

"Oh, God," she said, covering her mouth in horror. "Oh, Trace! I'm so sorry!" She threw herself against him, wrapping her arms tight around his neck and crushing herself to him with all of her might. "I'm an awful person! Just awful! I'm so sorry. I'm just such a mess! I'm paranoid and neurotic a-and stupid! Just stupid!"

"Stop saying that," he demanded softly against her cheek. "You aren't stupid."

Her sudden laugh took him by surprise until she pulled back and looked at him. "But I am neurotic and paranoid?"

He realized his omission and chuckled. "Well, just a little. But we all are, I think. Honey"—he reached up and cradled her slender face—"I want you to tell me what happened to you. If you can't do it now, I understand, but it would help me if I knew."

"Help you?"

"Yeah. Help me to not get pissed off the next time you freak out on me like that."

"Oh. Well, you need a lot of help, then, because that was a whole new world of pissed off you had going there. Not that I blame you." She took a breath and sighed. "Look, it was just your average run-of-the-mill child abuse at the hands of a religious fanatic. I . . ." She stopped when she saw the look he was giving her. "Right. No underplaying." This time her deep breath shuddered out of her. "From the first time she saw me heal with my hands at the age of five, my mother went completely off the deep end. Until Magnus told me why, I always thought it was just one of those random things—or maybe that I really was just so hateful that even my own mother couldn't love me."

"That is ridiculous!" he burst out. "That you should feel such things because you are the daughter of a dishonorable 'Dweller and an unfaithful woman?"

"She totally blamed me for her indiscretions. All those years!" Ashla was feeling her anger now even as she hurt. "I can't tell you how many times she caned me until something in my body broke. She was never afraid of what doctors would say, because my rapid healing would cover her tracks. She would beat me and lock me in the basement. Chain me in the basement," she corrected with a swallow, her hand rubbing at her throat telling him exactly how she had been tethered in the darkness. "She'd let me out days later, and if there were any remaining signs of the whipping, she would pass it off as my usual clumsiness. After all, she was a living saint in the community. Church, volunteering, four children and a husband. All of it. Who would ever suspect her of torturing her child?

"All the while, she had made me the family whipping boy.

If my brothers or sister did something bad, I would get beat for it. 'To teach them responsibility for others,' she said. The whole time she did these things, she would shout prayer at me. She made me repeat the Bible over and over, especially the passages where Satan speaks. I guess by hearing me use the voice of the devil she could justify what she was doing.

"When they got older, she made my brothers beat me for themselves. Malcolm hated it, but he did it and just tried not to be as bad. Joseph loved it. He would get in trouble on purpose." She laughed bitterly. "Apparently he's all the rage in . . . in the BDSM world. At least, according to Cristine. She read some e-mails by accident or something."

"That's why when I said you were submissive you freaked out a bit."

"Yeah."

"There is a very huge difference between what your brother no doubt enjoys and the way a natural sub responds." He ran two gentle fingertips down the side of her face. "It doesn't mean you enjoyed what happened to you, and what happened to you didn't necessarily make you this way. It also doesn't mean that it is what you will like all the time."

"I guess you know a lot about all kinds of stuff like that," she said, looking down at her hands in her lap. "Karri told me that you had those classes on sex."

"Ah. I see. That would be where the 'trained whore' remark came from."

Ashla winced, hearing it come from his lips like that. "I'm sorry."

"I know you are. I also know you don't understand my culture any more than I can claim to fully understand yours. Those classes are a requirement for everyone raised in this world. We consider it dishonorable to send inexperienced men and women into the adult world, cutting them loose on their own to figure everything out. The tragedy of shame, pain, and destroyed confidence that can occur from a single episode of bad intercourse can last throughout a lifetime, affecting every single lover that comes afterward in a ripple effect. But I don't have to tell you that, do I? You and your brutally bruised self-esteem at the hands of incompetent men prove my point far more soundly than anything."

"Yes. I suppose they do," she agreed quietly. "I hope you can understand why I was so upset, though. It sounded so . . . I don't know. So full of artifice, maybe? It sounds so stupid now. But in my culture, we are taught to keep our sexual past a secret so no one gets jealous or . . . or feels like they are in competition."

Trace laughed at that. "It's always a competition. Pretending you're an innocent virgin every time doesn't fool anyone, least of all yourself. Men love to compete, and frankly so do women. It is poor etiquette to put a lover on the spot and *ask* for those comparisons, but if it is offered, that is something else. This is why we 'Dwellers aren't considered adults until well after our thirties. Those are the mistakes of immaturity. It's better to expend them and learn otherwise while in a controlled environment like this."

He indicated the room around them.

"Like this? You mean, they teach sex in here?"

"Ashla, you can't learn everything from books and pictures. Live example is the next best thing to practical experience." He stood up and walked to a divan, sitting down to face her. Ashla realized then that all of the chairs in the room were facing the round bed in a staggered outward circular pattern to provide a large viewing range. The room could easily fit a class of thirty people.

Realizing suddenly what went on in the bed she was in, Ashla jumped nervously to her feet and backed away from it as if it were going to bite her. The reaction amazed and exasperated Trace. He could see the red flush of embarrassment all down the back of her neck.

Ashla nearly yelped when she suddenly backed up into him, not even realizing he had gotten up again. His hands closed around her arms and then gently rubbed them up and down. Trace could feel how thin she was, but already he could see improvement in her.

"The instructor walks around the bed," he informed softly against her ear, "and the students watch while the models in the bed demonstrate things like position and technique. I was sitting right over there the very first time I heard and saw a woman come. It was the most incredible thing I had ever experienced in my life, and I have never forgotten it. What's more, it wasn't even a man who brought her to it."

"A woman?"

"I see." He chuckled. "You only have heterosexual relations in your society?"

"Well, no. But I-I would have thought . . ."

"We see everything. Every kind of sex from masturbation to homosexual to orgies. BDSM, fetishists, and anything else you can think of as well as those you can't even conceive of. It is our belief that this is the only way to know what truly arouses us. It saves us from misunderstanding and mistakes; mistakes that can be painful and degrading at times. Usually we find out very quickly what works for our minds, and then we choose classes to focus on. There are those which are mandatory, and those which are voluntary."

"What if someone is like me. What if they are shy or if it upsets them to see something?"

"Mandatory doesn't mean forced. And no one is introduced to a class like this one until they are deemed prepared enough. There are also things you don't need to see to know you won't like it. By the time you reach that level, though, you are usually choosing your own direction anyway. We would hardly expose an adolescent boy of twelve to an extreme sadistic display. I didn't even begin to learn fetishes and the like until I was twenty or so. Believe me, it's enough just learning the basics of heterosexual lovemaking."

"I don't doubt that." Ashla tried to turn around, but he kept her still and facing the bed.

"The first time I ever saw a man penetrate a woman, I was

sitting right behind us. I was so close I could smell the scent of her excitement." Trace's fingertips came up and slowly stroked down the side of her neck and collarbone. She was wearing a traditional Shadowdweller *k'jeet*, a woman's high-waisted dress that gathered tight and low against the breasts before falling away in airy, thin folds of embroidered silk. It swept the floor and the toes of his boots, hiding her bare feet and legs. Traditionally, no undergarments were worn with it because it was a dress of privacy, for use in one's home. Women who lived in the temple and Sanctuary wore them all the time, and since she was living there as well, no one had thought anything of giving it to her to wear. He wondered if she was wearing it in the traditional style.

"We are often called up to see things more closely," he continued, watching her carefully as she stared at the bed. "Sometimes to touch."

"Touch!"

"Yes, touch," he said, stroking her throat up to under her chin. "We learn every touch. Touch classes take place long before we ever come to this room." He turned his hand so his knuckles skimmed her on the way back down to her breast-bone. "We are quite used to touching by then. And I am not talking about breasts and cock and pussy," he said, feeling her twitch with each bald English term he used. "I mean face, shoulders, and hands. Feet, calves, and back. We learn how to turn every nonsexual place into a sexual one. We learn how different one woman's hair will feel from an-other's. We are taught how what stimulates one person will not work on another. That is one of the most important lessons of all."

"That no two people are alike," she said, swallowing be-neath the touch of his fingers.

"Never. That's why, in the end, competition is such a fruit-less thing." He chuckled. "Not that it stops us. But it is good to have something to strive for." He reached up with both hands to filter his fingers through her golden hair. "The first time I came here, I thought I was going to see sex. Finally. And trust me, I was ready. Or so I thought. You see, we don't have television here, so films are not available to horny adolescent boys. Just thousands and thousands of pictures. Pictures of *your* race, because ours can't bear a flash. Unless they were artist renderings; for us it was like looking at alien sex. We couldn't always get past the differences in your looks. You will forgive me, but that, too, is a maturity issue.

"Anyway," he whispered warmly against her ear, "here I come, cocky as hell because I had made the cut to see a live class at last, not to mention overrun with hormones and horny young urges. I was ready to see the big hurrah."

"And?" she asked, already giving a little giggle.

"I spent an hour furious as hell with disappointment as I watched a nude couple engage in hair-brushing and hair-stroking techniques."

"Really?"

"A lesson I had to re-take later on," he added, his fingertips burrowing slowly and sensuously against her scalp until she shivered and sighed.

"I can see you paid attention *that* time," she said with a soft, kittenish movement into his hands. He let her direct his touch, watching her neck as a run of gooseflesh skipped along her skin down to her breasts. He saw her nipples become taut under the colored silk and smiled with satisfaction.

"But never think anything is 'practiced' or a 'routine.' We do practice, but only to familiarize. And anyone who tries the same pattern and routine on everyone they encounter is doomed to failure. We do build a repertoire, what we can do and like to do best."

Trace demonstrated by moving her hair off her shoulder and closing his mouth on the lowest curve of her neck. She gasped, then groaned as she slid silkily back against him while he used his lips, tongue, and teeth to stimulate the vulnerable nerve cluster there. He ended with a long lick that made her tremble.

"There, now, would you prefer I never do that because it is practiced and I have used it before?"

"If people used rules like that, we'd only be able to have sex with one person in our whole lives!"

"This is my exact point. We both know that you and I have had sex with others. When I was young, I confess it was a *lot* of others. Again, hormones." He chuckled. "But I have been highly selective of late." Trace slid his hands around the slender planes of her waist and onto her belly, the dress rubbing smooth and soft between his palms and her skin.

"You have?"

"Yes. And it is okay for you to ask me that because I brought it up first. I did so because I want you to understand something. Before I was with you in Shadowscape, I had not touched a woman in twelve years."

This time he let her spin around to face him. She stared up at him in surprise for a moment, but then he saw in the pale blue depths of her eyes as she came to an understanding.

"Because of what happened when you were a prisoner," she said with soft compassion.

"Mostly. Yes." He swallowed. "Did anyone explain euphoria to you?"

"Magnus did."

"I was playing with fire that day and I knew it. I couldn't resist kissing you, and then when you told me you had never felt an orgasm, I couldn't bear to leave until I made it right for you. But sometime just before you crested, I completely crossed into euphoria, and when I felt and heard you come . . . Darkness and Light have never heard anything as exquisite as you sounded to me. I forgot all about the woman who had tortured me with her evil touch. I forgot I couldn't bear to touch or to be touched by a woman. I forgot I despised the idea of ever again being naked and vulnerable in front of a female. All I wanted was to feel you around me, and once I did it was so glorious a feeling that I needed it again and again. Twelve years' worth and more.

"And you put up with every selfish second of it. To this day I don't know why. Any woman from my race would have cracked me but good for being so greedy and thoughtless. And then again in that post office. So damn impatient, I was. It was the opposite of everything I had learned."

"Maybe because you didn't take your lessons in spontaneity. I loved the post office," she whispered with a sexy little groan against his neck that sent a hot rush of blood pulsing down the half-erect shaft of his penis and finishing the fullness that had started at her first touch. "Mmm, I remember thinking how warm you were. You still are." He felt her reach out to caress his sides and belly. "And I was trying to plan all the things I wanted to do to you. I wanted to be brave enough to do it that time."

"And I just wanted to keep my head and get you home. But"—he breathed into her hair—"I catch your scent and everything unravels. Just like now."

Chapter 15

Trace didn't want to, but he glanced up at the rotunda ceiling, scanning the glass quickly.

"*Jei li*," he said quietly, swallowing back a pleasured sigh when her small hands ran up over his chest. "Don't forget we are in the temple proper. There are rules here."

"Rules?" she repeated. "And this is the temple?" She looked around at the room that in her world might very well have been illegal, depending on the age of the students.

"Yes. In our religion, we believe that all teaching and all learning is a blessing. We believe it should . . ." His voice skipped when her traveling hands began to slowly slide down the muscles of his belly, making them clench. "It should be done by our ministers."

That made her stop still, and he sighed with relief and regret. He couldn't think straight when she touched him. It was the most outstanding reaction, and it baffled him because he had never felt so profound an impact at anyone else's hands.

"You mean priests and nuns teach this class?" she asked in shock.

"Handmaidens. And yes. But that isn't my point. When in

the temple, we follow temple rules. No exception. And in this room, the rule is if you choose to make love, you are fair game for modeling to a class."

That made her jump away from him so fast that he had to chuckle.

"Oh my God!"

"Only if we're caught. But we will be." He pointed to the glass rotunda. "That's the second story. It's an observatory window that sits in the middle of a very busy hallway. This section of the school is very sex intensive, so it makes sense for students to be able to study whenever they want. The lectern's voice will carry and they can hear the lesson if they like."

"We have to leave! Why did you bring me in here?"

She grabbed his hand and tried to pull him toward the door.

"Because the rooms on either side of us are holding class," he informed her, making her stop still. "And the ones across the halls are the private lesson chambers. You came in this direction, I followed. It was my only choice when you pitched your fit at me. Every other room that might be remotely private was pretty far away, and I didn't want you screaming and cursing all through the Sanctuary."

"Oh," she said meekly. "I forgot . . . I wasn't thinking. I didn't mean to be rude."

"It's okay. No one expects you to learn all the rules instantly."

"But what about being in here?" She looked up nervously. "Are we going to have to do s-something? We should leave."

"A few more inches below my belt with those sweet little hands of yours and we would have," he told her as he drew her palm up for his kiss. "Any overtly sexual behavior makes us fair game. That means being caught crossing into any of the major erogenous zones." His eyes tracked down over the round swell of her breasts. "I want you to tell me where your rooms are."

"My . . . ? I'm in the women's dormitories."

"There are three floors to the women's dormitories," he reminded her with amusement, never once looking up from the memory replay he was having of how fair and pretty her breasts looked when she was naked.

"Oh." She backed away from him and waved a hand across his eyes. "Stop crossing my zones!" she whispered fiercely.

"I have no intention of sharing you with the entire winter semester," he rejoined in a low rumble as he closed the space between them, "but I very much intend on crossing every damn zone on your body, so you better tell me where your rooms are." He took hold of her by the back of her head, making her face the hard heat of need he knew was in his eyes. It had been banked there for two very long weeks as he had given her space and time to recover. "Unless you no longer want me for you, *jei li*. The choice will always be yours."

Ashla looked up at him with unreadable eyes for a moment, her expression closed in that way she could sometimes have when she wasn't afraid or nervous. He had watched her closely these past days and noticed she was not as afraid of everything as she had been in Shadowscape, despite the fact that the world she was in now was just as strange. Her wild show of temper had been a bracing example of that, but it made him nervous suddenly to not know what she was thinking. Despite his generosity of power of choice, he didn't want her to choose against the idea. Against him.

He cursed in his head as he looked back up at the rotunda ceiling. Anything he might do to best convince her would put them in danger of public display, and he knew Ashla would never be able to bear it. At least, not now. Perhaps in the future that might change, and just the thought of *that* made him painfully aware of the crying need in his body right then, but again he was losing sight of whose was the more critical need between them.

He drew her up close as he dared, bending to touch his forehead to hers. "What makes you hesitate?" he asked. "Why do you still doubt me?"

"It's not you I doubt," she admitted in a rush. "You are used to women who are trained and skilled in things that— that I am painfully ignorant of. I look different, act different; I *am* that alien you once found so strange as a boy."

"I am no longer a boy," he reminded her, roughly pulling her body into his to give her a physical reminder of that. "And you are no alien. We have been to this place before, Ashla. Don't you remember how you satisfied me? How my hunger for you raged then?"

"You weren't yourself then," she argued stubbornly. "You said it several times now. What if—"

"What if," he growled harshly as he swung her full around and began to back her quickly toward the door, "what if we find out for ourselves and then pass judgment, hmm? And let's do so quickly before I am forced to show a classroom of infants as well. Trust me when I tell you that for me to play model to a class would draw nearly every student in the Sanctuary."

He hadn't thought someone so pale could get any paler, but she managed it.

"I'm on the ground floor, just across the courtyard. My room faces it near the onyx fountain."

Trace didn't even bother to move. He knew every corner and every best shadowed spot in the building. He had skipped them time and time again in years of practice. He closed his eyes and skipped her quickly into the courtyard, then once again into the hall closest to where she had mentioned. When they materialized outside of the three doors suiting her description of her room, she drew in a loud breath.

"I thought men weren't allowed in the women's quarters," she breathed.

"They aren't," he said meaningfully, giving her a little shake to urge her on.

"This one," she said, pointing.

He moved them into the room so fast that Ashla barely had time to take a breath. Then the door was closed and everything was like pitch nothingness to her before she blinked and details of her room began to define themselves more clearly. Slowly colors arose out of the darkness, showing her how much her sight was improving over time. She realized now that this was what Trace saw when he looked into darkness, although perhaps even more clearly than she could.

That thought just as easily flew out the window, though, when her back was pushed against the door and his large hands curved around her waist and swiftly rode up the length of her torso. She gasped as he crossed one of those promised zones, taking the fullness of her breasts into his palms.

"I want to do this right," he said, his words like breath as they rushed from him. "But every time I touch you, everything hurries at me with a need I can't even explain. You fear disappointing me when it's impossible! Touch me, Ashla. Feel how my body shakes with anticipation."

Ashla didn't need to touch him; she could already feel the vibration of excitement resonating through him. But the invitation was irresistible. She curled a hand around his neck and drew him down to her, her lips parting as he came to kiss her. She melted against him the moment their mouths melded, sighing as his tongue sought deep for hers. His hands slid back and around her shape, gliding down the curve of her back and over her hips. She tried not to be self-conscious about how thin she knew she felt. It might be a coveted figure in American society, but here it was just thin and undernourished. All the women she saw here had curves and plenty of them. They couldn't even find clothes for her at first without needing to tailor them.

Trace felt her stiffen and was well aware of her reservations. It was completely ridiculous, of course, but he had to treat her doubts very seriously and very carefully.

"What will it take to convince you?" he asked her against her lips. "Will you be satisfied of the authenticity of my feelings only when I am coming wildly inside you? Tell me, what will it take?"

The imagery his words evoked took her breath away, just as the heated depth of his kisses did. Soon she was dizzy with the need to breathe, and when he finally released her mouth she did so in a drawing rush. Her heart raced hard against her ribs as she began to truly realize how much vital male she was daring to take hold of here. He dwarfed her like a mountain dwarfs a tiny goat, but all the same she wanted to be nimble enough to conquer her mountain. She wanted to grab hold of him and show him how to take and touch her, as if he was in need of the lessons. She wanted to leave fear and doubt behind and just do everything she wanted.

She suddenly realized that this was the one man alive she could ever safely do that with. Knowing what torture he had suffered secured her mind that he would never be cruel to her. He knew too well what it felt like. Just as she knew what it had been like for him.

I forgot I couldn't bear to touch or to be touched by a woman.

Yet he touched her. He'd had twelve years to touch any of those dark, curvaceous beauties, and he had wanted none of them. But he had wanted her . . .

"Yes," he whispered into her neck as he ran a provocative tongue over her carotid pulse. "No other will do for me what you do. They never have."

Ashla squirmed in delight at both his words and his playful tongue. The keen insight into her thoughts went completely unnoticed as her mind floated to a place of pleasure.

"Turn around."

Total stillness followed the command, and he raised his head with a lifted brow and amusement in his eyes. "Turn around?" he echoed.

"Yes," she breathed, flushing now that she had to assert her wishes while looking into his eyes.

But to her infinite surprise, her very dominant 'Dweller straightened up, took a step back, and did as she asked. Ashla licked her lips as she ran her eyes down the beautiful, high-powered length of him. From the broad scope of his shoulders to the tight narrowing of his waist, she could see the beauty of a truly fit male. Even the braced strength in his legs ran up tautly into an outrageously fine ass, which was accented, she felt, by the tailored cut of his slacks.

She had asked him to turn because she had barely gotten the chance to see him from behind last time. He had crowded and dominated her every movement. Now, this time, she wanted everything. Like him, she wanted it to be better.

Ashla stepped up behind him and slowly shaped her hands to the long muscles that crossed from his lower back around and down to his pelvis. Her fingertips bumped over his belts and their buckles. His katana was missing, but the second sword, the one he had told her was called a wakizashi sword, was in its scabbard on the other side. It was much shorter than the katana, but not as small as the one he kept strapped by his calf.

"Where is your katana?" she asked softly against the fabric of his thick woven shirt. She had to take the time to breathe in the scent of him, the richness and raw male message of power it imbued was heady and delicious.

"Ruined," he admitted, displaying his regret in his tone. "Saw-stars are notorious for their weight and force. Deflecting them damaged the blade badly, and then using it afterward fractured the steel."

"I'm sorry," she said sincerely. She had come to realize there was value to his blade that went beyond its ability to help guard his life. Now that she knew he was Magnus's foster son, it explained the similarity of their weapons and filled in the understanding that it had probably been a deeply treasured gift. "Can it be fixed?" she queried as her fingers closed around the buckle of the weapons belt.

"The master who made it has it. He will no doubt replace the tang." Trace exhaled a long, slow breath as she took away his belt and laid it aside. She smiled when she returned her fingers around him to find the belt to his pants and removed it as well. At first she was enjoying the way he would stiffen up, as if in reaction to her teasing slow touch, but then she realized it only happened when she brushed or touched against his spine.

"Take your shirt off," she demanded suddenly, pulling back so she could see his back once he did so. His hesitation gave him away and he knew it, so he turned to look at her.

"This is different than before," he reminded her with a pulse visibly racing in his throat. "I feel everything; I am aware of everything."

"Take your shirt off," she repeated slowly, reaching out to turn him away from her again. She watched the tension in his body increase, and even heard him fortifying himself under his breath. He skimmed off the first shirt, and she watched carefully as he scooped the second one over his head.

She gasped, unable to help herself as she looked in wide-eyed horror at the scars raked thickly up the length of his spine. Now that she knew where they had come from, her imagination raced in wild and terrible directions until she couldn't bear it anymore. Trace's hands curled into fists and he twitched to move, but she reached out and stayed him, giving herself time to look at him and to reconcile all she was coming to understand.

Ashla reached to touch him, amazed once again to find there wasn't texture to match what she could see. The white and pink tears in his dark skin were so stark and ugly that they ought to have a thickened feel to match the many, many streaks of pain he had suffered. But his body had healed everything except the disruption of color that showed his history of agony.

"Trace," she whispered softly, tears rimming her eyes. She leaned forward and kissed the first place of old hurt she could reach. Her arms wrapped around his sides and chest, her palms pressing flat against the crisply curling hair of his pectorals. She continued to rain kisses against the ghosts of the past, pausing only when he took hold of her hand to thread her fingers tightly through his.

Trace's eyes were sealed closed as he felt her lips and silent tears drifting down the length of his spine. The part of him that couldn't bear to be touched on his back dissolved away for her. Her pity did not insult him, because he knew exactly how she meant to give it to him. Her desire to heal him turned his heart over in an increasingly tight space. When she stopped to rub her face against him, her tears had gone and she was ready for the next step. He could sense it as strongly as he knew his own mind. He turned to face her, dark eyes rife with grief and reconciliation. There was powerful emotion to be found as he exposed it to her. Then he gathered her up tight and close, seeking her mouth with deep need and the starving strokes of his tongue. He kissed her until she could barely keep her balance; kissed her until she was holding on to his body as if he were there to save her life. She was everything he had needed all these long years of recovery, he thought starkly. Every touch was a balm and a fire; one to soothe, one to burn away the remnants of the evil past.

She aroused him madly, just as she had before, the planes and scope of her soft body just as craved as it had been in Shadowscape. It overran him like wildfire, again that blessed burning that told him he was alive and in need. Trace broke from her mouth by sinking to a single knee, his nose running the entire length of her sweet-smelling body. He couldn't believe how exotic the real depth of her scent was as it ran over and through him. The disparity in their heights brought him just beneath her breasts, and he instantly framed her between his hands, making an offering of gorgeous pale flesh under maroon silk. He found her easily through the material, her nipples already hard in anticipation of him. He bit at her gently, making her squeak softly in that way he was learning to get seriously turned on by.

The dress she wore was tied to her body in a knot beneath each breast and then together in between. They were small but serviceable ties, and they were also completely at his access.

But first . . .

Trace slid his hands down her slim sides, shaping her hips and thighs slowly as he distracted her with the flutter of his tongue through damp silk. She buried her hands in his hair, all but demanding he keep his mouth to her breast. She didn't seem to take note of his hands until she realized they were running quickly up the backs of her legs beneath her skirt. She tried to squirm, but stopped when a nip of his teeth warned her to keep still for him. He looked up, wanting to see her flushed face as his fingers met nothing but bare skin along the curve of her backside. Then he slid his fingers forward over the crests of her hips, enjoying how she shivered and trembled under his simplest touches. He nuzzled her slowly beneath one breast, and then the other, watching her pant for breath and feeling the restless shift of her legs. Just as his thumbs caressed the smooth mound of her sex, his teeth tugged free the last tie between her breasts and the dress slid down onto his arms.

Ashla hadn't expected to be suddenly naked in his hands, but she was. She was also feeling the combination of his mouth returning to her tender nipple even as his thumbs toyed against her sex, playing with the dampness already present at the very edges of her flesh.

"You've removed your hair," he noticed, sliding a fingertip into the cleft left exposed by her meticulous grooming.

"I . . ." She flushed, especially when he grinned up at her. They both knew very well why she had taken such special care in grooming herself. She had anticipated being with him again. "Don't get cocky," she breathed.

"Never," he assured her. "Now come down here."

He swept her dress out of their way, and then coaxed her down onto the floor. The dormitories all had mats covering the polished marble or wood, protecting it from the traffic and the rambunctious students. They were firm enough to walk on with comfort, but softer than perhaps even carpeting. Still, Trace took care as he laid her out before him. He felt as if he had not taken proper time to pay respect to her differences or even to her feminine body in general, and he was going to change that.

Ashla was racked with a continuous little shiver, but he knew that was from the intensity of her arousal and her curiosity over what he was planning. He cupped her knees in his hands and slowly stroked her legs along the insides of her thighs, methodically parting them as he went, until he could go no farther and his hands were framing the exposed heart of her. He simply drank in the sight for a moment, the display of pink flesh glistening with wetness he had inspired. It made his rock-hard cock pulse with randy anticipation. Impatient anticipation. He was bathed in the pure sexual scent of aroused woman, the power it had over him incredible as his heart raced in an effort to fuel the action his body wanted to take so badly.

"You are so magnificent," he uttered to her as he stared, the words tumbling out of him so roughly and so emotionally, she had no choice but to see the truth of them. She had felt self-conscious up until that very moment, but now Ashla's entire body relaxed into his guiding touch.

When he didn't take advantage of her wanton sprawl, she

moaned and squirmed with need. Instead, his hands were shaping all the bare swells of warm, smooth skin he could reach. Soon, she realized, there wasn't a single spot on her body that hadn't received his erotic attentions. Except the one place that craved him most. Her breasts ached with the stimulation of his caresses, her nipples throbbed with the dipping tugs of his teeth and tongue. Her hips lifted in offering as his hands sculpted them again.

"Tell me what you want," he said, his low tenor sly and sexy.

"Oh, please," she gasped.

She meant please don't make her voice her needs, because of her shyness and self-consciousness, and Trace wasn't going to stand for that. Not this time. He bent over her and, taking his hands away from her, blew a warm stream of breath against the swollen tip of her clitoris. She caught a spasm through her body, her back arching at the sensation and proving how incredibly sensitive she was.

"Tell me what you want," he echoed as he turned to kiss and then lick a line of stimulus up the inside of her thigh. The darker undertone of musk in her arousal increased so sharply it was enough to intoxicate senses as sensitive and starved for her as his were.

Suddenly he reached for her and rolled her over before she even realized what was happening. On her stomach now, she had to struggle to see him, but he reached out and turned her head back around, pressing her cheek to the floor.

"If you want to know what I am going to do back here, all you have to do is *tell me what you want*. Then that is what I will do. And believe me when I say far more than your curiosity will be satisfied."

She went hot along her skin at the promise, and again at the touch of his mouth against her spine. He bridged himself over her legs and took her hips in his hands, lifting her slightly so her bottom was in the air. He continued his slithery sensual kisses all down her spine until she was leaving a wet puddle on the mat beneath her and he had reached the line where her tailbone met her bottom. She felt him shift his grip until he was spreading her cheeks open for his ongoing progress. Ashla's heart reacted with panicked eroticism. She was screaming what she wanted in her head, but she couldn't connect it to her voice. She was afraid of what he was doing just because she wasn't used to the bold exploration or being the focus of so much attention.

"Trace!" she croaked out as his tongue danced in a wicked tease against her.

"Speak," he beckoned, breathing the word over damp places that fired with unexpected sensitivity.

"I w-want your mouth on me," she gasped, her face burning as she hid it against the floor.

"My mouth *is* on you," he pointed out, reminding her of it with a nip on one buttock.

"Please . . ."

"Say it, *jei li*. It's just you and me here. I want to hear it, and you want to say it. Don't think and don't hold back."

Say it, he begged her against the mind they sometimes shared. His body and psyche were screaming in need for her. His skin was damp with sweat from holding himself in careful, controlled reserve. Not to mention his exploration of her pretty backside had aroused all new hungers as well. But he wanted to untie her reserved tongue, to teach her that she had to tell him everything. Not just about the needs of her body, but all of her needs.

Trace was almost on the edge of a whole different kind of euphoria, and when she hesitated just long enough, he was actually grateful for it. He stole what he wanted, his tongue rimming the dark pink bud of nerves she probably never even realized she had. Humans attached shame and taboo to the strangest things, and then just as much eroticism to it when they thought to break those taboos. Ashla cried out in shock the first time he did it; then, confused response the next. The more she reacted, the harder Trace got. It was so intense for him that he groaned with savage need, gripping her tightly. If she didn't speak soon, he was going to give in to her. He didn't want her to get away with that, damn it! He wanted her to scream for what she deserved! For all she needed and wanted.

"Oh, God! Trace!"

Trace surged up the back of her body, finding her ear under the wild mess of curling gold. "What? Tell me. 'Oh God, Trace . . .' what?" He settled his hips against her bottom, his still clothed but very prominent erection nestling into her. "Tell me to suck your sweet little clit, honey," he coaxed her. "Tell me to lick your pretty pussy until you come in my mouth. Tell me you want my tongue deep inside you . . ."

"Yes! Oh, God, please! Yes. I want all of that!" she groaned, writhing under him in heat at the mere suggestions. Trace realized then what a truly passionate and sexual creature she could become once she had shed bad memories and ridiculous cultural hang-ups.

"But you didn't say it," he taunted softly, reaching to slide a hand beneath them, his fingertips tickling the drenched outer lips of her flushed and waiting sex. Searing Light, how he wanted to make her come! Not just once, but a thousand times. He wanted her to explode like a sun in supernova, even if it burned him up in the process.

"Yes! Lick my pussy and make me come," she gasped on a sob.

He was off her in a flash, flinging her onto her back and once again sliding hungry hands up her thighs until she was spread open like a pretty pink sacrifice just for him. He knew, even before he bent to do her bidding, that she was already about to burst. The tantalizing game of anticipation had chased full sensitivity and rich blood flow below her waist, making her plump, ripe, and ready. He skipped preliminaries, saving it for a less intense breaking point, and gently spread her labia to make a path for his tongue. When his mouth closed over her, Ashla bucked, filling his mouth with wet, swollen flesh. Her clitoris rubbed fat and demanding against his lips and he gave it a deep obliging sucking.

Ashla screamed, her hands latching hard in his hair, holding his head between her thighs as she burst into violent orgasm. Rich and sweet, a stream of juices burst into his mouth and Trace knew he could have climaxed just off the lusty flavor and scent, as well as her wild cries for him. It took everything inside him, every moment of discipline and control he had learned in his whole life just to keep that from happening. When he came, it would be deep, deep inside her, and nowhere else.

"Trace! *Trace!*" Ashla gasped and gasped for breaths as she rode the hard, unfamiliar crest that both thrilled and frightened. It was extreme, to feel so much at someone else's bidding! As her body trembled into weakness and repletion, making her limp and helpless beneath him, she could only stare at him in wonder and shock.

Trace rose up on his knees, very obviously licking his wet lips. Ashla flushed hot in more places than just across her face as she watched him reach for the front of his slacks. Then he seemed to think better of the idea, and stood up instead. She was too jellied with postorgasmic weakness to follow him, so she was grateful when he scooped her up off the floor easily. He brought her to her bed, laying her on the soft pillows spread over it in decorative style. Then he finished shedding his clothing, displaying the intensely colored length of his cock. She could see the urgency he was feeling in the visible throb of that amazing staff of flesh even before she saw it in his dark, molten eyes. He took hold of her under her knees and slid her to the very edge of the bed. He paused only long enough to slide another pillow under her, raising her up perfectly to meet him.

She could tell by the ticking of his jaw muscle that he had his teeth tightly clenched, a sign of how tautly he was reining himself in. The idea intrigued her, tempting the boldness he himself had been encouraging from her. With her focus slowly revolving around to Trace's needs, a sense of control slid through her. He had toyed with her, albeit for her own good and ultimate pleasure, but she wanted very much to know what that had felt like for him. The only way to know that . . .

Trace caught his furiously hard cock in his hand and moved forward toward her. All he could think about was the snug heat and bliss of plunging into her. It would be so sweet. So incredibly sweet.

"Wait."

He looked up with a blink of surprise, barely recognizing her voice in the low purr of command. There was something in her eyes he had never seen before, either, something strong and . . . wicked.

"Ashla," he warned her, knowing he was working on a hair trigger of patience.

"I've never tasted you," she said as she wriggled herself upright. Her hands slid up his chest as she gained her knees, her beautiful figure braced before him in a pose of striking feminine seduction. "I want to taste you," she whispered hotly against his stunned lips as he felt her hand drift down over his to touch him. He let go of himself to make way for her, his eager staff leaping up at her first light caress before she caught him snugly in her small hand.

How could he deny her after so much time spent making her voice her desires? She was just continuing the lesson, only he feared this time it would be him in the position of student. He had spent hours in classes learning how to pro-long his release in the face of unbelievable stimulus, but how could any of that prepare him for the sight of her licking her lips as she stroked him so lightly it made every nerve strain to her touch?

"Lie down on the bed," she instructed him, letting him free so she could shove pillows out of the way, dumping them to the floor impatiently. He obeyed her command with a smile in his eyes. He knew he was jumping into the sun, but damn it, he was proud of her fearless hunger.

When he was settled, she lay down perpendicular to him, her head pillowed on his belly and facing away from him. He stuck another pillow behind his head, raising himself up just far enough to watch her carefully study his body.

Ashla started with a single finger, touching the darkly purpled head where it was oozing slightly sticky fluid. She was overwhelmed with the raw scent of an aroused male, the sexual musk of animal desire making her shiver with delight. She could hear him breathing under her ear, the quickness quite telling.

She tracked her single finger down his length, all the way from the tip to the soft web of skin that led her through a nest of pubic curls before introducing her to the taut sac beneath. Here she used her full hand to cradle him, hearing him make a low, rumbling sound in his throat and smiling because she knew what it meant. He was malleable here, but she felt the hardness of his testicles within as a testament to his readiness for her. Her smile turned sly as she reversed her path slowly and stroked her fingers up along bumps, ridges, and prominent veins. He twitched and pulsed as her hand closed around him, and she felt his hand fall on her back and hold against her tightly.

Trace learned a whole new form of torture as her butterfly touch searched and explored him. When she finally rose up from his stomach, Trace was in a full sweat of need. Then she leaned over him and blew warm breath all along his shaft, trying his own trick against him and succeeding quite merrily. His cock jumped in its stimulated delight, drooling a fresh stream of pre-cum for her, and that was what finally lured her in. Her curiosity sent out a teasing pink tongue to touch the head of his penis, testing his taste almost cautiously.

That was when he realized she had never done this before.

It came to him in a dawning rush of clarity and overwhelming excitement. He was going to be her first taste of this decadent delight. Him and no other. Just as he had been the first to make her come.

Him and no other.

The possessive flood of emotion that broke over him made him tense and she felt it. She backed off, misinterpreting, and his soul cried in dismay, his erection weeping in reflection.

"Please, *jei li*, don't stop," he ground out, not caring what it was going to take to keep control. He would. Even if he died of heart seizure, he would maintain control for her.

It was all the encouragement she needed. Clearly pleased with her first taste, she returned for another, this one broader and using the whole flat of her silky little tongue. Trace groaned as his eyes rolled closed for a second to immerse himself in the sensation, but half the thrill was watching her. Beautiful, blessed Darkness, he could watch her forever. It was burning in his memory as she leaned closer and her gleaming curls of pale gold tumbled over him, dancing against his turgid flesh and tickling like hundreds of the tiniest fingers.

Then out of nowhere, she went for broke, shocking his entire system as she bravely closed her lips around him and sucked him into her mouth. Trace's hips lurched up from the bed even as his hand speared into her hair. He cried out in a low bark of pleasure, the sound strained as he tried to control the urge to thrust against the tongue that tormented him. Worse, she enjoyed making him react, so she did it again, only she wasn't as afraid to test the depths of her mouth as he might have expected her to be. He hadn't gambled on her curiosity or her driving need to get even with him. So he found himself deep in the warm seal of her mouth when she hummed in pleasure at the taste of him on her palate. The vibration skipped over his every erogenous nerve and shattered his reserve.

"Ashla. Do it. Please, baby, I need you to suck me hard. I need—!"

Trace gasped when she did just that, testing his tolerance for the draw and pressure she applied. She kept watching his face, checking him to see if she was doing anything to hurt him. She needn't have worried, he thought on the border of hysteria, he was so hard he could have deflected bullets.

And then she remembered she had hands, too.

She was imitating things she had seen somewhere else, he could tell, but it was a fabulous source, whatever it was. He'd never felt someone so inexperienced suit herself so naturally to giving head.

And that was exactly why he was in deep, deep trouble.

The urge to release blindsided him. He had thought himself in control, but he wasn't in the least. The burning sensation crawling up his thighs made that very clear.

"Stop," he choked gruffly, gripping her hair and coming just shy of pulling her off him. "I don't want to finish like this!" He was literally gasping for every word.

The little witch had the temerity to smile the smuggest smile he had ever seen in his life.

"Get your ass over me *right now*!" he demanded almost savagely as he grabbed for her arms.

Between their mutual efforts, she flew up over his body, straddling his hips in a heartbeat. He couldn't even breathe when she reached between her legs to take hold of his cock and poised herself to take him inside. When she slid his bulging head against her snug little entrance, he thought he would scream himself into pieces.

Ashla knew she had pushed him too far, though she wasn't entirely sure how. Regardless, she had never been so delighted in her life. The shift of power between them was a rush unlike anything she had ever known. So when he grabbed her almost brutally by the hips and plunged up into her even as he dragged her down onto him, she cried out in clear victory. Then the fullness of his wild penetration struck her and her whole body shuddered with pleasure. He was enormous! She could hardly believe he fit inside her. But not only did he fit then, but he did again and again. Trace spat an invective in Shadese as he whipped their joined bodies around. He drove her beneath him, gaining purchase with his powerful legs, and began to thrust into her in earnest.

"*Drenna shev ati mui!*" he ground out in a wild burst of native intensity. "Darkness is inside you!"

Heaven and rapture is inside of you.

She knew the meaning as well as she knew the power of his pistoning flesh inside her. He laid a large hand over her lower belly, as if he were treasuring the spot, and Trace shook his head hard, a denial that wouldn't work. He looked at her heated eyes with a sense of despair in his, and she understood his dismay at his hasty need.

She reached up and took his face between her hands.

"Come for me," she begged softly.

"*Jei li!*"

Trace couldn't have said another word even if he had wanted to. He felt his own body betraying him in violent screams of pleasure. He burst out into raw male cries as his body pulsed glorious, painful ecstasy. He came in hard, savage throbs of release, spitting his seed into her as wildly as he had taken her. It felt so good. Oh, so good. The roar of his own blood surging deafened him and his chest burned with the need for breath. He held her tightly in place, making certain she wouldn't so much as think of moving until he was done, completely ignoring the fact that it was obvious there was no place she would rather be at that moment.

"You destroy me."

He wrenched out the accusation as he fell onto his hands over her, gasping for his breath and trying to ride the shudders of postorgasmic spasms.

Trace's dark eyes were pained and savage as he looked

down into hers. To Ashla, it was almost like being stalked and targeted by a great jungle beast. The black of his lashes made his eyes lethally beautiful in the way a jaguar's eyes could be beautiful, but a deadly sight to see unless it was through a very long lens.

His hand was suddenly riding up over her belly and breasts, then closing around her throat. Ashla worked hard to keep from smiling at the intensity she had wrought from him, but the satisfaction she felt showed in her eyes. He hovered almost nose to nose with her for a moment of intensity before the corner of his mouth curled up in an almost challenging little grin.

"That, little temptress, will not happen again."

"Yeah, yeah, you said that before," she sighed, rolling her eyes.

Her audacity floored him.

Her challenge aroused him.

Trace almost laughed when her expression changed to one of surprise as she realized he was firming up inside her. They weren't in 'scape, and this wasn't fueled by euphoria this time. This was one hundred percent pure, unadulterated lust for her that he had been holding in check for what felt like a lifetime. But now that the short game had been played . . .

"It's time for the long game, *jei li*," he taunted her in warning.

Chapter 16

Malaya cursed softly in her native tongue, pacing her bedroom chamber nervously.

Something was *wrong*.

Every Shadowdweller could Fade, and most could skip through connected shadows, but every so often, a 'Dweller was born with a significant third ability that was different from most everyone else. For Trace, it was the ability to skip unconnected shadows; for Rika, it was the remarkable power of locus, which allowed her to sense or track specific psychic energy.

For Malaya, it had always been the redoubtable power of precognition.

And she hated it because it lied to her. Well, not lied, but played games with her. It presented itself in instincts or even dreams, flashing sometimes dire warnings or bracing information at her when she was asleep and unprepared for it. Sometimes, it didn't wait for sleep to come and it rode over her in a vision with pictures of clarity and meanings as clouded as mud. They could be sharp, ringing and accurate, easy to understand and read. But here was the trick, because the next time everything would come sharp and ringing, but only accurate to a point. The power would create imagery in her mind using alternative representations, transposing objects and people so they became representatives of what would occur instead of the clarity of the actual occurrence.

For example, the dream she kept having about Guin.

She had said nothing to anyone, her fear so crippling that she dreaded that to speak aloud of it would solidify the reality of it. Time and again, with increasing frequency, the vision came to her. Always the same.

Her brave and rough Guin, falling to his knees in defeat, turning his eyes to her before declaring, "I have found your traitor, *K'yatsume*."

Then that sound . . . that awful sound! The whine of steel ringing through air right before slicing through the neck of her beautiful warrior protector!

Thank Darkness, sweet with comfort, that it had ended there. Bad enough to watch him die over and over so horribly; she didn't think she could bear the gore of it as well.

Malaya sobbed softly into her hand, her frustration and fear getting the better of her. Was it an accurate vision, or did it mean something else? It had been the driving force of her denial to release him. She didn't want him to find out who the traitor was. It was probably fruitless and ridiculous, but if he was ignorant, then he could never speak those words to her, and then she could ensure his continued life. What use were her premonitions if she couldn't prevent the tragedies she saw from forming? She had done it before, and she would do it this time as well. She didn't care what it took. She didn't care how furious he became with her. Of course, if he ever found out why she was keeping him tied to her side, furious wouldn't be a powerful enough word to describe his reaction. She knew Guin and his temper quite well, thank you.

The vision couldn't be accurate, she told herself as she paced a bit faster. Guin on his knees? Beaten? Impossible! Laughable! The behemoth who protected her was a legend on the field of battle. He was even more deadly in the darkest slips of shadows, using silence and stealth that belied all the bone and muscle he managed. No, it had to be something else. If it was, she dreaded it just as much. There weren't many things to mistake such a mental representation for. The slaughter of that which she loved? Death to someone loyal to her? The destruction of that which made her feel safe and secure in this world?

Just then, Guin entered the room, carefully hesitating to give her the opportunity to demand privacy. Malaya quickly composed herself, brushing dampness from her cheeks and sitting down on a chaise with a flounce, facing away from him. She affected a sigh.

"I'm bored, Guin," she complained with distracting energy just in case he had caught sight of her troubled expression.

"Well, don't expect me to entertain you. I'm not in the mood," he grumbled, making her turn to look at him. Guin had learned that he was free to speak to her almost any way he pleased as long as they were in private or company was limited to those in the upper entourage like Trace and Rika. He was never one for politesse, so he generally kept silent in company. But even with freedom to do so, he rarely expressed emotions of a moody nature. He rarely expressed emotions at all. He simply kept silent behind a stone wall of inexpressive features and muscle that stood at rigid attention.

So she was a little surprised when he moved to her side of the room like a storm and sat down on the edge of the chaise she occupied. He was every inch the picture of a man who had an issue to raise, and she feared she knew exactly which one he was going to go for.

"How is Rika today?" he asked instead, once again catching her off guard.

"S-she is better. Or as well as she can be." Just speaking of her vizier's unstable health saddened her. "She has not said so, but I believe she is completely blind now. Not even color to guide her." Malaya swallowed. "She stopped beading. She could still do it when she could see color, but now . . ."

Guin nodded. He had noticed other similar things. It had pained him to watch the active, brilliant artisan in the vizier slowly wither away as blindness stole her best loved tools of artistic expression. How the sweet-natured Rika kept her spirits was beyond him. She never once complained. Never became angry at her fate. It wouldn't do any good, except to maybe make her feel better, but he supposed raging in a temper was against her elegant, sophisticated mind.

Malaya wept for her good friend in her darkest corners and most private moments. Guin was too observant not to notice how she had covered up when he had entered the room. Some days, she didn't want to be seen; others she would lean against him or curl into his lap as she sobbed openly.

But Guin didn't realize he was mistaken and that it was him she shed tears over this time.

"I just saw Magnus at the forge."

Guin was leaving her side a lot. It was not normal, and it was risky behavior on his part, but she knew he was torn between his restriction to her side and his duty to protect her. He was doing what she had asked him not to do in little snippets of stolen time. If she was with her brother and Xenia in the palace, he would excuse himself, leaving the other bodyguard in charge of both royals' lives. Or he would send the good-natured Killian in to be with her, though he never did this if he thought they would end up alone together. He didn't even trust the head of their own security forces.

Guin would never be gone more than an hour total in a day, but even her brother was beginning to frown on it, and Tristan had taken the threat of traitors with a minimum of concern.

Until they had poisoned Trace.

Now Tristan was a black, brooding presence, his usual

joviality vanished, his boisterous sexual escapades confined to the deep privacy of his rooms where they had always belonged. He dogged his sister's steps frequently, moving his work into her offices, which they had not done since the time during the wars. But it was actually nice having him at a desk across the room again, even if it was a threat that had brought him there. When this was over, she would insist that he stay this time. They simply worked better when they were together anyway.

"Repairing Trace's weapon," she said softly, toying with her necklace. When she turned her head, the delicate chain that strung from her pierced ear in a low curve to connect to the piercing in her nose would shimmer against her face. Guin loved the beauty of her unadorned face and form, but when she wore the chain that accented the prominent curve of her cheek in gold and drew attention to the black liner that rimmed her whiskey-colored eyes, he had to marvel at her. She always knew how to present herself perfectly. Be it looks or manners, she had that which he sorely lacked when it came to appealing to mass society.

"Yes. And quickly, too. Magnus does nothing with haste, as you well know."

"He is worried Trace is still a target. That he is an unarmed target."

"He is hardly that," Guin assured her. "But the katana is Trace's best strength."

"But the point is," she said, turning her dark eyes onto him, "Magnus is worried. Magnus is not known for fretting, Guin."

"I know," he agreed with a short nod. It had been his point, and he was glad she had already intuited as much. "His son has almost died twice. If not for the half-breed, Trace would already be dead. And . . . I am worried as well, *K'yatsume.*"

"You have said as much many times, *Ajai.*"

"*Drenna!*" he burst out, surging to his feet suddenly and

rounding on her. He reached to grab the back of the chaise, trapping her between his arms as he loomed over her and nearly touched noses with her. "Did it not occur to you, *K'yatsume*, that after failing twice they might decide to move on to an easier target? Hmm? Think, you obstinate girl! Think who they will choose!"

"If you mean me, then all the more reason for you to stay close!"

"You think I mean you?" He laughed in rough and insubordinate mocking. "My, my, princess, you are self-important, hmm? And do you think you are an easier target than Trace when you have me attached to that shapely backside of yours?"

Malaya gasped softly at the crude behavior and remarks from him. She had never seen him so mutinous toward her before. Every muscle in his body bulged with repressed anger, even the exposed armband over his biceps looking ready to burst under the strain of them. Yet his breath came deep and rock steady as it poured warmly against her cheek and lips.

"Think!" he shouted at her, so hard and sudden that she jolted in shock and surprise. She swallowed nervously, for the first time truly facing the tiger she had held tamed to her side for so many years. It reminded her of the stories where those who raised such beasts always said they could never turn their backs on them and never forget that they were born and bred for the kill. Nothing that wild could ever be perfectly tamed. "Think of who is weakest among us. Who, if we lost her, we would suffer from the loss like a mortal wound pours out life's blood!"

Guin knew by the appalled widening of her eyes that she finally understood. She wasn't this dense and stubborn; it wasn't like her. There was something else going on, and he could feel it deep in his bones. But unless she told him what it was, he would continue to stumble around in this inhibiting ignorance. It was enough to make him want to strangle his own charge.

His gaze drifted down her face briefly, settling for an agonizing moment on her sensually formed mouth. It, like everything else about her, was designed for one thing and one thing only. At least, to his mind. She'd been carved out of pure sexuality, forged in heat like a fine precision blade. At times like this, Guin could think of better alternatives to strangling her that could work just as well . . . if not better.

He looked back up to her eyes, swallowing as he heaved his mind out of that forbidden gutter before she took notice.

"Your blind Rika would be dead before she could scream," he growled at her, being cruel on purpose. "A single saw-star and her delicate little throat would be laid wide open, severing everything straight to her vocal cords." He meanly cut a hard finger across the middle of her arched throat to drive his point deeply home. "An assassin could come up behind her with a drawn blade, and with a single swing—"

"No!"

She screamed in true terror, making him jolt back several inches in surprise. Malaya was not easily frightened, and he had fully expected her to all but kick his ass for his bullying tactics. He wasn't expecting tears, a wrenching sob of dismay and then . . .

She threw her arms around his thick neck, scooping herself up tight against him, her body curving exquisitely flush to his even as he was still bent over her. Then she pressed her lips against his with a sense of desperation, the salt of her tears sneaking in to touch his tongue. Guin was so stunned that, for the first time in his life, he simply could not react. She could have run him through on the spot and he wouldn't have been able to move the flicker of an eyelash to defend himself. His large hand spread over her back, holding her to him for an achingly sinful moment of realized impossibilities. Five decades of repressed emotion threatened to swamp him all at once, clamoring against the gates of reality and sense he kept them locked behind.

And then he saved himself, an instant before he would

have turned the kiss back on her and given himself completely away. He realized she meant nothing sexual, and nothing beyond the friendship alone that she thought they shared. She loved him, he knew, but not . . .

Just *not*.

He drew himself away from her painfully sweet mouth, reaching to stroke his hand back through her thick, beautiful hair as he slowly lowered to a single knee.

"*Jei li*," he said softly, his heart aching for her fear and devastation, and for his own. "What is this?"

"Don't ask me anymore. Don't ask me to leave. I can't bear it! I see death . . . I smell the blood! You, on your knees before me, your knowledge killing you!"

She wrapped tight around him again, all but throttling him with her sleek strength and desperation. He held her tightly, comforting her as best he could though it tested the strength of his racing heart. He had known her long enough by now to understand the rambling way she spoke and glean meaning from it.

"You have a vision?" he asked gently.

Her reaction was to tense tightly in his hold, a shudder running through her. It was beginning to unnerve him, seeing her like this. Next to Xenia, Malaya was one of the strongest women he knew. But while Xenia's mind was so much like his own, it was the way Malaya could find answers without resorting to violence that so impressed him. She was beautiful and powerful, and it was true that this went a long way to making it happen, but he knew that even had she been the lowest citizen, she would have stood ground for what was right and made her impact.

And with her lithe dancer's body and the speed and flexibility it bore, she was also the most graceful and swiftly deadly fighter he had even seen. However, Malaya had made no secret of her disgust with the need for battle and had shouted her pleasure when fighting for their lives had no longer become a daily activity. For her, this all must be like a nightmare time distortion, throwing them back into the war she had hated, however necessary it had been at the time.

"*K'yatsume,*" he said, allowing himself another moment of her lush warmth and the sweet jasmine scent of her hair as he held her. "You see me, on my knees before you? This, now, is the only way you will ever see me in such submission. To respect you, to show my devotion and loyalty to you, but never to let anyone shed my blood on you. I swear it to you, it will never happen. If you wish me to stay, if you wish me to truly end my investigation, I will. I will pass the task to Magnus. He is the only one I can trust with this now. Besides Tristan, he is the one who would do anything to save your life, including sacrifice his own."

She made a sound of distress into the fabric of his shirt at his shoulder, and he would swear she was biting the thick cloth. The vision she had seen had to have been graphic and terrible to affect her so.

"Besides, I believe now that this goes beyond the Senate and includes Sanctuary as well," he informed her as gently as he could. It was hard, shocking news, so he expected her gasp and the way she jerked back to meet his eyes. Her face was speckled with tears, the black around her eyes streaked wildly. He reached up with his thumbs, smiling a little as he wiped away the smudges that had changed her magnetic loveliness into instant, vulnerable adorableness. "No one will better root out corruption there than Magnus will. Once he begins, it will lead him to others. My time and efforts are now best spent close beside you. You and Rika. I would be better pleased if you would have her share your suite, *K'yatsume.* There is one other bedroom besides yours and mine."

"You barely use yours," she pointed out. "You still sleep on the floor, though the war is long over."

"And newly begun again. I am grateful I kept the habit." He was sorry that pointing that out made her flinch, but he would always speak plain truths with her.

"Very well," she said, her voice stronger now as she composed herself. Then for a moment she hesitated, and her whiskey-warm eyes searched his slowly. It was moments like this he most feared, feeling as though she could see straight down into his soul where all his secrets were buried, but for all her intuitive and insightful ways, she never did. She simply reached to smooth back a strand of his hair where it had escaped the thick plait at the back of his neck. "Move Rika here, *Ajai*. Keep close to us both if it suits you. Speak with Magnus and tell me what he thinks."

"Magnus thinks I am right. I told you, I saw him earlier. Trace began my mind working when he mentioned that only Sanctuary personnel knew he had entered Shadowscape that day. That means at the very least there is an informant within. The idea is as a personal betrayal to Magnus. He had already begun to realize this long before I approached him, though. But I am glad I did. It comforts me to think we are coordinating. All I need is for him to find the spy in his ranks and then I can . . . we can trace it back to the source."

"And then this will be over? We can end this?"

"It could be that easy," he assured her. "You should pray for that."

"I will." She smiled at him. "You don't believe in prayer."

"No, but you do. That is enough for us both."

Trace knew that as long as education was in session for the day, he didn't have to worry about the dormitory rules. No one would be around to catch them until after lessons came to a close. And despite the closed door and that no one had seen him enter, they were quite easily going to get caught.

Because his Ashla had quite a set of lungs on her.

"Trace!" she begged him, her head thrashing on her pillow as her calves clung to his back and her fingers grasped at his hair.

He had to admit to his part of the problem. He was completely obsessed with the taste of her. Well, that and the way she was grabbing at him, just as she did every time she came really close to orgasm. Something about the unexpected strength and demand she used sent pure pleasure ripping down through his body. The excitement went straight to his already aching cock, shifting his heartbeat into a higher rpm. Then, to top it off, he could slide two fingers inside her . . . just there, right at the edge of her breaking point, and everything inside her would clamp down like a vise. Now all it would take was that flutter of his tongue dancing relentlessly around her chubby little clit, and she would rebound like the snap of a whip.

Ashla tried to shout, but she was hoarse after an hour of his relentless focus on her, so it came out as a rush of air and a pitch a canine could hear. She trapped his fingers inside her with the squeeze and clutch of her walls as they went into spasm, and she held so tight with her clenching legs he figured he was going to bruise for a bit.

Now, he thought with satisfaction as she went limp enough for him to work free of the way she held him trapped to her body, now he was ready to take this to the next level. Now he was going to do what he should have done long ago. He was going to make her shatter like she just had while he was inside her. No impatience, no loss of control, none of it. Then he was going to damn well do it again. Then maybe . . . *perhaps* . . . he would have a little mercy on himself and allow himself to climax again.

Maybe.

First, Trace needed to decide on a position. That was a tough one. He had to consider all he was learning about her and her sensitivities, while admittedly satisfying his hard desire to watch her beautiful face flush pink with the ecstasy that rippled over her expression so vividly. Without a doubt, he knew he would get around to everything eventually, retracing his steps from their previous time together but rewriting his role as he went and paying attention to details this time.

Trace settled on his knees on the mattress, cupping both

hands under her backside as he lifted her up the plane of his braced thighs and draped her legs loosely around his waist. She was still wobbly and limp, and he grinned down at her as she tried to focus on him through passion-drunk eyes and golden lashes she couldn't lift above half-mast.

"You got A's, didn't you?" she asked, her small voice rasping hoarsely.

"I'm sorry?"

"Your grades. You got all A's in your sex classes, didn't you?"

He chuckled at that. "We didn't get graded."

She licked her lips, luring him unwittingly with the urge to kiss her, but he focused on what he was doing instead, more than happy to settle for the feel of sliding himself along the center part of her legs. His stiff cock was so ready for the wet glide between her swollen labia that he couldn't contain the groan of pleasure that followed the sensation the hot, wet feel of her sent shimmering up his shaft.

Not even inside her yet, and already losing his mind.

No, no, no. Not this time.

Holding her to him, he continued to slither through that flushed, pink flesh. He could see, especially, the little bundle of sensitivity that was her clit, and he made very certain to rub himself there again and again. It wasn't long before she was making those sounds of surprise combined with frustration again. She wanted more, the unkept promise he teased her with every time he slid back and forth over the mouth of her vagina. A couple of times, he tormented her with notching himself snug to her, clearly only a proper thrust away from invading her completely. But he denied her again and again until she actually flung a hand out and smacked his shoulder in frustration.

"What?" he teased, his cocky merriment blatant in his eyes, he knew.

"Trace, quit teasing me!" she complained, squirming restlessly between his hands.

"Now, you don't really mean that," he chided her. "The teasing is half the fun. Mmm. And you have no idea how hot it makes you against me." The latter was said a bit breathlessly as her scorching heat rode over him almost suddenly. He felt himself pulsing with the urge to plunge into her, and with each pass it was harder to resist. She was drenching him, writhing to try to capture him, and almost succeeding more than once.

"This time," he ground out in stern lecture to himself more than to her, "it's going to be very different."

Ashla was going to tease him about how she had heard that one before, but the beginning probe of his swollen sex made every function of her body go into overload from the sensation. She heard the harsh change in the cadence of his breathing and knew he wasn't as in control as he had hoped to be, and she took satisfaction in that. Deep satisfaction.

He painstakingly worked himself into her, just until the glans of his penis disappeared into her hot little core, and then paused for a much-needed breath as she continued to wriggle in frustration, her movements tightening her around him repetitively. He exhaled hard several times when she did this, but for the most part it was the fascinating contrasts of their skin that saved him from loss of focus. He was so dark, and she, even along the rich, blood-engorged flesh of her sex, was so fair. He became completely enthralled as he inched himself so very slowly into her, thinking rather fantastically that it was like being swallowed by pure light, even the searing heat everything he would have expected.

Except instead of the promised pain of such a fate, he was in glorious pleasure. He put his hands on her then, his fingers framing her pubic bone, his thumbs sliding down either side of her clitoris for several strokes, then one went to pull her hood taut, exposing her to the sweep and swirl of the other. All the while, he made shallow movements into her, just enough to remind her every nerve that he was there.

"Trace!" She reached up for his arms, her fingers clinging to his biceps where she could barely reach him. But she needed something to anchor her as he toyed with her so successfully. She went tight from head to toe, spirals of tension pulling her like a winding spring. She watched his hot black eyes flick up to hers for a moment of fierce possession, and nearly wept when he removed his thumb from her clit just long enough to give the digit a meaningful lick before returning it saliva-slick into place.

Her fingers dug into his arms, flesh on one side and metal on the other resisting her small strength. It didn't matter, though. All she needed was to hold on to him as her whole being swept around in time to the circling of his thumb. Then, just before she could cry out, he shot deeply forward into her, seating himself hard and deep, the movement stuttering her orgasm to a standstill for five whole seconds.

Trace felt her lock down around his cock like a constrictor relishing its victim. He felt his balance stagger away, the sensation rippling through him until he felt like he was on the front lines of a raging wildfire. The roaring burn threatened to engulf him completely, forcing him to face how insignificant his hard-won skill and focus could truly be when faced with that *one thing* it couldn't hope to defeat. Then she boiled up around him, oozing liquid heat until he was drowning in the bliss of it. He had to move. *He had to move.* No one could possibly fault him for it, he thought almost desperately as he began to do just that. And even as he did so, he wondered with shock and appalled disbelief how anyone could have possibly cast her aside.

He laughed with blind glee as he bent to his rhythm and to take her gasps and cries into his mouth. After over an hour of listening to how responsive she could be, the chaining glory of her voice raised in passion, he needed her with the same desperation all over again. He realized then it might never change. Perhaps a little, enough to allow him to treat her right, but he knew it would always be like this. Like coming home after the war. Like liberation after torture. Like euphoria in Shadowscape.

"Shh," he whispered soft and quick against her lips as he did things to her that refused to keep her silent, "it's okay, *jei li*. I will love you again and again. There is no rush anymore."

Ashla didn't fully hear, never mind understand the depth behind his words. She didn't know she had snared the emotions of a man of total logic. That she was healing an entire people by becoming the salve to the soul of their king's advisor. Trace himself didn't realize just how deeply he was being penetrated, even as he himself did the penetrating.

And then there was the friction of their meshed bodies as well, the erotic sound of wet flesh squeezing into wet flesh, the scent of it rising from their skin in a sensual cloud as they struggled to find breath and balance. It was all fruitless. Here was where instinct alone could survive. Trace's thrusts became nature's metronome, the rapid tattoo seemingly driving his heartbeats as well. His vision went dark—*it actually went dark*—and he gasped in dismay as he heard her little cries climbing up to pitch once again. He wanted to see this. More than anything.

"I want to see you!" he cried out. "I want to see you come around me!"

Feel and see. Know and forever remember. And like a wish granted, his vision cleared, just in time for that final kick of burning desperation that ran through his whole body. He double-timed his stroke, then tripled. He shook his head, peppering her with his perspiration even as she went tighter and tighter around his pumping cock. Ashla arched under him, her back bowing off the bed as she gasped in and over again, still drawing for breath as sky blue eyes went wide with dilated astonishment.

Her walls rippled, clutching around him like her fingers around his arms, only the tight grip of her sheath was far more demanding, much more potent. Ashla's entire body whipped with an undulation of ecstasy, her mouth open wide and robbed of every scream she was trying to make. Trace had never seen a woman look so glorious as his Ashla did surrendering herself body and soul to her pleasure. But just as sense-stealing as watching her was, so was feeling her. There was that sensation of rushing up on the moment, his lungs and chest burning in ridiculous demand even as Trace turned inside out, everything inside himself bursting to the outside, jetting in concentrated pulses as his orgasm rocketed to match hers. Her spasms were so blissfully grasped around him that they would stutter the stream of his relief into hard stops, making him growl low groans of pained pleasure, dragging out the intensity as he held on to the world with just the tips of his fingers. Pushed another inch, he would have fallen away forever.

He couldn't fall on her, though, her small body already a victim of his significant size and strength, but he couldn't help the collapse that came in the wake of his finish, either. He rolled, the only thing he had coordination for, dumping her carelessly over himself and feeling it harshly in his gut when he slid free of her body without intention or desire. He would have stayed. He felt it like a need, or even a craving as sharp as his desire for her in the first place. Separating from her felt wrong. It was too much like loss.

His fingers found a home in her hair. The silky gold was soft, and the sigh she released sweet. His eyes were closed, unable to open as his respirations calmed. The room was drifting with them, slow and lazy lifts and turns, like a tiny ballerina in a child's music box.

He heard voices, irritating him despite being almost melodic in their feminine rise and fall. He only wanted to hear his Ashla's breathing as she continued to calm and gravitate toward the opposite end of the spectrum: sleep.

Trace's eyes flew open.

Sure enough, he heard students returning to the dormito-

ries. They were outside the glass in the courtyard and beyond the door to the hallway. The etched windows were
sparsely designed, and the curtains almost as sheer, but it
was enough to protect them from sight from the courtyard.
Idiotic detail to notice now! he reprimanded himself fiercely.
He had been so focused on his partner, he'd never even
thought about it.

But regardless of visual impairments, they would be *sensed*.
As he had said to Ashla, there were rules . . .

Consenting adults or not, free of chaperones and family
and protocol they might be, but Sanctuary was different. The
rules kept students from engaging in—well, exactly what he
and Ashla were engaging in. At least, they were meant to
make it much harder. These students were taken in with a
promise of responsibility and guidance, not to be sent home
pregnant or worse because they had been given opportunity
to ruin themselves before they were emotionally and physically mature enough to know restraint. It set a poor example,
to break the rules at whim. And if he and Ashla were caught
and given exception, others would take that for permission
to do the same.

Magnus would serve him his penance himself, Trace
thought with a wince. Compensation for rule-breaking with
Magnus had never gone easy. He had no tolerance for dis-
obedience. There was right and there was wrong. Magnus
was not known for his willingness to explore the gray areas
of rules. But this again was what made him the most formidable warrior at the beck and call of Darkness and Light.

"Ashla," he whispered. "I have to go."

She was fully awake in an instant, her head shooting up
so she could narrow those eyes of silly insecurity at him. He
couldn't resist reaching out and flicking her on the forehead
in punishment.

"Ow," she pouted, her kiss-swollen lips immediately tempting. She rubbed her forehead though they both knew it hadn't
hurt.

"Stop it," he scolded softly. "I have to go because the women have returned. If a handmaiden catches me here, there will be Light to pay."

She looked to the door and the noises outside. She bit her lips and looked back to him. He knew her reluctance to let him go just as he knew his own to leave. He should have exercised more patience, taken her to the royal house and his rooms in the palace. They could have spent hours together alone without a second thought.

"Can't I come with you?"

That made him smile as bright as light. "Aren't you tired?" He didn't want her to walk all that way after he had worn her out so well.

"Yes, of course I am. But I'll have a second wind by the time we get out of here," she returned urgently. She rolled off him, scurrying quickly to her clothes, pulling the provocative *k'jeet* against her bosom.

"No!" He hissed the command as he followed her to the floor where his own things lay. "You are not wearing that outside of Sanctuary."

The utter surprise on her face must have been pretty funny, because Ashla caught him smothering a chuckle as he quickly began to dress.

"But—"

"Are you going to argue and waste time?" he demanded.

"But I don't—"

"Arguing," he pointed out sharply.

She huffed a sigh and hurried to her dresser. She only had three outfits. The one he wouldn't allow, a handmaiden's sari, and a bolero and skirt set she thought was much more revealing than the *k'jeet*. She wasn't about to run around like a handmaiden, as if she were pretending to be culturally something she wasn't. She would get enough stares as it was in the belly-baring outfit left as her only choice . . .

"Fuck it," she muttered, yanking the thing out and hurrying into it.

"*Paj!*" he whispered across to her as he shrugged into his shirt.

"What the hell does that mean?"

"*Paj*. The pants you wear under that skirt."

"I never knew you were such a slave to fashion," she hissed in irritation. "There is no *paj*! Are no *paj*. Whatever!"

She heard him mutter a string of Shadese under his breath she just *knew* was very uncomplimentary.

"Come on, let's go." He gestured her to his side and she hurried to him, flouncing down to her knees beside him in a swish of satin skirts. "*Aiya*," he groused as the pale length of her leg appeared up to above her knee. "You save my life only to be the death of me," he complained before taking hold of her.

"Hey, if you don't want to be seen with the uncouth white girl, I can keep my ass right here," she bit out temperamentally.

"That is the most ridiculous thing you have ever said in the time I have known you!" he shot back.

She opened her mouth to give him something in return for that remark, too, but he slapped a hand over her mouth and quickly skipped them out of the room just as the doorknob was turning.

"Ashla?" Karri asked, announcing herself politely before opening the door a bit wider. The room was a shambles, and the handmaiden could swear she had heard arguing. She frowned as she looked around, making sure to check even the darkest corners where someone could hide. Her sensitive senses couldn't be fooled, though. The room reeked of sex and the dress Ashla had been wearing earlier lay on the floor. The bed was a rumpled mess, an obvious testament to rules being quite broken. Karri smiled a little in amusement. "I guess we kissed and made up." She chuckled.

She left the room, closing the door behind her.

Chapter 17

Magnus had gotten very little sleep.

He was used to lack of rest and other hardships, especially when he was on a hunt for a Sinner, but this time he was far more weary than usual.

He was disheartened. The increasing understanding that there was a taint in his own house was wreaking havoc on everything he had held perfect confidence in. Oh, he had always known there were personality issues here and there. He was far more aware of Shiloh's power-grubby attitude than Trace credited him with. However, he had control over those minor issues. Shiloh was pushing for a transfer or demotion, depending on which of Magnus's nerves he decided to dance on at the last minute. Everything else could be handled with creative care and thinking.

Or so he had thought.

Then they had tried to murder his son.

Magnus's fists curled tight as he sat on the edge of his bed in tense temper. He didn't like to be so angry. At heart, he was a man of wisdom and peace. It was why he had so thoroughly supported the regime that now ruled their people. The warrior within him was relegated to whatever was necessary to see religious law obeyed, and appeared only to bring balance in the dire moments of unfairly disadvantaged victims.

He didn't dislike his warrior's victories, especially when it saved lives and souls, it was just that he preferred when Darkness guided him to chores of education and guidance, his role as a professor to the young being his favorite. But he did thrive on his supervisory tasks as well. Like a master of chess, he had to manage everyone with precise care if they were to best function and maintain Sanctuary for doing what it was destined to do best. In this way he would protect the young, the beliefs of the law, and the spiritual heart of their nation. It was his true calling, and he had devoted his entire existence to it.

The sound of soft footsteps on cool stone approached him and he drew up a welcoming smile for Karri.

"*M'jan?* Are you well?" she asked as she moved to kneel on the bed beside him. She had a cup of warm, honeyed *frousi* juice between her hands and held it out to him.

"Yes, pet, I am well," he assured her, taking the cup and reaching to rub his thumb over her lightly freckled cheek. Those freckles had always amused him. Her skin was a pretty even mocha color, except those tiny dots of darkness.

She smiled under his affectionate touch and waited quietly while he enjoyed his morning drink. Once he went to put the cup down, though, she spoke. "You slept poorly last night. I wish you had called me in. I could have tried to help."

"No, no, *jei li*," he corrected her, "your herbs and medicines would have done no good for a troubled mind. It was just thoughts, not illness."

"Well"—she gave him a sly feminine smile as she leaned her warmth against him—"I have more than herbs at my disposal to quiet your mind, *M'jan*."

Magnus was surprised by her bold offering out of the blue, and it made him laugh. He studied her a moment, curious as she rubbed her chin against his shoulder. Karri was quite pretty and very provocative in her way, he admitted easily, his eyes running down her body warmly. He had never had issue with her attractiveness. But after knowing her for so long, he was quite aware of how out of step her playfulness was for their routine.

"Of that I have no doubt," he agreed. He tilted his head and studied her. "But this is not like you. Is all well with you?"

"Quite well," she assured him.

Then to his unending surprise, she moved to throw a leg over his thighs, hiking up her night dress and exposing herself almost to her sex. She then snaked an arm around his neck and bent to nuzzle her lips against his cheek. Magnus reflexively caught her around her ribs, fruitlessly trying to hold on to her as she slid provocatively against him.

"Let me rest your mind, *M'jan*," she invited softly against his ear, the warm rush of her breath seeking out his spine and flooding him with delighted response. He felt heat blooming in his belly, his blood warming to her quickly.

Puzzled as well as becoming aroused, Magnus suddenly turned with her, swinging her onto her back on his bed and looming over her.

"Karri, why are you playing with me?" he demanded suddenly of her, trying to shake off his unexpected response to the feel of her beneath him. "I have enough on my mind right now without you—"

"This is exactly my point," she purred as her long, lovely legs suddenly snaked out to wrap around his hips. She drew his big, braw body down onto hers, tightening their intimacy with her lithe strength. "What is the harm in losing yourself from your thoughts for a while? *M'jan*, you are so hard on yourself. So strict in all you do. It is my duty to urge you to rest and relax. Come and sate yourself, Magnus," she beckoned temptingly.

Magnus would be damned if that wasn't the finest idea

he'd heard in weeks. The desire to fulfill her request rode through him like a wild herd of mustangs, thundering through his blood and body until he was deafened by it. She was triumphant in her expression just before he swooped down to catch her mouth and kissed her as deeply as his racing pulse could goad him into doing. He was amazed by his own virulent passion, the hardening of his penis a swift and fiery sensation.

A bracing sensation.

Magnus jerked back away from Karri's eager kiss, a jolt of denial and shock rushing through him. He launched himself off her and away from the bed, stumbling back a little in graceless confusion.

"*Drenna, K'yan*, what in Light are you thinking?" he demanded of her angrily. *What had* I *been thinking?* he wanted to know of himself.

"Why?" she exclaimed, sitting up suddenly. "It's not as though it is forbidden! Magnus, we are allowed to be with each other."

"Karri, I'll not talk of this," Magnus snapped irritably as he marched away from her. "Damn it, I have enough on my mind without you adding to it!"

"Forgive me," she said in a small voice behind him. "I was only trying to help."

That made him stop and turn around to look back at her. He sighed when he saw the despondent little ball she had curled up into by drawing her knees to her chest and clinging to them.

"*Aiya*," he sighed, moving back to her and kneeling on the floor in front of her. "Karri, honey, I know you were. You are always trying to help me. It is the very definition of your role by my side. And if I do not say so enough, I am eternally grateful for it. You make my life and my job so very easy and I am proud to have you as my maiden." He took a deep breath as she loosened her hold on herself a little and let him kiss her forehead in gentle affection. "But this is not like you. The seduction and the sensitivity. It tells me there is something else beneath all of this."

She shook her head mutely, trying to slide past him but only gaining his hand around her arm and an insistent little shake as he frowned sternly at her.

"No, Magnus. It's nothing," she insisted, the telltale biting of her lip saying otherwise. "I was just overthinking, I guess. Really."

"*K'yan*," he scolded gently, "you cannot fool me. You should not even try. Speak to me."

She sighed heavily, her doe's eyes looking terribly caught, telling him she was having a struggle of conscience. "Very well," she relented at last. "I had a conversation with the halfbreed girl the other day about sex and the nature of a handmaiden's and priest's relationship, and I suppose I was thinking I could do more to make you happy than I had been. Like I said, I was overthinking. Anyway, I upset Ashla with my remarks somehow, and when I went to apologize, I found her room in the dormitories . . . umm . . . used."

"Used?" he echoed suspiciously.

"Yes. I didn't want to get anyone in any trouble, so I have been agonizing over it for two days. I guess between that conversation with Ashla and coming upon the scene of your son's sexual congress, it made me obsess a little about sex. I'm sorry."

"*My son?*" The bellow of anger belted into the handmaiden and she winced.

"Yes. It was Trace with Ashla, of course."

"In the women's dormitories?" he demanded furiously. "He knows that is forbidden!"

"Please don't be so mad, *M'jan*," she begged him.

"Do not tell me what to feel," he barked at her, releasing her sharply. "That is twice you have tried today. Do not let there be a third!"

Magnus turned and began to dress so he could hunt down his son.

*   *   *

"*Ajai* Trace!"

Trace knew that displeased bellow anywhere. He had, after all, grown up with it. While Magnus tended to be even-tempered and mellow in speech, he had a voice of incredible power that he put to magnificent use whenever he was angry, formally lecturing, or calling out a Sinner.

Trace knew instantly that he had been caught.

It didn't matter that the incident in Ashla's rooms had taken place two days earlier. He still knew. Firstly, there was no other reason why Magnus would be that furious with him. Secondly, it was simple logic. Thirdly, he was his son and he just knew. He just knew.

"Here, *M'jan*," he called, sitting back at his desk.

Magnus, like most male 'Dwellers, wore boots. The clipped and ominous approach almost had the power to make Trace feel fifteen years old again, despite that having been a very long time ago. Still, he was a man and had lived a man's hard, convoluted life, so *almost* wasn't enough. He did feel bad, however, for disrespecting his father's house.

Magnus rounded the doorway in full stride and impressive temper. It compelled Trace to his feet as he faced his foster father.

"Damn you, boy, how dare you?" he demanded right off, the father knowing full well the son was aware of his own indiscretions. "I raised you better!" he bit out, his free hand pointing to Trace in emphasis. "You know I cannot let this slide! Penance for an adolescent's trick, at your age!"

"Yes, *M'jan*. I am sorry to disappoint you," he said with quiet sincerity.

"I just don't understand. This isn't like you. No one respects temple and Sanctuary like you do who is not priest or handmaiden. And what is worse, I had to hear it from my own handmaiden! It took the poor woman two days of distress before she finally relented and did what she had to do. How dare you put her in such a position of crossed loyalties?"

"I had not realized that, *M'jan*," Trace said with honest regret.

"Whether it was Karri or a student or anyone else, their loyalties would have been torn. To pit yourself against me in the eyes of my students and those I call my colleagues—it is unconscionable!"

"Yes, *M'jan*." It was all Trace could say. Magnus was right. What was worse, until this moment he had not felt a moment of regret for his reckless acts. He had even laughed with Ashla for escaping unscathed. Magnus was right, it *was* beneath him. He quickly came around from behind his desk and supplicated to his father, lowering his head as he dropped to a knee. "*M'jan*, I know I deserve no consideration when I gave none to you and your house, but I beg you not to hold Ashla responsible. She doesn't understand our ways, our religion, and certainly she will not understand penance."

More importantly, Trace thought, she would not be able to bear it.

"She will quickly come to," Magnus promised him with no small level of threat.

For the first time in his life, Trace felt a surge of temper at his father's unrelenting interpretation of the rules. He rose sharply to his feet, facing him squarely. "That is unfair. What of understanding? What of compassion? She is a babe among us. I will not allow you to punish her for my misguidance!"

"You will not allow?" Magnus was absolutely and utterly flabbergasted. "*You will not allow? Just how will you prevent me when you yourself will be on your knees in the penance chamber? If she lives in my house, she abides by my rules and my disciplines. You know that. You were all but born of that!"

"Then she will no longer live in your house!" Trace shot back harshly. "She will live in mine. And here she will stay, under *my* compassion and *my* understanding."

"The future does not change the past," Magnus hissed, disbelieving his son's hard-line opposition against him. Magnus had never seen him do anything like this. Not against him. Trace was a formidable man, of that there was no doubt, and Magnus was quite proud, but he had also raised him to have ultimate respect for his father above all others. He was stunned to see him undermine that for the sake of the half-breed girl.

And had Magnus not already been blindsided by the devastating realization that there was a viper within his carefully constructed nest, he might have slowed his temper and asked for clarification. He was a stickler for discipline, true, but he was also a priest and a man of great reasoning. However, his understanding that he was housing a devil that had been directly responsible for the near murder of his one and only son made him forget all of it as he took it out on the closest target presently pissing him off.

"Father, don't do this. Don't make me square against you any more than I have. I alone have wronged, not Ashla. She has been through enough."

"Having a bitch for a mother doesn't exclude or excuse her from the rules, Trace."

"What does, hmm?" Trace challenged him. "You say that as if there are exclusions and excuses, but there never have been with you. I understand, *M'jan*, that this is what makes Sanctuary the great institution that it is. I respect the scope of your accomplishment for our people, but you cannot be so absolute and unbending this time."

"What is wrong with you?" Magnus roared in sudden fury. "You say you respect, but you do not speak with respect!"

"Neither do you!"

"Let penance be done and that is the end to it!"

"Over my dead, rotting, mutilated body!"

"*Ajai! M'jan!*"

Both men took several beats to stop glaring at each other before finally looking toward the Chancellor who commanded their attention. Malaya was heaving for breath, clearly having run fast and hard to arrive there, and probably from some distance, since she didn't wind easily. She stood braced between the archway, Guin hard and ominous at her back as always, and beyond him a small crowd of palace personnel who had been drawn by the shouting.

"What is the meaning of this?" Malaya demanded.

"This is none of your affair, child," Magnus said sharply. "This is between a father and his son."

"It is my affair when it shouts down the walls of my home!"

"Or does respect stop at your door alone, *M'jan*?" Trace shot out at his father with a mean and accurate point.

"*Bituth amec!*" Magnus reached for his sword in his anger, but despite his shock, Trace was there along with him, his hand catching the tsuba of his father's weapon at the bottom of the hilt. He pushed the quarter-drawn blade back into its scabbard, using Magnus's own grip on the sheath against him. Then he grabbed both and held them together, facing his father's furious eyes.

"If you draw a blade with intent to harm in the royal household, *M'jan*, you commit a high crime. To do it in the presence of the Chancellor marks your throat with a dotted line," Trace hissed. "*Think!* What has gotten into you?"

Magnus's eyes went wide for a moment, but Trace's words sank in quick and sharp. His son had just literally saved his neck. Had his blade cleared its wooden scabbard, it would have been enough to invoke the laws his own fosterling had created as vizier. He was in the act of doing the very disrespect he was accusing his son of.

And now it was moments later and he had no idea why he had become so angry as to want to draw a blade on the one person he loved like he loved his gods and his duty.

"I don't . . ." Magnus shook his head.

Trace's hand snaked out on instinct to seize Magnus around his upper arm. He couldn't ever have described the heart-stopping shock he felt to watch this invincible man stagger back on unsteady legs.

"Guin! *Septh apt mui!*" Trace barked the order without thought, even as he grabbed for his collapsing parent. Guin was there in a heartbeat, as was Malaya, and all three of them guided Magnus down to the floor. "*Drenna!* I should have known! You would never be so unreasonable. Forgive me," he whispered at last as he touched his forehead to his father's chill, clammy one.

"*M'jan*," Malaya said with clear worry, "what is wrong?"

"Drugs. Poison. Or both," Trace answered for him, as Magnus tried to get a grip on himself.

"Poison again," Guin ground out. "And how convenient it is you, *M'jan*, after you begin investigating your house."

"It is affecting my mood," Magnus realized slowly, although the others had already gleaned as much. "Worsened my temper. Enraged me."

"Some can do that, *M'jan*," Malaya said tightly. She looked up at Trace and Guin with worried eyes. "What do we do? All the healers we have are in Sanctuary. We could end up laying him at the feet of a murderer."

"Not all," Trace said softly.

"No, Trace," Magnus rebounded sharply, his wits coming quick this time. "Ashla is no guinea pig. The last time she was poisoned, it was only because she was half human that she survived healing you. The poison was a synthetic designed to destroy the blood of a Shadowdweller. A genetic tag, if you will. Only her mutation kept it from destroying her. If they are using such sophistication, you can only assume they aren't going to let her ruin their plans twice. I could be a trap. You understand? A triple cocktail meant to snare me, a powerful young healer, and to shatter your spirit like glass, my son."

"*M'jan*, I won't just sit here and let you die," Trace argued in soft despair.

"Maybe Karri's herbs can help. Her gift for healing is miraculous, and surely you trust your own handmaiden," Malaya said, her shaking fingertips clenching around Magnus's hand.

"Trust no one any longer," Magnus warned her as his waning strength dropped him back prone on the floor. "None but this echelon among you. Trace, Rika, Xenia, and Guin. Only these." Tristan, of course, went without saying.

"And yourself, *M'jan*," she reminded him, her tender touch continuing. Despair was in her eyes as she looked to Guin. The guard could see what she was thinking, how she was feeling her visions were coming to pass in the worst way.

"Your katana is complete, the new tang a thing of great beauty," Magnus said as he reached to grasp his son around his arm. "In my chambers. I meant to bring it, but my temper . . ."

"You will bring it soon," Trace said firmly. He pried Magnus's grip away and surged to his feet. "Watch him. I will get Ashla. Keep him calm."

Trace was on his feet and running before Magnus could protest again. As much as he wanted to, Trace didn't shadowskip. It burned precious resources and energy, and if he was entering that den of danger he had once called home, he needed every trick at his disposal.

Drenna, the distance was so great! It had never felt so before, but now the sloping streets and convoluted passages between the palace and Sanctuary seemed to take forever. But finally he was there, rushing into the vestibule, his booted feet sliding on the high polish of the marble floor as he came to a stop. Courtyard first, then rooms, he thought.

Luckily, they were right next to each other. In his momentary panic he forgot all about the draw within him that would always lead him directly to her.

When he saw her sitting and laughing with Karri, he was doubly relieved. Despite Magnus's warning, he knew that he had not meant Karri should be suspected. Priest and handmaiden had been together since Trace's boyhood. He had been about eighteen when she had been Chosen. She had been not much older herself.

Ashla felt him before she saw him. But it wasn't the usual effervescent call that warned her. This was an alarm, plain and true, and she knew before she met his eyes that something was terribly wrong. She put down the box of confection candy she held, apologizing to Karri with her eyes as she rose quickly to her feet and raced across the courtyard to meet Trace.

"My father has been poisoned," he said without preamble. He raised his eyes from her to include his father's handmaiden in the announcement. "A traitor in this house has him in his grasp, just as sure as they thought to have me."

"I will get my herbs," Karri said, her face folding into an awful distress as she put the back of a hand to her mouth and ran as quickly as her sari would allow.

"She will catch up to us," Trace said, taking Ashla's arm and urging her forward quickly.

"Don't worry. I know I can do this," she said, grabbing for his hand in firm reassurance.

"Magnus doesn't think so. Not without costing your life. I am afraid he might be right."

"Trace, I can do this."

Her amazing confidence brought him to hesitate, turning her toward him so he could search her steady eyes for a moment. Where, he wondered, was all her fear? Darkness knew, *he* was terrified. She couldn't possibly realize how dire the situation was. Nothing, absolutely nothing, could bring Magnus to his knees. Didn't she understand that?

Just then, Ashla reached up to him, caressing the side of his face with gentle self-assurance. "I will not let your father die, Trace."

And in that brief moment, he could almost believe her.

Ashla was afraid, but that was to be expected, and it wasn't the crippling fear she had seemed to always suffer. Maybe that was because, for once in her life, this thing inside her wasn't the worst of curses. After already saving Trace's life twice, she knew she was grateful for it for the first time, too. Trace had, and still was, saving her life in return. Every day of his careful wisdom and his volatile hunger for her was changing her. Just as darkness and food were reforming her starving body, his affections and righteous demand that she respect herself as he did were reforming her spirit.

The more time she spent with Magnus, too, the more she saw the dynamic that had formed his charge into such a good man. He had been very kind and extremely patient with her as she had spent these weeks asking every raw question there was. Neither he nor anyone else in Sanctuary had ever complained. He had clearly made her a priority, though why such an important man would spend so much time tending to one sick half-breed girl was beyond her. *K'yan* Karri or any of the other handmaidens would have served just as well, she was sure.

She kept hold of Trace's hand, sensing how badly he needed even the smallest comfort. Just that small physical connection intensified her sense of his raging emotions. The fear she had seen, but there was also a tremendous guilt and no small amount of anger. He felt responsible for this somehow. Since she knew he would never do anything to harm Magnus, she wondered why.

It would be all right, though, and it made her feel settled and good that it would be because of what she could do. She would heal Magnus and everything would be fine. Maybe she'd get a few more days of feeling like total shit out of it for herself, but it would be worth it if it returned something to Trace, who had already given her so much.

She had been to the palace before, but she still couldn't get over the sudden grandeur of it. The entrance was nonde-script mud-colored plaster to smooth the man-made edges of haste left behind by the miners of the long past, but once you stepped over the threshold it was like the grandest and most magnificent buildings in the human world. She always imag-ined this was what the Taj Mahal would look like on the in-side. She couldn't say for sure because she had only ever seen pictures of the splendid exterior, but those smoothly sculpted minarets and the gold and marble so artfully laid in accent were very much like the floors and walls she now rushed past, only much darker.

The situation in Trace's office had worsened dramatically in their absence. It was written across the faces of those who were there as they all looked up to Trace on his hasty en-trance. Ashla felt the sinking of his heart and could even taste his terror on her tongue. He all but dragged her as he fell to the floor beside Magnus.

The priest's coloring was frighteningly pale. He was drenched in a sickly sweat and shivering in violent tremors. He was fighting for consciousness, his pride the only thing letting him succeed. His body clearly wanted to curl into it-self, but Magnus refused to obey the need. He had, however, allowed Malaya to slide her lap beneath his head, her touch the only comfort he could find. He was furious with himself for being so brutally stupid. He should have expected this deceitful sort of trick from those low enough to plot in the shadows with the use of hired swords. But he had resisted the idea of corruption beneath his own roof just a little too long. He had wasted energy trying to figure out if something else could possibly explain it. He had sulked at the forge, shaping his son's new blade with a fury, as if his speed and temper would give the blade the power to protect where he could not.

He cursed softly when his son drew the tiny blond healer down beside him. He didn't want this. Better he should die than be responsible for the death of an innocent. The feel of his blood writhing painfully through his veins told him how unique this weapon inside him was. Trace was mad if he thought someone so frail could take on such a demon.

But before Magnus could protest with the force he wanted to, the poison sank its fangs into his vulnerable brain and sent him into seizure.

"Holy Light. *Drenna*, save him!" Malaya cried out as the giant of her spiritual world snapped into a contortion of muscles so violent she expected to hear the sound of breaking bone any moment. She protected his head as the men reached to contain him. The floor beneath them was so hard! So painfully hard, she thought with distress. But none of them could stop what was happening. Not Guin, her most powerful protector; not Trace, their dependable expert on all solutions. And she with her useless visions, who had seen this coming, yet had been unable to understand. She had seen Guin's face, but it had never been Guin. The supplication, the act of being on his knees, was representative of the prayer position Magnus so frequently guided her to. Guin himself was a backbone of strength, just as Magnus was a backbone of spirit. And Magnus had certainly found her traitor and now lay low before her. If he died, it would literally be cutting off the head of the strongest institution in their culture. Even now, she could feel in her heart the ripple of shock and destructiveness this poisoning could fashion now that there were deceivers in the temple.

But they were all powerless to do anything about it, and Malaya had never known such a horrible feeling in her life. She felt as though her very spirit was dying in her lap, her faith shattering and her purpose withering. She looked up, seeking her twin, knowing he had arrived. The Chancellor knew he could see and feel straight to her heart because the look that crossed his steady features was anything but steady. He was beside her in a flash. Everyone else focused on Magnus, but Tristan buried his hands into her hair and turned her eyes to him. Another of her great men, on his knees now in front of her.

"This will not defeat us," he whispered fiercely to her, his eyes, perfectly matched to her own, radiating the savage strength and will that was unraveling within her. He fed it to her with all of his might, his hands tight around her head with his intensity. "This will not destroy what we have made here. *Claro? Sedna, istu veenima, K'yatsume.* Do you hear me, beloved?"

"Yes. Tristan, help him, please."

Tristan knew he could not. The realization that he would fail his sister when she no doubt needed him most brought him low, humbling him. All he could do was lay his own dark hands on the dying man before her, joining all those others of power that tried to hold back what was coming.

And in amongst so many dusky hands and sienna-skinned arms, there appeared two of soft, pale white. The contrast was stark as she reached to quickly slide them each back to points farther away from the center of Magnus's body. Then she quickly unbuttoned and stripped aside Magnus's shirt. When Ashla reached the undershirt, she turned to her lover and simply held out her hand. He was already there, the tanto's handle fitting into her palm carefully.

The blade made her nervous, but it cut through the fabric like air. She handed it back quickly, Magnus's writhing body making her afraid of a sudden accident should one of the men lose grip of him. She needn't have feared. They weren't going to let that happen.

The Shadowdwellers watched with morbid curiosity, fascination, and hope as Ashla shucked off the outer drape of the handmaiden's sari she wore. It left her in a half-shirt and skirt, which she promptly hiked up around her thighs. She threw her leg over the priest, something she might have resisted had she a choice, but she wasn't thinking about any of that as she settled over him.

"No! Don't!" They all looked up as *K'yan* Karri rushed into the room. "Do not put yourself at risk, *Anai* Ashla! Let me do this! Magnus would never forgive himself if anything happened to you!" She hurried to them with her box of herbs in hand, kneeling with them all. "Please! *Ajai* Trace, I beg you! I will not let him die and will spare your woman in the process. Trust me!"

Trust no one.

Trace would have been torn between the options the two women presented had Magnus's last words not sang so sharply into his mind. It upset him to doubt Karri. She was the closest thing to a mother he had, her closeness to Magnus as natural to his father's presence as his katana was.

Why should he distrust this woman who he had grown up with, but trust an alien who knew so little of them? Because he felt lust for her and she gave him such pleasure? No, he knew it was more than that; more even than the Sainting between them. He knew to the depths of his soul that his beautiful Ashla would not let his father die, even at the cost of her own life. The idea of losing her paralyzed him with a fear unlike any other, made him want to choose the safer methods of Karri's herbs, but he knew their world could not afford to lose Magnus. Though his desire to be selfish was overwhelming, Trace had given up far too much of himself for this culture and political structure he so devoutly believed in. Too much to stop giving now.

"I'm sorry," he whispered to Ashla, his eyes full of his devastation and terror. Full of his sacrifice.

Ashla did not misunderstand, although Karri did. The handmaiden sighed in relief and moved closer, but was surprised when the half-breed girl didn't make way for her. Ashla paused just long enough to touch Trace's desperate features. She knew he was not telling her he regretted making her leave, but that he regretted needing her to stay. He was trading her life for his father's; she could see he was convinced of it, and her throat tightened in empathy at the pain she felt roaring through him.

She prayed, for his sake, that she survived this.

Ashla turned back and laid her hands on Magnus's bared skin.

"Wait. What are you doing?" Karri demanded. "Trace, you are killing her!" she cried in near panic. "Don't make her do this!"

"*K'yan! Shut up!*" Malaya shouted with sudden ferocity, making the other woman jolt back in shock.

"*K'yan*, I know you have come to care for Ashla, but you must trust my choice," Trace rasped hoarsely. He wasn't very convincing because he barely trusted his own choice. "Ashla, hurry."

Ashla was already doing that. She ignored those around her as she breathed softly through her lips, touching Magnus in a sure, slow movement. She closed her eyes, her fair head tilting and sending her little fall of curlicues bouncing over her shoulder. Her expression was one of concentrating, of seeking. Her fingers moved up to his mouth and Trace watched as his father's clenching jaw relaxed, opened, and gave her entrance. She ran gentle fingertips over his teeth and tongue.

"He ingested it," she said softly. They had suspected as much, but her surety convinced them. Trace watched as her fingers came back down his throat, following the poison's path to his belly. "Very recently. It is quick and brutal. It toys with his emotions. Desire intensifies to lust. Anger explodes to rage. Trepidation to full terror." There was a sob, soft and desperate, from Karri, but she covered her mouth to prevent any further sounds.

Ashla bent forward, laying her cheek to Magnus's chest over his poisoned heart, her small hands covering what she could reach of him, drawing the sickness into herself. Her eyes opened and she focused on Trace, her breathing picking up in tempo. She stroked gentle hands over the priest's head, and suddenly the seizing stopped. Magnus relaxed into oblivion with a long, rattling sigh.

"*Jei li*," Trace whispered, his terror choking him as he realized she had committed them to this course now. She was absorbing into her tiny body that which had laid low the strongest man Trace knew.

It was a mistake. She could never survive.

"No," she whispered to him when he would have moved to snatch her away. He wanted to stop it. He had to stop her! He couldn't lose her. His heart, he knew, would no more survive this than it would the loss of Magnus. How could he have thought he could make this choice? How did he dare think it was his right? "*I* made this choice," she said as she sat back up again, exhaling long and slow as she reached out to Trace. She caught the back of his head, leaning in to kiss his cold lips.

Ashla could taste his guilt and devastation as sure as she could feel the wicked heat of poison filtering slowly through her veins. She knew the pain would begin soon, that she had very little time. She kissed him until his mouth warmed to hers and then crushed against hers in desperate expression. He dragged her from astride his father, wrapping her into his arms and against his chest. He kissed her still, the heat between them putting the burn of poison inside her to shame. His hand burrowed through her curls, his tongue tunneling between her parting lips. They kissed as if it were the last time they ever would, both of their hearts straining with pain of impending loss.

"I need you to survive," he gasped against her, his beautiful dark eyes spilling sharp sudden tears into their kiss. "I need you to live, *jei li*. Like Darkness, I need you. Don't leave me."

"I don't want to leave you," she said, his emotion overwhelming her until her whole soul smarted with its clarity of understanding.

He loved her.

This man of deep passion, deep loyalty, and even some-times militant devotion *loved her*. Ashla knew he gave noth-ing of himself easily or on a whim. He only threw himself into those causes that were justly deserving of all he could give them. And though she did not feel that deserving, he still loved her.

She wished she had the time to tell him she loved him, too.

But she didn't.

Trace was still kissing her when her body jerked with its first cruel spasm of pain. She threw her head back, making a low sound that he had actually heard her make before . . . though it had been in pleasure that time. His soul screamed in denial as she jolted again and again. Her eyes went wide, tears of pain to match the horror of it leaking out of their corners and racing down her face.

"Hurts," she whispered, clutching at him in desperation.

"Baby? Oh, honey, don't," he begged her, even though he knew it was a fruitless plea as her body bent fully back in a hard seizing of muscles. Only his strength supported her, her clawing fingers tearing his shirt, destroying its usefulness as her anchor. He couldn't bear to subject her to cold, hard mar-ble, and he tried to contain her to himself. The other men helped him, their big, gruff hands so tender as they arranged her gently back against his chest, giving her legs room to kick and flail.

"Karri," Trace said roughly, looking up to find the hand-maiden over his father, weeping as she touched his face, a vial of herbal extract in her hand. "Come help me! Magnus will be well now."

"I have to be sure," she cried. "I have to give him this. It's the only way to be sure!"

"Karri, he doesn't need it! I need your help!"

He saw her thumb flick off the small cork to the vial as she ignored him.

That was when he remembered that no priest was served so much as a drink of water without his handmaiden's lips touching it first. She served him everything, and she tasted everything that she served. It was a tradition as old as time.

Magnus had realized this as he lay incapacitated. That was why he had warned them at the mention of Karri's name not to trust anyone. He had suspected her himself.

But *Karri*? Sweet and plainly pretty Karri was one of the senior handmaidens, devoted to her work and her priest, most of her two hundred years spent behind Sanctuary walls. Why would she ever want to betray that life? Why would she want to murder Magnus, who had Chosen her, raised her up, and given her more than she could ever have dreamed of?

The why, he realized, was unimportant. Even with his dying Ashla in his lap, he twisted and reached for the wak-izashi and its scabbard, drawing the weapon with singing speed. The pitch of the blade in the air was only thrown off when the super-sharp tip came to rest at the back of her neck after severing half her braid.

"Move so much as to breathe and I will take off your head," he warned in a low, slow threat. Malaya gasped, horrified that he would dare to do something like this. "*K'yat-sume*, remain quiet and still," he instructed her carefully. "Guin, if I meant your mistress harm she would be dead already." The remark stopped the guard's hand on the hilt of his own weapon and Trace met his eyes steadily even as he clutched his love to his chest and felt her dying. "*M'itisume, K'yatsume*, I have found my father's viper. Take the venom from her fingers before I am forced to shed blood upon you both."

Like a frozen photograph, no one moved for the longest time, save the seizing girl in the vizier's lap. Then Malaya reached out the flat of her palm to Karri.

"Give me the vial, *K'yan*. Whatever he thinks, it can be disproved simply and you will have nothing to fear. Let us not test his emotions. He has been through much."

The patronizing words grated down Trace's spine like Acadian's claws. However, he couldn't care less so long as the snake at his father's breast was defanged and removed.

"It's not poison," Karri insisted with an aghast laugh. "*Ajai* Trace is clearly out of his mind! How many years have I worked by his father's side? I am a healer!"

"You are a murderous bitch," Trace hissed sharply. "Back away or die!"

Karri turned her head slowly against the wakizashi's blade when the foul name slapped at her from him. She narrowed her eyes on him.

"Your father thinks you are so perfect!" she spat with scorn. "If he heard you speak to me in such a way, he would have your head!"

"You, little viper, will tell me nothing about my father that I do not already know!" He turned his wrist slowly, turning the sharp blade up tight beneath the back hinge of her jaw.

"You think so? Know him so well, do you?" She was mocking him, her sneer ugly and alien to the woman he knew. "Did you ritually bathe him every day? Lay out his clothes and dress him? Taste his food and then serve it to him? Were you his maid and squire every minute of every day for two centuries? He is a proud man, a beautiful warrior, and deserved the best maiden to serve his every insignificant need so he could lay all his focus on those that were deadly and great! He chose me for that! He made me his!" She drew a wild breath. "But then he cut out my heart, serving it to me again and again and again.

"There is one woman, and only one, whom he might take

to his bed, and that is his handmaiden. How many times did I offer myself, only to be turned away? Rejected! What is wrong with me? Am I ugly? Deformed and unpleasant? Am I cursed or a Sinner? No! I did everything! I was perfect! Yet he would not touch me! He was never even tempted! Not for two centuries! *Two hundred years!* Did you know *that* about your father? That he is a eunuch, for all his masculine swagger and bravado?" She laughed at him in a bark of disgust. "Or so I thought, all of this time. I even pitied him for his sexual dysfunction! I thought I was the only one who knew he suffered in such silence. I pitied myself as well. A handmaiden is just as bound to her priest as he is to her. I may take only him to my bed and no other. Since he couldn't make love to me, I thought of it as *Drenna*'s test. Darkness was testing my worthiness by giving me so difficult a hurdle to overcome.

"And I have faced it. Decade after decade I faced it. I battled with need, temptation, and the desolation of feeling unwanted as a woman. I did it for the love of our gods and because, damn him, I loved your father with all my soul!"

"*Loved*," Trace bit out, his arm as steady as ever to his sword.

"Oh yes. Although even now I know my heart is his, it is no longer ignorantly his. I saw him, one day, when he was in the privacy of his rooms. I was shown the truth that day. I watched him take himself in hand, watched him lie back and fantasize about gods know what! He easily brought himself to orgasm not once, but three separate times within the hour. Three times! He turned to his own hand like it was an old and beautiful lover, rather than me!"

Karri's pain and hurt could be heard in the harsh break of her voice as she bent forward into sobs, cutting herself on the end of Trace's blade. "Imagine how I felt," she begged hoarsely. "To be so made a fool of. So shunned and rejected!"

"So you poisoned him? Thought to murder him?" Trace hissed.

"No!" she shouted back at him. "I was told it would arouse his passions. It would break through whatever was keeping him so reserved and controlled! All I wanted was him to need me. I wanted him to love me with the desperation you have for her!" Karri pointed to Ashla, who was slowly going limp against him. "I had been forbidden from ever taking another lover by religious law, so what choice did I have?"

"This doesn't explain the poison in your hand, witch," Trace urged her, watching with satisfaction the trail of blood that began to drip down her neck.

"When I fed Magnus the aphrodisiac and failed to seduce him this morning, I was angry. I told him about your little escapade in the women's dormitories just to spite, and he was livid. I knew he would seek you out. When you came in crying of poisoning, I knew—I knew I had done it. I swear I had not meant to! But none of you who are so perfect would ever believe me! I found the one who gave me the potion and made them give me an antidote!"

"Made them? How would you make someone so treacherous give you an antidote?" Trace demanded fiercely. "You are no warrior. No fighter."

"Don't you see? It was an accident! A mistake. They would never have hurt Magnus. No more than I would have! It—it must be some kind of allergic reaction." She looked at Magnus, desperate to believe her own lies.

Trace burst out in an animal's sound of fury. "Look! Look, you deceitful bitch! Look at my love and tell me again this is no poison!" Trace's entire body shook with his rage, the vibration traveling up the tang of his blade with a hum. "Tell me again," he begged her. "Tell me, so I can cut your lying throat."

"Not until she tells us who the maker of the poison is," Malaya stipulated.

Hearing the Chancellor's bloodthirsty tone visibly

shocked the handmaiden. She looked to Malaya with plead-
ing. *"K'yatsume*, it's all just a mistake! I beg you, you know
I would never . . ."

Then Karri made another mistake—she reached out in
supplication to touch Malaya.

It always awed Malaya, the sleek speed which which her
big bodyguard could move. Guin leapt over Magnus, his
hands a blur as one pushed Malaya safely into her brother
and the other spun Karri around at the shoulder. When Guin
landed on the opposite side, he turned slowly, the threat neu-
tralized now so haste was no longer required.

Karri's body fell to the floor at his feet, her throat finally
laid open by Trace's blade, which he had pushed her onto.
The handmaiden looked surprised as she searched for
breath, her hand going to her gushing wound.

"Guin! She needs to tell us who it was!" Trace cried out.

"While she kills Malaya?" he countered sharply as he
knelt beside the dying woman. He picked up the hand that
had been reaching for the Chancellor, turning it over and
pulling her wrist back. The sharp movement sent a spike of
steel spitting out from the long-sleeved blouse beneath her
sari. It was thin and painted black with venom. Malaya
gasped in righteous indignation. She had believed Karri!
She had begun to think it was all just a misguided woman's
mistake!

"That's an assassin's blade!" Trace was overrun with confusion and outrage. "How is she an assassin? She's a handmaiden! An herbal healer at that! Magnus never taught her
how to fight. She served him every day! When would she—?"

"She wouldn't. She didn't. Look." Guin turned her wrist
and showed the strap securing the weapon. "It's secured
wrong and in haste. The ties are tied from my direction.
Someone put this on her."

"Guin, careful! The poison," Malaya breathed as the sharp
spike came too close to him for her to bear.

Guin ignored the warning, leaning over the maiden dying

on the floor. Life was half gone from her eyes, spreading quickly over the tiles beneath her. "Tell us, unfortunate girl, who led you to this. You spoke the truth, I believe, when you spoke of your fury and hurt. But someone else knew of it and manipulated you with it. Someone spoke softly in your ear, feeding your rage and desire for revenge. Who? Who twisted your mind away from your priest, girl?"

"I l-loved him," she croaked.

"Guin! I swear I will mutilate her if I don't see an end to this now!" Trace exploded. "I cannot bear to hear her say how she loved my father again!"

"That's just it," Guin said grimly as he looked up at them all. "I don't think she means Magnus anymore." He looked down again, watching the last of her life ebb out of her eyes. "You were lucky," he ground out to her. "Had I to do it over again, I wouldn't have let you find your time in the Light so quickly. Burn, treacherous creature. You will spend eternity becoming cinder and ash."

Chapter 18

Trace drifted gentle fingertips over Ashla's clammy and gray face, his brow wrinkled in distress to match the rattling labor of her breathing.

He had wanted her in his bed. If she was going to die, he wanted her here, where they had loved each other so thoroughly. Here, where he could hold on to her in peace. He wanted to do something to help her, but he trusted none of the healers. His father lay quiet in another room, recovering with sleep. Sanctuary awaited Magnus's return, trembling silently at the coming fall of what Trace knew would be his righteous fury. Magnus would find any other deception in his house, of that Trace had no doubt.

He kicked off his boots, stripped away his weapons, and climbed into the bed beside Ashla. He drew her chilled body against him, fitting her to his chest and rolling under her. He was her mattress now, his warmth her blanket. Her head settled beneath the constant brush and rebrush of his lips, his breath sharing its steady stream with her. Their touching hearts beat out of time with each other in a staccato cacophony of death in chorus with life.

"When you are well," he said softly to her, "I will tell you how I love you, *jei li*. Believe me, had I realized it sooner, I would have confessed it before this. Strange, how blind I can be when something sits so close to me. But I had no idea what to make of how you affect me. How could someone so small and so meek be so powerful? I mistook your fear for cowardice at first, you know. Then I realized that it is nothing to fight when you have no fear, and everything courageous to fight when you have to overcome absolute terror. Had I consulted with my father over this, he would have seen this. No doubt, he would have. He would have shaken the idiocy out of me, for certain.

"Did I tell you that when I was young he had this way of smacking me across my ass with the flat of his working blade? I would try and dodge him every time, and fail miserably. He did it whenever I was being dense or arrogant. I swear I still feel the sting of it sometimes, keeping me in line.

"When you are well," he continued hoarsely, "I will ask him to join us. If he agrees, then I will beg you to become my blessing, my child's mother, my permanent heart. And I'll hear none of this nonsense about you being a half-breed. I wouldn't care if you were fully human with barely half a century left to live. I would take every minute. Oh, honey," he breathed, kissing her hard against her forehead as he tightened his hold. It was as though he could keep her alive with will and strength alone. "I need you to survive. Can you forgive me for this? For all my mistakes? I never meant to cause you pain."

"*Ajai* Trace."

Trace looked up as his bedroom door eased open.

"Leave me be unless you bring me a miracle," he said in a bitter, emotion rough voice.

"Fortunate, then, that I do," Tristan remarked softly as he pushed the door open wider.

Trace watched with confusion and doubt as he did this, revealing the presence of a tall, silver-haired male Trace had never seen before. By his skin tone he might have been a 'Dweller, but his sterling hair and matching eyes of mercury dispelled that notion instantly. He also wore light colors: tan breeches and black boots; a white shirt of loose, billowing fabric. He wore silver daggers strapped to his lean legs, the worn leather wrapped around the weapons' hilts telling Trace how familiar they were to his hands.

"*Ajai* Trace, I would like for you to meet Gideon. He is one of the Demons I met during the Nightwalker summit."

Demon! Trace was absolutely shocked. He had met very few of this race in his lifetime, and then only by rare accident. Only recently had serious contact taken place between their breeds. Their efforts toward mutual peace were in the infant stages at best. What had made Tristan think to call on a creature so distant from their culture in geographical and essential ways?

"Welcome, Gideon," he said softly. "You will forgive me if I do not rise to meet you."

"Understood, *Ajai* Trace," the Demon said with low-voiced respect.

"Gideon lives in the Russian territories. He and his mate are ambassadors to the Lycanthrope court for their king," Tristan explained.

So, he had been much closer than Trace had thought. Tristan must have traveled through Shadowscape to reach the Demon. But how had he brought him back so quickly? And what good could a Demon do a dying Shadowdweller?

"I understand your confusion and your doubt, as well," Gideon said, his eyes steady and deep with a wisdom Trace was very familiar with whenever he looked into his father's age-traveled eyes. This Demon, he realized, was very old. For all his young, healthy form, he had seen life through many centuries, and it was written there in those silvery eyes. "I am a medic. A healer for my people. A very powerful one. Chancellor Tristan believes I can be of help to your woman, and he may not be wrong."

Trace didn't want to feel the surge of hope rushing through him if it was unfounded. He was worn out, thrashed by all the abuse his emotions had taken since the day Baylor had attacked him.

Since the day he had met his Ashla.

"Forgive me, but I don't see how. A Demon healer cannot heal a Shadowdweller. Not that I know of."

"Not that I know of, either. However, as I am understanding this, your woman is not entirely Shadow."

Not entirely Shadow.

Half-breed!

"You can heal humans!" Trace exclaimed, sitting up suddenly and gathering Ashla up tight in his hold. Dared he hope for this?

"I can heal her human half. Perhaps that will be enough to let her Shadow half come the rest of the way." Gideon walked across the room to Trace and Ashla. "I was skeptical when Tristan suggested it. Our bodies do not work in absolute halves. She does not have half-Shadow blood cells and half-human blood cells circulating through her. She is a fusion of both, of course. However, now that I see her, it is plain her human genetics are dominant. In theory, this will be critical to saving her. That and the fact that I am unlike any other healer."

"Please."

It was all Trace could think of to say. He held Ashla forward to this would-be savior, ready to settle to his knees if he had to in order to make this happen.

"Lay her on the bed and either step away or move to the other side. I also ask you to please be aware that a healer touches to focus power, and I will need to do this."

"I know," Trace said quickly as he obeyed the command to lay Ashla out and then hurried to the opposite side of the bed. "Ashla is a healer. She touches as much skin as possible to do it. May I hold her hand?"

"Of course. It will not disrupt me." The Ancient Demon

reached down to draw a fingertip over Ashla's forehead. "A healer is strange for your breed, is it not? Or am I mistaken? There is much we are ignorant about with one another."

"Something that we will one day change," Tristan promised.

"Soon, I hope," Gideon remarked.

Tristan did not respond. He could make no promises when the future was so uncertain beneath his feet. Whatever was happening in their world, it would take time to discover it and then repair its damage. Until then, their truce with the other Nightwalkers would have to hold its own. For the time, however, they had eradicated the most immediate threat. From this point, they could work their way backward through any veins of destructive disease that remained.

Gideon turned his knuckles against the cold dampness of the girl's face. He closed his eyes and sought to sink inside her ravaged systems. Unlike Ashla, when he healed, he was not affected other than by the power he used. This backlash that she suffered, he considered, might be a flaw of her cross-heritage. While the Druids who had blended with human DNA and created hybrids had made intensely powerful descendents, it seemed that first-generation hybrids between humans and Shadows were not so fortunate. At least not in this instance.

As he searched through Ashla's system, he was surrounded by the black specificity of the poison within her. It was attached to her 'Dweller DNA like an engineered virus. This could be a tragic obstacle in his healing. He could heal and strengthen that which was human within her, but what would that matter when her Shadowdweller half was the part of her under attack? But again, it was the fusion of the two that might make the difference. That and the curiosity of her own healing power. Perhaps he could fortify this anomalous gift.

He reached down and closed his hand around her throat gently, focusing his power into a beam of searching light within her, seeking her strengths and her healing aspect. He called it to him, coaxing it from its desperate work of trying to win a losing battle. She had burned all her energy taking in the poison, sparing nothing for herself. A typical human trait, to do something in this all-or-nothing manner. Had she used half her ability and saved the other half to heal herself, then she might have been better off. Still, it was a brave thing for her to do.

Foolish, but brave.

Trace was forced to sit by and watch, with nothing but prayers and love in his arsenal to help her return to him. To lay faith at the feet of this Demon stranger was almost as insane as the rest of his existence had become. But within the space of a minute, he watched Ashla take the first full and deep breath of hours.

"Blessed, beautiful Darkness," he uttered in his choked relief.

"Just a step," the Demon warned him. "Only a step in a long journey."

Ashla opened her eyes in a slow, sticky flutter of lashes. Grit scraped her eyelids and she opened her mouth to take in air. Her tongue felt like it was wrapped in cotton, and her jaw ached at its hinges. She was raging with thirst as she focused on the men ringing her bed.

"I could use a Coke," she said thickly.

"Last I checked, we don't have a McDonald's down here," Tristan remarked with amusement.

"I imagine the neon and fluorescents would have something to do with that," a stranger with shining silver hair returned.

"Trace." Ashla turned to where he was in bed beside her.

"Yes, love?" he asked, his voice a rush of taut emotion and relief, his eyes shining with nearly shed tears.

"I'm not naked, am I?" she asked in a whisper.

"No, love." He chuckled. "I wouldn't allow that."

"Good," she sighed with relief. "So I guess I'm going to live," she theorized.

"Not for much longer unless you learn reserve and measure in use of your power, youngling," the silver-haired man said with stern authority. "You need someone to teach you both. Plus, I believe you can do much more with your gifts one day if you can manage to keep yourself healthy. I also do not recommend any more such risks as this last one until after your child is born. Luckily, she is part human herself and I was able to strengthen her. I do confess, though, that she was well protected by your womb in the first place. A surprise, considering how undernourished you are."

Ashla blinked and turned to look at Trace. Trace was gaping at the other man in absolute shock, so that pretty much confirmed for her that she hadn't heard that last part wrong.

"Uh . . . Trace . . . ?" she asked uneasily. "Just, um, how accurate is this guy?"

"I-I have no idea." Trace rose fully to his feet, meeting the Ancient healer's eyes dead-on. The blasé lift of one silvered eyebrow told him in an instant that this was a man who was never wrong about anything, and that if he suggested otherwise, he might end up paying for it. "But . . . there's this method we use to prevent this from happening," he tried to explain, the numbness filtering into his body making speech awkward and slow. "Our males take oral contraceptives. *I* take them, I mean. I always protect my partner. To do otherwise would be . . ."

"Dishonorable," Ashla chimed in for him, pausing long enough to give the only other non-'Dweller in the room a significant eye-roll. She was surprised when the austere man actually smiled. "Do me a favor," she said as she tried to make her weary body sit upright, "say something before he sticks his foot down his throat or I stick mine up his butt."

"Ashla!" Trace was aghast she would speak to a visiting dignitary in such a way.

"What?" she shot back.

"I realize how you might be surprised by this pregnancy," the Ancient speculated, "if what you say is true. I would have to know more about this contraceptive to explain the anomaly with any certainty. However, I assure you she is indeed harboring a fetus, and that fetus is three-quarters genetic Shadowdweller. All I can say is, I hope the one-quarter part that is human does not include her mouth."

"Hey!"

Trace exploded in a shocked laugh even as Ashla scowled at the blatant insult. He supposed he ought to have taken just as much insult on her behalf, but frankly he was a little too overwhelmed after the day he had had. All he knew now was that she was clearly going to be all right. She was alive.

And gestating.

"Burning Light," he choked out suddenly. "My father is going to kill me."

"Oh, brother. I'm tired and I'm going to sleep," Ashla announced, scooting back down in bed and getting comfortable. "Someone wake me after this episode of *Shotgun Wedding* is over."

"Ashla, this is serious! We must be joined as soon as possible!"

Ashla wasn't sure, seeing as how she was feeling really crappy at the moment, but that had to be the worst and most unromantic marriage proposal on earth. His only saving grace was that she had realized the depths of his emotions for her before this news had sent him spiraling into his cultural heart attack over her unwed and knocked-up state.

"Yeah, yeah, whatever. Just at least let me sleep a few hours first," she said, closing her eyes and trying not to smile. She figured a sucky proposal deserved an equally lackadaisical acceptance.

"Gideon," Tristan said, clearing his throat. "I am sure Ashla and Trace mean to thank you for your help."

"Yeah, thanks, Gideon," Ashla acknowledged with a

wave before closing her eyes again. "We'll have to name the kid after you."

"It's a girl," Gideon reminded her dryly.

"Oh. Well, next time, then."

"We should go," Tristan said with a sigh as he reached to guide the medic to the door. "This only promises to get worse."

"Did you or did you not describe her to me as a 'shy, mouselike girl afraid to even say hello'?" Gideon was asking as Tristan took him away.

"Must be the poison," he said with a shrug before beginning to close the door.

"I am actually more apt to suspect New York state," she heard him reply.

The door shut with a click and left Ashla and Trace alone in the silent room. Then she heard Trace move, clamping his hand on her shoulder and rolling her hard onto her back as he swung a leg over her, astride her as he leaned down nose to nose with her.

"You were all but dead in my arms," he informed her hotly. "Every suffering breath you drew, I suffered as well. I thought I would never speak with you again! I thought I had sent you to your death in order to spare my father's life!"

"Trace, your father is the backbone of the religion your people need for strength and guidance. He runs the institution responsible for all of the education in this city! I knew all of that when I offered to heal him. You didn't ask and you didn't beg. You didn't force me, either. I would have forced you to let me!" She took a breath. "Did it work? Tell me it worked, please."

"Yes," he breathed, his hands curving around her precious face with exquisite care. "He is resting. And so must you. Ashla . . . *jei li*, you are with my child."

"I know. I wonder how that happened," she said, her eyes flashing with wicked amusement.

"It had to be in Shadowscape," he realized. "But I don't see how . . . when your body was not completely present."

"It was present enough, I guess," she returned, reaching up to touch his mouth, rubbing away his consternation.

"*Drenna*, can you imagine if Magnus had not sought you out? You would have been pregnant in both 'scapes . . . with no explanation for it in Realscape. Your mother and the hospital, they probably would have . . ."

He swallowed loud and hard, unable to put words to the understanding. His sensitivity touched her heart. "It's okay, Trace," she soothed him softly. "I am here now. Safe and sound in your protection."

"Some protection," he sighed as he gathered her up and rolled her to him. "I tucked you into the nest where vipers lay waiting. I knew it, too. I came to watch over you, but I should have brought you to be with me here at the palace. I just . . . I didn't want to overwhelm you or pressure you. I wanted to give you the opportunity to heal and choose fairly."

"I see. I totally got that feeling when you demanded I marry you for the sake of your honor just now."

Trace saw no irony in that whatsoever, of course. "It is the right thing to do. The only thing. If I speak to Tristan, this could perhaps remain quiet between us. My father wouldn't have to know, per se."

"Babe?"

"Yes?"

"He'll know," she reminded him.

Trace sighed heavily.

"I know. You're right. And I'm sure it seems pretty foolish to you."

"Actually, once you stop panicking, I think you're probably going to be pretty sweet about it." She paused to nervously tug at his shirt a moment. "I am, of course, scared shitless."

Trace smiled at that, sympathy in his eyes. He knew exactly how she felt. "Me, too," he admitted. "For many reasons. This combination of DNA has no guarantees to it, and that worries me. I have never entertained fatherhood before. *Aiya*, until a few weeks ago I wasn't even entertaining the idea of a woman."

"Given the choice, you wouldn't be doing this," she noted softly.

"With threat and treachery all around us? No. Absolutely not. But there is no choice, and that's okay. We will make this work."

"There's always a choice," she reminded him. "I could go back. To the human world, I mean. Trustworthy hospitals there, too, by the way." She had already gleaned his feelings on other choices, so she didn't voice them.

"Full of light and sunlight! You would birth my child into that hell?" He was aghast, and when he put it that way, so was she.

"No. I'm sorry. I wasn't . . . I just don't want to force you into anyth—"

"Force?" He grasped her chin and met her eyes. "I am never forced to do anything," he said roughly. She remembered his history and winced at her word choice. "Gestating or not, I would have you, Ashla, be assured of that. You have crawled into my heart and my soul, picking off parts of me day by day and making them your own. Your heart, your goodness, your sheer generosity—they are all I could desire in a woman and more. Your passion," he continued, the change coming over him on the single word both obvious and alluring, "leaves me breathless, and mine for you simply can't be measured. What, in any of this, do you read as being forced? Unless . . ."

It finally occurred to him that she might not want to be with him. She could tell by the absolute fear and panic that flew through his eyes. Ashla would have loved to mess with him just a little bit, but she didn't have the heart to torment him.

"Yeah, okay, but can I please have a drink of water first? I'm dying of thirst here."

Relief warred with amusement in his expression, and she smiled at that. She didn't want to see him endure any more pain. He had been through more than enough. He got up, fetched her cold water twice before she slowed down to breathe, and then helped her into the bath when she begged him to. He lowered her sore little body into hot, soothing water and talked softly to her as he helped to bathe her.

"I know my ideas seem old-fashioned and silly to you at times," he said, "but we do things with precision for good reason in this society."

"You are a very careful and thoughtful culture, Trace. I can see that, and I can see the good in that. I am hardly complaining."

"You should be," he said with a frown. "I trust no one outside of the upper echelon in the palace. I can't bear to think of you in childbirth at Sanctuary when it is rotten with creatures like Karri who would do you harm."

"*Karri!*" She thought he was putting her on for a millisecond, but his face told the stark truth. "Karri?"

He carefully explained the confusion of emotion and deceit as they had best understood it from Karri's reprehensible mind. He edited some of it, for the sake of his father's honor, but it made an impact on Ashla just the same.

"But she was so nice to me. She was always spending time and . . ."

Trace looked at her with sympathy as she understood why Karri had no doubt paid extraordinary attention to her.

"She was a spy," he said gently, "and she did what spies do. She gathered information from wherever and whomever she could. As Magnus's handmaiden, she was set high in the most critical goings-on in Sanctuary and in the palace. He spent as much time here with Malaya as he did there. No doubt, over time, we will discover just how widespread her treachery was. Darkness knows, this could have been going on for years. I am hoping, however, that the recent rush of activity against this household is indicative of it being a shorter time span than that.

"I am almost certain that whoever was twisting her to his needs is also in Sanctuary. Who else would have access to a handmaiden? It is hard to say, though. I take nothing for granted in this. But now it is up to Magnus to find the truth. You and I are done risking our lives for the time being. I would keep you safe, my pretty love," he promised her with soft intensity as he nuzzled her cheek with a warm kiss. He dipped the sponge into the heated water, drawing soap and warmth up over her shoulders. "You and my child." He closed his eyes after he said it, exhaling slowly. "I have to be ready for this. I . . . I have to be ready."

"Luckily, you have nine months to get ready," she noted. "And please tell me you aren't going to freak out all of the time like this because, honestly, you're supposed to be the strong and brave one in this setup. I'm getting a little scared."

"I'm the brave one? *Jei li*, you sell yourself cheaply if you think you are not brave. You have taken on new worlds, new peoples, and self-alterations with an impressive aplomb. I am so proud of my courageous woman who would gamble her life for the sake of others."

"I did it for you," she said, turning to face him with a soft slosh of water in the unusual shell-shaped tub. She reached out to run tender fingers through the crisply short hairs around his ear. "I think I would do anything for you. Especially have this baby, even though it terrifies me."

"Why do I think we're afraid of two different things?" he asked her, catching her hand and kissing the tips of her fingers slowly, each in their turn.

"I'm afraid of everything, remember? Is it ironic to say a Shadowdweller is afraid of her own shadow?" she joked weakly.

"Just tell me what you're afraid of," he coaxed her, his light kisses including each knuckle on the back of her hand now.

"I'm afraid she . . . she'll be different."

"*Jei li*, everyone is different."

"You know what I mean," she said, looking away from him so she could toy with droplets of water on the edge of the tub. "She could be like me. White-skinned. Blond. She would . . . it would be hard for her, wouldn't it? Harder for her to use Shadowdweller methods, harder to socialize—just harder. It feels like it wouldn't be fair."

"*Jei li*, it's true that you're a curiosity and that people need to get used to you, but it's just curiosity. It's not hostile or un-welcoming. It isn't intolerant like it can be in the human world. Our troubles have always been clan related. One clan versus another and the prejudice that comes with it, or hard feelings from issues of the past. This is not going to be an issue for you because you have no clan affiliation. And anyway, the clans have mostly dissolved since the war ended. It will take more time, of course, before they truly are a thing of the past, but it will happen.

"I have faith that no matter what she looks like, our child will meet with a tolerance that will make me proud of my peo-ple. If there are troubles, she will have a very powerful father to set things better. Don't you trust me to take care of her?"

"Of course I do," Ashla said, a little mortified that she sounded as if she were questioning his ability to protect their child. "I love you, Trace. You are a good man. I feel like I have won some sort of megaprize just by finding you, never mind somehow getting you to love me. I'm very fortunate."

"*Aiya, jei li, Drenna* knows you deserve such fortune. Your life has been hard enough to start. Relax and enjoy this now. Let me worry about all of this for you. Let me love you and keep you safe."

He reached to kiss her, a painstakingly gentle kiss that

kept her engaged for several long, sweet minutes before she finally drew back for a breath. She looked into his dark eyes and smiled when she saw the slow-rising passion readily burning for her there. But they both knew he would not say or do anything about it just now. She had healing left to do, and Trace's sense of honor would not let him cross any more lines than he already had in his history with her.

"Magnus will join us once you are fully recovered," he told her. Then he seemed to rethink his rather dominant tone. "I mean, that is what I would like."

"I would like it, too." She smiled. "Unfortunately, you will have to extend all the invitations. I don't have any family or friends any longer."

"You will. And quite soon, at that. Although I should warn you that gestation for Shadowdweller females is, um . . . somewhat different than for humans. It will be hard to say which you might tend toward."

"What do you mean 'somewhat different'?" she asked, her eyes narrowing on him when he tried to act a little too nonchalant about it.

He shrugged. The casual movement simply looked wrong on him. It reeked of evasiveness, and he was not by nature an evasive man.

"Okay, remember the part where I asked you to stop scaring the crap out of me? Well, you're doing it again!"

He had the nerve to look surprised and aghast at the idea. "No, *jei li!* Don't be afraid. Different is just different. It isn't bad. I just know you're not fond of unpredictability."

"You know, specifics would be good here," she said coldly.

"Honestly," he said, sounding very sincere and convincing, "it's just minor things. For instance, it may be a bit longer than nine months. This is true of most Nightwalker breeds."

"Longer?" She gave him a dirty look. "Like a month?"

"Or three. Possibly four. It varies."

She gasped in a stunned little laugh. "Oh, is that all? Just a month or four here or there, right?"

"Now, see, you are looking at this the wrong way. It gives us more time to prepare, right?"

"What else?" she asked.

"Honey, it's nothing for you to get upset o—"

"*What else?*" she demanded.

"You can't enter Shadowscape for more than the briefest times while pregnant. Euphoria sets in too quickly for gestating women."

"Oh. Well, I can't Fade yet anyway. I don't even know if I can do it again."

"You can. You will. I can tell."

"Oh." She licked her lips nervously. "Well, that's okay. I don't need to go into Shadowscape, do I?"

"We will try to avoid it, of course."

"Of course." She rolled her eyes. "Anything else?"

"Not really. Except . . . well, I am certain this won't apply to you since you are so pale, but there are the skin tone changes."

"The what what now?"

Trace knew this was just going to get worse by the tone of her voice and the increased use of human idioms. He sighed and wondered, for a moment, if this was any sign of how she was going to react to the traditional wedding practices of his people.

He decided he wouldn't get into that until much, much later.

For now, he leaned in and caught her frowning mouth in a slow, warm kiss and decided to keep kissing her until he could think of a better way of handling her fear.

And it actually seemed to work.

Epilogue

Magnus returned to Sanctuary with a brooding step to match his austere frown. No one approached him, and no one said a word while he was present. Speculation and gossip, however, would continue as soon as his office doors closed behind him.

Especially when he refused a temporary handmaiden to replace Karri.

No, Magnus thought darkly. When he chose another handmaiden, it would be very, very different. There would be no one else involved in his choice this time. No committee of approval, no suggestions from others. He was wise enough to realize, however, that Karri had not been some evil entity, spoiled from the very start. That would be too easy an explanation for too complicated a tragedy. In fact, it was her kindness and her sensitivity that had left her open to the manipulations of some deceptive *bituth amec* within the walls of his church.

Church and state.

Sanctuary and Senate.

It unnerved and disturbed him to know this taint had touched both crucial strongholds of their society. He knew it was affecting Tristan and Malaya as well. They would need his guidance now more than ever.

The question was, how could he overcome such a deep betrayal in order to preach hope and faith to them once again? How and who could he trust in his very own home after discovering his most trusted companion was as treacherous as the winter night was long?

He also wanted to know just how much of what was happening would turn out to be his fault.

And keep the magic going with ELIJAH,
the sexy warrior captain. . . .

They are called the Demons, one of the elusive Nightwalker races living in shadow and struggling for survival against their human enemies. Their proudest warrior is Elijah, a man who bends for nothing and no one . . . until one woman brings him to his knees . . .

Some Feelings You Just Can't Fight.

He is known as the Warrior Captain—a master of every weapon, a fierce soldier sworn to protect his kind. Powerful, relentless, merciless, Elijah has always won every battle he's ever taken on—until now. Ambushed by necromancers, he is left for dead only to be discovered by the woman who could very well deliver the final blow . . . Siena, the Lycanthrope Queen.

With three centuries of warring, little more than a decade of uneasy peace has existed between the Lycanthropes and Elijah's people. Now, after a lifetime of suspicion, the warrior in Elijah is consumed with a different battle—winning Siena's heart by giving her pleasure beyond all boundaries. What starts as attraction and arousal soon burns into a passion with consequences that will echo through the ages for both their people. And as would-be enemies become inseparable lovers, another threat approaches, one with the power to destroy them all . . .

Surrender to the night.

The story continues with DAMIEN,
available now from Zebra. . . .

They are the Nightwalkers, mysterious beings who dwell in the shadows of our world, and Damien, the Vampire Prince, is among the most powerful of them all. But one woman will tempt him with a desire unlike anything he has known, and together they will face a terrifying and relentless foe . . .

He'd Never Loved.
But She Was Irresistible.

As reigning Vampire Prince, Damien has tasted every pleasure the world has to offer—consorting with kings and queens and delighting in sensual adventure. Now, tired of such pursuits, he devotes his energies to protecting his people. The war between human necromancers and Nightwalkers has escalated, and when the enemy makes a daring move, kidnapping Syreena, a Lycanthrope Princess, Damien boldly follows. He succeeds in rescuing her, but is unprepared for the erotic longing her lush sensuality awakens in him.

Gifted with rare abilities, Syreena grew up in a cloistered setting and was forbidden to form attachments to others, yet the connection Damien feels with her is immediate, intoxicating, and impossible for either to resist. But claiming Syreena as his mate could have shattering repercussions for every Nightwalker—and leave their enemies more dangerous than ever before . . .

Temptation tastes sweetest at night.

And get excited about Jacquelyn's newest book,
the second in the Shadowdwellers series,
RAPTURE,
coming in July 2009.

Turn the page for a sneak peek!

"A handmaiden," Daenaira said speculatively, "bathes her priest, I was told. She dresses him, undresses him, and tends his body and his wounds. She is a maid and a squire, seeing to all of his needs as a domestic wife and assistant would, freeing him to fight for their beliefs and their people. My mother told me this. She said it sounded so romantic."

Dae smiled a little, taking a moment to feel the textures of his shirt, but more importantly to marvel over the absolute hardness of the rippled muscles beneath. He was very warm, almost hot she could say. He radiated strong heat from even stronger muscles that processed energy and motion at peak efficiency. For male attributes, they were surprisingly appealing.

Magnus was wrong, though, when he assumed she had had no sexual education. Not formal, perhaps, but a bar rat got to see more than her share of bawdy behavior between waitresses, customers, and even her own mother. She had seen expert methods of flirtation and temptation; not to mention that last minute flip of denial. What men liked to call a tease. What they *loved* to call a tease. They stomped and growled about it, but they always hung around for more.

It wasn't that she wanted to be that mean or anything, or even that she wanted to play the tease, because frankly she shouldn't tempt fate when this arrangement was actually beginning to appeal to her a bit more.

"I am very young," she noted as she moved a little closer to him, just because she was enjoying his warmth and because the rich scents of him reminded her so much of a time when big, brawny men had been really nice to her. "Don't you think it's unfair to ask me to decide right now what sacrifices I am willing to make for the rest of my life? Especially sacrificing things I have never experienced? Aren't you concerned that I will always wonder what I'm missing? Aren't you concerned I won't abide by your rules and decisions or I will become tired of them?"

Dae couldn't have realized how close to the raw wound in Magnus's soul she was striking against, but she found out instantly when he grabbed hold of her arms with sudden and barely leashed violence. He drew her up so hard and high against his body that her still weary muscles made her clack against him like a loose marionette. Then everything settled and there was only the bruising force of his grip around her and the fast, hot rush of his breath against the right side of her face and neck.

"Oh, yes," he said softly, his voice so even that she could feel the rage broiling beneath it in each and every breath. "Believe me when I tell you, I have considered this quite a lot. In fact, I agree that you are young and uneducated in some of the ways of the world and that you are in no position to decide loyalties and faith when nothing in your experience seems to have generated either one in your heart. Light, I don't even know if you believe in our gods."

Daenaira felt the touch of his lips then, firm and warm and dry against the sensitive edge of her ear. It gave her a queer and powerful chill that coiled in a rapid spiral along the outer edges of her body.

"But," he continued tightly, "my beloved goddess of

Darkness, in her infinite wisdom, has plagued me with visions of a girl with strange red hair and the face and form of a beautiful warrior. She didn't even wait until that . . ." He swallowed what he was going to say and she felt the repressed fury shudder through him. "My previous handmaiden was five minutes from death the first time *Drenna* showed you to me. She wasted no time at all before driving me all but insane with the need for you. You were Chosen, *K'yindara*, and not by me. And *you* considered this fate for a week before you agreed to it. Knowing now what your alternative was, I can only imagine you thought very carefully about it if you considered saying no and risking yourself for a few more years in your relatives' house."

"You never asked me a thing!" she gasped.

"I did. I entered Dreamscape while you slept and I found you there. I made my proposal, and you turned me down quite quickly. You made me woo you, my little *K'yindara*. Every night I came and spoke with you, quelled your concerns and answered your questions. I spoke to your soul, sweet girl, and all but begged you to come to me. Anything. I would have done anything to ease these visions of you as they haunted me in ways I can't even begin to describe. I know you don't remember this, and *Drenna* designs it this way, so now I will have to woo you all over again here in Realscape where it will count just as much. But make no mistake, this was your choice and you have already made it. The price was paid and I doubt you will ever fully realize which of us bled the most for it."

There was pain. Oh, so very much pain in those last words that Daenaira physically felt it shredding through her. Yet his voice and tenor never wavered, never changed. She sensed in that moment that, though their worlds were so vastly different, they were far more similar than it appeared.